DEFCON DARCY

A Teenage Sleuth Thriller

A. J. LAPE

A.J. LAPE

ISBN-13: 978-0-9882641-6-8

Cover by Qamber Designs

To the best parents in the world who have always been on call 24/7. I love you.

Chapter One

TRUE CONFESSIONS

*M*aybe I should have a sex change operation.

A sex change operation might be the answer to becoming anonymous again. Here lately, guys noticed me—a fact that not only befuddled me but the legitimately gorgeous girls of Valley High School. To my right, Ben Ryan acted as though he'd cuff my wrists and force a marriage proposal. To my left, Jagger Cane looked like he'd jump in my pants and teach me the ways of the world. I had no intention of losing my V-card anytime soon, and if I did? Well, that led to the third guy who made my love triangle an official square. It would be with my best friend who was now my official boyfriend. Yup, in a rare moment of insanity, I agreed to be the regular kissing partner of the hottest guy I'd ever met. And let me confess, there had been some great kissing. Total. Spiritual. Awakening. But I was truly out of my league because if the world thought Ben Ryan and Jagger Cane were naughty dream material, Dylan Taylor was the benchmark on things that would make your girl parts quiver.

Like I said. Too many guys.

For a girl who swore to her father she would remain a virgin for life.

Why did I stay with Dylan? For one thing, he wasn't a *fastard*—that was Darcyspeak for a guy who fed a girl a line of bull, only for her to find out he shoveled the same crap to other unsuspecting victims. But with Dylan? Sigh. His words were genuine. He could kiss with the endurance of an Olympic athlete, and let's face it, he was big, bad, and deadly—number one on my zombie apocalypse team if the world ever came to that. The problem was, love sucks. When you loved someone, you should step aside and let that person evolve into what he or she was intended to be—their dreams should become yours. The challenge was to find that delicate balance of give and take where more often than not you were on the same page. All last semester, Dylan and I bickered because our relationship had failed to be symbiotic. Why? Because I couldn't show him the real me—the me he would've rather cut off his right arm than rubberstamp the things I considered recreational. Why was it, you say, did I want our relationship anyway? A relationship I sometimes, eh, *lied* to keep copacetic? I'd tell you why. Dylan's body was nothing short of dirty poetry.

Shoving that stuff down would be criminal.

My name's Darcy Walker, and I live in a suburb of Cincinnati called Valley, Ohio. Where some students were destined to be the leaders of tomorrow, some of us were your inspiration to try a little harder. Maybe that was why I couldn't take any of those guys seriously because I fell into that group and buried the competition. Some of us, no matter how hard we tried, were doomed to bring up the rear regardless of the assignment. We were the class clowns, the kids who stared out the windows, the note passers, and the ones not able to get our point across. People like me had a shelf life, and it ended senior year, diploma in hand...if we were lucky.

Thank God, I had one more year to find my calling. Well, I *had* a calling, but I wasn't sure I could make regular money by finding dead bodies and figuring out *who* or *what* had stolen their oxygen. Maybe I could if I did things on the up-and-up. At the moment, I preferred the down-low.

I flipped over a paper I'd written for my English lit class, biting down a plethora of four-lettered words.

"Shoot, dang it, and darn," I mumbled, eyeing a please-see-me note from the teacher. Tapping Finn Lively on the shoulder, I whispered in his ear, "Do three semi-curse words count as one big one?" Because God knew I needed an outlet.

Finn ran a hand through his platinum-blond hair and wadded up his paper, three-pointing it in the trashcan by the door. "I guess the answer is about as subjective as that paper. What do you want it to mean?"

"Something so dirty the Mother Superior puts me on the FBI's Most Wanted List."

"Then yes," he said and chuckled. "Darcy Walker is a really naughty girl." Finn didn't divulge his letter grade, but more than likely it had been an A. Finn recently joined Mensa but hated the textbook and pencil gig as much as I did. I had ADHD...translation? Paying attention and sitting still were not my strong suits. Oh, I was supposedly smart, but short of a miracle not much would help me amp up the performance.

Period. Endo facto. The end.

That thought had me regularly busting for the door.

As far as looks went, I was an okay girl. My muscles were well defined with slim hips and long legs but nothing that screamed pin-up on teenage boys' walls or the grin on dirty, old men's faces. I had almost-green eyes and straight, white teeth comple-ments of braces and Crest White Strips. I also possessed a melting pot of blonde hair, including every yellow hue in a crayon box. The look of the day was a white turtleneck with a black infinity scarf, pair of holey jeans, and silver down-filled coat I hadn't removed since lunch. Add UGGs, and I basically resem-bled an Eskimo.

Finn swung a beat-up leather messenger bag over his shoulder, brushing his knuckles down my cheek. "Ciao, bella," he said with a smile, picking Italy as his accent of the day.

"Ciao," I muttered back.

Beating my head against the desk two times, I stuffed my paper in a Spiderman folder and shoved it in my backpack, zipping the thing shut. I didn't waste time trying to find a silver lining. By God, there wasn't one.

"Later, babe," I heard a voice breathe in my ear. Jagger's voice—the lady-killer type that could send you to therapy for a month.

I half-waved, half coughed out, "You're stupid."

"How'd it go, Darcy?" Ben then asked.

Hmm. Let's see. One foot dangled over the ledge...same old,

same old. "It could've been better," I muttered, not knowing if he heard and honestly not caring.

"I can give you some pointers next time," he flirted.

What the H...I just stared. Ben transferred from another school in December when his father took a new post at Wright Patterson Air Force Base in Dayton. For some reason, he had a huge crush on me. A fact I needed to put the skids on, especially since he continued to ask me out when Dylan and I had gone official. Ben was tenacious, though, and happened to be a five-time mixed martial arts world champion. Losing wasn't in his vocabulary.

That hand-to-hand combat hadn't hurt his face. Ben was gorgeous...with a splash of arrogant jerk. Born in Great Britain, he had a sexy British accent and what I referred to as the "rocker snarl." His grin crept up at one corner and sucked me in, even when I knew it might steal my breath. The look was totally unexpected for someone who dressed as preppy as a Ralph Lauren model. Per usual, he sported a white button-down shirt and khaki pants, starched and as perfect as his grade point average. He was unbelievably sharp, tall at six foot one with coppery-colored hair and screaming silver eyes.

"Study buddies?" he persisted. Ben took an inordinate amount of pleasure in watching me squirm. The blush on my face deepened as it traveled to little red blotches on my neck—a trait I'd tried since childhood to overpower, but my dermatological tendencies rendered unsuccessful. With a deep chuckle, he strode over and parked himself beside my desk. "Come on, angel," he said and grinned. "This could be the beginning of a long, prosperous, and very intimate relationship." Ben loved the word "angel." As far as I knew he only bestowed the winged creature on me.

A throat cleared. "Hey, Darc, let's bug out of here. The sharks are circling."

With an exhale, I turned to the voice of my archangel, standing two aisles over—Dylan Taylor. His tiger eyes were warm, and Heaven help me, my brain scrambled for a beat. Dylan had a Chippendale's body that made my tongue sweat. I shot him an air-kiss in answer while Ben slowly nodded once in Dylan's direction—almost as if he recognized his territory. Dylan's face remained masked and unreadable. I'd seen him take guys to the mat for less, but with Ben he was still in the observation stage.

Ben strutted out the door, swinging his jacket over his shoulder in one fell swoop. Ultimately unaffected. "The offer always stands," he said, chuckling deeply.

I looked at the back of Ben's head and thought, *May you rest in peace*.

"Dylan and Darcy. Come here a sec," interrupted my English teacher, Mrs. Conner. Thin but shapely, she stood around five foot five with curly, shoulder-length strawberry-blonde hair and the cerulean-blue eyes of the Vikings. Trendy in all black, she'd tutored me off and on since grade school, trying her best to get one side of my brain to make nice with the other. Eh, so far I hadn't been a glowing testimonial to her tutoring skills.

In an attempt for privacy, she waited until most of the class had exited the room. My lips twisted ruefully. I'd bet my Chuck Taylors Dylan had been tapped for moral support because he basically grabbed a pencil on test day and blew the bell curve away for the rest of us. The universe just served up another big plate of *Somebody Shoot Me*.

"Okiedokie," I answered flatly. Looking at my feet, I strolled toward one of the few teachers who'd thrown me a lifeline all year—and it was still as appealing as rotten ground beef. Here was how I was feeling: Awkward. Embarrassed. My brain said, *Back away... slowly*. At the last second, I gave them both a look of apology, hit reverse, and left them standing like I was late for a date with God.

"Darcy!" Dylan shouted.

I heard a feminine sigh, followed by a, "Let her go, son."

———

I opened my locker, dug around in my gym bag, and popped an ibuprofen in my mouth. My left shoulder killed, and I was bent over in my own version of Quasimodo. I'd dislocated it in the fall riding The Beast rollercoaster with Jon Bradshaw, and even though I was sixteen, I swear I had arthritis.

Swallowing it down with my own spit, I noticed Fisher Stanton out of the corner of my eye. He just stood there, like he wanted to ask me something but feared I might bite a chunk out of his hand. Fisher was not one of my favorite people. A couple of inches taller than me, he was the junior class student council representative who always had his nose in everyone's business. Plus, he bordered skeevy with his flirty comments that played 24/7. Fisher sported pink chinos, brown tasseled loafers, a white oxford rolled to his elbows, and a red crew neck sweater tied around his shoulders. I referred to him as an octoman because he was "all hands" with the opposite sex.

His Polo cologne smelled like it came from the scent glands of a wolverine. "Why are you stalking me, Fisher?" I asked, turning toward him and rubbing my nose.

Fisher's baby blues flew wide. "I'm not stalking you."

"Yeah, you are. You've been lurking in the shadows for over a minute."

Fisher laughed, sliding a hand through his sandy-blond hair. "We haven't made eye contact one time, Darcy. How would you know?"

"Let's just say I've gotten good at feeling people." Er, no kidding. In the past year, I'd discovered numerous dead bodies and had guns aimed at my back, head, and chest—knives shoved up against my neck and brainstem. So far, none of them had hit the mark, but I'd developed a keen sense of awareness the normal might call paranoia. To me, it was survival.

I closed the door to locker number twelve. "Speak."

Fisher nervously looked over both shoulders and absentmind-edly played with the leather band on his watch. "I need help with something."

"And what would said something be?" I asked. Fisher dramatically sighed. "Cut to the chase, Fisher, or I'm outta here."

He spat out, "I think my girlfriend is cheating on me."

I cocked a brow. "And what makes you think I'm the Lone Ranger?"

"She's in Spanish class with you, and you've developed quite a reputation as Valley's Nancy Drew."

Seriously, if flying unicorns took over the Kentucky Derby, it would've been more believable. Fisher and I weren't friends. And I honestly hadn't seen him with anyone other than his theater groupies who typically remained stag, hosting the occasional back-room rager at the guitar shop where Fisher worked. The fact Fisher had a girlfriend I didn't know about was a red flag on its own. I kept up with the who's-with-who stuff.

"What's her name?"

Another dramatic sigh. "Indigo Chase," he answered. Egads. When I thought of Indigo, all I heard was thong-*th*-thong-thong-thong. Indigo always wore pink thong underwear and was known as having the biggest butt in school. The ringtone on her phone was even Sir Mix-A-Lot's "Baby Got Back." I didn't know her very well —other than her penchant to wear pink stilettos and big, black pageant hair she wore to balance out her hips—but I had to admire a girl who embraced her glutes with the I-like-big-butts song.

Classy.

I glanced over my shoulder for Dylan, knowing that closing a deal with Fisher would be less likely if he showed up on the scene. "What makes you think she's cheating on you?"

"She won't return my calls, and when she does, she's rudely aloof and manufactures an excuse to not see me."

"Does she say she *wants* to pull the trigger?"

"No, just strings me along," he muttered.

That didn't sound good, but in my experience, it would come down to the guy she allegedly cheated on him with. I wasn't a fan of cheats, but after dating Dylan, I had to admit there might be some guys a girl just couldn't say no to. "What guy are we talking about?"

Fisher grunted, "Marek Ransom."

Holy crap on a cracker. He thought she'd been messing with Marek Ransom? I would agree that presented a problem because he made Jagger Cane look like a choirboy. And Marek was one fine-looking guy too. He played basketball and football for our rival school in Rook County, and I'd only become familiar with him in the past few months. During our last basketball game against the Blue Devils, Marek was teamed up against Dylan, and apparently Dylan's skills caused Marek to suffer from small gonads syndrome. He jumped Dylan in a brawl that made national news, and although Dylan attempted to make nice after the game, let's just say it had been reciprocated with bellowing and a middle finger.

"How long have you been dating?"

"Six months."

I considered his request a DIY project, but if Fisher was willing to pay for my services, then I'd be willing to rob him blind. Besides, the task would be easy. All I had to do was follow the chick and ask questions along the trail. Believe me, somebody would be willing to spill if Indigo was a cheat. Find the appropriate wallflowers, and their bitterness for being single might make them pee on Indigo's perceived happiness.

"Give me something to work with," I requested.

"That new place in town, Club Need. Management started a Friday night gig that's booze-free, trying to attract the teen crowd. We'd been talking about trying it out tonight. Her last text said she wanted to make a GNO out of it instead."

A Girls' Night Out at a bar definitely spelled trouble. If she didn't have plans to cheat, she would once she walked through the door. Music, half-dressed girls, and guys on the prowl could definitely make one stray out of one's normal backyard.

"If I take on your case, I've got a few stipulations," I said.

"Name them."

"You're available to me day or night. If I need to speak with you, you pick up my call or consider our business relationship severed."

"I can do that."

"You also talk to my associates if they are sent in my stead."

He furrowed both brows into a unibrow. "You have associates?"

I pinched the space between my eyes, wishing it were Fisher's head. "I'm losing my patience."

"Agreed."

I took one menacing step toward him. "If I find out you've lied to me on any of the details, we're also done."

Fisher blanched, acting as if I'd hurt his feelings. "I don't lie, Darcy. I'm as straightforward and honest as they come."

Fisher pledged that statement with the utmost sincerity—but really, his words were more full of crap than Valley's sewage system. He was a bullshiz artist. "Then answer this. Did you do something to make her *want* to cheat? I'm not saying cheating is right, but what kind of boyfriend are you?"

Fisher's looked like I'd stuck him with a sharp instrument and commenced to twist. "I thought we were cool. Maybe I didn't tell her I loved her enough. Do you think I shouldn't ask her to brush her teeth every time we kissed? Is that weird?"

Tylenol, anyone??

"Hey," I said, softening my voice. "I'm sure you're a great boyfriend. It's not my place to judge what happened between you and Indigo anyway. I just need to know if she knew you really cared."

"She knew."

"Then let's talk price."

Fisher's eyes went as big as a freaked-out lemur's. "There's a charge?"

"New policy as of January," I said giggling. "Payment can be in the form of United Dairy Farmers, Pink, Visa, Starbucks, or Target gift cards. If gift cards don't work for you, then I'll always take cash. And for this particular job my fee is fifty bucks."

"Wow." He whistled. "Does UDF do gift cards?"

"Not my problem," I said, "and I can deliver within the week. If I deliver before next Friday, the price is doubled."

Before we could shake on it, the ground underneath me metaphorically trembled. Only one person held the absolute power to make or break my day. When I met Dylan's eyes, my first thought was I wish he'd get hit with an ugly stick. At six foot two, two hundred and twenty pounds, he was a powerhouse of muscle. Dark skin adorned his body, showcasing a face and abs so chiseled they could cut you. His jet-black hair was the type a girl wanted to run her hands through—everything to make her a ten on the perv scale. Wearing faded jeans and a black letterman jacket, his stride was confident and sexy. Laughter plus a hormonally anxious prayer left my lips. He'd ruin things for me. One snap of his fingers, and I'd go Pavlov's dog and wag my freaking tail.

"Here comes Dylan," I said, nervously giggling. "Help me distract him."

Fisher looked like I'd asked him to walk on water. "I can't distract Taylor. That's like asking someone to distract God when he formed the Earth. He's everywhere, Darcy," he said and shuddered. "Scares the pants off of me actually."

I rolled my eyes. Dylan definitely cast a long shadow, but Fisher put the "C" in coward. "Just distract him. I don't expect you to shoot fireworks out of your butt, but come up with something when he starts asking questions."

"Hey, baby," I said, grinning when he sidled up next to me and kissed my cheek.

"Where in the world have you been?" Dylan grumbled. "The only place I didn't look for you was on the back of a milk carton."

"Right here patiently waiting," I said, grinning deeper.

"And what were you doing as you patiently waited?"

"Talking."

"Talking," he echoed, frowning at Fisher. "And what would you be talking about?" Again, eyes raked over Fisher.

"That's private."

"Private," he echoed.

Eye roll number two. "Kill your mockingbird, Dylan." Dylan had an annoying habit of mocking what I said in an effort to make me cave.

"Pinky swear you have nothing to hide," he said, gazing into my eyes.

Ah, the pinky swear. Dylan and I made a pact at age eight to never lie to one another as we twined our pinkies in solidarity. We existed in a world where we wrote the rules and bylaws ourselves, governed by nothing less than total honesty and devotion to the other. But here was the problem with that. It came a tad bit easier for him than me. Ugh...I had a tiny touch of liar in me, although I sucked at the delivery.

"This is very entertaining, watching you flail," he said. Dylan tucked my hair behind my ear, unleashing The Dimples—*the* dimples I fell victim to one hundred percent of the time.

Darn you, Dylan Taylor. Darn you.

"Uh, we were just...oh, crap. What were we doing, Fisher?" I asked, glancing over at Fisher, tongue-tied.

Fisher dumbly replied. "I've hired Darcy to find out if my girl-friend is cheating on me."

Dylan was intensely and maybe even insanely possessive. My particular lifestyle, however, placed those naturally inborn qualities on steroids.

"Why do I not find this odd?" Dylan muttered. Fisher dumbly shrugged. "Can she trust you, Stanton?"

"Yeah," Fisher said, confused.

Dylan gave better empty-face than anyone. Trouble was, a lot lurked beneath it. "Here's my advice to you anyway. Mess with Darcy, and I'll put you on a hospital diet for life." Fisher gulped so loudly we actually heard his Adam's apple bob. "Good to know we're on the same page," Dylan murmured.

Mr. Do-The-Right-Thing wasn't such a rule follower when it came to PDA. He tilted his head and took my mouth in a hard kiss —a kiss tinged with anger and maybe a little bit of desperation. I didn't care. Whatever he'd dish out, I'd more than enthusiastically take. When I shivered a little, his smug chuckle vibrated from his mouth down into my chest.

"You're such a jerk," I mumbled when he pulled back.

"True, but you love it. Now I'll leave you two alone to solidify the details while I open my locker and wish my girlfriend was the type that left me bored."

I wiped my mouth, shakily turning back to Fisher.

Fisher, God help me, looked turned on. "Wow," he whispered.

Dylan's growl threw off a don't-screw-with-me vibe. It wasn't wise to stand in the epicenter of his temper. Fisher, dumbly, couldn't read between the lines and recapped his specific request in front of my boyfriend, ad infinitum. When Fisher added whom he thought the girlfriend had been cheating with, Dylan made a noise that was more savage than civilized. Yup, Marek had a reputation, and Dylan had probably guessed how I'd get the damning details.

Fisher said goodbye with a brisk nod, and I immediately turned to my boyfriend. "Don't say another word," I ordered.

Dylan made the hands-up, don't-shoot gesture. "I've said nothing."

"You're thinking so hard I can hear it," I muttered, and I knew his reservations before he even named them. Here was the problem with a business relationship or *any* type of relationship with Fisher Stanton. He was the former best friend of the guy who almost killed me at Christmastime. And how, pray tell, could he be a best friend and be totally ignorant of what his BFF had been doing? Well, I'd tell Dylan it was totally possible, but then I'd have to use our relationship as an example. And let me tell you, Fisher's best friend put the antipsychotics in crazy.

"Should I have said no?" I asked.

Dylan opened his mouth and closed it, procrastinating an

answer. Dylan was never in a hurry with me. Whether in a conversation or a simple hug, I always had his undivided attention. But regarding Fisher? I honest to God wanted the lecture over, so I could get a jumpstart on the fifty-dollar bonus.

"Let me start by saying I'm proud of you for requiring payment," he murmured.

Ah, the discipline sandwich. Start out with something good, layer constructive criticism in the middle (your beef), and then end with a positive that more than likely was total BS. Dylan was an optimist to the core, but he was an idiot if he believed the tactic would work on me.

"You've been reading your dad's business manuals."

Silence, wherein Dylan gazed at me like I was a lab rat. "Did it work?"

"No."

"Would you like another kiss instead?" he asked, winking and dropping the subject.

Um, please and freaking thank you...and all that. "You're going to cross-contaminate me with your boy germs," I joked.

"Yeah, and cross-contamination tastes great."

I glanced down to his hands, skilled and capable of such strength it was alarming at sixteen years of age. But they were also hands that held such sensitivity it would leave me breathless. He anchored me—well, as much as possible. I wound my fingers between his as he took my lips in a tender kiss. "Are you okay?" he murmured into them. "Mrs. Conner said you didn't finish your paper. She claims it was the best piece of writing she'd read in years, Darc. Her actual quote was that it was brilliant, but you just stopped."

I combed my mind for an explanation but simply said the obvious.

"Maybe it was the subject matter," I said, sighing and still in a partial kiss. Because let me confirm...the subject matter was like a stake to the heart. My mother was murdered when I was nine years old, and unfortunately, I had a front row seat. Gemma Walker had been the lead singer for a popular local band called The Minstrel Cramps. They were on the tail leg of their ten-year reunion tour when a psycho stalker, who'd become obsessed with her a decade earlier, gunned her down. Over the band's ten-year hiatus, no one had seen neither hide nor hair of the SOB, but evidently he'd been lying in wait. I learned then some people were very patient with what they wanted. And for the stalker, it was either my mother or no one else would have her at all.

Our English lit assignment had been to write an essay over the single, most important event that shaped our lives. I got halfway through the retelling and shut down, turning in my paper and leaving the room. I even jokingly yelled, "I'm going for a smoke break," like a total buffoon. Did I realize I'd get partial credit? Absolutely. But I couldn't finish. Not even seven years later could I retell it on paper, and I think that was because she died on Valentine's Day—mere days away.

Dylan's eyes were wrought with understanding. "I thought so," he said softly. "And Mrs. Conner feels terrible. She wants to give you the opportunity for another grade...on a topic not so raw. You know she loves you, yeah? And that I love you more?"

Dylan and I had this thing. When one of us said, "I love you," the other followed up with an "always." Problem was, since we'd started dating, Dylan used those words more fluidly than me. In fact, he said, he love-loved me—you know, the in-love kind. The idiot in me couldn't even say I "friend" loved him anymore, and I'd uttered the L-word phrase since we were six. In fact, every single time he said the words, my vocal cords clamped up, and I became a stuttering fool. It humored Dylan, but true to character he hadn't been deterred. Our relationship had certainly been buzzworthy. We'd trended on Twitter before the weekend was out. At first, I was like, "Mmm, sorry, haters...he's taken." But then the pithy comments and whispered-shock started. I saw his perfection, and the crowd reminded me of my deficiencies.

There you have it. True confessions. Deep thoughts by Darcy Walker.

"You're going to be okay?" he murmured.

"I always am," I said, sighing into his mouth.

"You're lying," he said tenderly.

My voice evidently lacked the necessary conviction. "Yeah," I admitted, "but it's what I do. One day you're going to leave me because of all of the things I do."

Dylan pulled back, grabbing my gaze. "Never going to happen."

There was a mighty fine line between stubborn and pigheaded determination. I wasn't sure Dylan knew the difference. His voice was thick, intimate, and deep with emotion. "I love you. Play, rewind, and repeat that statement over and over until you get it. For me, it will never change. Which means, I will never leave."

Be still my heart...

Chapter Two

NECESSARY EVIL

*A*ccording to my feet on the ground—in this case, Oliver "Bean" Anatoly—Indigo Chase was definitely the overly exuberant type when it came to the opposite sex. But one had to consider the source when recon came from a guy like Bean. If a girl looked at him sideways, he thought he had a chance. So if he thought Indigo had some 'ho-bag easy in her, the reality could range from a friendly blink to removing her bra in public.

Dylan, Bean, and I were in the Beemer Friday night, heading to Club Need. I could confidently say Dylan had never fantasized about Bean in the backseat of his car. Heck, I'd never fantasized about Bean in the backseat of Dylan's car, but I'd commissioned him to help, and his cut of the money stipulated he be in attendance. Bean did have a tendency to be the big mouth express when it came to our ventures, but after browbeating him that secrets were mandatory, he'd dialed back on the enthusiasm...somewhat.

For some reason, Dylan had been beyond supportive. He still lived in some kind of blissed-out state two months into our relationship when I figured our first date as a one-and-done. But I waited for the moment when he'd blink his eyes open and remember that the things I did were wrong...*and mostly illegal*. Our relationship was a walking PSA about opposites attracting. Only time would tell if it would compute into an HEA or become a statistic of how opposites wound up metaphorically killing the other and ultimately settling for boredom.

Dylan maneuvered his black BMW to a stop in a nearby parking garage. Bean jumped out and started singing a Lady Gaga song, whereas I barely got my door opened when my boyfriend cracked it wide and extended his hand in that chivalry-is-not-dead thing.

One look at him and I wanted to stop, drop, and roll...

Dressed in dark-washed jeans, he sported a mock black turtle-neck sweater that tugged at every muscle in his chest, his armor underneath the skin. He also sported loafers, which boasted a private shoemaker in every stitch. His black onyx hair was bed-head messy like he'd rolled off the mattress and decided to grace the world with his presence. My eyes glazed over like a doughnut, and I mentally punched myself before my hands did something they shouldn't in front of Bean.

"What's that look?" he murmured and grinned with amusement, knowing full well I appreciated the view.

Every neuron and synapse in my body lit on fire, charging at a rate that could arguably arm a nuclear weapon. Forcing my inner-bad girl into hibernation, I unloaded the God's honest truth. "I'm thinking the local fire department would approve of what I'd like to do to you." Dylan's face had a brief moment of confusion, and then he read my mind and burst into laughter. "Yeah, stop, drop, and roll," I said, grinning wickedly.

Dylan got his flirt on. "Being in the company of Bean isn't exactly conducive to what you had in mind, sweetheart, but I promise to make it up to you on the dance floor."

We both took a moment to gaze at Bean—who brandished a purple velour leisure suit—practicing his dance moves as we walked. Up and down he went, and then with humanity as my witness, he went Gangnam style followed by a running split leap, coming down like a ballet dancer in a plié.

"You owe me," Dylan grumbled. "Oh, God, do you owe me."

No shiz. Bean fell out of "the stupid tree" and snapped every branch on the way to the ground. Case in point, he carried a dead stuffed gerbil with him wherever he went named Mr. Pongo. Most usually, they dressed as twinsies, and Mr. Pongo's blue-gray rodent self was predictably dressed like Bean, attached to a white cowboy hat Bean wore on his head.

"And what would the payment be?" I giggled, watching Bean strut in vintage *Saturday Night Fever* style.

Dylan leaned in and whispered, "Use your imagination," in my ear.

Dude, if I used my imagination, I was positive it would include a one-way pass to Slutville. But if Dylan assumed we'd have an intimate outing for two, he'd been sorely mistaken. He needed to wrap his head around why I was here before he walked through the door and blew his image of me as Little Miss Perfect. "D," I said with a wince, "about tonight..."

"Mmm?"

"I need to appear single, so I can zero in on Marek."

Dylan was so close I could taste his breath. "Zero in on Marek," he repeated. "And you think that's the right thing to do?"

"I didn't say it was *right*...it's merely the tactic I'm going to employ. Think of it as a necessary evil."

Dylan slid his right hand underneath my jacket and sweater as we walked, the warmth of his touch making me shiver. Once again... stop, drop, and roll blinked in my mind. "You play dirty," I whispered, glancing up at him.

A smile tempted his dimples to show. "Taste my lips, sweetheart. They're best friend tested, government approved."

Major LOL moment, but before I could finish the laugh, he slanted his lips over mine and proceeded to suck the common sense and air right out of my body. Dylan took me to France and all over Europe with his kiss. I mean, we took the slooooow boat to fan-freaking-Paris.

After I got my shiz together, Dylan, Bean, and I assimilated into the fifty-foot line at the entrance of Club Need, cordoned off by a gold velvet rope. Here was the story with Club Need. Apparently, it was a happening club back in the day but was shut down due to underage drinking, nightly brawls, and a handful of teens last seen walking into the place but never returning home. In fact, it was called the Bermuda Triangle for teenagers. That was a recap from Rookie when I told him where we were headed. My Uncle Rookie,

AKA Shepard Johnson, happened to be the head honcho at the Prosecutor's Office in the town where Club Need was located. He wasn't necessarily the paranoid type, but prosecutors never liked cases that remained unsolved. It made them fear perpetrators still lurked, continuing their lives of crime.

By the looks of the crowd, I'd say the place pulled down a hefty penny every night, even on High School Night when booze was not on the menu.

One couldn't escape the fascination with Club Need. The outside glowed bright and glittery—a neon sign claiming the party to be inside. It was hard to fathom teens had allegedly disappeared once they'd entered the place years earlier. Unfortunately, my inner-verb didn't consider that a deterrent. Two sunglassed, muscle-bound men dressed in generic black unhooked the golden rope, allowing patrons access. Some paid cover charges. Others were simply nodded through the door. When we made our way to the front of the line, Dylan slid his hand to his wallet, but the tall brunette touched his left ear like someone spoke into it, glanced at me, and then nodded us through. Dylan's deep chuckle told me it might be one of those times it was good to be blonde.

"You're a VIP, and you didn't even know it, Darcy," Bean said, smiling and smacking my hand in a high-five. "Cool."

Yeah, my guess was I had been typecast as the good-time girl.

Two steps inside, and it felt like a bomb had gone off in my head...with the heat of hundreds of hormonal teenagers. A Black female DJ spun a techno-mix of "Wobble Baby" by V.I.C., and floodlights illuminated the dance floor with a technician choreographing a show for the song. Next to the DJ stood a large man—a floodlight haloing them both on a massive fifteen-foot high stage. Where she had a reggae look about her with a multi-colored poncho and dreadlocks, he was built similarly to Dylan, dressed in black designer threads. Not a brown hair was out of place next to his rugged good looks.

"Interesting, huh?" I said as we placed our jackets in a booth.

Dylan didn't answer one way or the other, but I could tell he'd been as intrigued by the spectacle as much as I'd been. Everyone on staff dressed in black with up-to-date haircuts, which seemed to complement the modern warehouse feel of silver metal fixtures, a black ceiling, and contemporary wall hangings. A bar area with red leather booths sat in the upper right corner with room for more patrons. A quick estimate netted just as many teens upstairs as on the dance floor.

Overall assessment? Not a bad seat in the house.

A hulk of a man came from the shadows and stood next to the host. Tipping the scale around three bucks, he was bald, wooden in appearance, and standing close to seven feet. His station in life? Bodyguard. But why would the host need a shadow larger than the security detail on POTUS?

Bean squeezed my hand, jerking his head toward the east side of the dance floor, right in front of the stage. "There's Indigo," he shouted over the music. "Fisher was right."

Time would tell...

I texted Fisher earlier and said I needed visual proof of his relationship with Indigo. He returned a picture of them together along with a chocolate chip cookie cake that bragged, *Happy Sixth Month Anniversary*. Eh, it didn't get more committed than a celebratory cake. The clincher? The date listed was last weekend. He also said the photographs had been posted on his Instagram account. That told me one of three things: the mystery man wasn't a friend of Fisher's, he didn't care, or maybe he was in the dark about Indigo's cheating ways as Fisher had been. I leaned toward that explanation since Indigo had no proof of hers and Fisher's relationship anywhere on her social media pages. To the world, she was single and ready to mingle.

Fisher had also forwarded their last two text exchanges where she'd told him about the Girls' Night Out. He straight up asked if there was someone else. Indigo swore on her pink stilettos there wasn't (serious stuff in Indigoland). She merely needed some time to "shake her a-s-s"—er, verbatim.

I spotted Indigo's big butt immediately, taking up the space of two dancers, in black, shiny leggings that gave prominence to glutes resembling cottage cheese. She'd paired the leggings with a V-neck pink sweater that fit her like a second skin, her boobs as big as two ripe melons. Rumor said they were Double-Ds, but I'd lay money they lay farther down the alphabet.

Right as DJ Khaled's "All I Do Is Win" lit up the air, a group of guys from another high school motioned for us to join them. Here was the thing with Dylan. He was arguably one of the best athletes in the whole state—heck, the dang country—but for some reason guys liked him. Where some were very methodical in their attacks, Dylan went on pure instinct. A player lined up against him, and in a split second he had the guy's number. He knew where to pivot, where to hit the ball, and which knee to take out first. No wonder many fell into the love-to-hate-you camp. But the odd thing was, there were just as many or more in the love-to-love you camp.

A question for the sphinx.

Dylan grunted in my ear, "I'll make sure to stay close," and after a quick peck on the cheek, Dylan and Co. convened on the west end of the floor.

Indigo spied me almost as quickly, beelining it my way with half a smile, half a face that said she'd just seen Big Foot when she'd been led to believe he was a fable.

Indigo gasped, "Where's Dylan?" as a greeting. Like I said, Indigo and I didn't know one another very well, but *everyone* knew I dated Dylan. And the suspicion in her voice would've been clear to a deaf man. She wondered if I was being unfaithful to him like her two-timing butt was allegedly doing to Fisher. First off, who would cheat on Dylan Taylor? And secondly, who would cheat on Dylan Taylor?

"Dylan is with the guys tonight," I told her.

I baited Indigo with that question, hoping she'd conversely say, *Hey I'm with the girls tonight too.* Instead, she replied, "Oh," like I'd probably already been dumped.

Here's what I knew about cheats—and the info came from my father, Murphy, who'd been a notorious cheat before he met my mother. *Cheats are dishonest by nature, kid*, he'd said. *And those kinds tend to think everyone else is dishonest as a result of their paranoia.*

I'd never given it much credence since Dylan was faithful, but seeing the speculation in Indigo's eyes led me to believe my father had a valid point. I didn't want to play my hand that she was supposedly taken too—not until I had concrete proof of who exactly Marek Ransom was to her. Right then, she was stag, but that didn't mean Marek wouldn't show or was hidden somewhere in the crowd.

"So are you by yourself?" I asked. Indigo and I stood in the middle of the dance floor. It felt stupid to take up space and not dance, so I pulled out some of my best moves while maintaining eye contact.

"No," she said bubbly, bumping me with her butt in a turn. "I'm here with some girlfriends."

Indigo's girlfriends were carbon copies of her—big butts, boobs, and hair that should've been annexed in the 1980s. After chitchat so moronic it left me with a migraine, my hip jingled with a text. I pulled my iPhone from my back pocket and registered it came from Dylan:

Duty calls. Marek just hit the floor.

While I sent back a red lipstick emoji kiss, Bean twerked up against me right as Indigo's ringtone sang "Baby Got Back." She pulled it from the waistband of her leggings with a flirty grin. Bean stepped up the twerking. God. Help. Me. All twerkers were not created equally.

"Good news?" I smiled.

Indigo played coy. "Yeah," she purred. Uh-huh, my gut knew that was Marek. We waited until Indigo left for the restroom, and the moment she was out of sight, Bean and I dirty danced our way to Marek. Dylan's eyes followed me across the floor even though he stayed next to his friends. A non-threatening gesture from most people—downright mother-trucking scary from Dylan.

"Hey," I said, sidling up next to Marek.

Marek was a player. And players shot off a scent to mate that either crumbled a girl's resolve or left her running for a shower. A little taller than my five foot nine, Marek had chocolate brown hair that touched the tip of his black Henley. His chest bulged underneath his shirt, and he either worked out regularly or was one of the few gifted with a great torso without lifting a finger. Relaxed fit jeans bottomed out the look, hugging muscular legs that showcased his athletic ability. Marek's electric-blue eyes, my guess, were the asset that made girls buckle faster than his natural mojo. Let's just say somebody in the baby factory tapped him as a favorite.

After a brief, "Back atcha," his eyes traveled to my oatmeal-colored giraffe sweater from Hollister. Dylan had given it to me for Christmas along with a Tiffany's silver heart necklace...various stocking stuffers...gift cards...a cell phone charger...vintage T-shirts...and a partridge in a pear tree. Not exactly on the pear tree, but you get my drift. I'd paired the sweater with my skinniest of jeans I had to lay on the bed to snap. A matching beanie with sparkly thread adorned my head, and tan leather boots hit me at the knee. With Dylan, I didn't worry about the extra three inches...it made me closer to his mouth.

"Marek Ransom," he greeted, semi-formally.

"Darcy Walker," I said.

"Are you here with a date?" Marek grinned and pulled on his bad boy, but I wasn't impressed. Ho. Hum.

When I didn't respond, to my utter embarrassment he reached out and touched the top of my sweater—um, like right above my left you-know-what.

I angrily swatted his hand away from my habaneros, fueled by a whole lot of righteous indignation. "Seriously, dude. I don't want to play in your sandbox."

Marek laughed so loudly the couples next to us jumped like kangaroos. "I wasn't coming on to you," he explained, "you just have food on your giraffe."

Glancing down, sure enough the light show lit up a big glop of salsa verdé. I'd wolfed down a beef chalupa from Taco Bell during the car ride—about four hundred unneeded calories. Unfortunately, I'd left about fifty on the top of my giraffe's head.

When Marek dumbly touched the sweater again, I felt Dylan's presence behind me, throwing off radioactive rays that'd probably make our offspring have three eyeballs.

"Hello, Marek," Dylan murmured, throwing a possessive arm around my waist. "If you touch her again, if you so much as put a frown line on her pretty little head, I'm going to rip your balls out of their sac, and you'll be singing soprano. You feel me? Tell me you don't. My mother lives for a good opera."

Taylor diplomacy. Hardcore.

Marek grunted a laughing mommy-effer when Dylan's anger dehydrated like water in the Arizona heat. Thing was, it hadn't gone anywhere. What we were looking at was merely Dylan's game face. "Surely you mean that as a term of endearment," Dylan muttered.

I placed a tender hand on Dylan's solar plexus (BTW, it felt mighty fine), attempting to force his beast back on the chain. Likewise, I placed a tentative palm on Marek's arm. "Enough of the pleasantries, boys," I said, nervously giggling.

"He started it," Marek joked. Um, wrong move.

"You started it by touching my girlfriend," Dylan said, adding an angry snort.

I didn't think it was possible to find peace here, you know, Jesus-style. A détente was probably all I could hope for. But then Marek abruptly changed from the confrontational badass when he played basketball to happy-go-lucky, man's best friend.

"Hey," he said, back to dancing. "You have nothing to worry about. Darcy told me she didn't want to play in my sandbox. Granted, it hurt my feelings, but the girl gets points for most creative turndown ever."

Dylan's smile quirked up at one corner as he fought a laugh. "Darcy is definitely the indisputable owner of creative dot com."

"I'd say," Marek said, half laughing, half cursing. "How'd you get all the luck, man?"

I saw that as my chance. Besides, all the love-on-Darcy, Darcy's-the-greatest stuff crap had me self-conscious. Let's not forget I had verdé sauce on my boob. "Come on, Marek," I said. "What would your girlfriend think?"

Marek gave a fake shiver. "She's kinda the jealous type. Do you know her? She's Valley born and bred. Indigo Chase."

I had to hand it to Dylan. He never missed a beat, continuing to dance with a stoic face and no response.

"Indigo?" I said aghast.

Marek pinched his eyes together in a frown. "Yeah, what's wrong?"

"Nothing," I said aloof. "It's none of my business."

"Hey," he said, frowning deeper. "You can't leave a man hanging."

"If I tell you, you can't let anyone know it came from me."

"Agreed."

I touched him on the forearm, cultivating a kindred concern. Once again, Dylan dialed down the alpha male crap and let the conversation roll. "Did you know she has a boyfriend?" I whispered.

Marek stopped dancing altogether. "Nuh-uh," he said.

"Uh-huh," I verified.

"No freaking way," he whispered.

"Freaking way," I repeated.

Leaving Bean to dance, I pulled Marek by the elbow off the floor to talk in private. Dylan followed, but point for him he pulled out his phone and acted disinterested. Sliding my iPhone out of my back pocket, I accessed Fisher's Instagram feed and showed the last post of his and Indigo's six-month anniversary cookie cake, accompanied with a dozen emoticons of kissy lips and red hearts. Switching to Indigo's wall, I proved Fisher might as well be a passenger bird...totally extinct.

Marek whistled out, "Noooo waaaaay."

"It's still *way*, Marek." I sighed. "Are you meeting Indigo here tonight? Because I just talked to her."

Marek gave the club a once-over and scratched the back of his neck like he had a bad case of eczema. Listen, I think there's someone for everyone, but Marek could do better than Indigo Chase. My word, I wasn't even sure Indigo's butt could fit in his car.

"Yeah," he mumbled.

"Believe me, Marek. I've got a myriad of sympathies coming your way, but you need to ask her. Maybe if you just—"

Marek cut me off. "We've been going out for a while."

My heart broke a little, and I secretly prayed Indigo got what Karma had planned for her cheating pink stilettos. "I'm sorry."

"A whole two weeks," he said aghast. "And we talk every three days. Her idea, so we won't get tired of each other."

They'd talked, what? Four times? Marek was proof there was no shortage of supply on stupid. "I'm sorry," I said, trying to find a genuine tone. "That has to hurt for you to have invested so much time."

"I know, right?" he said frowning.

Dylan fought a chuckle then coughed, hoping to cover it up. At that second, Bean and Indigo bounced our way with Marek as the target. Marek's jaw opened to, my guess, call her out, but Indigo literally stuck her entire tongue down his proverbial hatch. Guh. Shudder. I swear, I coughed for them whereas Bean stopped mid-move and clicked off a selfie with duck lips, their unappetizing display of PDA as the backdrop. When her hands went straight to his um, jeans, Bean snapped another with a peace sign. Number three was my favorite—Bean popped-out a hip, arm slung over some chick whose V-neck sweater showcased cleavage he could smother in. And that was why Bean was on the payroll. Indigo was busted. Photo cred: Bean. I texted Fisher, telling him I'd email proof later and meet him Monday for payment.

Marek took his time enjoying Indigo's attempt to suck out his soul, but after a few minutes—seriously, it felt that long—he grabbed her by the shoulders and pushed her away like she had leprosy. "Whaaa?" she asked confused. "What's wrong, baby?"

Marek went for total transparency. "I know you have a boyfriend, Indigo." Indigo's eyes darted to me, her scowl contemplating going *Jersey Shore* on my butt. But Lord help me, I'd practiced my dumb-blonde face for years. I conjured that sucker up—a wide-eyed innocence mixed with bargain basement intelligence. Indigo blinked twice, looked at Dylan who gave her a toothy grin, and bought it hook, line, and sinker.

After a few, *I don't believe yous* and *Where's your proofs,* Marek's jaw set into a hard line, and he went for the jugular. "It's over," he said. "You don't even kiss that good anyway."

Ooh burn!

If someone, ahem Dylan, said that to me, I'd either come up swinging or dissolve into sissy tears. Okay, it would def be sissy tears, but I liked to think I was more badass than I actually was. Marek angrily split the crowd, and Indigo—pageant hair posse in tow—clicked after him, her thong almost giving me whiplash. Here was the issue. I think Indigo might really care for Marek—Fisher had merely been a stand-in until she felt confident Marek was a sure thing. But Indigo was one messed up chick if she felt no remorse in stringing along two guys.

Strong arms encased my waist as Dylan rested his head over my left shoulder. "How do you feel?"

"Slimy," I muttered. "But money aside, isn't it best he knows?"

"Absolutely. You did your part. Let them work things out and back away."

Listen, folks. I wasn't good at backing away. Dylan must've gone temporarily insane to even think I was capable. "What if one of those relationships was meant to be," I said, "and I just screwed it ten ways from Sunday?"

Dylan kissed the side of my neck, trailing his lips up to murmur in my ear. "Neither relationship was good, sweetheart. And I don't believe you can mess up what's meant to be anyway."

Ah, Dylantopia. If only the rest of us were smoking what he was.

Chapter Three

GILDED CAGE

I didn't mean to toot my own horn, but um, toot-toot.

Fisher texted back I'd have my money Monday at school, bonus included. A half an hour had bled by, and Dylan and I were cozied up in the booth. It was a victory celebration of sorts, only for the love and togetherness moment to be crashed by Marek. Male posturing ensued when he slid into the seat, but once it ran its course, Marek and Dylan had a pseudo nice convo. The potential blood bath, temporarily over.

Marek seemed to be over his jilted-lover thingy. Indigo was MIA, and ergo he hit on every female who had two legs. Marek apparently didn't have a type because the girl he chased onto the dance floor was tall and leggy with red and purple hair she'd gotten from an aerosol can.

As they say, love (or lust) is blind.

The bass on the sound system jackhammered in my chest while Dylan grabbed me by the hand and ushered us onto the floor, close but not too close to Bean. Dylan had developed a soft spot for Bean —almost like he was a puppy too young to wean...too naïve to understand the big, bad world. "No more work tonight, Darc," he murmured. "Let's have fun."

Eh, good point.

While "Black Widow" growled through the sound system, my eyes fell on the man Marek named as our host, Lars van der Hart.

With gold Aviators shading his eyes, he jammed next to the DJ, watching customers and the subsequent cha-ching in his bank account. Other than random couples hooking up, High School Night seemed pretty sedate, but maybe that was the verb in me itching for action.

We cut the rug through another set of music when nature called. I kicked the lovin' up a notch and pecked Dylan's lips, taking off for the restroom, navigating through a crowd that had almost tripled. It ticked close to eleven o'clock, and if I didn't make my curfew of midnight, Murphy would mobilize the Marines. Plus, we had to drop off Bean in the boonies. Murphy—yes, I was on a first name basis with my father—had taken the upgrade in Dylan's and my relationship as well as could be expected. But if Dylan didn't have one foot out the door by one a.m., Murphy would stumble downstairs and take a clothing count.

A long narrow corridor cut a path to the restroom. I immediately discovered that area was the land of wallflower. Girls huddled up against one wall. Guys huddled against the other. All of them stared—wondering who, if anyone, would make a move on the opposite sex. I nervously smiled and walked as fast as I could, remembering what it felt like to be invisible. Heck, I still felt invisible and worried I'd one day wake up, and it would be: Me, Darcy. You, Dylan. We, best friends. Our relationship and kissing evolution would've all been a dream.

With one hand on the bathroom door, I shoved inside and quickly took care of business. When I stepped to the sink for a mirror check, I was smacked in the face with the stain on my sweater. Yup, verdé sauce ruined the look. Turning the faucet to cool, I snagged a paper towel from the automatic dispenser, doused it with water, and wiped the stain away in four swipes. Fluffing my hookerfied hair (humidity, the culprit), I repositioned my beanie when the ambiance went loco. Four girls muscled their ways inside —decked out in I'm-on-the-market clothing—some trendy, some embracing their Miss Slut.

I made an attempt to slide around them but was forced into reverse and backed into the sink. My butt hit the porcelain, but before I could mutter, "Watch it, 'hos," a catfight ensued between two girls fighting over one guy. Girls like that I referred to as skanks...not because of their looks...but because they believed their time and space on the planet was more important than anyone else's. For a skank, the bathroom was her palace—a place where she busted on everyone and delivered mental torture, not caring if the victim was present or not.

"I saw you looking at him!" Skank Number One screamed.

"He sure as heck wasn't looking at you," Skank Number Two said, snorting in laughter. "Seriously, your outfit is so five minutes ago. Totally ratchet." I didn't know much about clothing but thought Skank Number One looked rad. Heck, her outfit was similar to mine. Skank Number Two, however, put the nymph in nympho with five-inch, candy-apple red heels and a silver jump suit. If she thought she was the epitome of sophistication, she'd fallen face-first off the *Vogue* wagon and hit spaceship.

"Oh, get a clue," Skank Number One said. "You can have Marek Ransom. I'm more interested in his friend." Ah, good ole Marek had been making his rounds.

"And you think you have a chance with his friend?" Skank Number Two added. At the mention of Marek's friend, the skanks got all dreamy-eyed with sighs and pornographic moans. *Dayum*... the guy must be hot, or these girls were desperate and delusional—a land I wasn't completely unfamiliar with. I had one hand splayed on the door when Skank Number Two stopped me dead in my tracks. "Dylan Taylor has a reputation as a lady killer. And yeah," she said and giggled, "he can kill my lady parts any time he feels like it." It felt like someone ripped my heart out and batted it around with a Louisville Slugger. Dylan had a rep that followed him everywhere. I mean, ugh. Even in a foreign place, girls fought over my boyfriend, but I knew in my bones he probably hadn't even spoken to them. "Unfortunately, I hear he's off the market with some chick named Darby-something," Skank Number Two finished.

Sigh. I might as well have a secret identity. No one ever got my name right.

The skanks talked amongst themselves, wondering who I was, what I looked like, and so on and so forth. When one of the girls sounded like a hog in heat, I did my own DIY counseling session and told myself I was beautiful, I could have any guy I wanted, and one day soon I'd be on the cover of *Playboy* as Playmate of the Year.

Throwing my shoulders back, I hitched my chin up to beeyotch league and muscled my way outside. Looking at my boots as I walked, I reminded myself Dylan said the L-word. Still, the hot mist of tears dotted the backs of my eyes. When I dabbed at them with my fingertips, I ran right smack into some man's chest—causing him to make a death grip on the two coffees he held in is hands. Unfortunately, the phone cradled under his ear tumbled to the tile where its screen cracked like a frozen lake in springtime. File that under *Total Disaster*. Let's hope he had insurance or didn't worship his amenities like I did.

I snatched it off the floor, my hand violently shaking even though I commanded it to not give a shiz. "I'm so sorry," I said grimacing. "I'll replace it...not today...because I haven't gotten paid yet...but I will...um, fifty, er one hundred dollars is coming...crap. Double crap."

I realized my eyes were closed when a deep voice gently murmured, "It's only a phone. Look at me."

Cracking open one lid at a time, I met eyes with our host himself, Mr. Lars van der Hart. Wow. Big OMG moment with capital EEEs afterward. I stood stock-still, my ribcage forgetting to do the inhale/exhale gig. Tall and lean, he was ripped and cut like Chris Hemsworth with the BMI of one of those cyclists in the Tour de France. Around Murphy's age, his hair was chestnut-brown, his eyes green like the Atlantic Ocean. But his face...the face came accompanied with a story. At one time, he'd been über good-looking, but something or someone had hardened his features. Four one-inch scars marked his right cheek, and one had been cut so deeply a layer of flesh had been removed. It was not hyperbole to say I waited an eternity to speak. The man reminded me of someone, but I couldn't place a face to a name.

"You're new," he said, "and beautiful." *Yes, to the first*, I thought. *The jury's still out on the second.* When I stood there like a moron, he asked, "Hey, are you okay?"

"I, uh, I'm sorry...sort of a klutzy...they were talking...about my boyfri...I shouldn't...jeez, I suck."

"What a command of the English language you have," he murmured.

"Yeah, I never fail to impress." I looked at the coffee in his left hand the way a bloodsucker admired a fresh vein.

"Would you like one?" he asked, toasting one toward me.

"Is it roofie-free?"

Van der Hart nearly peed himself with laughter. "It's roofie-free," he said.

I grabbed on to that coffee like it was the last drop of H2O on Earth. "About your phone," I said, admitting the mea culpa.

He took a disinterested glance at his broken phone and opened his Armani jacket, sliding it in the side pocket. I wasn't one to scope-out labels, but I could spot an Armani anywhere. "Again, nothing to worry about. Everything okay in there?" he murmured and grinned, pitching his head toward the ladies' restroom door. "It had gotten rather loud."

"It was one nasty catfight, but I think the fur has cleared."

The grin ballooned into a full-fledged smile. "Did you win?"

"Not my style. I'll save my gunpowder for something bigger."

A deep chuckle warmed my bones. "Smart girl."

A memory niggled at my skull, just far enough away I couldn't grab it at first try. "Smart girl"—where had I heard that in the context of a conversation? God knew it wasn't at school. "Do I know you?" I asked.

"I'm Lars van der Hart."

"Darcy Walker."

Something flashed in his eyes, but just as quickly as it came, even quicker was it snuffed out like a candle. "So how do you like the place, Darcy?" he asked.

"It's great but not my normal scene. Besides the fact I played with fire as a kid, I guess I'm sorta boring."

"I wouldn't categorize you as boring."

He had a black and white flier tucked under his arm that said "Underground Fight Club" in bold across the top. I nodded toward the flier, grinning. "Not so underground if you advertise it's underground."

He chuckled, bringing it to his eyes for deeper perusal. "My thoughts exactly."

"Isn't that illegal?" I asked.

He folded the paper and shoved it in the left side of his jacket.

"Fights aren't illegal, but betting on them is. Someone hung this in the mens' restroom. It's not something I promote, so hopefully I got it pulled down in time."

Yeah, well, uh...good luck with that. "Hey, I've gotta scram. My dad's gonna go bonkers if I miss my curfew. It's not exactly a gilded cage, but it's close."

His gaze glittered with amusement. "Ah, well, carry on, um—"

"Darcy," I reminded him, reaching for a handshake.

His long fingers wrapped around mine in a strong and stately grip. Instead of returning the shake, he pulled my hand to his lips in a gallant kiss. "Good evening." With that, he turned on his designer shoes and walked back toward what I assumed was his office, taking a left.

Dude was a god.

———

Someone lifted me up—several someone's to be precise—as soon as Drowning Pool's "Bodies" hit the airwaves. Oh. Lordy. "Bodies" was the ultimate mosh-pit song, and somehow I'd been chosen to crowd-surf amongst a group that'd morphed into a bunch of teenagers off the leash. It was one of those occasions a person either fought the group or went with it because mosh-dancing could prove deadly. I wasn't afraid of death (obviously), but I wasn't ready to retire the kissing thing yet. It actually had been the main reason for my feet hitting the floor each morning.

Guys and gals alike grabbed my bum, legs, and torso as I stayed hoisted above heads, sometimes ten feet in the air. A thick grip fondled my rear, and my ankle was twisted in a hand-off to someone not ready for my buck-thirty pounds. I took a quick dip to the floor, only to be saved by two overly handsy guys. I craned my neck to make eye contact with the pervs, gave up, and gazed at the twirling strobe lights. After I'd been successfully passed off to a dozen other people (uh, partly), those releasing me chested and slam-danced into one another. While bodies sloshed and groaned, my untouched coffee spilled, and when the crowd grew even rowdier, I clocked on the budding emotion of panic.

Oh. Shiz.

Oh shiz. Oh shiz. OH SHIZ.

When I heard a panicked, "Darcy!" I swiveled my head and saw Dylan wide-eyed, muscling people out of the way and frantically grabbing at the air in front of him. "What the...!" he growled. Yup. Dylan dropped the F-bomb as he grabbed me around the waist and gently lowered me to the floor. Right then, the song abruptly transitioned into another tune and the moshers lost their pep. When I glanced a shaky eyeball to the stage, I spotted a PO'd Lars van der Hart jawing with the DJ. Guess he didn't want the liability of a mosh pit. After he ripped her a new blowhole, our eyes collided—him, angry like a doper without a syringe...me, grinning like a fool.

Dylan was like a Glade Plugin of hormones. After one sniff, I silenced his nerves with a kiss, taking a rocket ship to 'hotown. My heart hammered. I couldn't breathe. And the blood roared like a lion in my ears. Normal SOP. Every once in a while Dylan would kiss me with abandon. As a rule, he tried to remain in control since I turned out to be a more than willing participant. On the rare occasion where he gave into his feelings, the world disappeared and viewer discretion was strongly advised.

As "Thinking Out Loud" crooned in the background, after a few beats at my lips, he trickled tiny bites up my chin, kissing hungrily down my neck. We pushed the limits on my curfew, but any girl would if Dylan had her wrapped in his arms in a passionate lip-lock, right there in front of God and everybody.

Group shots and selfies popped all around us—the flash lighting up my closed lids. *Do not let this shiz go viral* was all I thought because I honest to God was close to licking his armpit if he'd let me. Why the viral concern? Murphy had recently turned stalker on my social media accounts. He'd never cared before, but now he trolled every waking hour and even commissioned two of his cronies to assist. After several lip-smacking smooches, my control was seriously off the chain, purring and growling like a feral cat in heat. I pulled back with a dizzying shiver and uneasy feeling in my stomach. Le sigh. I was in so much emotional trouble I was afraid to explore its depths. I shook off the self-doubt before it settled in and convinced myself our love was forever. And if it *wasn't* forever, it would only be because I chose to live alone, found someone hotter, or decided to reside on the freaking space station. Eh, none of those were possible, but the little L-word kept popping onto my tongue, and it had grown harder and harder to force into dormancy.

"I love you," Dylan murmured, almost as if he'd read my mind.

My breath came out in ragged, gaspy chunks, like a car engine trying to turn over. I wimped-out with a right-back-atcha grin, leaving him in no way deterred. Both his dimples imploded. I had to admit our relationship had been pretty epic so far, but let's be real... I pushed the limits of his patience.

"Ever want to go back to that best-friends-only thang?" I teased.

Dylan hooked a finger in my belt loop, pulling me to him. "Over my dead body," he murmured.

As they say, famous last words. The ground shook, the ceiling rumbled, and the wall standing next to us crumbled to the ground in four large pieces. White plaster, ductwork, and powdered dust hit the air in a puff of smoke as Mother Earth commenced to tell us she was in charge, not us. It was an earthquake...strange. Screaming girls could barely be heard above the screeching of the music. Dylan came for me at light speed, curling me into his stomach and trying to shield me from tremors from which there was no refuge. Once the quake had ended, a dead body tumbled down in slow-mo in front of us.

Chapter Four

TORTURE CHAMBER

*N*ow there's some material for your next nightmare.

A dead body. Yup, a d-e-a-d body. Who would've thought a gasp-inducing make-out session would end that way? Thing was, dead bodies had become the norm for me. I'd found a body in a dumpster, a head buried in the sand, and a skeleton in a closet...for those who wanted the particulars.

When the aftershocks abated, the mood grew eerily silent. Most were in a white-knuckled shock, but then all hell broke loose when they registered a body with a striped shirt and jeans on decaying bones. Probably a girl. No way could one superglue her back together and add skin. In fact, the flesh that remained resembled beef jerky.

Dylan took the three steps separating us, getting between the body and me. He gulped hard and prayed, "Holy Mother."

Dude, there wasn't anything holy about the body. And P.S., whatever put it there was even unholier. I swallowed down the chalupa begging to make an encore and glanced back to the plaster walls that had hidden the body away. It was a small compartment of some kind, maybe a closet, and when the idiot in me stepped inside, I realized it resembled a prison. Three pairs of shackles hung from the wall—with no way in, no way out. Had it been hidden there? Tortured?

Dylan and I simultaneously had the exact thought. "Where's

Bean?" we asked the other. Let that thought incubate no more because Bean hovered overtop the bodily remains, attempting to do CPR when it had died with the dinosaurs. For the love of God, if I believed my superhero mindset was bad, Bean was channeling his inner-EMT. The corpse cracked and crunched with the weight of his palms as he totally contaminated and FUBAR'd what was probably a crime scene.

"Bean, it's dead!" I screamed, half mortified, half laughing my head off. Bean still went at it with total gusto. Problem was, in Bean's dedicated efforts Mr. Pongo fell out and lodged into the body's gaping jaw.

Hello face, meet palm.

Dylan grabbed Bean around the waist, coaching him the body was evidence as Bean ran in the air still trying to get to it. Bean punched and kicked while tears rolled down his face like he hadn't made it to the scene on time. Dear, God. There was a story there. Like me, a single father raised Bean. His mother was dead. I knew it, and by his reaction he felt a boatload of guilt.

Fifteen minutes later, Detective Christian O'Brien had Dylan cornered, asking for specifics. When I gave him my side of the story, he immediately moved on for Dylan's take. I was thinking I used too many adjectives, or Dylan appeared more stable. He only gave me the five-minute treatment where Dylan was going on twenty. Bean was still one breath away from needing a sedative and had held my hand since Dylan pried him away from Dead Girl. He'd calmed a smidgeon when the coroner returned Mr. Pongo, but whether he was sane again—or as close as Bean could be—was TBD.

The coroner right then threw a sheet over the remains while bouncers and policemen attempted to corral the handful of us left. Normal MO would've been to kick everyone out ASAP and contain the area. Problem was, the temperature had dropped to seven degrees, and the cops didn't want the liability of unchaperoned teens wandering the streets and freezing. So the handful of us remaining had been ordered to stand and/or sit quietly by the bar and wait for a ride home while detectives did their thing. Since Dylan's interview portion was taking for-freaking-ever, for once I did as I was told.

Standing in the corner talking to another detective was the DJ and manager of the digs, Lars van der Hart. My eyes ping-pong'd between them and the body. The DJ seemed beyond nervous, twisting and twining a dreadlock around her fingers. Lars, however, had that look like his new investment had sunk deeper than the Titanic. While my eyes scanned the crowd for anything or anyone suspicious, I tugged Bean over to a section of the bar not being worked by CSIs, looking for a seat. As soon as I neared the eight seats still vacant, I recognized the voice of my secret mentor, Tito Westbrook, on the barstool to my left. Well, hallelujah, but I almost wet myself.

Tito was the go-to crime reporter for *The Cincinnati Enquirer*, and I'd followed his work since I could read the back of a cereal box. He had his checking account hacked over Christmas, and I helped him uncover the perp. The crook robbed several people blind, killing a few in the process, but was ultimately unmasked by my hand. So far, Tito only knew me under my alter ego's mononym of Jester, but seriously, if a few key criminals chose to talk, in the words of Ricky Ricardo, I'd have some s'plainin' to do.

Tito stood at average weight and height, dark-skinned with black hair slightly balding at the crown. My initial estimate placed him at early to mid-forties. His clothing was business casual, wearing khaki pants, a brown golf shirt, with lace-up leather shoes along the lines of something my father would wear. His features were strong with eyes a dark brown, lips stained a beefy red, and cheeks aglow with the same color. Tito was good-looking, but he wasn't great looking, but he possessed something that made a person take a double look. He had that "it" factor, but one could spend his or her entire life trying to figure out what that "it" was. I suppose if someone was a journalist like Tito, trying to get people to divulge their dark secrets or details of someone else's was the best gift the universe could've doled out.

He spoke quietly into the cell gripped in his left hand. "It comes as no surprise," he said. "We need the body ID'd, Sophie. If I'm right, this is going to blow the lid off of everything." A pause. "Darlin', I know I'm right on this one, and it's an answer to prayer. Get your flirt on and pull a favor at the coroner's office. Capeesh?"

How innnnnnneresting. Why would Tito not go all reporter on

everyone here? I expected him to have his notebook flipped open, interviewing whomever he could before the cops kiboshed his efforts. It was almost like he waited patiently for the third act in a play to be over so he could make his grand exit.

In my head, I knew it was a bad idea, but my body hadn't quite heeded the warning. My hand gripped him on the shoulder, tight enough that it wouldn't be considered nice. "Don't turn around. It's Jester."

The coffee cup in his right hand halted midair, and his back went ramrod-straight. The bar had been closed, so what could I conclude? The man had been here for a long time, and his coffee had to be cold. "Jester," he drawled with Southern charm. "The pleasure is all mine."

Tito slowly drew the cup to his lips, took a drink, and deposited the mug back on the counter. Tito'd played that game before because he craned his neck around the booze to see if he could catch my reflection in the mirror behind them. Fortunately, the liquor bottles had been restacked to capacity after the tremor, so getting a visual would prove difficult. I'd been smart enough to snuggle up next to a group of girls of varying shapes and hair color, turning my body sideways. Plus, my profile was shadowed by Bean's ten-gallon hat. Tito couldn't see me, but he could still hear my voice.

"What exactly is your interest here, Tito?"

"I could ask you the same."

"I wanted to be a big time wrestler when I was eight. When that didn't work out, I decided to grab life by the gonads and squeeze," I answered. Tito reluctantly chuckled. "There's a story with that body, Tito. I stepped inside the wall from which it fell. It looked like a closet, and there were three sets of shackles mounted inside, giving it a creepy medieval vibe. Someone kept people prisoners. The dead girl—if she *is* a girl—had no shackles around her. Question is, why not? We know she didn't die under restraints. Did she die because she discovered other people *had*?"

"Leave it alone, Jester."

And when had I ever done that? That's right...never. "Maybe I can help."

"Darlin', you're talented. I'm not sure who you are, but this one is definitely over your head."

"I never took you as the Doubting Thomas type."

"Okay," he conceded. "Maybe it's not over your head, but I don't think you have access to the information I need."

"Why don't you let me be the judge of that?"

Tito laughed again. "I'm not playing, Jester. I worried myself sick over you back in December. I can't chance you becoming the next corpse."

A smart person would run right out the door, but the part of my brain that was smart just took a ride on the "stupid bus." I said, "So you admit what happened here tonight was a crime? Did you know her, Tito?"

A tiny pause that the normal wouldn't notice...but I did. "No," he said.

Grade A, mother-trucking baloney. "Fine, I'll go this one alone."

"Jester," he said, rising out of his seat. "You do not want to swim too close to a drowning man. Trust me. Stay home. This ain't for you, darlin'."

Thank the good Lord his effort to stand had been dashed when a man the size of a mountain sidled up next to him, asking the bartender if he could use the house phone.

A bead of sweat trickled down Tito's temple. My word, he was nervous, so nervous his sweat glands had gone haywire. But why? Right then, Dylan whisked Bean and me toward the door while Tito continued to talk to dead air. Bean walked stoically between us. Dylan and I linked our arms through his in an attempt to keep him vertical.

"What did you think of the place, D?" I asked when we hit the sidewalk. "You know, other than the dead body that fell out of the wall," I added in a nervous giggle.

Even though Dylan was choirboy clean, he was street smart, discerning, and had the uncanny ability to read people. I wanted his take on things, although I could've predicted the response. "The place didn't feel right," he answered.

No doubt. "How in God's name, could someone not realize a dead body was in the wall, even after the place had been inspected?"

Dylan's gaze hardened, and a vertical worry line appeared between his eyes as he craned around Bean to meet my face. "My sentiments exactly. Stay out of it, hound dog. I prefer my girlfriend warm."

———

Bzzz, bzzz, bzzz.

Bzzz, bzzz, bzzz. What in the H was that? Did flies live in the dead of an ice-cold winter? Rolling over, I attempted to drown out the sound with a pillow when it slowly dawned on me it was the annoying vibration of my iPhone...not flies making love to a trashcan.

"You've got to be kidding," I groaned from the premature wake-up call. My hand floundered around on the nightstand, coming up with nothing.

Dylan Taylor. Who else in the world would be insane enough to text me at seven a.m. on a Saturday morning? Dylan had been my personal alarm clock for years, albeit at a respectful hour. Here lately, his calls shaved fifteen minutes off our agreed upon time. It sucked to work on the weekends, but if I wanted cash to burn, then I needed to chase the pavement. When my phone buzzed again, my hand went for a repeat on the flailing thing, finding my phone and pulling it to my eyes.

U up??? the text said.

No, moron, I typed with one eye closed.

Ha-ha, rise and shine, sweetheart. I'll bring coffee.

Bite me.

Apparently, Dylan grew tired of texting because my phone rang, scaring the bejeezus out of me. Dropping it to the floor, I rose back up and banged my head on the nightstand. Rubbing my throbbing crown, I finally snatched it up and brought it to my ear.

"That's assault and battery, baby," I grumbled. And yeah, I occasionally called my best friend-slash-boyfriend *baby*. Ugh. How mortifying.

"Good morning, sweetheart," he said, chuckling deeply. "I've missed you."

"Do you even *know* what time it is?"

"It's seven o'clock. Sorry, but *Dylan's* up, and I want *Darcy* up. Besides, there's something I need to talk to you about."

I dropped anchor on the topic before Dylan made any headway. "Now?" I mumbled. "I'm not sure I'd understand what you're saying. I need fifteen minutes for my brain to reboot and a shot of caffeine."

A short pause. "Okay. In the car, but it's important."

"Everything is always life or death with you," I muttered.

A low chuckle reverberated in my ear as he shut the convo down with a baritone, "I love you." Sigh. So dreamy. I so was going to kiss him later.

Coaxing my feet to stand, I slid into my robe and peeped inside Marjorie's adjoining room. No Marjorie present. My money said she'd slept with Murphy. That could only mean there'd been a crisis situation in the nightmare department. My little sister had endured nightmares of late, and it all had to do with this time of year. Believe me, I got it. It was the anniversary of my mother's murder. M-U-R-D-E-R. And no, we had never delved into the specifics, but she found an article on the Internet that went into minute detail.

Um, thank you, Information Highway.

I tried not to dwell on my mother for more than short bursts, but seeing how it affected Marjorie thrust her back into the forefront whether I liked it or not. All these years later, the wound was still jagged, but Murphy could pull me out of the dumps—even if the endgame would ultimately be the same.

Most of the time my father was a ticking time bomb, but the universe gave him two daughters, and he found a maternal side. At six foot two with curly brown hair and Cherokee Indian lineage, he wasn't short in the looks department either. With cheekbones that could chisel granite, his thick eyebrows framed deep-set, chocolate eyes the color of a candy bar. Thing was, people could get lost in those eyes, but if they didn't know him, they could get scared to death in them too.

Creeping into his room, I found Marjorie curled in a tight little ball oblivious to Murphy's heavy breathing. Realizing all family members were accounted for, I schlepped back to the shower, discarded my PJs, and switched the spray to the hottest setting. Stepped inside. I needed to think about some things—the today, the tomorrow, *all* of it. Those tomorrow conversations made me crazy because my life was circling the drain. I didn't have an ace in the hole where my future was concerned, but that was the nature of the beast. One had to appear marketable before anyone would buy what he or she had to offer.

Problem was, there was a statute of limitations on my attention span. I was bored. Bored...with compulsion issues. Not a winning combo. And what did a girl do when she had compulsive behaviors? She most usually surrendered to the compulsions. And guess who stumbled upon Dead Girl the night before? Yeah, little ole me. I had a feeling Dead Girl was number one on Dylan's we-need-to-talk agenda.

Punching off the shower, I padded outside, did the towel thing, and dressed in black yoga pants and a bookstore T-shirt that claimed "Belinski's is the Bomb." Next, I grabbed matching black and red Asics. Twenty-five jumping jacks later, I let my hair dry naturally, slapped on lip gloss, and swiped mascara over the mongrel green eyes of a crossbreed. Taking the steps two at a time, I'd somehow mastered the art of not waking Murphy and Marjorie—an accomplishment because every other step had a loud squeak. Fixing them was on Murphy's list of "things to do," right up there with banning junk food and going to anger management classes.

Breakfast was leftover pizza. Swallowing a slice down with a can of Coke, I pulled a powdered doughnut out of its package, opened the front door, and snagged the morning paper. Lead story: *Club Need Leads to Death*. You don't say. Now I knew why Tito Westbrook hadn't hopped on the psycho train with the rest of the crowd...he'd already fired a cannon across the bow.

Club Need Leads to Death
By Tito Westbrook

Sometimes questions arise in life, and one is forced to answer. What job should I take? Which college should I attend? Should I get married? The biggest question these days is will Club Need kill patrons like last time?

By my calculations, Cincinnati lost close to 50 of its citizens in deaths or disappearances once they stepped foot inside Club Need. A quarter of those were found dead. The other three-fourths merely disappeared into the wind. Those found dead were teenagers or early twenties, but just the same, they were all individuals looking for a night out on the town.

A rational person tries to piece it altogether. There are deaths. What causes the deaths or better yet *whom*? There is always a paradigm among disappearances and deaths that are related to serial killers: hair color, height, weight, age, and various other physical properties that exist in the mind of the criminal. The only pattern in these deaths is the victims' youth and fascination with Club Need.

Tito always went for the big story, so whatever happened decades earlier still chipped away at his curiosity. In fact, he'd acted as if it was still alive. And that thing, er person rather, contributed to the demise of Dead Girl. He must have some credible intel because the article bordered libel and defamation of character if one could put a name to the accused.

I barely finished the last paragraph when I heard the sound of a high-pitched beep. What the shiz? Then it went on repeat. *Beep! Beep!*

"Dylan," I shrieked as if it were a curse word.

Chapter Five
THE F-WORD

Shoving both arms through my coat, I hauled my purse over a shoulder, stuffed the paper under an arm, and made a mad dash for the door. Stepping out onto the porch, cold air punched me in the face like a heavyweight. Dylan, however, didn't seem to mind the arctic air. He sat on the hood of his recently waxed BMW, coffee in hand...*my coffee*...since he didn't pollute his body with the nectar of the gods.

Munching my doughnut as I walked, once I neared him, he took me by surprise and stopped me with his moving legs. He wound them around my waist, hooking them together at his ankles and drawing me up to where our eyes lay within inches of one another. I had to catch my breath. Stumbling forward, I braced myself on one of his muscled legs. It wasn't like Dylan had never hugged me, but I'd never been wrapped between his legs and up into his grill.

When he leaned forward, my codependent self closed my eyes for what I expected to be my first kiss of the day. Instead, he lightly took his tongue and licked away the doughnut's white powder from the corner of my mouth. I dropped my doughnut and heard Def Leppard's "Pour Some Sugar on Me."

Yup, I'd died and gone to Badgirlville.

Dazed and confused, I gripped his thighs and mumbled, "You like the effect you have on me."

"And just think," he said, smiling and picking the doughnut up and placing it back between my teeth, "I wasn't even trying."

I took a big bite, rolling my eyes. "You are one cocky dude, son."

Dylan winked, suddenly tight-lipped. That was unusual because it wasn't like him to not continue the flirtathon and go for the last word. Unhooking his legs from my waist, he slid off the car, suddenly introspective. Disappointment pierced my heart when our contact was broken. Once again, Badgirlville, people. I was a charter member.

Remaining true to his gentlemanly nature, he strolled around to open my door. Once I'd hit the seat, he tweaked my nose and handed me the coffee as I swallowed down the last bite of dough-nut. Closing me inside, he made his way to the driver's side, slid into the seat, and punched the key in the ignition.

"I'm fRRRREEEzzzing," I chattered through my teeth when I felt the Beemer's heated seats. Dylan pulled me into a hug that had the heat of a blast furnace. As soon as I warmed up, I started mackin' on him. Like. All. Over. Him. I tasted the doughnut, mixed with the coffee on his tongue and decided Heaven couldn't be better. "I've missed you," I breathed into his neck, ending with a kiss under his chin.

Dylan moaned. I moaned deeper. "Good morning, sweetheart," he eventually said. "I love it when you go au naturel." Leaning forward, I glanced into the rearview mirror, appraising the bangs I'd been trying to grow out. Murphy had curly hair. Evidently, I inher-ited a couple of cowlicks because my hair was lifted off my head at a forty-five degree angle.

Collapsing back into the seat, I giggled. "I love it when you're stupid, D."

Fulfilling the unspoken creed of the gorgeous, he looked ready for a fashion magazine. Dylan sported a black baseball cap and wore a white sweatshirt underneath a black bomber. For all I knew, he rolled out of bed, shoved a cap on, and qualified as paradise to women both young and old. The good ones didn't have to do much. The blessed didn't even have to try.

"How's my girl?" he murmured while he backed out of the drive-way. Even before we were a cohesive unit, Dylan often shuttled me to work when most teenage boys lay facedown in the pillow. Dylan swore he was up anyway, and the way his wake-up calls nudged the sunlight, I'd begun to believe it. I still wanted my own car...unfortunately, there was a little requirement called cash.

I took a sip of coffee. "Just peachy. And you?"

"I'm still trying to recover from last night. A video of you crowd surfing made Club Need's website. I'd say you made an impression on management."

"Duuuuuudddde," I drawled out. "I'm like famous!"

"Or infamous," he said and chuckled. "And by the way," he added, glancing over with a humored eye. "Dad isn't too happy you were crowd surfing."

Dylan's father, Colton, was sometimes worse than Murphy in the hovering camp. Some collected stamps, others cars, but Dylan's father collected people. Unfortunately, I fell into the assortment of objects he liked to keep tabs on. "It's not like I was dropping acid, and I can't say I blame Club Need management for using the mosh-pit as a marketing ploy. They couldn't exactly post a video of the person who fell out of the wall."

"Makes total sense," Dylan said sarcastically. "How naïve of me."

"Come on, baby," I said grinning. "You're a worrywart. And you worry more now that we're all kissy-official." Dylan's dimples tempted to show, but he squelched back the urge. "Okay," I whined, "I could've put up more of a fight, but I promise to work out all of my rebellion. And if not—"

"That's why we have prisons," he deadpanned.

Hardy, har-har-har.

Dylan's favorite road? My way or the highway...

I leaned over and grabbed his right hand, some serious smoochery on my mind. After two quick pecks on his knuckles, I said, "Fire away, D. What did you want to discuss?"

Dylan's swallow was almost audible. Releasing my hand, he rearranged his cap. Up and down. Side to side, side to side. Back and forth, back and forth. Dylan had one mannerism that was as predictable as him touching his heart when something moved him. He'd rake his hand through his hair or rearrange his hat. "I have a video interview today with the University of Alabama head football coach," he exhaled. The baby-fine hair on my arms stood on end. I waited for my mind to grace me with a spectacular riposte. Didn't happen. "You're upset," he whispered.

My mind cursed, @#$%^&*, but I didn't want to upchuck my panic all over him. I pumped the brakes on the dead air. "I'm just shocked," I answered. "You had all last night to tell me, and you didn't."

Dylan had a great poker face. He gave me nothing, but then a crack in the dam formed. His knuckles tightened on the steering wheel. "Bean was with us," was his sighing excuse. "And I didn't want to go to bed with either of us feeling—"

"I can see your point," I interrupted...but still.

"Does this bother you?" he murmured softly.

Um, duh...

The thought fell somewhere between Michael Myers and *The Shining* music scary. For a split second, I considered going Pinocchio, but there was no room for little, white lies or your casual stretching of the truth. I was determined to not be a mega-crazy damsel in distress, although worry tugged at my heart that our epic romance would blow up in my face.

"I hate it," I said honestly, "but it's coming at us like a runaway train. I'm proud of you, D. Just follow your heart."

"That's the problem. My heart is with you. Here."

I twisted my body toward him, reaching for his hand. "But here may not have the best opportunity. And then everything you've worked for would be for naught."

Listen, I hit the best friend lottery with Dylan. He was full of compliments, endlessly encouraging, and always loyal. Thing was, the roles needed to reverse. I didn't have the talent he had or opportunity knocking at my door. I needed to pull on my cheerleader even if I hated the "rah."

"We all have a natural path, and yours is clear," I said. "You've trained hard, and people have noticed. It would be wrong to not follow through on what you've started. That's what you'd tell me, and you know I'd do what you'd asked." Dylan kept one eye on the road, the other on the eye roll I commanded to go dormant. "I have faith in you. Just wait, the world is gonna be your oyster."

I didn't use that particular F-word often. Sometimes the Fates had something else planned. Something extremely distressing and unbeatable.

"I'm not sure anyone else has such unequivocal faith in me. You always have."

After an intense stare down that left me feeling naked, Dylan winked and held his arm wide for me to snuggle up against him. Believe me, he didn't have to ask twice. But once inside his embrace, I wasn't ready to be touched so intimately. A big part of my soul could never get close enough, but here lately, I'd developed a pang when we had to part. Like the person who completed me might someday find someone else who completed him more.

I whispered, "I'm proud of you. Play this out, D. You have to."

"It's just an interview. We'll cross that bridge when we come to it."

Dylan always substituted optimism for reality, but it seemed to me he already had one foot on the flipping bridge. Signing day was coming up fast. Universities didn't always wait until senior year to sign athletic prospects. They signed junior year, sometimes getting promises even sooner. And believe me, the nightmares of the day were not blurry on recall. I'd been plagued by panic attacks since I realized what college would do to Dylan and me. And that was before we'd even gone official as a boyfriend and girlfriend unit. Now that we had, it was one huge slice of the pie called reality I could do without.

As the seconds ticked on, Dylan broke the silence first. "You do believe in us, yeah?"

My answer? Sort of a yes-ish. Dylan grabbed his heart, almost as though he tried to convince it to pump its next beat. Let's just say I'd learned to lower my expectations in the love department. Distances most usually tore people apart, but if I didn't encourage Dylan to do what was best for him, then that wouldn't make me his best friend. Likewise, if I encouraged him to leave, then the Fat Lady might as well tune up her pipes.

I gave him more teeth. "It's not like I'm going to delete your ringtones," I joked.

That loosened him up. "Please," he begged in a whisper, "don't ever stop doing that."

"Joking?" I said, stupidly laughing. "Most find it annoying."

"Being *you*. I crave you, Darcy. I'm up to my eyeballs in you."

"Well, I'm drowning in you, pal. And sometimes I don't like the feeling."

Dylan and I had a moment—the moment I knew was coming—where I pretty much admitted I was scared of the L-word. It didn't offend him. In fact, he acted as if he waited for his pulse to return to normal because the prospect excited him so much.

I felt the beginnings of a mammoth migraine. I dug around in my purse for some change, planning to raid the vending machine. Sugar was my go-to drug and would hopefully help me ignore the clamor of my heart. When I came up empty-handed, Dylan clicked open one of those secret compartment thingys only Beemers have and placed a twenty-dollar bill in my palm.

Dylan's wallet, AKA, the Darcy Walker slush fund. "Thanks, D. I'll pay you back."

Dylan's eyes softened into a shade of amber that made me want to lose my clothes. "No, you won't. What I have is yours, Darc. Always has been. Always will be."

My breath twisted in my throat...would that always be the case? Because let me confess, if this thing went south and a new girlfriend entered the picture, the first person on her hit list would be me.

If she was smart...

By the time we'd made it to Belinski's Bookstore, things with Dylan were a blinding blur of unsettled emotion. He blinked rapidly as I offered a smiling, "Bye, baby. And thanks for the ride."

"I love you," he murmured. The leather of the seat crackled as he leaned across the console and brushed his lips against mine. I squeezed him hard and answered in a fevery kiss. Let's just say if we were wound tightly before, Dylan pulled the coil and the resulting heat bounced us to the moon. After a make-out session that steamed the windows, I cut through the door, threw my things behind the counter, and ran to the restroom. I had one of those heart-wrenching, soul baring wails females have in the middle of the rom-com when the guy gives her the heave-ho.

Oh shiz. The day had gone to shiz already.

———

That conversation murdered my sense of humor. Well, almost. After a few laps around the store on my RipStik, I lied to myself that all was right in Darcyville. Thing was, Dylan and I didn't discuss things like we used to. Now that we sucked face regularly, we'd developed a tendency to allow all things physical to correct the misunderstandings. In the past, even if there had been a hotheaded blowup, we would come back, sit down, and duke it out at the bargaining table. We didn't duke out anything these days. Well, maybe our mouths did, but I got the feeling that wasn't a healthy resolution to anything.

Baby steps, I guess.

My fingers tugged on my lower lip with the recall, deep in thought, and I robotically got on with my NCIP day. No Crap in Particular, that is. Belinski's Bookstore—or The Double-B as customers called it—barely saw any business, let alone be accused of housing books that sent the mind up in flames. Mr. B recognized the problem. In fact, in an attempt to reach a younger demographic, he bought the staff fire-themed T-shirts. The "O" was the fireball of a grenade whose pin had been pulled. Problem was, inventory was probably one-third of what your basic bookstore stocked, so to turn a profit he marked everything up by an obscene amount. Embarrassing, but somehow the man produced a paycheck for me every two weeks. As long as I hauled in the green, I'd continue the daily grind.

I poured a cup of joe and puttered back to the break room. Slipping a buck fifty in the vending machine, I watched a Hershey's bar and bag of Famous Amos cookies kerplunk to the bottom. Shoving half the bar in my mouth, I stole a glance at the faux leather, lime-green couch. Mr. B had passed out on it, breathing like a whale whose blowhole had been clogged.

Dead to the world.

Sleeping off a bender.

Mr. B was three hundred pounds and had three necks. There might've been a fourth, but that would require an investigation I didn't want to assign the energy to. His face was dusty red, his eyes were blue-gray, and his standard bibbed overalls were littered with a snowstorm of dandruff. If the theory was true that every person had a soulmate, then a Mrs. Shamu existed somewhere knocking back some hardcore liquor.

Propping him up on his side (the universe had named me rehab by de facto), I trekked to the customer service desk. The day's shift was Rudi, myself, and Bean...yes, I said Bean. Coralue, the senior citizen I'd worked with since age thirteen, up and moved to Florida with her boyfriend of two months. He was twenty years younger and spray-tanned like someone on *Dancing with the Stars*. Here's to hoping he didn't love her social security check more than her.

I sidled up next to Rudi who had thirty percent hearing but didn't mind talking at work. "How's it hanging?" I signed.

Rudi blushed. I know, cue the filter.

Rudi qualified as the quietest girl in the junior class, reserved only because she was deaf. Up until Christmas, neither of us had had a date, been kissed, or anything with the opposite sex other than the occasional dirty dream. In Teenagerland, we'd been the losers. Now that I'd had a taste of the committed life, it was my goal for Rudi to have a sample. So far, she'd been unwilling. Why? Because I think she had a crush on one of the biggest fastards in school and had been keeping it on the down-low. Yeah, insert Jagger Cane.

"What's his name?" I asked even though I knew the answer.

At barely five feet, Rudi had brunette hair styled in an asymmetrical bob and wire-rimmed, Ben Franklin glasses. She shied away from the dialogue, embarrassed but smiling deeply, smoothing out her Double-B shirt and skinny jeans. Instinctively, I knew there was a story there, but if it was who I thought it to be, Rudi needed a bodyguard on standby just to stay virginal.

The thermometer hovered in the teens. Ringing up the first customer who'd braved the cold, I slid my arms in a black Adidas jacket and zipped it halfway when Bean blew through the door. I brokered him a deal for his job last weekend. I know...idiot move, but I'd begun to feel responsible for him. Bean had helped with Tito's case in December, and he'd done it by introducing me to his regular friends in Valley High's detention. Things snowballed from there.

Bean needed better influences. It was a sorry state of affairs when I was the upgrade.

Behind Bean was who I assumed was his father. When I say his father was old, I mean *old*. Like he could've speared a T-Rex or shared a smoke with Thomas Jefferson. Something about him reminded me of Bob Cratchit in *A Christmas Carol*. Laugh lines surrounded his eyes, but a sadness had perhaps made them deeper than age. After a quick goodbye hug, Bean lined his belongings up right next to mine (seriously OCD move) and headed for the restroom...a trip to the restroom he'd asked me to accompany him to.

Bean was afraid of getting eaten by the toilet. I could see the issue. Toilets could be loud. Problem was, I'd been under the impression he'd grown out of it in fifth grade. Just my guess, but I was thinking Dead Girl might've brought back the fear of the unknown.

Standing outside the door, I prayed his nerves would level out because come Monday morning I'd pass the torch to someone with gonads if he didn't get with the program. After a few seconds of feeling like a perv, I heard the toilet flush and the faucet switch on. Right then, a black furry spider crawled across my sneakered foot. That sucker was as big as a silver dollar, and the bloody bugger had fur! I screamed a bloodcurdling scream nightmares were made of. Grabbing a Stephenie Meyer off the shelf, I played a game of whac-a-mole until its furry legs splatted out and moved no more. Next thing you knew, Bean flew open the bathroom door like an F5 tornado, spied the smashed arachnid, Stephenie Meyer in my hand, and shrieked, "That's murder!"

Technically, I thought, but the quiver in my hands told me that might be a lie. I steadied my breath, looked at Exhibit A on the carpet, Exhibit B in my hand, and realized my defense would not stand up in a court of law. "It's not homicide if the bug looked threatening," I told him.

Bean's eyes flew out of their sockets and then jumped back inside his head. "Swear it?" he asked.

I ripped my pinky nail off with my teeth. Dang, telling the truth surely wasn't as painful as covering up a murder. "He, uh, just went to Heaven early, Bean. It was his time. Why don't you go help Rudi?"

Bean seemed to buy the Heaven comment, but by the time I flicked the furry monster off of *New Moon*, my head pounded so badly I'd seriously begun to reconsider my caffeine addiction. That was the life of the sugar addict. We binged and paid for it later.

My iPhone rumbled right as I dumped the spider into the nearest wastebasket. Oh, God. Cue the *Jaws* soundtrack. Duunnn-dunn...duunnn-dunn...dun-dun-dun-dun-dun-dun-dun! Jaws was an 18-karat thug who lived in Cincinnati's underbelly with all the other lowlifes and mobsters. For some reason, he'd developed an affinity for me but was the type who would kill people and then use their bones as wind chimes.

At first, I wasn't allowed to know his real phone number, but the last four times he'd phoned, the same digits appeared, so I gave him a ringtone. The number was still untraceable because I'd *69'd it and got nowhere fast. In fact, he texted back he'd feed me my own eyeballs if I kept trying to find him.

Chapter Six

THE FIFTH AMENDMENT

"*S*peak," I grumbled.

The deep bass voice I'd come to recognize answered. "Why were you on the Club Need website, Jester? I don't approve of you going there. Need I remind you that I saved your ass twice?"

True dat.

I'd first become acquainted with Jaws sophomore year when he helped me uncover the leaders of the Northside 12 gang at school. A bunch of hair-raising stuff went down, and I almost got murdered, but I considered that a small detail on the road to success—just another day in the life of Darcy Walker. Eventually, one of Jaws's mysterious friends shoved me in the trunk of a yellow Dodge Charger...so we could chat. As a result, I'd become obsessed with finding Dodge Charger Man, in a you-need-shock-therapy sort of way.

Initially, I had zero clue he and Jaws were connected, but in retrospect I should've assumed as much. Jaws admitted he had details about my mother's death, and that information only came when I backed him into a corner about this friend of his. Dodge Charger Man had a knack for showing up when I was about to eat lead, and I had a feeling his interest likewise had something to do with my mother.

Shoving the copy of *New Moon* back on the shelf, I peeked in at a still snoring Mr. B and made my way to the cash register. "You're quiet," Jaws said. "What's wrong?"

I sighed. "I'm exercising my fifth amendment rights."

Jaws chuckled low in his throat, the sound waking something female in me that was so appalling I considered ripping out my own ovaries. "Babe, you make me laugh."

I rolled my eyes. "Exactly why did you call, Jaws? Other than to lecture me."

"I called because you're too nosy."

"A character flaw I've never tried to deny. Judge away."

I heard a door quietly close. "I'm in no place to cast judgment, but I did call to nominate you for the posthumous award for biggest dumbass."

"Don't talk to me that way, Jaws. Not one brother talks to me that way except you, and I can debrotherize you at any time." And um, yeah…I had a band of misfit brothers who did dirty work for me on the DL, and I dumbly—let me say again, *dumbly*—inducted Jaws into my own misfit society mob.

I heard the grin in his voice…and unfortunately, there was some sex appeal in it. "I don't talk to anyone this way except you."

"And why is that?"

"I suppose that means I care about you the most."

Leaning beneath the counter, I pulled out an aerosol can of antibacterial spray and squirted a stream on the countertop. Bean was afraid of germs. I figured I owed him since he'd fallen back into the land where the toilet was his enemy. "No one else gets on your nerves?"

"Tons of people get on my nerves, but I just shoot them."

My hand stopped the 360-swipe of the countertop. I debated a retort but decided to let it die a natural death. "I'm assuming you know about Dead Girl?"

I think he laughed but wasn't sure. "I heard, ergo your nomination for the dumbass award. How in God's name do you keep attracting the dead? If I didn't have firsthand knowledge, I wouldn't believe it."

"She just kind of fell out of the wall. You know, the earthquake… in freaking February."

"Meteorologists say an earthquake can happen at any time, Jester. But like you, I wonder if it's the end of time. So why were you there?" he pushed.

I couldn't believe I had plans to tell him, but Jaws was like Dylan. If I didn't give him the truth or a version of it, he'd keep calling until he was satisfied with my explanation. I unloaded the deets. "I was spying on a girl at school named Indigo Chase. Her boyfriend hired me to find out if she was cheating...which she was. The beeyotch scored so high on the BS meter he should've smelled it."

Jaws cackled so loudly it quickly morphed into a wheeze-fest. "Jester, you never fail to shock. So did you go into this with a plan, or were you flying blind as usual?"

"Sometimes the stupid part of my brain overrides the side that's a rapacious planner."

An even lustier laughter. "Double word score on rapacious, babe, but you rarely plan anything." True, and I hated it that he knew me so well.

I put the cap back on the can, returning it beneath the counter. "Ouch. That hurt."

"You aren't hurt. In fact, you're intrigued."

"I don't deal in innuendo. Speak now or forever hold your peace."

"You only deal in innuendo," he said chuckling. "If you catch my drift."

I rolled my eyes. "Maybe I'd like a life that was innuendo-free for once. I'm guessing you called specifically about Dead Girl. Do you know who she is? How long she's been dead?"

"She could be a number of people, but it wouldn't surprise me if she was Lyric Armstrong."

Acquiring that information had been pretty easy, which meant Jaws was up to something. "Lyric Armstrong," I verified. "Any other info on Lyric?"

Another deep chuckle. "I won't squeal, Jester, but I will role play."

Of course. How stupid of me. Falling into the seat behind the counter, I massaged my temple with one hand, giving Jaws the proverbial finger with the other. "You've given me a migraine," I groaned, "but I'll play. Let's just say you knew of her. Am I getting warm?"

"Keep going."

"She suddenly disappears, and you and all of her friends were devastated."

A weary sigh. "You're boring me. And I was quasi-sure you could do this."

What an insufferable tool. "Let's say she disappears, and your curiosity is piqued why she suddenly is gone." No answer. "You believe she was murdered."

"Aye."

"Then that means you suspect someone in her inner circle of being bad."

I got a low, "You're good."

"But bad to you means this someone probably double-crossed you because you aren't exactly what I'd consider a paragon of clean living." Jaws laughed and the sound shivered through my body as if he were right behind me, whispering into my hair. "You want this person to pay."

"Retribution is not always a bad thing."

"My guess is you want me to link Lyric to this person, but if you didn't know Lyric, then my guess is she merely serves as a means to an end."

A whispering, "You scare me."

I was on a roll. "Since her death isn't keeping you up at night, the person who killed her *does*. So much that you want to settle a score that is—"

"Nearly two decades old," he interrupted darkly. When Jaws said those four words, the warm rush in my blood told me I'd better beware. Um, wow. Whatever happened was unfathomable.

"So anything else in this two-decade span to ruffle your feathers?"

"A person who deserves all my hate definitely does more than one thing. The beef between us began almost two decades ago and set off a Lemony Snicket series of events that affected someone I care about. Point blank, he doesn't deserve air in his body. And I want you to find him for me."

"And you want me to help you remove the air from his body?"

"I want you to give me his name."

My eyes flew wide in shock. "You don't know his name?"

"He switches identities. I've known him by various aliases and looks, but there is one specific name I'm after."

"Which is?"

"Julius Marx. I need you to tie the death of Lyric Armstrong to Julius Marx. Regardless of what you hear, it was murder. And if you can point me to Julius Marx...if I get close enough...I'll recognize the rat by the smell."

Poetic...but I knew what that meant: Jaws had a bullet in his gun, and I'd pull the trigger. "You call me to tell me I'm stupid, Jaws, yet you want me to dive into this dangerous world of Lyric? To be specific, you're molding the bullet, and you want me to shoot it? Dude, that would make me as guilty as you."

"Do not misunderstand me. I want you to feed me information, but I do not want you personally doing a thing. In fact, I forbid it. I don't like many people, Jester, but somehow you've wormed your way into my dead heart. Anyone else, I'd rather pull the trigger on and shove out with the trash. This is too dangerous for you, but I trust you enough to know you can do this discreetly."

Nice endorsement. I wasn't sure I should be flattered since it came from Jaws who I was positive was a psychopathic schizoid. My inner-verb told me I was moments from missing out on some action that might be bigger than what I'd ever experienced. "Give me a starting place."

"You don't want to swim too close to a drowning man, babe," Jaws muttered and then disconnected. Cue the record scratch. Good. God. Almighty. Those had been Tito Westbrook's parting words the night before at Club Need. Was Tito the drowning man? Or did Jaws simply mean Tito had the information I needed?

Ugh, I thought, wincing my eyes shut. Why was Jaws doing this to me? Whatever the specifics, it meant the donkey himself had been in attendance. Amend that: he was in attendance practically stealing my air because I'd lay money he was the big guy who muscled his way between Tito and me. I almost had him...but he'd outplayed me again.

———

I went Disney in my iTunes library. The seven dwarves and I boogied down to *Snow White's* "Heigh Ho" as I tried to convince myself Bean's brain wasn't on the express train to insanity. He'd been in the back section of the store since opening—dusting, realigning spines, and practicing his ballroom dancing to "The Blue Danube."

Nope...he didn't have a partner. Didn't look good.

The boredom had eaten up five hours, and the only thing interesting about the day was Marek Ransom and one of his friends now sat at the table in the middle of the store, the three of us shooting the breeze with Rudi. I was confused how Marek had found me until he confessed the tattletale had been Instagram. Hmmm, guess I shouldn't have uploaded the pic of the mutant spider that scared the shiz out of me. They came to see its remains.

"I still can't believe Indigo was a cheat," Marek said solemnly.

Listen, I had no idea Indigo and Marek had been dating, but their under-publicized relationship and über-publicized breakup had lit up social media for the past twenty-four hours. Thankfully, my name didn't enter the threads, but let me just say I'd been sweating it like a hooker in a squad car.

"Seriously, dude," his wrestler friend, Canyon Cavanaugh, said. "She wasn't even that cute."

I couldn't see Indigo from a guy's perspective, but Canyon's words were crass and totally heartless. It decapitated Marek's pride, and for a guy as good-looking as Marek, I thought that a crying shame. Canyon either was the type that never considered his words or he felt the need to cut Marek down. Neither scenario was good for Marek. Made me wonder why he hadn't kicked Canyon's butt to the curb.

Marek stiffened, letting out a curse directed at his butt wipe of a friend. "At least, I had a girlfriend, idiot. That's more than I can say for you."

"There's better out there, Marek," I promised, reaching to squeeze his forearm.

"I'm thinking the best might be taken." Marek smiled, pitching his chin to Dylan's class ring on my hand. The ring was white gold with a round black onyx stone, a silver "V" stamped on top. A diamond decorated each side. Totally masculine. And totally rich.

He'd proudly given it to me the night we'd gone official. It was an old school practice, but I either wore it around my neck dangling from a matching chain or on my left middle finger with yarn to make it smaller.

When I sheepishly shrugged, Marek winked, his roguish smile deadly to a virginal female. He and Canyon were similarly dressed—school hoodies, jeans, and sneakers. I let my eyes slowly linger over Marek, ending on Canyon. Both were in the beautiful crowd in their own respective rights. Strike that thought. A mustard stain dotted the front of Canyon's hoodie. I smiled inside. It couldn't have happened to a nicer guy.

Canyon ran a hand through his shoulder-length, dark blond hair —hair so unkempt I briefly wondered if things lived inside with their own ecosystem. His eyes burned and cut like blue lasers. When he raked his eyes over Rudi's chest and my Barely-Bs, Rudi blushed and nervously shifted toward me. When Canyon saw her reaction, he gave me a grin like name-the-time-and-place. Just a guess he didn't know Dylan Taylor was my boyfriend. Dylan could make you a eunuch from states away. "I'm not interested," I said, acknowledging his play for me. "In fact, I'd rather bail headfirst out of a hot air balloon and kiss the grass."

Canyon didn't know whether to laugh or be offended. Marek made the decision for him, bursting into giggles that had a hint of karma's-a-beeyotch in it. "Ah, Darcy, it's a shame you're in a relationship. My life could use your sense of humor."

Canyon wasn't deterred, shoveling a crapload of BS he was sure I'd bite into. He propped his Nike KDs on the table, leaning back and threading both hands behind his head. "Come on, girls. Don't make me try so hard. Unless that's what you like?"

Up yours, you mother-trucker, I thought. The testosterone was choking me. I had a feeling whatever came out of Canyon's mouth would be a tsunami of lies. Plus, he was too smarmy for my taste. "Let's talk about Dead Girl," I said, changing the subject. "Have you guys heard anything?"

Marek leaned forward in his chair, ready to dispense gossip. "Negatory from my end, but Canyon's dad's a detective with the city of Cincinnati."

Listen, I'd practiced my I'm-a-nobody face for years, so I casually slid my eyes over to Canyon, calling up a little bit of dumb and blonde.

Canyon said, "I don't know much. Only that the body is female, aged fourteen to twenty-five, and probably been dead a good fifteen to twenty years."

That would jive with what Jaws said earlier. Since Jaws claimed he had a nearly two-decades-old axe to grind, it was logical to assume Dead Girl's death fell within that timeframe. What little I knew about forensics, we might legitimately be weeks from getting a positive identification though. After I quickly signed the details of Dead Girl to Rudi, I pulled on my twenty questions. "Um, wow. How do you think no one ever noticed her?"

"Your guess is as good as mine," he said shrugging. "But no matter what, there should've been a smell at one time or another."

So (A) there was either no smell—not possible with decomp; or (B) she died after the place had been shut down. If she died after the original doors to Club Need closed, then it was logical to conclude future tenants never had reason to assume she'd haunted their walls. But who would have access to the place after it closed? Only a few people—a realtor or the owner, presale.

"Then she must've died after the place had closed," I surmised. Canyon shifted uncomfortably in his seat, his reaction almost worth as much as his three-figured sneakers. "Any suspects?" I asked. "Former owner of the club, boyfriend, coworker? Did she work at Club Need the first time around? Before it was shut down for not being on the up-and-up?"

One more shift and Canyon went as silent as the grave. He knew something, but by the firm set of his jaw, my guess was the info dried up like the Rio Grande. While Canyon reconvened hitting on Rudi, I slid my eyes over to Marek. "I'll see what I can find out," he said, chuckling and then he dropped his voice to a whisper. "Taylor's a lucky dude. Makes me want to hate him all the more."

I tried not to make eye contact, but when his face was practically in my mouth I honestly had no choice. "No one can successfully hate Dylan once they know him."

"True," he admitted. "I was disappointed to know he wasn't an a-hole. Hey," he said, suddenly jumping subjects. "Did you hear about that underground fight club thing?"

It took a moment for me to remember what he referred to, but Marek must've seen the flier in the Club Need restroom the manager had pulled down. "Yeah."

Marek's eyes lit up. "I'm gonna do it. I've never done any MMA stuff, but I can take a punch. Besides, Canyon will show me some moves."

"I'm not sure it's legit, Marek. In fact, the manager yanked it down because it was even posted in his place."

Marek shrugged my doubt away. "It was legit enough for someone to print up a flier. It's at least worth a call."

Worry knocked on my brain, but I didn't have time to allot brain cells to Marek's pretty face. After twenty minutes of Canyon scoring a date with Rudi—gah, I'd kill her in private—I rang up a customer as Rudi gave Canyon the directions to her home. Point for Canyon, he didn't seem intimidated by her hearing impairment, and Rudi surprisingly spoke in front of him. But it'd take more than one act of class for Canyon to score a green light from Darcy Walker.

Jumping on my RipStik, I wobbled my way to Marek as he opened the door to exit The Double-B. An onslaught of ice-cube flavored air blew my hair into the Albert Einstein league. When I struggled to remove it from my face, Marek lost control of the door. My RipStik chose that moment to bust-a-uey, and my legs went out from underneath me. Unfortunately, Marek went for my hand, and the glass door came crashing around our fingers with a loud thwack. By that time, Canyon entered the fray and tried to stand me aright...he on one side of the door, Marek on the outside, looking in. When they both pulled at the same time, I heard the crunch of a breaking bone. That's right. Crunching. Bone. My left hand got jammed between the door and Dylan's class ring. When I pulled it out, blood spurted and stained the floor like Dan Aykroyd's when he channeled Julia Child on *Saturday Night Live*. I went breathless. Swallowed vomit. Mother of pearl, maybe I had brittle bone disease because that was just flat-out weird.

Marek had a volcanic temper. I'd seen it when he'd been paired up against Dylan in basketball. When I turned green and muttered, "I'm going to hurl," Marek put two-and-two together I was one digit shy of a peace sign. He pushed the door wide, growling at Canyon who'd already propped me against his chest. "You just broke Dylan Taylor's girlfriend's finger," he barked.

Canyon's face said he'd stepped into a den of rattlesnakes. "Dylan effing Taylor?" he whispered profanely.

"Yeah," Marek muttered. "Apocalypse now."

Chapter Seven

JOY JUICE

"*W*hy does pain and trouble follow you, kid?"

"I dunno. Just lucky, I guess."

"Not a question...just a statement," Murphy muttered. "God knows there truly is no answer."

I'd just made it back from a trip to the X-ray machine. Yup, the idiots definitely broke my finger. My bloody digit looked like an appendage on a prehistoric caveman, the middle phalange gnarled and snapped in two. Consequently, Dylan's class ring had been moved to my right hand.

Murphy had drunk six cups of coffee as we waited for an ER doc to stitch me up. I sort of had stitches in third grade when a six-pack of Mountain Dew tumbled off a grocery store shelf and smacked me in the forehead. But those were stupid butterfly Band-Aids they give kids to make them feel invincible. Plus, my head was stapled on the first day of school last fall for a head wound. Murphy was experiencing some post-traumatic flashback because he'd said the P-word, the D-word, and I was pretty sure he considered the F-word. I'd said them in my mind when the orthopedist popped my bones back in place five minutes earlier. It was painful, right up there with dreaming I sat in school naked. I'd texted Dylan after the torture was behind me, trying to break the details gently without having Marek and Canyon lose their cojones as fallout. He'd been on his way to the hospital when the nurse swore we were next on the patient assembly line. So he stayed put—my guess sticking pins in his Marek and Canyon voodoo dolls. But seriously, I floated peacefully on a narcotic cloud. All was right with our going-to-Hell world.

Murphy stepped in a slushy puddle back in the parking lot, and his black tie-ups squeaked like a dog toy. He gave Marjorie, nick-named M, a second bag of Skittles while he stuck his head out in the hall, attempting to bully the doctor into making an early appearance.

Dressed in an all pink tracksuit, my little sister sat on the exam-ining table next to me, smacking her lips. "I wuv candy," she said, followed by a swallow. "I wuv it better than anything elth." Her lisp —a product of two missing front teeth—became more prominent when she was nervous. It came as no surprise her lisp had my name on it.

"That's right, kid," Murphy said. "Sugar can put a temporary bandage over the crap the world dishes out. But the mood I'm in, I'd rather kiss up to a salt mound."

Marjorie's almond-shaped eyes scrunched up like Murphy's when she was happy. At the moment, they were so bugged-out it looked like she had thyroid disease. Attempting to fluff her fire-engine-red hair, I gave up and picked off lint balls instead.

Murphy opened and closed cabinet doors, banging them louder than necessary. "I wonder how much this stuff costs?" he grumbled. "Do you know I read an article in *U.S. News & World Report* that swears I should put it all in my pocket and take it home? It is *mine*, you know. That piece of paper your butt is sitting on probably cost two hundred bucks, and the hidden cost is going to show up some-where in my bill." A short pause. "Dang it."

"Maybe you should just chill," I said.

Murphy slid his brown eyes over with a snort. "I'm ten centime-ters dilated here with no indication of an easy birth." Another lengthy pause. "Ask, and it shall be given you. Seek, and ye shall find."

Murphy went King James, throwing out Bible verses when he needed extra patience. "Is that your s-sermon of the d-day?" I asked.

Ruh-roh. I'd begun to slur my words. What exactly was in that IV drip anyway?

"Consider me your spiritual advisor," he grumbled. Murphy dropped a JC. Something he rarely did.

At that moment, Dr. I'm-Definitely-A-Russian strolled in. He had brown hair and freckles, was string bean skinny, and obscenely tall. His eyes were a steely blue, and the clothing he wore was dialed up too. Pink shirt. Purple-dotted tie. Flashy. The expression on his face, however, was dead—like he needed caffeine to jumpstart his heart. In other words, he'd treat me and street me and grab a nap in the nearest bed. Fine by me.

Drunk on drugs, I greeted him with a "Dasvidanya."

"Jesus, Mary, and Joseph," Murphy said, actually performing a face palm. "Even I know that's goodbye, kid. How much joy juice did they give you?"

The doctor offered a handshake to Murphy. "I'm Doctor Popov."

"Hello, I'm the man who pays your salary," Murphy grumbled. "Can you explain why—"

"I'm s-ssorry," I interrupted. "This is Murphy, my spiritual advisor. Are you American?"

Dr. Popov didn't even crack a smile. "I'm from Scranton."

"Bless him, Lord," Murphy muttered. Once again, a Bible reference. That particular phrase was Murphy's way of saying "you're screwed."

Dr. Popov thoroughly washed his hands and snapped on purple latex gloves. Gently picking up my left hand, he frowned and sat on the stool at the end of the bed. Walking it to my side with his feet, he opened a rolling cart and removed a needle and thread. Marjorie jumped off the table, licking the Skittles from her fingers, immediately moving to hide behind Murphy. He patted her on the head like someone would a pet. Even drunk on joy juice, I could tell my father had hit the ceiling on single parenting. As much as I hated to admit it, he might need a girlfriend.

"Do they have R-russians in Scranton?" I asked.

"We're everywhere," he answered.

"Long live the R-russians, I say. Murphy's from Kentucky...and I think he's inbred."

Dr. Popov actually chuckled. "Good God," Murphy mumbled.

Weaving the pinkish-red thread through the needle, Dr. Popov made eye contact, unexpectedly painting on a confused frown. "What's wrong?" I asked giggling.

"Your hair is blue," he said.

"Yeah," Murphy said snorting. "I could've sworn Smurfette didn't leave the house with blue hair. But who am I? I'm just the father. No one calls to ask me if it's okay to make her hair blue. And no one calls to ask if it's okay to break her gosh-danged finger. You messed up my basketball afternoon, kid. I'm not sure when or if I can ever forgive you for that. UK was up by twenty. The only thing good about your hair is it's blue."

Murphy referred to my ombré hair and how it matched the uniform color of the Kentucky Wildcats. Rudi and I'd colored my dirty-blonde head during lunch. We boiled a powder packet in water, and the bottom third was a Kool-Aid royal blue.

"Do you think it'll come out?" I asked.

"Not anytime soon," Murphy grumbled. "I swear, kid. Your brain might be a ten, but your mouth is a two. No...one point three."

"Probably should've put more thought into it," I said and shrugged.

"How are you doing?" Dr. Popov asked. I hadn't noticed, but he already had one stitch in and was working on number two. The numbing gel definitely did its job. In fact, I was numb all the way up to my wrist.

"I'm good," I said. "May I ask a question?"

Dr. Popov finished stitch number two and expeditiously moved on to number three. "I'm not sure I have a choice," he muttered.

"If someone dies, how long does it take for the dead body c-ccooties to set in?"

He stopped stitching and looked me square in the face. "The what?"

"The smell," I clarified, "and then how long before the smell goes away?"

He slid skeptical eyes and one raised brow over to Murphy. Murphy went *Romeo & Juliet*. "Loaded gun, loaded gun," he muttered. "Wherefore art thou, loaded gun?"

M yanked on Murphy's hand. "Daddy, I gotta pee."

Marjorie normally wasn't squeamish, but once again, I think her seven-year-old threshold of weird had been lowered. "Sure, kid," Murphy said softly.

He glanced over to me as if to ask silent permission. "All is well in D-Darcyville," I slurred.

Murphy growled like an angry bear. "Yeah, I can see that. All the same, if she starts getting defiant, give her another hit of whatever she's taking. I think it's making her more agreeable."

I twisted my fingers in a cross-my-fingers-hope-to-die gesture. "Now where were we, Doctor Popov?" I asked when Murphy and Marjorie made like Elvis.

"Dead body cooties," he said.

Here's what I knew about dead bodies. Unfortunately, it came from firsthand experience at nine years old. When a person's heart stopped beating, the cells and organs were deprived of oxygen and immediately began to die. At that point, all the blood drained from the circulatory system and traveled to the lower portions of the body. I was a little rusty on the timeframe, but after a short period, the body stiffened in a stage called rigor mortis. It stayed that way for a while but eventually subsided, and the body became limp again (secondary flaccidity). What I referred to with that particular question was the death smell. When would it be hard to deny something was dead within your vicinity?

"Right, the dead body smell. To keep things scientific," he muttered sarcastically, "the cootie smell comes quickly, especially if there was trauma with leaking blood. As soon as a person dies, the body stops producing white blood cells, so bacteria on the skin begin to break down tissue. The tissue adopts a pasty pallor, and the more time elapses you'll get this lovely oxblood ooze or opaque-white, sinewy fluid. It can vary."

"The cooties," I said.

"Cooties. And dependent upon weather—"

"Just for giggles, let's say the body was locked up in a wall."

Another raised brow. "I love it that you aren't one to mince words."

"There's too much game playing in relationships today. Personally, I'd rather cut to the chase."

An abysmally idiotic response, but then again, I was drunk on joy juice.

"If the body was in a wall and the temperature was controlled," he said, "you're still going to smell things at twenty-four hours. Perhaps before, dependent upon the trauma wound."

"What if it was an interior wall, old building with plaster?"

"That changes everything. I worked in construction before med school and dependent upon the frame of the building, feasibly you may *never* smell it. If it was an old building that didn't use today's drywall, then the body can go through all stages without anyone smelling a thing."

Dr. Popov explained a plaster-like substance had been used in construction before drywall, and plaster could be like concrete, with no air passing in or out. So the body may have been there while the business was still in operation, not necessarily after it closed like I'd initially thought.

"What's a body going to look like after about fifteen years?"

"The body will begin to liquefy in three hours. So at fifteen years it will be a leathery blob stuck to the floor. There would be skin, hair, possibly fingernails preserved, according to how dry it had been kept if rodents didn't consider it lunch. If it's a skeleton, then something fed on it, or it weathered somehow. In what condition was this body discovered?" he asked suspiciously.

I saw no harm in telling the truth. "It fell out of the wall last night at Club Need during the earthquake. It kinda looked like a mummy."

"Aye," he said, loosening up some. "Nothing stays hidden for long, but cooties can actually eat through linoleum, Darcy. If it was undetected for that long, then the plaster and structure of an old building preserved it."

Or someone made sure it remained hidden.

"Do you think the cootie ooze weakened the floor?" I asked.

"Hard to say. But older buildings are more durable with double-layer flooring. So even if it weakened the top level of flooring, it may have dried before it even had a chance to drain to a basement. Just remember, plaster doesn't mold even with the liquefaction. Is there anything else I can do for you, Miss Walker?"

"I'd rather impale myself on a rusty railroad spike than get stuck by another needle. I'd say we're done."

After the sixth stitch, Dr. Popov quickly cast my hand, telling me to suck down painkillers as needed and to schedule an appointment with my pediatrician for the stitches to be removed and Velcro buddy-straps to be applied. Jumping off the table, I waved my injured hand as he retreated, knowing full well that would probably be the only time I could legitimately give someone the condor and get away with it.

It was sevenish, Saturday night. After I showered the ER scuzz off of me, Murphy dropped me off at Dylan's for some sort of froufrou, unexpected business dinner of his father's. In the for-what-it's-worth department, I hated parties. Especially where I was supposed to make small talk with guests I didn't know. Why? I had a tendency to say naughty things, always at inappropriate times. But Dylan wore me down with the Dylan lovin', so here I was waiting to make a public spectacle of myself.

Colton Taylor's official title at Go Glam! was Vice President of Fraud Containment and Global Relations. Counterfeit products cost Go Glam! close to a billion dollars a year, and the job had Colton performing cloak and dagger routines, uncovering those giving Go Glam! the shaft. He headed up their own police force, so to speak, that brought down the bad guys draining their bank account.

Colton landed on the Go Glam! radar after he brokered a deal for his little sister to become the face of their products. A former undercover detective like his father, Colton quit the life when a bullet hit him in the back by a colleague he suspicioned as being corrupt—a detail we'd only recently discovered. In a serious eval, he gave the businessman gig a whirl and found success. After dominating the world of sales, when the cloak and dagger opportunity arose, he enthusiastically jumped into the foray since it brought him back to his crime-stopping roots.

The crime of the night? The Mexican city of Tijuana was giving Go Glam! the screws.

A sweatshop had churned out eyelash curlers using subpar metal. When a customer complained their new product broke, it was sent into Go Glam! for a replacement where a quality check discovered it to not be legit. Colton strong-armed the owner of the store where the customer purchased it, and he coughed up the location of the sweatshop that supplied him. Colton then led a raid where over a million dollars' worth of products were found in someone's basement, along with a metal press and children younger than ten working the machines. The Mexican government envoy vowed to be on the situation like stink on a skunk.

I was in the second floor game room with Colton. It had a huge a-s-s television on the wall in front of a comfy leather sectional that'd initiated many ZZZs over the years. A *Star Wars* pinball machine, vintage *Tetris*, and *Pac-Man* arcade games anchored one wall, and a foosball game was stationed in the middle of the floor. Family pictures decorated the walls, some capturing Dylan and me from all eras of our life—playing tee-ball, snowboarding, waterskiing, and even kissing under the mistletoe last Christmas. Made me feel slightly incestuous, but I let the thought slide since kissing was a feature I didn't plan on parting with anytime soon.

"Blue hair?" Colton asked.

"Azul," I verified in Spanish.

Colton swallowed down a stiff cup of coffee probably wishing it was an adult beverage. "I just wanted to make sure my eyes weren't failing me. How's the finger? Does it hurt?"

"It only hurts if I do this…" I slid my black cast to the right. "Or this…" I moved it to the left. "Or hold it down too long…." I dropped it south with an accompanying wince.

"Good Lord," he muttered, pulling me into a hug. Dylan was a duplicate of his father. They had the same raven-black hair, knockout face, olive complexion, deep dimples, and sexy-as-sin mole in the corner of their left eye. The eye color was the only exception. Colton's eyes gleamed like black diamonds. Dylan's boiled like melted butter that had an affair with toffee. Even their hugs felt the same. The Taylor men were all alpha, and it was extremely addicting being embraced by someone who believed he could attack a running buzzsaw and win.

"Yeah, try going to the bathroom with this thing," I muttered. Colton spewed his coffee out. "TMI?" I added with a giggle.

Well, you asked.

A bathroom lay across the hall. I snatched a thick towel off the rack and cleaned up the mess before it sunk into the carpet. After I'd wiped into oblivion, Colton left me crashed on the couch, café au lait drippings staining his pinpoint cotton shirt. After a peck on the forehead, he hoofed it to his room, mumbling how he never got a weekend off. My pain meds had taken a toll, and sleep closed in like ISIS in the Middle East. While Dylan sang in the shower next door, I crossed my arms over my chest, fluttered my eyes closed, and dreamt of Jaws.

If Jaws claimed Dead Girl was probably Lyric Armstrong, then by God she was probably Lyric Armstrong. But to make sure I didn't bark up the wrong tree, I'd ask my pal, Vinnie Vecchione, to see what he could ferret out. After I had a starting place with Vinnie, next up would be to nail down how Dylan's interview had gone. What exactly had he agreed to? Turned down? Negotiated? Maybe I didn't want to know because next thing I knew I heard myself sawing logs. My iPhone startled me awake with Jason Derulo's "Talk Dirty to Me." Only one person had that designated ringtone, and Dylan held that honor. I fished my phone out of the pocket of my fave Seven jeans. Glancing at Dylan's mug, I smiled and swiped my finger over the answer button.

"Talk dirty to me, sweetheart."

Dylan had a dirty mind, a mouth even dirtier. "Where are you?" I asked sleepily.

"Come to my room," he murmured. Then he introduced me to the proverbial dial tone.

Sliding off the couch, I held my left hand up and repositioned my gray, long-sleeved sweater. I performed the same routine to its matching scarf, awkwardly retying its knot. I shuffled inside Dylan's room—broken finger up, my good hand stuffed in the back pocket of my jeans. "Yes, master?" I said and grinned.

Dylan stood in front of his bed and grabbed a handful of shirt behind his neck, yanking it over his head. Dylan's chest...first thing I thought was exclamation mark. If that hadn't been enough to make me squirm, he wore his butt-hugging jeans that could make the Mona Lisa smile. His hair was modern-messy with a touch of gel. I felt something strange on my lips when it dawned on me it was my tongue licking them. *Doh! I'm so easy!* While I reacquainted myself with the proper technique on breathing, one of his muscled legs followed the other until he stopped right in front of me.

"So how's my favorite girl?" he murmured. Dylan twined a strand of my ombré-blue hair around his index finger in a playful tug. "Your hair is blue."

"You're beating a dead horse, D. Half the world has established it's blue."

He winked. "I swear, you can make anything look good. Let me see your finger, sweetheart."

"I'd really like to kiss you," I breathed.

The glint in his eye held the promise of heated lovin' later. "First things first," he said and grinned. "Show me your finger."

I stood there, unable to focus. When he repeated the same phrase, I came back to the land of the living and waved my middle finger around in a slow-mo three-sixty. Dylan burst out laughing, immediately dissolving into little girl giggles. "You're going to have fun with this, aren't you?"

"You gotta admit the bird flipper is the most fun finger to break. You've broken all of yours."

Dylan had at one time or another broken all of his digits during roughhousing or sports. He held up his hands, flipping them backward then palms out as though he remembered each injury. "I survived," he said, "but I hate it that you got hurt, Darc. The only reason I didn't kill them was because you made them both brothers, and I know you don't date brothers."

"Baby," I flirted, "you have a jealous streak."

"Jealousy would insinuate 9mm handguns and a GPS tracker in your purse. I simply don't appreciate poachers. Canyon, I've never met, so the jury's still out. But with Marek, I'm good. He not only called but texted three times."

"How very un-Marek."

"Yeah," he murmured, bringing my broken finger to his lips in a kiss. "He's an enigma. Did he tell you about some fight club deal?"

"Yeah. Weird."

"Weird and probably illegal. I get the feeling he doesn't always think things through...I've missed you, and you look gorgeous." His eyes strayed down my body and up to my eyes with a smirk. Unfortunately, I didn't wake up acceptable. That only happened after a shower and a lot of prayer. "Now about that kiss," he flirted, nipping at my lower lip. Listen, I was always in the mood to go to first base, but he'd made me wait...turnabout was fair play.

I pulled away, kick-starting the conversation. "Nope, I'm good. I want to talk about your interview. How was it? And by the way, your naked chest is not going to distract me. Well, maybe a little," I admitted laughing, "but I'm going to pretend you have the face and body of a fat donkey."

He gave me an aw-shucks look, resting both hands on my waist. "No more talking. Show me some love."

I swatted his hand away, giggling. "Get off of me!"

On me!

Off of me!

Errrrgggh!!

Dylan snickered because he recognized the tug-of-war in my face. He gently grabbed both my arms by the wrists. "Kiss me first, and then we talk."

"You drive a hard bargain," I said grinning.

Our lips collided in one of those oxygen-stealing kisses. Problem was, one kiss from Dylan gave my already overactive libido a real shot in the arm. Tunneling his fingers in the hair at the base of my neck, he latched ahold and tilted my head backward. Somebody. Save. Me. I really dug it when he released his inner-caveman. He kissed hungrily down my neck, trying to distract me from the conversation. Believe me, he was extremely talented in the distracting department, but he was stalling.

Mustering up the strength, I put both palms on his chest and pushed. "Ttt-alk," I stammered.

Dylan had gone somewhere else. He appeared thunderstruck, his eyes fogged like an addict who'd just had a hit of coke. *Dude, that isn't even my best material.* I laughed to myself.

When his neurons came back online, his voice sounded wispy. "It was just an interview." He blinked.

"Then do me a favor and rewind."

Dylan's face instantly humored, but when he clocked on my

unnatural stubborn streak, he paused and collapsed back on his unmade bed. The big story here was he never...and I mean *never*... conceded so easily. Dylan was silent for a moment, sucked in a bunch of air, and ran both hands through his hair. "He offered me a full-ride," he said clinically.

Mommy fudger. Add on a sniff. "Congratulations," I managed, tears pooling under my lashes. "You deserve it."

My voice pitched so high I could practically hear the fine china breaking downstairs. Dylan pulled me between his legs and clasped my face in his hands, thumbing away the tears. "I didn't accept," he murmured.

"Why? They've got a great record."

"It's too far away from you."

I bit my lip so more tears wouldn't spill. "Did you decline altogether?"

His face turned grave. "No, I told him I needed time."

"So that means you're still considering."

"I didn't say that."

"Well, you didn't *not* say that."

He snickered, "Are you sure you don't want to be a lawyer?"

I rolled my eyes with a snort. "People won't wait forever, D."

Dylan went ice-cold, a tinge of panic marking his gaze. "Is there a hidden message in those words?"

"No," I quickly assured him, turning my head and gently kissing each palm. "I would wait an eternity for you, but for them...it's business. They have a slot to fill."

Dylan's sigh ran deeper than mine. "If he wants me, he'll give me the time I requested."

"The time you're still considering," I clarified.

Another hungry kiss down my neck. "I liked him," he said. "It was an easy conversation, but was I bowled over like I was with you? Like I knew this was where I was meant to be? No."

File that under *The Hottest Thing Anyone Has Ever Said To Me*.

I was all over Dylan like black on an emo. We tumbled back onto the bed, and he held my injured hand away from us on the way down. For the love of virgins everywhere, we were tangled together like Rapunzel's hair in howling winds. Here were my thoughts: Muy caliente! Shirt off! Sweat! I normally wouldn't end three thoughts with exclamation marks, but my hormones were lit up like the northern lights. Dylan rolled over to where he was on top, kissing my mouth like he intended on sucking out my soul. Ho. Ly. You. Know. What. He could have it. Running my hands up and down his back, my hormones took off at a rolling boil. After ten sweat producing minutes, I panted like a dog, my heart pulsing with desire. I sent out an S.O.S. for some self-control, and when I came up empty-handed, I prayed to God Dylan still thought me to be desirable and not some skanky 'ho-bag. The moment I wanted to round third and go for home, he abruptly put on the brakes.

Drats.

"Darc...it's getting...too hot. We need to tame the flame."

I deepened our next kiss, hoping to put that thought on ice. "Maybe I don't want to tame the flame," I breathed into his mouth.

It didn't help when Dylan's mouth said one thing, and his body said another. "Darcy," he warned, gasping as he came up for air. "If you get any closer, you're going to be behind me." Dylan could definitely be a buzzkill. A problem since the biggest predisposition I had was to get as close as possible to Dylan Taylor's soul.

"I..." *L-word*, I thought, "missed you," I settled on.

Dylan kissed harder, and when I followed with the fervor of a religious zealot, he abruptly pulled back the reins again. Just like that, he propped us both up to a sitting position. And that, my friends, was a sneak peek at our relationship. He had control...eh, I'd been prepared to go at it until the twelfth of never. The only thing that made me feel better was seeing sweat all over his chest while his breath convulsed more than mine.

Abrupt withdrawal is painful! my brain screamed. I had a brief toddleresque tantrum, spitting in his direction and wondering what it would take to get him past the point of no return. I had a feeling it wouldn't take much for me. Not a good thing for my moral standards. "Why thank you, sweetheart," Dylan said, giggling like a little girl. "I actually need another shower, but I would've preferred water from the showerhead."

I rubbed my eyes, trying to gain focus. "If we can't have any over the top kissing, can I at least have a meaningful hug?" I asked, batting my eyelashes.

Dylan held his arms wide, and I immediately settled up against his heart. Kissing the top of my head, he lovingly caressed the side of my face with his fingertips. Our relationship was shaky—or at least my worst fears said it was shaky—but I didn't want to verbally acknowledge the doubt and perhaps make things worse. Right then, I needed to get my aforementioned virginity out of here before my clothes melted off.

Chapter Eight

CHASING PHANTOMS

"Hey, Vinnie, it's me. Are you busy?"

"I'm running lines with Donatella."

While Dylan changed into dinner party-appropriate clothing, I got my verb on and quietly phoned Vinnie Vecchione for a quick rundown on the situation at Club Need. Vinnie played football at Ohio State University, and his *running lines* wasn't football talk for learning plays. No, Vinnie's aspiration was to become the next big Hollywood movie star. He'd just finished a project named *100 Proof Stud* and had been rehearsing for its spinoff *Fat Men From Venus*, set to film during the summer. I supported Vinnie's dream, but I had two problems: number one, I wasn't so sure it wasn't soft porn; and number two, he needed to get away from the Donatella chick.

Donatella Ricci had morphed Vinnie into someone none of us recognized. Pre-Donatella, Vinnie had been a dirty man-slut. At the moment, he was so nauseatingly infatuated and monogamous it was hard to stomach. I'd never met Donatella, but I'd seen photographs, and I had a hard time thinking Vinnie landed a girl with the face of a goddess and legs up to her armpits. She was using him, and I suspected she'd blown through the fifty grand he'd made off the stud film. Biggest question mark? She was on a full academic scholarship. They had a brief one-week engagement but decided to pull back when her parents vetoed a marriage before graduation. Made sense, but I worried she'd put Vinnie's heart through the wringer. Don't get me wrong. I could understand loving Vinnie, but Vinnie and I had a connection that went beyond logic.

"So you're in, V?" I asked after I gave him a sixty-second rewind.

The Lion King's "Can You Feel the Love Tonight" spun in the background. I miraculously kept a laugh to myself. No knock against jungle love, but the song wasn't exactly what I'd call mood music. "I'm in, Dolce," Vinnie responded, calling me by his Italian nickname. "But let me get the key points straight about Club Need. There's missing people and a dead body. You need the name of the perp and victim."

"Yes," I said quickly. "I need to verify the body found was a girl named Lyric Armstrong. I also need to find out if the cops have any leads on who they think killed her because I'm pretty confident it was murder."

I'd tell Vinnie later why Jaws requested I find Lyric's killer. Vinnie would keep my secret, but right then, he was distracted.

Vinnie responded with his normal, "Totally doable."

Maybe, but Vinnie also believed in unicorns.

I barely had a, "Thanks," out of my mouth when I heard Donatella whisper, "I love you, babe." Hmmm, I should probably acknowledge her, but she gave me a bad feeling in the pit of my stomach. After Vinnie kissed her—believe me, I heard the smack of disgust—he said, "And this is your business how, Dolce?"

Was it any of my business? I decided not to answer because I knew the reply Heaven would give if I cared to listen. But who in their right mind could walk away now? (A) Jaws knew secrets about my mother; and (B) he knew the man in the yellow Dodge Charger. If I landed the information he requested, then that could provide leverage *if* and *when* I decided to blackmail him. Yeah, I had plans to blackmail Jaws and wouldn't give him answers unless he provided *me* with answers, seven years in the making.

My explanation to Vinnie? "The usual. I'm bored."

"I'll have my cousin help out," he murmured. Good move. Vinnie and I'd used his cousin before to score coroner's reports in the past. Come to find out, his cousin was a runner in a law firm. He worked for an ambulance chaser to be specific, with a more than questionable clientele. In fact, he brokered a meet-and-greet with Jaws a few months back. Vinnie had never divulged what chip he had to cash in for that meeting, but I had a feeling it was something big that'd make me feel guiltier than sin.

"Interesting the name of the joint is Club Need, Dolce."

Vinnie Vecchione didn't normally put a lot of deep thought into our shenanigans. He mainly acquired information, and I was the one to execute. But Vinnie's words struck a chord. I'd done a little Internet search on Club Need while waiting in the ER exam room. Apparently, the first time it opened for business, a membership fee had been required. The fee wasn't required to frequent the place, but if people wanted to go deeper into the perks it offered, they had to sign on the customary dotted line.

"While I'm getting my stuff, what'll you be doing?" Vinnie asked.

"I'm making a plan...*to make a plan*."

A deep cackle. "I've missed you, Dolce. So it's just the two of us again?"

"I'll probably give Bean a job." Vinnie burst into laughter, coughing and wheezing like he had the lungs of a chain smoker. "The kid with the dead gerbil?"

"It's Mister Pongo, Vinnie. Address him by his name. Just do your part, and I'll worry about Bean."

What did it say that I had no doubt of my success even with Bean and a probable adult industry star at my side? In short, it said I liked playing with a handicap, or perhaps it said the obvious: I was stupid.

The moment I 86'd the call, Dylan finished changing and threw an arm around my shoulder while we made our way downstairs. The Taylors' ten thousand square foot home had an Old World vibe. A romantic winding staircase marked a two-story marble entry. The main double-doors opened to an open floor plan under graceful arches. The rooms included a parlor with a ten-foot fireplace, library/office, seven bedrooms, private guest apartment, exercise studio, and pool in the basement...in a lower level to die for. We stopped at the dining room.

Dressed in an off-white sweater and slacks, Dylan's mother blinded me with perfection. Impeccable as usual, she was equally as striking as her husband. Her tawny hair fell to her shoulders, her beauty topped off with honey-colored eyes. She conversed with whom I'd bet was the Mexican diplomat's sidepiece because she had booty-call written all over her. When the airhead gave me a smile, Dylan's mother grinned and pitched her head to a man entering the buffet line. My eyes went wide with disbelief.

Lincoln Taylor was in the building, better known as Dylan's grandfather, and the originator of his and Colton's pretty boy genes. With mocha-brown hair and eyes, turning heads when he was younger no doubt carried over into this era of his life because men like that never went bad, they just got better. From experience, I knew his temper could clear a room on impact. And one look at the leather strap over his shoulder, he came prepared to rumble by way of his GLOCK he'd nicknamed Jackal.

"Lincoln!" I screamed, breaking free from Dylan's grasp.

I came at Lincoln with the speed of one of those idiot road-runner birds, knocking him back against some party guests with a thud. His plate flew high, but he snagged it in the air, and that right there, folks, was why I should never go anywhere without a child harness.

"I never get greetings like that," Dylan pouted and laughed from behind. Oh, yeah, he did. And in those, he normally wound up going horizontal with me drooling on him.

"So how's my favorite blonde?" Lincoln chuckled, and then he got a load of my ombré-blue locks. Wrapping a strand around his finger, he pulled it to his eyes to verify the oddity. "Thank God it's not a tattoo."

Lincoln happened to be an undercover detective for the city of Los Angeles, California. Last summer I did the usual and stuck my nose in his business while we vacationed together. As a result, when his enemies wanted to send him a message, Dylan, two of our buddies, and me had been targeted on the first day of school in a car accident...that wasn't so much of an accident. We all lived, but recovery had not been a piece of cake.

Word in the Taylor camp said Lincoln was close to nailing his enemies to the wall. "So what have you been up to?" I asked as I grabbed a white dish and joined him.

"The usual. Chasing phantoms."

After some small talk with guests that qualified more as micro-scopic, Lincoln and I ditched the oxford shirts and took our plates to the basement. Three basketball games played on their triplet of flatscreens. Last I saw, some of Colton's colleagues and the guest of honor had Dylan backed into a corner, quizzing him about his future. He'd make an appearance soon, but an unexpected visit from his grandfather meant trouble brewed somewhere. Trouble I wanted to put a name to.

I desperately tried to cut into my chicken to no avail. Lincoln watched my chicken bounce off the plate with a deep chuckle. "The little punks messed you up, huh?"

"It's a great conversation piece," I said, shrugging and waving around my middle finger. When Lincoln cut my chicken into bite-sized chunks, I noticed new tattoos on his left hand. "Did you get new tats?"

He glanced down at them with a nod almost as if he'd forgotten. Lincoln went under so deep he occasionally not only wore facial disguises but tattoos that washed off by the time an assignment was over.

I commenced with the Q&A. "Why the visit? Are you staying long?"

Lincoln stuffed a bite of chicken in his mouth, chasing it with a drink of coffee. "Colton told me my grandson was having difficulty making some decisions. I thought I'd pop in and see what I could do."

My heart tightened up. "The scholarship offer?" I asked quietly. He answered in another nod.

"Believe it or not, the boy listens to me," he said, lightly chuckling. "But I've had a lot of practice. He's got a temper like his grandmother, but they mostly get upset because their emotions are so powerful they can't navigate them. I merely try to help them piece things together. He's a good kid. It's not going to be hard, and I feel like it's the least I can do for Colt. Colt didn't grow up in the best of circumstances with me going under like I do. A lot of the time he raised himself, and the fact he asked for help with his son is a blessing this old man probably doesn't deserve."

That could not be further from the truth. If anyone deserved respect and good things, it was Lincoln Taylor. "How long are you staying?" I asked, forking some potatoes.

"Until Friday, and then I'm going to fly to Orlando to see Willow when Dylan and Colt meet with the football staff at the University of Florida."

For a moment, my mouth was incapable of speech. Once again, Dylan had kept me in the dark. "I beg your pardon?" I finally said in shock. Lincoln wiped his mouth on a napkin, repeating his words. "That's what I thought you said," I mumbled.

And the plot thickens...

I couldn't say I blamed Dylan for the interest in that specific college. The Valley roads at the moment were a dirt-peppered slush. Florida's sunshine looked mighty fine mid-winter when Cincinnati was basically blah. Besides, Lincoln's daughter and Colton's little sister, Willow, lived nearby. He'd have the comfort of family if he ever got homesick.

"Did I just let the cat out of the bag?" he asked sighing.

"I'm sure Dylan was going to tell me. Like maybe Thursday...in a text or something."

"I apologize, dear. Sounds like my grandson needs a tutorial on communication."

"He's stuck," I said, defending him.

"It's still no excuse, but I see his quandary. Try getting one hundred offers in less than a week, in all three sports. That would do it to anyone."

My mind spun like a record table. One hundred offers? I only knew of one. Something in my gut began to twitch on overdrive. File that under *Clueless*. I had no idea. *No freaking idea*. Doing the math, he'd had a few days to tell me and hadn't. What that boiled down to was my boyfriend had been keeping secrets. I could understand keeping secrets from his girlfriend but from his best friend?

Admittedly, I'd expected everyone would be after him.

As an athlete, Dylan was unmatched, calling up a primal need to conquer and dominate only few were born with. And even though he played all three major sports, his first love was football, his dream to play professionally.

I slumped down into the couch, my mind attempting to leapfrog over the confusion. Sometimes a girl had to gear up for the undeniable. It was a thing called destiny. Dylan was in demand. People in demand eventually accepted an offer.

Lincoln attacked his scalloped potatoes like he hadn't eaten in ages. Knowing what he did for a living, the last thing he consumed could've been a dead rat. "Try not to be too upset, dear. I think my grandson is riding the love boat and refuses to think about anything except you."

"Perhaps, but he's sorta treading water. I'll encourage him to be more proactive." Problem was, Dylan had been treading H2O because of me. *Me*, I thought, and the last thing I wanted was for him to not accept the offers coming his way...even if it was a conflict of interest on my part.

I swear, when I glanced around I discovered the person mouthing that sentence was me.

Lincoln winked. "No one blames you, Darcy. Dylan has been in love with you for so long we all think it's entertaining. His cup definitely runneth over."

I swallowed down a bite of cheesy broccoli. "He has been rather serendipitous."

A cunning grin creased Lincoln's features. "Ah, dear, I've missed you, and no wonder my grandson has been under your spell for so long. I've never met a sixteen-year-old girl who says the word serendipitous."

"Electric shock treatments might help him find normal," I muttered...maybe. But Dylan felt we were by divine decree.

Lincoln dropped his head back, laughing heartily. "Not on his part. My grandson gets bored. You've never bored him."

I wasn't sure that was an endorsement, but I was proud to say I kept my laugh in check. Blowing a light breath into my coffee, the reed of steam filled my nostrils with a false feeling of warmth and security—God knew the subject matter didn't. Why? Well, here was a reality check for you. When your boyfriend doesn't tell you life-changing details, he just might not include you in them. But then again, I guess Lincoln could be right. Dylan was still drunk and drowsy on love. Me? I was paranoid as shiz.

Dylan picked that moment to thunder down the steps. Glancing over my left shoulder, he had not one plate balanced but two, while carrying a drink in his teeth. "Let me first thank the two of you for ditching me to talk to Mister I'm-In-Love-With-Myself," he joked through a clenched jaw.

Lincoln deadpanned, "You look like you had it handled, son. I had all the faith in the world in you. So what's the story upstairs?"

Dylan settled next to me, diving into his food after a quick peck on my cheek. "The official line is that the Mexican government abhors the counterfeiting of Go Glam! products, and they'll uphold the NAFTA agreement to the letter of the law. The unofficial? I'll look the other way if it keeps food on someone's table."

Couldn't blame them. Who wanted their people to starve?

"I predict the dinner will be over soon," Dylan added. "All the guy did was talk about his new Lamborghini and look at Mom's chest." Sheesh. His next statement was directed at his grandfather. "All I can say is you'd better not be offering my girlfriend a job."

Lincoln winked. "Darcy has to do something when you're doing your thing, son. I never took you for the chauvinistic type."

"I'm not a chauvinist. It's just that *your* idea of fun is *Darcy's* idea of fun."

Nothing would get a person's butt caught up in a sling faster than crossing Lincoln Taylor. Except when it was Dylan, and then I think it humored him.

Lincoln had recruited me into going to LA's cop school, under his tutelage, last summer. Maybe I would. Maybe Dylan and I both needed to be thinking about our futures. My thoughts never made it past incubation because everything always came back to Marjorie. I couldn't leave her like I'd been left. It was too gosh-darned painful to think about.

Dylan suddenly went quiet. In my experience, a lack of words was never a good sign.

I swallowed down some acid, my eyes darting back and forth between the three basketball games. While Lincoln took a phone call from his partner, Paddy O'Leary, I leaned over to Dylan, trying to draw him into conversation.

"May I ask you a question?"

"Shoot," he murmured.

"When were you going to tell me about the hundreds of offers, D? That hurt."

He muttered to himself, "Lincoln has a big mouth."

I refused to sound too clingy, keeping things factual to get my point across. "Was I supposed to act like I didn't know? I'm not picking a fight. I'd just like to know where I stand in the grand scheme of things."

Dylan wiped his mouth, placing his fork on his plate and turning toward me. "You stand where you always have...right beside me. I swear it was going to be tonight, and I'm aware this is totally out of character for the one hundred percent honesty shtick I preach."

I muttered, "Must be something in the water."

"Don't joke, please. I just didn't want to see pain in your face. Pain that I'd caused."

"But you put pain in my face by excluding me."

Dylan buried his face in his hands right as Lincoln glanced over his shoulder with a look of sympathy, shaking his head. No, I didn't relish being left out, but by Dylan's actions and Lincoln's response to it, my boyfriend must really be troubled. "I'm sorry," I said, reaching for his hand.

"No, I'm sorry," he whispered, pulling my fingers to his lips. "I don't want to do anything that will ever hurt *you* or jeopardize *us*. Tell me what to do, Darc. Everyone wants a piece of me, but all I want is to be with you."

Listen, he should ask Yahoo before he asked me, but Dylan acted like someone tried to explain the laws of the universe when his own personal body went against gravity. Nonetheless, his words were like a physical blow. Hearing his small gasp for breath, he blinked away his tears before they could fall. Normally, I was a horrible liar. I'd giggle and get twitchy lipped, but when I was acting I was so darn good I deserved an Oscar.

I whispered in his ear, "Try not to worry so much...or about us. I'm going nowhere. I swear, it'll work out." And with those words I backed out of the conversation, immediately talking about a basketball game that had gone into overtime. Dylan normally didn't divert so easily, but on that one he gladly took a pass.

Lincoln looked like he'd gotten caught up in the middle of a hurricane. A tinge of worry lined his forehead, and his immediate curse said shiz had hit the fan. The case he worked on at the moment, chasing Turkey Cardoza, was a case that could make or break a career. But Lincoln had made his career decades earlier when he uncovered evidence a prominent actor murdered his wife. Lincoln said the actor didn't smell right, so he plugged away and wore the man down until he snapped. Maybe Lincoln was afraid Cardoza would break his career. By the looks of things, it might be closer to breaking his sanity.

"Somehow she knows his playbook," he murmured into the receiver. "She has to be inside." More jawing from Paddy—something was said which made Lincoln snort in disbelief. "I don't think he's all of a sudden grown a conscience, but remind me to send him a fruit basket at Christmas. Dear, get me an ink pen," he said to me. I popped up from the couch and found a black BIC on the countertop at the bar and tossed it to Lincoln while he grabbed a nearby napkin, jotting down notes. "Hold your trigger finger, Paddy. I would never hire someone without vetting them first. Sounds to me like Iggy and I have some business." I heard Paddy laugh through the receiver. "Yes, Walter Ivanhoe's Cincinnati connection, and since Walter works for me now, Iggy does too."

Talk about a blast from the past. Walter Ivanhoe, AKA The Grizzly and crime lord of Orlando, had the hots for me when I chased a kidnapped boy last summer. A late night visit to one of his warehouses had me almost losing my head. "What's up?" I asked, acting as if the name registered nothing.

Lincoln's two-worded answer said it all. "Pixie's back."

Pixie was his informant...here's to hoping she brought luck along with her.

Chapter Nine

STUCK IN REVERSE

Valley High is one of the largest schools in Ohio. Navigating through halls that big, there was always a little bit of grab-arsing that went down. The trick was to walk fast and have one fist ready in a swing at all times. Dylan had upped my street cred amongst the guys at VHS. Now that someone like Dylan Taylor was playing kissy-face with me, it seemed every guy on the planet wanted a piece of me too.

Speaking of my boyfriend, after a quick peck of "goodbye" in the parking lot, he jogged to the gym for a basketball meeting he was five minutes late for. Thing was, his "goodbye" was practically the most he'd said all morning. No flirting. Nothing. Zip. Heck, Dylan could flirt when he only breathed, but I wasn't sure his lungs remembered they had a job. Regardless, even if we never uttered a word, there was always electricity. And since Saturday night, the energy rolled off him in waves.

My body hummed with the memory.

My usual breakfast of processed sugar and/or leftovers didn't happen since my stomach hadn't stopped the gurgle of nausea. Before we parted ways Saturday night, Dylan laid his soul bare by detailing all of his offers, what the fine points were, what positions they had in mind for him, but he still couldn't rank the top ten. My guess was that would be where Lincoln would come in handy. By the time the conversation was over, I'd missed my midnight curfew by an hour. Murphy didn't mind when I'd asked for the extra time because he knew Dylan's time was running short. To help things along, I actually emailed Lincoln and Dylan, telling them who I thought Dylan's top ten should be—the top ten that didn't take proximity to me into consideration but rather what would be best for Dylan's career. Lincoln returned a message that said his rankings mirrored mine, he loved me, and that he appreciated where my heart was and had faith Dylan and I could make things work.

Dylan's three-worded response…"I worship you."

Of course, I boohoo'd like the nerdy wallflower who finally got asked to the prom. But the insecure part of my brain still wouldn't allow me to believe a forever-after was possible. College was a long four years to be away from one another. And let's face it, I had a tendency to eff things up.

Boogying my way to my locker, I needed to find Fisher before he quote-unquote forgot he owed me money, plus a bonus. Fisher lurked there as expected, sad-faced and as broody as Murphy when his lottery ticket turned out to be a loser.

Sliding out of my jacket, I opened my locker and immediately pulled on my relationship counselor. Like I said, Fisher had some douche in him with his octoman ways, but publicly being cuckold stung like a scorpion to the happies. His eyes were bloodshot, and he'd either chugged Jack Daniels all night or just survived a crying jag. "I'm sorry I confirmed your fears, Fisher. That has to sting."

Fisher kicked at an imaginary pebble with a brown loafer. Once again he'd dressed like an upper crust New Englander. "Yeah," he said. "Stinks is definitely one word for it."

That was the ugly part of relationships. They had a beginning, a middle, and an end. Fisher hadn't even realized he was in the middle, let alone have it end for Indigo, and he found out by accident. At the risk of sounding insensitive, I gave him my transparent thoughts. "You deserve better. Anyone deserves the truth and not to be cheated on. It's not cool."

Fisher absentmindedly rolled the sleeves of his powder-blue Ralph Lauren oxford up to his elbows. He understood it, but evidently the reality couldn't come out of his mouth. I got that. My word, I only uttered the words "Gemma Walker" like maybe twice a year. Come to think of it, maybe I just said the word "Mom."

Putting an identity to someone or a situation that hurt could be like a shovel to the face.

"She's just so beautiful," he said, sighing sadly.

I guess if a guy liked big butts that wiggled. "Beauty is only skin-deep," I said. "Her heart didn't seem to be beautiful. I mean, people can make mistakes, but she should've fessed up. You do realize you're better off, right?"

Even by my standards, that was psycho mumbo-jumbo overkill, but the boy looked like he was headed for the nearest semi to jump in front of. I couldn't say I blamed him. Getting dumped didn't exactly make a guy feel like God's gift to womankind.

"It doesn't feel better," he mumbled. "I didn't even want to come to school today."

Ugh and double ugh. Fisher's confidence was still a no-show. "Hey, running is the last thing you should do. Face it now, or somewhere down the road a therapist is going to make you work it out with dolls."

"I guess," he muttered, back to kicking that imaginary pebble.

"I promise it'll come. The day you can put words to what happened, you're looking at coming out on the other side."

My words went in one ear and out the other, but down deep I felt like a hypocrite. Sometimes seven years later a person was still stuck in reverse.

"Hey, I heard about the dead body," he said. "Totally gross."

"Seriously, the dead body only enhanced the ambience, Fisher. It was sorta awesome."

"Do you have the 411?"

"I wish," I mumbled. "If you hear anything about what went down, float it my way." I gave Fisher my show-me-the-moolah face when the late-bell rang, signaling students were minutes from tardy status. As Fisher took a Benji out of his Michael Kors wallet, I quickly dropped it in my purse, grabbed my math book, and closed the locker door.

While I spun the combination lock to secure it, Fisher exhaled like a steam engine about to blow. "This stays confidential, agreed?"

"I'm not going to rat-out the person paying my bills, Fisher." Besides, I liked my hands clean of anything resembling collusion, where it wasn't obvious I'd been whoring out my detective skills.

"Good, then I've got a friend who could also use your help. Are you game?"

"I'm always game. Question is, can he pay?"

"*She* can, and she's good for double what I paid."

I heard the cash clink in my piggy bank. "Then give her my number. A girl's gotta eat."

Fisher gave me a nod, and when he attempted to tack on a hug, I delivered two stiff pats on the back and watched as he slunk away. A throat cleared near me, and as I turned toward the baritone sound, I realized Dylan had been leaning up against the wall, quietly watching the entire exchange.

He looked downright scrumptious. Let your imagination soar.

It was game day, and athletic department policy dictated players come dressed to kill. Dylan sported tailored charcoal trousers, a crisp white shirt, and a red tie the hue of breaking hearts. It nearly threw me into V-fib.

When our eyes met, he unloaded a thirsty gaze. Uh-oh. He had that I-want-to-kiss-you look, but a little bit of a come-to-Jesus meeting was mixed inside. I held up a palm, mentally straightening my I-don't-care look, which consisted of little makeup, a ponytail, and glasses. Suddenly my skinny jeans and vintage Ninja Turtles T-shirt that said "Say Yes to Pizza" seemed out of place. I said, "I realize my ways are unorthodox, but you're off your rocker, D, if you think I'm going to turn down a personal endorsement from a satisfied customer."

He jerked me toward him by my belt loop. "I take back what I said to my grandfather last night about him recruiting you for a job. You're talented, sweetheart, and you delivered horrible news in a nice way. That alone was worth the price of admission."

I blew out a puff of air. "I thought it would be a simple assignment. But simple turned out to be sucky."

Dylan gave my belt loop another tug, pulling me even closer. I readjusted his tie, running my hands down the front of his shirt, ending with a hug to his waist. "I agree," he murmured. "The thought of not seeing you every day paralyzes me, but I can't keep you on a chain."

I glanced up into his eyes, one eyebrow raised. "This is a change of pace."

"Let me finish," he said. "If I go somewhere away from you, it's only fair you turn into who you are meant to be. And if I trust anyone to do right by you, it's my grandfather."

FYI, when a guy says something like that...you cry. I blubbered like the blubber on a whale. By the grace of God I got my crap together before first period, but I was pretty sure I sat down with a face like my dog had just died.

———

The first three periods were a blur. No food mixed with a painkiller, and I couldn't tell if I was nauseous or just plain stoned. As a result, I had a raging case of heartburn, and being in the company of Herman Himmel was tantamount to guzzling battery acid. I was sitting (er, daydreaming) in science listening to him drone on about thermal inversions. I didn't give a shizzle about thermal inversions, but evidently the educational system said I had to know its details to be a Valley graduate.

It was safe to say Mr. Himmel would rather have a prostate exam than have me as a student. We had a tumultuous relationship dating all the way back to junior high. He hated me. I hated him. And part of that was due to the fact I was a student with issues.

Schoolwork and me...a hesitant partnership.

There had been a rift in our partnership because I had ADHD. With ADHD, the mind had one idea, but it competed with a body that demanded something else. But having ADHD wasn't always such a bad thing. The pros? I could multitask like a mofo. I came out of the womb with high energy and could follow through when most had fallen over from exhaustion. In fact, the more pressure on me, the better I performed...especially if I liked the assignment.

Here were the cons. When I was focused it was like a dang laser beam, and I forgot the world around me. If stimulation got too high, my brain could short circuit, and I needed an Australian walk-about to find myself again. And if I was bored, God help anyone near because I could drive him or her insane with incessant chatter or picking what I thought to be harmless fights.

So why that particular daydreaming episode? It was twofold. Rudi informed me her date with Canyon had been a bust, so I plotted how to land her a boyfriend with some staying power. And the second part was a mere continuation of my latest bout of insomnia. As soon as I'd crashed at command central, I had my nose to the grindstone regarding Lyric Armstrong—trying to figure out what I'd do with Vinnie's information once he acquired it. My creativity, however, conked out long before I did. I stared at the clock until two a.m. Point for my corner, I was Darcy Walker. Darcy Walker didn't give up when things appeared impossible. In fact, that was when I was at my best.

"So what's your opinion on that, Miss Walker?" Mr. Himmel asked, placing his chalk on the tray behind him and crossing his arms over his chest. Short as a troll, Mr. Himmel wore all gray, à la JC Penney, with mousy-blond hair and a red-scaly face that belonged on *Jurassic Park*. Problem was, his Velociraptor smile looked like it contemplated a bite out of my head. My stomach twisted, and my left eye developed a twitch. The man had given me PTSD.

"Could you repeat the question, Mister Himmel?" I grimaced.

"It's Doctor Himmel," he groaned.

Oh, yes...Dr. Himmel. That might be another reason our relationship hadn't been so kosher. I was the only student who refused to address him by the title he liked to thrust in our faces. But it wasn't for reasons of disrespect—at least not at the moment. I had done it as a joke for so long it had become a hard habit to break.

"Sorry, sir. I mean, *Doctor* Himmel."

Dylan sat behind me and lightly touched my shoulder, no doubt offering moral support. I opened my mouth to attempt an answer, but Mr. Himmel talked over me. "Straighten up, Walker, or you're never going to amount to anything. I heard about your IQ. My guess is your father paid someone off."

That comment was horrifying. He referred to the fact Murphy claimed I had an intelligence quotient of 160. That was genius league or the league for individuals too dumb to know when to get out of the rain. Thing was, I knew to get out of the rain. My guess was someone scored the test wrong, or my father resided in Utopia where his best friends were talking animals.

"That's offensive," Dylan barked. Then I heard him mutter, "You mother-effer."

"What was that you said, Mister Taylor?"

"I *said*—" Dylan repeated, prepared to add the profane ending.

I wisely cut him off and spun around, grabbing Dylan by the hand. His face was hard, PO'd, and contemplating where he'd bury Mr. Himmel's body. "What you said was kinda degrading, Mister Himmel. And I don't think it's a good idea to call my father a liar."

Oh. My. Stars. If that was my attempt to defuse a situation, then please let me stay at home.

Mr. Himmel thundered up the aisle, his squatty legs hitting the brakes right beside my seat. His cologne tickled my nose with an aroma so pungent it smelled like he'd done the nasty with a skunk. "You weren't addressed, Miss Walker."

I viciously rubbed my nose to keep from sneezing but gave up, succumbing to a cough. "I'm sorry," I finally said. "Hair ball."

"You're being as disrespectful as ever," Mr. Himmel said, snorting in one of those you're-an-idiot snorts.

"No," Dylan said, snorting back. "She's defending herself, and the fact that you've busted on her father—"

Mr. Himmel cut Dylan off. "Would you like to leave this class permanently, Mister Taylor?"

Once again, Dylan opened his mouth. That time with an accompanying chair screech.

Oh. Crap. Dylan was about to go wrecking ball. Mr. Himmel, however, had one leg up on me. "Where are your shoes?" he asked me.

I let out a sigh longer than Mr. Himmel's lecture and got a heck-no when I felt around for my Chucks. I'd kicked them off as soon as I'd sat down, and I clued-in Jon Bradshaw, AKA Grumpy, must've stolen them.

He sat in front of me and grunted, "Oh, crap."

"They're here some place," I said, giggling nervously. "Some idiot stole them."

"Are you insinuating that idiot was me?" Mr. Himmel barked.

My vocab could use a good soap scrub, for sure, but if I said the idiot was Grumpy, then he'd be exiled to the land of no return like me. "No," I said, "I mean, yes...ugh, this isn't coming out right. Please forgive me for my actions, Mister Himmel. I'm dealing with my stress by attacking the authority that placed the restrictions on me."

Heard that on the Disney Channel last night. Um, thank you, Mickey.

"Is that right?" he still pushed. "I think it's just you being *you*. A failure."

Cue *The Good, The Bad, and The Ugly* record.

Problem with a teacher like Mr. Himmel, one heard his words long enough, and they eventually became a self-fulfilling prophecy. He was definitely an initiative-sucker. My ADHD demanded I go for a jailbreak, but I chained myself to my desk and listened to Dylan and Mr. Himmel go at it like a hissing cobra and mongoose. To make matters worse, God's monthly gift came to visit at lunch. I was tired, achy, and on the verge of tears.

"I'm sorry, Mister Himmel. Er, Doctor Himmel," I interrupted, trying to recover from the snafu, but honestly I wasn't sure what I'd even apologized for. All I knew was Himmel's class felt like *Shark Week*, and I was the dang seal.

Mr. Himmel's dirt-brown eyes were unforgiving. "Not accepted," he sneered.

"May I at least ask what I did wrong?"

"Why does this not surprise me that you don't know?" he grunted. He went Aretha Franklin and said something about respect.

"I do respect you, Mister Himmel," I said nervously. "In fact, Dylan and I are going to name our first illegitimate lovechild after you." Jeez, just cut my tongue out already.

The class burst into laughter.

Hand to God, I didn't mean that as a joke, but sometimes my mouth made me do things I immediately regretted. When his frown grew deeper, I sighed and opened my mouth, hoping something profound would spew out. Nope, nothing but spittle.

Dylan went vertical, unleashing unholy hell as Mr. Himmel continued to give me the third degree. I had experience enough with Dylan's dark side. My guess was Mr. Himmel had a shallow grave waiting somewhere cold and dark, where animals would dig him up and eat the remains. Luckily, we didn't have to find out what came next because the bell rang right as Dylan was about to get kicked out permanently. My self-esteem just bit the dirt, and I gave

Dylan a look like, *Pardon me while I find a corner and lick my wounds.* For once, he let me, and I only figured out why when he angrily strutted past me, thundering down the stairs and straight to the office of our new principal, Vance Unger.

How, you ask, did our former assistant principal get promoted mid-year? Our sex-crazed substitute, Collette Reynolds, came down with a little case of pregnancy over Christmas break. Principal Ward had been the one to infect her. What was the big deal? After all, they were both married...just not to each other.

Upshot was that AP Unger had been named principal. Vance Unger was one of my father's best friends, and God help me, that did not always bode well in the Darcy Walker Camp. Why? Principal Unger had adopted Draconian tactics where I was concerned —his discipline completely over the top for what I considered minor offenses. He would feel differently if he knew I saved his sorry butt from bleeding out when a school shooter used him as target practice sophomore year.

I'd kept the details zipped up nice and tight in my mind—maybe I should reconsider.

"Walker!" he yelled when Dylan had him cornered. "Get your gosh-danged tail over here!"

Ah, there it was, the Kentucky connection...not totally PC in principal land, but oh well. I gave him a one finger wave as I shuffled over. "You should be good to me," I muttered, wondering why he'd blocked out the shooting incident. Maybe the better question would be, *Why hadn't I?*

"I *am* being good to you. Murphy is one of my closest friends. Me being good to you is allowing you to not be in detention every gosh-danged weekend."

Detention. I knew it well. I had a preferred guest membership card.

"And I appreciate it, sir. Let me reaffirm that."

"Exactly what is the problem?" he asked.

Dylan started running his mouth again, but Principal Unger laid a hand on his shoulder, signaling he wanted things from my perspective.

I swallowed a sob, giving him the SparkNotes recap. "Here's an overview. Mister Himmel just threw a crap-ton of shade on me, so

I'm having some quality time with my low self-esteem. And even though it's taken a toll on my mental health, I'm used to it."

I heard Queen Elsa from *Frozen* sing "Let It Go."

"What do you mean you're used to it?" he pushed.

"It means I'm going to let it go," I said. What the H...I hummed a few bars.

Dylan didn't appreciate my attempt at a diversion. "He doesn't like her," Dylan bellowed. "Don't you remember what he did to her at Christmas?"

At Christmas, Mr. Himmel (um, Dr. Himmel) threw me out of class under similar circumstances. Once again, charges were I hadn't been paying attention. When he confronted me with the accompanying threat I'd be kicked out, I stupidly responded, "Oh, goody." Let me tell you right now, "oh, goody" was never an appropriate response. We had a science project due, but I wound up acing it and was somehow on target to get a B minus for the quarter.

Principal Unger frowned. "I thought that to be a one-time occurrence."

"Try again," Dylan snapped.

"Relax, son," Principal Unger said, sighing deeply. Right. Good luck with that.

"I'm okay," I said. "I've been called stupid by people smarter than Himmel. Actually, dumber too. I'm over it."

You couldn't escape the defiance in Dylan's jaw. Mark my words. Things were far from over, verified when Dylan's voice rose to the unfriendliest of tones. "No one should be used to it!" he screamed. "He called you a failure!"

Principal Unger's voice dropped an octave. "And your statements are free of embellishment?"

Anger played at the flex in Dylan's jaw. "What would I gain by embellishing things, sir?"

"I believe you," Principal Unger said, sighing heavily. "Unfortunately, Walker isn't the only student Doctor Himmel enjoys picking on."

"And what exactly are you going to do about it?" Dylan grated out.

"Son," Principal Unger scolded. "Consider your tone."

"I won't consider anything. It comes with being a Taylor. You screw over someone I love, and believe me, you're going to feel some sort of retaliation."

Dylan was brazen by nature, but the extra ballsy attitude came from Lincoln being on the premises. Lincoln was known to have a mouth, but he had a gun to back it up. "No need to retaliate," Principal Unger told him. "I'll take care of it."

Wow, and world order was restored.

Principal Unger glanced over at me one last time. "I swear it," I said. "I did nothing this time. Maybe this was backlash for last week."

"What happened last week?" he asked. Here was what happened. I got busted binge watching *Pretty Little Liars* on my iPhone. I thought for sure they would reveal whom A was, but alas, it was not meant to be.

"The usual, sir," I said, "but today he got extra dirty. He called Murphy a liar."

If Principal Unger hadn't ruptured a blood vessel earlier, he was pretty darn close at the moment. "He what?!" he roared. And furthermore, I wasn't sure if he defended Murphy's honor, or if he merely tried to lessen Murphy's odds of a Murder One charge.

"I hadn't planned on telling him," I muttered.

"Tell him the truth," he said and then thundered up the stairs for Mr. Himmel's classroom.

There are only two mistakes one can make along the road to truth—not going all the way, and not starting.

—*Buddha*

Chapter Ten

BULLET DODGED

"**Y**our chariot awaits, milady," Dylan murmured as he opened my door with a broad sweeping motion of his arm. Grumpy fell into the backseat of the Beemer, gagging out a snort. One glance at him, and he reminded me of someone who got trampled by wild horses. His hair was a hot mess, and his blue necktie hung cockeyed like a drunk trying to scale the yellow line. He needed a permanent woman. Therein lay the problem.

"Nice touch, Taylor," he grunted snidely, "but I really wouldn't call your ride a chariot. It's kind of insulting to the Germans."

"Since when were you named Goodwill Ambassador?" I said, laughing and cutting him off mid-rant.

Grumpy didn't grace us with an answer, slamming his door shut a little harder than required. Generously listed at six feet and built like a linebacker, he seemed quiet and more pensive than normal. The first initiate into my secret brotherhood clan, our union began freshman year when we wrecked his dirt bike. I symbolically mixed my road rash with his, and as they say, the rest is history.

History or misery.

The temperature rose right above freezing but had been enough for the salt to melt a tiny bit of snow on the February ground. I kicked the slush out of my UGGs and slid into the seat while the

Big Man gently shut the passenger side door. Last summer, I started calling Dylan the Big Man because he kept getting bigger and bigger. To my chagrin, most girls lusted after his bigness. Blah.

"Blah, *bl*-blah, blah, blah," I muttered aloud.

Dylan punched his key in the ignition, grinning. "Blah?" he said.

"Blah," Grumpy agreed.

"Okay, all you blah-ers. What kind of tunes? Top 40, alternative, jazz," he paused cheerily, "classic rock?"

"Take a pass on the classic," I mumbled.

The last thing I wanted to do was think about my mother, and listening to classic rock paraded the loss of Gemma Walker like a big red balloon down Central Park West. My mother's band performed cover tunes of classic rock albums. With the anniversary of her death looming like the plague, I needed to hold that memory off as long as possible.

Dylan thumbed the Beemer's preset to a Top 40 station, motioning for me to strap in. Resting my head against the window, I rehashed the fourth period from Hell. Word on the Valley grapevine had been that Mr. (um, Dr.) Himmel and Principal Unger had a verbal nuclear war. I wish I could've been a spectator, but I didn't like being the arrow in Principal Unger's proverbial bow. My source, Oscar Small, said it had been all kinds of spectacular, and that honestly was the biggest use of vocab I'd ever heard Oscar use. Anyway, my guess was Murphy would call Principal Unger later, and I'd prepare myself for the repercussions sure to come.

"You're coming to the game tonight, yeah?" Dylan asked as he pulled into traffic, jarring me from my thoughts.

When I gave him my clueless face, he repeated the question with a dimpled grin. Of course, I would go. Dylan and multiple guys in short pants would be like turning down a visit by Keebler elves, packing cookies. "With bells on, dude," I said. "With bells on."

Dylan leaned across the console and nipped at my lips. I tapped the camera on my iPhone and held it above our heads, clicking in the middle of him nibbling down my throat. Yeah, I'd upload to my social media accounts later, along with the caption: He's all mine, haters.

"Shazam," I whispered into his ear. "I just got the shivers."

Dylan pulled back and rubbed his nose up against mine. Oh, jeez. Getting all cozy had not been a good idea in front of Grumpy.

"So much for solitude," Grumpy interrupted. "I'd just been thinking about how great it was to just chill, and then I have to witness Taylor eating your neck like a freaking cannibal."

Right then, Dylan slammed on the Beemer's brakes and threw his right arm in front of me protectively, shoving me back against the seat. Not soon enough because I snapped my neck when it landed back on the window it had rested on seconds earlier.

"You just gave me *whiplash*," I whined.

Grumpy took the Lord's name in vain accompanied with the d-a-m-n word. In the second those complaints were born, I glanced up and noticed the reason for the abrupt stop—Jagger Cane. My immediate Twitteresque thoughts? Hashtag jealous. Hashtag fastard. Hashtag misunderstood. Jagger had loads of potential but couldn't get out of his own way. A little taller than my five foot nine, he was raunchy good-looking with spiked, brown hair and razor-sharp, black eyes—similar to Dylan but harder, darker, more edgy.

And here was the issue. Ivy Morrison was with him.

Ivy...Jagger...together...*not good*.

"Man, I *hate* that guy!" Dylan fumed, leaning over to massage the back of my neck. Dylan and Jagger hated one another—like Luke Skywalker and Darth Vader kind of hate. Here lately, I'd grown fond of Jagger though. Maybe fond was too strong a word. It was more like tolerable, but when he did things like that, it was one step forward, two steps back.

"Someone's gonna get chlamydia," I sang at the thought of him and Ivy together.

"Darcy!" Dylan gasped and then chuckled.

I didn't know what the big deal was. Everyone was thinking it...I just said it.

Ivy might've read my lips because she unloaded a smile that'd melt a nuclear reactor, accompanied with a one-fingered salute. I peeled my lip back in anger, wishing her a cold sore and zit on her butt. Not for the bird episode. It was just that as far as anyone knew she had been semi-dating Grumpy for the past two weeks. Ugh. Not the way a guy wanted to find out that his pseudo-relationship was over.

Sucked.

Grumpy leaned forward, and when he got a load of Ivy and Jagger, he went quiet—appearing lost in thought. He didn't want to give any kind of emotion or vulnerability to either one. Smart move.

"I'm assuming Ivy dumped me," he muttered, falling back into his seat, riddled with anxiety.

A logical assumption since she was in the car with Jagger. But here were my feelings...bullet dodged. Ivy was one hundred percent witch and my archenemy. She told lies on me, bullied me, and peeked under the bathroom stall during my *me time*. I should rip her hair out for that alone. She and Jagger had an on-again, off-again romantic history. Both had been expelled for a week in January when naked selfies were accidentally group-mailed to the entire junior class. The photo served as corroboration Ivy had recently had a boob job. I didn't care how young a female was. No one's boobs were perky and symmetrically round like softballs.

On their latest breakup, they actually had Jubilee Mueller draw up a post-breakup document where they decided not to stalk...or steal the other's dog...or key the other's car...or take naked selfies with anyone else but the other...SOUNDED REASONABLE.

Jagger had cut us off and laughed hysterically as he shot a quick wave, squealing out of the parking lot in his Mercedes SUV. Right. Another imported car. VHS was full of the haves and have-nots in every sense of the word.

"You can do better," I said, turning to look at Grumpy. A grunt was all I received. "What about Clementine?"

Grumpy dated Clementine Miriam Rabinowitz around Christmastime, but they broke up in January under mysterious circumstances. He wouldn't talk about it, which I found extremely odd since all he ever wanted to speak of was the opposite sex. "It's complicated," was his official answer.

Dylan met his eyes in the rearview mirror, serious as a heart attack. "Listen, Bradshaw, you're better off without Ivy Morrison, and you know it. We've had this conversation more than once."

Can I get an amen?

"Is your mouth broken, Grumpy?" I asked.

Grumpy channeled his inner-dwarf. "I wish yours was broken, but we can't be so lucky."

I hadn't been offended. Most people probably felt that way about Darcy Walker.

While Dylan distracted him with thoughts of the game, intermixed with a dozen reasons why it constituted a blessing in disguise, we pulled into my neighborhood. I live in Buffalo Trails Country Club at the end of the cul-de-sac on Bison Boulevard. We started out as a country club community, but the club dried up before anyone could ever *swing* a club. Four holes had been built, but the developer ran off with home-owners' deposits before the course had been completed with eighteen holes. Houses were brick and siding and a cookie-cutter of the one next to it. Our particular unit was traditional red brick with black shutters, coach lights lining the drive. By no means were we the tony crowd. We were a neighborhood of the duct tape and plastic toys crowd.

After I kissed Dylan goodbye and grunted to Grumpy, I trudged into an empty house, kicked off my shoes, dropping my coat and backpack on the couch. I nuked a leftover tamale, slid it onto a paper plate, and carried it upstairs along with an ice-cold Coke.

The walls in my room were painted in a gray mist. My furniture consisted of a white wrought-iron bed with a matching desk directly in front of it, scooched up against the wall. On my bed lay a white comforter with different shapes and sizes of matching throw pillows, plus a sock monkey I'd had since age four. On the wall hung a flatscreen TV, my best friend on insomniac nights.

Killing the tamale in four bites, I picked up a container of fish food, grabbed a healthy pinch, and dropped the flakes in the tank to feed Roosevelt, my goldfish. Dylan gave him-slash-her (who knew) to me for Christmas. For reasons unknown, keeping fish sucking in oxygen had been challenging. I changed the water regularly, treated for diseases, etcetera, etcetera fish stuff. But like clockwork, they would kick the bucket and travel on a one way cruise to Valley's sewer after a few weeks. Roosevelt had survived the longest.

When Roosevelt darted to the surface to munch a flake, I tossed a handful of birdseed in the cage for my lovebirds, Churro and Chimichanga. Falling back onto the bed, I tapped the notepad on my phone, scrolling through notes on Lyric Armstrong. During English lit, we had some downtime, so I might have googled and researched her. Question was, who was she? After a few clicks, come to find out Lyric had money. Like cash coming out of her rear. She disappeared exactly fifteen years earlier, and her parents launched a nationwide search complete with the best of private investigators, no expenses spared.

The only information I discerned from reading the article was that Lyric had been concerned about the disappearance of her best friend, Ryder Beck. The quote in the story had been given by Beck's girlfriend, Gabrielle Allen. And here was the interesting part. Tito Westbrook had interviewed her...guess he couldn't let sleeping dogs lie.

Beck had last been seen entering Club Need, never to return home. Two weeks after his disappearance, Lyric likewise disappeared. My common sense walked off the face of the Earth when I phoned Vinnie and asked if his cousin had had any success in finding out Lyric's cause of death yet.

"Caesar is tied up with a big case, Dolce," Vinnie explained. "I promise I'll make him do it tomorrow."

Tomorrow sounded like an eternity away, especially when I knew Vinnie could acquire the information himself. Last spring, he'd taken on the coroner's office and scored two death reports by citing the badge number of a Detective Russo...I'd hoped he'd do it again. "V, do you remember how you used a badge number for a Detective Russo before?" Vinnie went mute. The only thing audible was the wheezing lungs of an overweight football player. "I need you to call today, okay?" I decided to play all of my cards. "If I find this out, then the person requesting it can feed me information about my moth—"

Vinnie interrupted before I confessed the requestor had been Jaws, and my endgame was information about my mom. "No need to beg," Vinnie murmured. "You know I love you, Dolce. I'll give you whatever you want."

"Okay, then work your magic and have Detective Russo ask questions. I heard Tito Westbrook ask someone named Sophie to get her flirt-on, so she could ID the body. So someone down there is willing to talk."

"I'll do a lot of things, Dolce, but I'm not going to flirt with a guy," he grumbled.

I rolled my eyes. "Of course not. Just find the person with loose lips and promise them the moon."

Patience was not one of my virtues...but drastic times called for drastic measures, and right then I had a bajillion reasons why it was a good thing. "Okay," he said. "Give me ten minutes to finish up a shopping spree with Donatella, and I'm on it."

Yup, Donatella was riding Vinnie's gravy train, running through the bills like a 'ho ran through johns.

Twenty minutes later, Vinnie called back with confirmation the body was indeed Lyric Armstrong. I had a momentary rush of guilt, wondering what he had to promise because he'd done that sort of thing for me before. Unfortunately, the rush of guilt didn't last long. Vinnie had a smorgasbord of details. Evidently, Lyric's body had been confirmed through dental records, and although the official cause of death might not be known for weeks, initial findings pointed to the fact she might have expired from starvation and hypothermia.

She'd been trapped in the ductwork, and CSIs theorized it could have collapsed with her weight when she'd used it as a means to sneak inside the building—ergo, she may have fallen into the torture chamber, which would explain why she had no shackles on her arms. In other words, she hadn't originally been placed inside to rot or scream or whatever...she'd just unluckily wound up there. If the theory was correct, that meant the duct-work she'd used was not the ductwork in use during that time or even now—exactly as Dr. Popov surmised. If it had been the same, the dead body smell would've permeated the building like a frat party where marijuana headlined the menu. So (A) she fell from old ductwork into (B) a plaster-lined room. No smell would escape anywhere.

What a cold and bleak way to die, I thought. Unless there had been a massive head wound that killed her instantly, she knew what was happening. But why sneak in? If she was pretty, more than likely she would've been given free entry. The only probable answer would be she snuck in because she didn't want anyone to notice her—she'd been spying. But on what?

Padding to the restroom, I pumped a dollop of skin cleaner into my palm, hit the speaker, and dialed Marek Ransom. Other than the name from Vinnie, Marek was my only starting place, but I wasn't so sure he could deliver.

"Hey, gorgeous," he said in a rich bass voice. "You and Taylor still an item?"

"Happy as clams," I said quickly.

"Darn," he muttered. "What's up?"

Switching on the faucet, I cupped some water in my palms and doused my face. "Do you remember when you said you'd get information for me on Dead Girl?"

"Yeah."

"Any luck?"

A deep chuckle. "I actually asked Canyon's father Saturday night. He said if the body was who he suspicioned it to be, then there'd been some leads the first go around. Unfortunately, the guy who was the biggest blip on the radar has been confirmed dead. He wouldn't give me the names of either because it hasn't hit the press yet. But he did say if he's right, the victim came from a wealthy family...and even if there's no likely suspect, they'll put men on the street anyway because of who the victim was."

My mind hopped around like popcorn on a hot-oiled skillet. The old article I'd read earlier by Tito claimed Lyric came from money. So Jaws banked on the fact that IDing her as the body would open up an old, high profile case. That bugger—he knew who she was. He hadn't been guessing—and merely tried to smoke the person responsible out. But why not tell me? He knew I was nosy enough to do the job for free.

Blindly grabbing for a towel, I dabbed at my face. "Thanks. If you find out anything else, buzz me, okay?"

"Will do, gorgeous. Hey," he said hurriedly, "I'm fighting Saturday night and could use some moral support. I dialed the number on that flier about the underground fight club. I got some automated message, telling me to show up at eight p.m., prepared to throwdown."

You know that thing that killed the cat? It just grabbed ahold of me. "Seriously?"

"Yeah, the number's since been disconnected, but I'm showing up anyway. I know it's stupid, but oh well..." And then he chuckled.

Hmmm, didn't sound good.

Math homework and two Tylenols later, I thumbed the speed dial into my iPhone keypad, striking the digits I'd programmed for Jaws. His contact was listed under the name "Chief Brody," after the lead character in Peter Benchley's *Jaws*. Not especially original, but since no one knew we had a relationship, then I assumed we were sufficiently incognito. I had nothing to report, other than to verify a snitch at the coroner's office had corroborated his suspicions.

Point blank, Jaws had been playing me. Why?

"Jester," he drawled when he answered. "I assume this call comes with a reason?"

"You knew, you mother-trucking *ponkey*," I hissed.

"I'm going to need a definition, babe."

In Darcyspeak, a ponkey was when the punk in someone made a donkey out of his or her a-s-s. I hated him and decided not to grace him with a definition. "You knew if Lyric was the body, the county would be obligated to reopen a high profile case, even if it was determined she died accidentally."

"Is the coroner claiming it was accidental?" he said oddly.

"And what makes you think I'd tell you if I knew?" I spat. Jaws and I spoke the same language...bluff. And it was underscored by a whole heckuvalot of getting even.

"You're angry."

"You used me."

"And Hell hath no fury like Darcy Walker scorned, eh?" he murmured, chuckling in a deep voice. "Babe, you'd planned to blackmail me. So we're even."

I swear to God—I swear to G-O-Almighty-D, I would gut him like a tuna if I had a knife. And I had not let one inkling of an offhanded remark slip I intended to blackmail him. Just another reason why I hated him—that he knew me so well. "And what would I blackmail you with?" I snarled.

Jaws growled. "Do you actually want me to mention the name of your mother? I was trying to be damn sensitive, Jester."

My breath caught in my throat. Tears of anger burned my eyes, and I literally looked around for that tuna knife even though I knew it didn't exist. Once I got my wits together, I realized it officially might be the best day of my sorry life. Unofficially, it might be the stupidest. We both breathed for a while until I was the first to cave. I had zero leads regarding my mom other than Jaws. Plus, the man in the yellow Dodge Charger lived in the wind. If I waited for him to surface again, I might be ninety and too senile to care.

My voice boiled in anger. "I swear you have the skill to irk me with pinpoint accuracy. Name what you want, so I can go plot your murder."

"I told you what I wanted."

"You said you wanted me to tie the death of Lyric Armstrong to Julius Marx."

"That has not changed."

"Is Julius Marx who the cops initially think did it? If so, they claim he's dead."

"Claiming to be dead and *being* dead are two different things. I know he's alive. That can only mean they chased another alias because Marx's passport has been active."

"I'm going to need more than that."

"If I cannot get him on the crimes he's done to me, at least I can nail him with Lyric Armstrong's death and that will suffice."

"Until you can make your case."

I heard it in his lack of words. He was unwavering and nonnegotiable. The trail of Julius Marx was crucial, and the situation was some of the freakiest, freaked up stuff ever. That brought to mind a slew of thoughts and emotions. Relief because I could put another feather in my so-called detective cap but a guilt I'd not been prepared for. If Jaws was double crossing me, I could be leading Julius Marx to his death. Jaws had me in the palm of his hand, and he knew it.

"Once I tie Marx to Lyric's death, then that's all you'll require of me?" Because at one time he insinuated we get to know each other Adam and Eve style...not gonna happen.

"We made a deal, Jester. I will not renege."

I recycled one of Murphy's famous lines. "Half a truth is still a lie, Jaws. My guess is you'll string me along because you know how much this means to my family. If you double cross me, let's just say contracting flesh-eating bacteria where your gonads fall off like rotten grapes would be better than what I have planned."

Jaws burst into the barking laughter of a herd of sea lions. "Can I get a halle-freakin'-lujah?! Atta girl, babe. If someone uses you, then manipulate them back until you are the driver."

"So manipulation begets manipulation," I muttered.

"Always." Jaws laughed and killed the call. Sadly, I agreed.

Chapter Eleven

JANE Q. PUBLIC

*T*hat conversation was more confusing than an M. Night Shyamalan movie.

Point blank, I wouldn't glean a single thing about my mother's death until I delivered Julius Marx...the definition of SOL.

When I heard a female giggle, "Come downstairs, big mouth," my ears snapped to attention. My aunt was in the building. She'd texted an hour earlier, saying she had a bag of designer hand-me-downs for my "skinny a-s-s." The plus side hadn't been the free threads, it was that she was the Assistant Hamilton County Prosecutor. If anyone knew details about Lyric Armstrong, she'd be the person. I gazed up to the ceiling with a grin. I was tempted to say the windfall was Divine Intervention but feared I'd contract leprosy on the spot.

I tugged out my ponytail and ran my fingers through my hair in an attempt to find a style of this decade. After gazing in the mirror at my almost-green eyes and sometimes-blonde hair, I realized I'd be standing next to my aunt—my aunt who couldn't look bad if her facial cartilage had been marred in a pay-per-view catfight. Stripping out of my clothes, I punched my legs into H&M imitation leather leggings and delicately coaxed my broken hand through a VHS "Fighting Buffalos" hoodie. Switching up the usual make-up duo of lip gloss and mascara, I went for the trifecta and added blush. After I scrubbed my teeth, I took thirty seconds to affix temporary tattoos of Dylan's jersey number eleven on each cheek. Shoving my lucky houndstooth hat on my head, I took the stairs in a jog, hopping into my UGGs one boot at a time.

Murphy and Red were crashed on the sofa with Marjorie dozing on the floor underneath their feet. I hurdled over the back of the couch, landing between them. "Well, well, well, look what the cat drug in," I said with laughter.

At five foot ten, Tabitha Arthur was a natural redheaded spitfire with the constitution of a man but a body that was all woman. Her dyed-blonde hair (this season's look) had been pulled back into a low ponytail. Clad in a khaki pantsuit tailored to her small waist, the ensemble screamed of four figures while she wore gold jewelry that shouted five...maybe six. A gift, my guess, that came from her ex-husband who didn't understand what the prefix "ex" signified.

Red was not only my aunt, she'd been Murphy's best friend since freshman year in college—his best friend who forever changed his life when he discovered she had a twin sister raising hell in the art department. Murphy's life changed because...well, because he'd been dating a married woman at the time (shhh, family secret). My mother tamed his fastard self, and I became the offspring of said hell raiser and dear old dad.

Who'da thunk it.

What Red could squeeze out of one twenty-four-hour period would take most people seven days. She not only spent her time putting away bad guys but taking up the slack from the absence of my mother. When Murphy needed a wingman, she accompanied him to school conferences where they analyzed and ran credit checks, references, and rap sheets on everyone they met. Paranoia seemed like a trite word.

"Hey, baby," she said, grinning and squeezing my cheeks in one hand while she planted a kiss on my lips. That was her standard greeting. She claimed kissing the cheek was for people too intimidated by real intimacy. Funny coming from her quadruple-divorced self.

Red picked up the silver Sharpie on the coffee table and grabbed my left hand, autographing my cast. I got a few sigs earlier, but my Sharpie ran out of gas, so Murphy brought one from work. Red drew a big heart with the word "dumbass" in the middle of it, pitching her head to two oversized Nordstrom's bags in the recliner that looked nine months pregnant. "Muchas gracias," I gushed, dropping the Sharpie in my boot when she finished.

I squatted down in front of the bags and pilfered through jeans, sweaters, and an orgy of tangled scarves. It didn't take a rocket scientist to figure out I'd interrupted a classified conversation. How'd I know that? Red always whistled, and Murphy grunted about how much he'd just paid for a tank of gas. I wish I wasn't a perceptive person. It made for a lot of awkward moments where the parental bureaucracy decided how much of the truth they would BS the kids with.

When I glanced up, Red stared at me with an almost guilty grin. "Do you want to go to the game with me?" I asked, eyes darting back and forth between them.

Murphy's hands were laced behind his head while he stared off into thin air. "Yes, but no, kid," he grumbled. "I've got a report due tomorrow. Tell your boy I'm sorry."

My eyes slid back to Red. "Sure, baby," she said.

Murphy met her gaze. "You're not going to stay for the brown beans I made for dinner?"

"Heck to the no," she said and laughed.

Murphy snorted in offense. "That meal is five-star in the South."

Murphy's last go at brown beans and cornbread tasted so nauseatingly bad, it was like the vomit birds threw up into their babies' mouths. I usually supported his efforts to recapture his southern roots, but I had gas for days.

"We'll grab a hot dog at the game," I said.

I could almost see him rolling his eyes. "Do you have food money?"

"Yeah, it's upstairs. Right next to my furry handcuffs and edible underwear."

Murphy muttered, "You know that comment wasn't quite as horrifying as I'd originally imagined it to be."

Red pitched her faux blonde tresses back, laughing. "I'll take care of her, Murphy. And uh, I'll call tomorrow so we can finish our chat."

She should've dropped the subject. Now I had no choice but to push for answers.

I got my lawyer on. "You two look guilty, like you're hiding money under your mattress or something."

Red glanced over to me wide-eyed, and my twisting gut immediately knew a joke had been a mistake. Their actions were an odd occurrence. Usually, they buckled when I pushed for an answer. In fact, I had one vivid memory where I walked in on Red giving Murphy crime scene particulars on a rapist she'd put away. That launched Date Rape Lecture Number One where they both gave me more than my ten-year-old ears could process.

"It's nothing," Red promised.

Murphy squirmed in his seat, puking out the details. "Some idiot guy sending you black roses, stealing your mail, and returning it with some cheap aftershave is not *nothing*, Red," he barked. "It's a guy looking for a secluded log cabin where he can strip you bare and chain you to the staircase while he talks to his dead mother."

Red didn't laugh. I inappropriately did. "Do you have a stalker?" I asked, half mortified, half intrigued.

"A very aggressive admirer," she said diplomatically, but her bold devil-may-care attitude for once seemed shaken.

Scratching the back of his neck, Murphy pushed off the couch and gazed at the last family portrait taken with my mother, hanging above the mantle. Murphy lounged in a chair with his arms lovingly draped over his wife's shoulders as she sat between his legs with a one-month-old Marjorie dozing in her lap. That was the way I remembered them—Murphy protecting the woman he loved with me swinging like a half-witted monkey from his back.

"God knows we've had our fair share of stalkers," he groaned.

The uncharacteristic laugh that followed dripped with sarcasm. Red and I glanced at one another. Holy shiz balls. Not a typical reaction from my father. His normal MO would be to let the anniversary of my mother's death come and go like any other day, only to be heard crying his eyes out in his bedroom privately at night. I wasn't sure how to take the evolution of his feelings. A newfound peace? An instability that had grown so large it had become too hard to harness? My money went on the latter.

But here was my latest experience with the subject of stalkers. I spent the night at Rookie's, Red's ex (I think) husband, last Christmas. When I answered his ringing cell, Tito Westbrook was on the other end. That had been our first introduction to one another—me posing as Red. Tito eventually caught on to me, and when he phoned Rookie to inform him someone had confiscated his cell phone, Rookie uncharacteristically passed the incident off as a psycho-stalker. Right then, I knew the reason why. Apparently, a psycho stalker had already been in play.

File that under *News That Will Keep You Up At Night*. "You are taking precautions, right?" I asked. I mean, they hadn't forgotten what had happened to my mother, had they?

Red knew exactly the chain of events I referred to. Stalker + victim x opportunity = death.

"Don't worry. I'm not afraid," she said while Murphy mumbled to himself. "Annoyed is more like it." A deeper groan as Murphy continued to stare at the photograph. "Stalkers are men with little cojones who think it's their gift to society to force themselves upon us," she continued. "I'm going to hire the men at Rafaeli Investigations to get the little creep." Last year Red worked for a PI firm while she recovered from her fourth divorce from Rookie. I'd never had the pleasure of meeting that crew, but reputation said the owner could find a white cat in a snowstorm. "Keep your nose out of it," she said to me, "because I can smell your bloodhound from here." Like me, Red was nosy. So nosy, she always felt people gave her half the story and left out the juicy details.

Going vertical, she slid her feet into black, four-inch pumps. "Enough about stalkers. Tell me what's going on with you?" *Puh-LLLLLEASE*! She was keeping something from me. Did they not know I did this stuff (sorta) for a living?

Since Murphy teetered over a bottomless abyss, I dropped the subject, planning to gaslight her in private. "Crappy day," I said.

"Define the crap," she said.

Tell the truth, Murphy would have a heart attack. Lie, Principal Unger would eventually out the story of Mr. Himmel anyway. Thing was, it was one thing to be mistreated. It was something else to admit I'd been wronged and then watch others feel sorry for me. Sometimes that could be more demoralizing than the initial slight.

"Um, Mister Himmel might've picked on me today."

Murphy's head snapped around like a crocodile snagging a wild pig. "Is that why Vance called? Come to think of it, I have an unanswered text from your new boyfriend too. Sweet Jesus," he said, glancing to the ceiling. "This day just keeps getting better and better."

And to answer his question, that was exactly why both of them had attempted a little convo. I organized the clothes and accessories, crossing my fingers in my mind that both experienced a moment of ADHD forgetfulness.

"What was the offense?" he predictably asked.

"Himmel's class is a snoozapalooza."

"And you were caught snoozing?" Red tag-teamed.

I held my right hand up like I stood in a court of law. "So help me God I hadn't been snoozing more than anyone else," I promised.

"Did you talk back?" Murphy pushed. "I told you to keep your nose clean in his class."

"I thought that was like a guideline or something," I joked.

"Sweet Jesus, learn to filter your thoughts," Murphy grunted, massaging his forehead. "Give me the details, aiight?" he said ghetto.

"Mister, I mean *Doctor* Himmel, retaliated when I asked him what I'd done by calling me a failure and you a liar. His douchiest offense yet."

Murphy narrowed his gaze. "Run that by me again?" he said lowly. Murphy could knock someone over with a whisper if he so chose. Red actually repeated the words for me while I tacked on the details of Dylan going berserk, me trying to act as if it was no big deal.

"Just SOP for my life, Murphy. I'm sure he feels bad."

"And you're okay with SOP?" Red frowned and squatted down to pat Marjorie on the head. She sashayed past me, heading to the refrigerator for a Dr. Pepper Murphy kept on hand, specifically for her.

"Major suckage," I mumbled.

"This Himmel man is making you insecure," Red said all lawyery while she cracked open the refrigerator door. Bending down, she grabbed a dark red can on the bottom row. "I can tell by your body language."

"My body language isn't saying anything. In fact, I vomit sparkles and rainbows."

She placed a thumbnail carefully under the silver tab and popped open the can. The sound of carbonation broke the tension in the air. "Yeah, me too," she muttered. "That's why I know it hurts."

Outwardly, it appeared as if I didn't care. Inwardly, I'd birthed an ulcer. I wasn't sure why I was perpetually insecure. Maybe my looks were the culprit. Maybe my grades did me in. Maybe it was the fact I believed my mother died because of me, and I didn't deserve to live.

The list went on...

So in the grand scheme of things, the standard operating procedure for my life was "feet hit the floor, the shiz hits the fan." I wasn't sure that defined insecure...it just *was*.

———

The night air had dropped to the digit fourteen and was so cold it felt like razor blades cut into my skin. Red and I held hands as we jetted out of her black Benz like Mercury on a mission. Once inside, we grabbed some snacks and zigzagged through the student section, taking a seat at the outer edge so I could cheer with the pep band, and she could maintain her sanity.

While Red snacked on popcorn, I found Dylan at the end of the court strutting with the poise of a panther. His long, muscular arms and legs flexed as he participated in the team's pregame routine of lay-ups. I let out a wolf whistle, lassoing his attention. His head snapped, and he locked eyes on mine with a deep dimpled grin. *No, no, no. Stay where you are.* I giggled to myself. But Dylan had a habit of leaving a required venue to seek me out even if it qualified as inappropriate.

Wearing a white uniform that left absolutely nothing to the imagination, he made one step like he planned to join me but faked me out with a loud chuckle.

I toasted my hot dog in his direction while saliva figuratively driveled down my chin.

Dylan was *meltinyourmouthnothingbutsin*—one word, folks, and polyester was my new best friend.

"Nice move," Red said, giggling sultrily next to me. "You landed a good one, baby. I'd say you have the boy wrapped around your delinquent little finger."

Maybe. "Speaking of delinquency," I asked, licking mustard from my lips. "Can you give me the scoop on the body that fell from its grave at Club Need?"

She slid over an inquiring brow. "Murphy told me you happened to be in attendance. How lucky for your nosy self."

Grabbing some popcorn from her over-sized bag, I tried to act nonchalant but was not sure I managed it. "It was kinda disgusting," I said, thinking that to be an appropriate response. "Sad too."

"I'd say. Why are you so curious?"

Me? I blinked. "I'm just Jane Q. Public," was my official answer.

"Then hear this, Jane," she said, tossing more popcorn in her mouth. "The place scares me, and Rookie is ate up with the possibilities. You're never to go there. No exceptions."

I believed a devil hid behind every angel, but when Red was spooked, I wondered if we should triple the number. "Bad, huh?"

"Bad. Do you understand?" she spoke firmly.

"Of course," I said and smiled...unfortunately, she then made me want to go.

Red tossed a few more kernels in her mouth, chasing them with a Dr. Pepper. "Point out Brynn to me," she said. "How's she taking the upgrade in your relationship status with Dylan?" Brynn Hathaway was a ranking national gymnast, last year's Homecoming Queen, and the VHS cheer captain. I pointed to the group of eight girls in six-inch, white skirts and debated whether to bow down or flip them the bird.

If someone put a group of little girls together, four out of five would say they wanted to be a cheerleader. I had no scientific research to back that up. It was merely based on the assertion that little girls like to be thought of as peppy and beautiful. Unfortunately, I came out of the womb wanting to play manhunt with the guys.

My polar opposite? Brynn Hathaway. She came into the world hoping Dylan Taylor would put a ring on her hand or at least introduce her to the backseat of his car. She made a major play for him last year, and he even admitted to dating her a couple of times. He claimed he'd merely tried to find a stand-in for me. Major face slap in the confidence category, but I could see the allure. She was the good girl, soft-spoken type—the prototype of the girl a guy wanted to mother his children. Her body was fit, petite, several inches shorter than mine, and less than a zero size. Plus, her signature chestnut waves framed a heart-shaped face that was angelic. I wasn't Brynn. I drank milk out of the carton, had cold pizza for breakfast, used my running sneakers as book ends, and occasionally still played with Barbies. And let's face it, I probably had a death wish.

One thing about Brynn, when she was excited she became extra effervescent...cheer captain material. She happened to be one of those people that no matter what she said, those around her agreed. Her cobra-like tactics were in full swing too. She said something salacious, I'm sure, and Clementine Miriam Rabinowitz, Ivy Morrison, Trudi Hatchett, and the others leaned in for the juicy details. Heck, even *I* wanted to track forward until I registered the snickering was about me when they glanced my way.

To Red's amusement, I unloaded a ha-ha grin in Brynn's direction and pointed to Dylan who'd just sunk a three-pointer. If there'd been any doubt before of her intentions, there sure as heck wasn't then. Insert an icy stare. She still felt proprietary. Brynn and I had a little meeting of the minds. *Congratulations*, I imagined her saying. *But don't get used to it.*

Hear that? That's the sound of heartbreak, people. Grab your tissues.

Red zeroed in on Brynn with a scientific face, as if she compared two specimens underneath a microscope. "She's no threat to you," she murmured. "She's not his type."

When I glanced back at Brynn, she gave a version of the evil eye that would leave me a Barely-B for the rest of my life. I couldn't let that slam go unanswered. Once I typed WTF on a text to Justice Becker and autocorrect changed it to the word "ergonomics." I looked Brynn in the eyes and went ergonomics on her butt.

Right then, Justice dropped down beside me with Bean. "Yo, Darcy," she greeted. Justice was my jock soulmate. Cruising at six feet, she was biracial with auburn-colored hair and dark chocolate eyes. Justice lived vicariously through me in the boyfriend department, but I was pretty sure she had a thing with Bean a few weeks back. I pushed. She said little...only that...buckle your seatbelts...he was a good kisser.

Um. Wow.

To each his own.

"Yo," I said back. I snagged the Sharpie out of my UGG and gave it to her. After she and Bean signed their John Hancocks, she took the bag of popcorn Red offered, grabbing a handful and passing it back. "I need a date," she said, munching down on a kernel. "As far as I'm concerned, dates are fruits in your exotic section's grocery aisle. I had a semi-date with Bean at the winter formal and a total disaster with my cousin's neighbor on New Year's Eve. He spent the entire evening wearing a patch over his nose that was never explained." Red burst out laughing beside me. "Yeah," Justice muttered.

My eyes slid over to Bean to see if he was copacetic with Justice talking so openly. Bean was...*Bean*. He didn't seem to harbor any ill will. In fact, when I'd asked what went down between them, he'd been nothing but a gentleman.

"Hey, Bean," I said grinning.

Bean wore a white Valley sweatshirt and ballcap, sporting a soul patch so bushy it resembled a black caterpillar. Slung over his shoulder was a man-purse, which definitely made him bully bait. Justice noticed it as soon as I had and slung it over her shoulder, acting as if it were hers. Mr. Pongo was nowhere in sight, but like an American Express, Bean never left home without him.

In the five minutes Justice had sat down, I learned Grumpy had phoned Ivy (the idiot), she rebuffed a reunion (the beeyotch), and Frank and Oscar Small had found Jesus Christ over the weekend (stranger things had happened). Frank and Oscar were Valley's resident dipshits. Justice said they huffed gasoline on a dare. Oscar almost bought the farm but claimed he went to Heaven anyway. That, in itself, was probably the most creative burst of energy Oscar's brain had ever produced—so much so I almost believed him on the JC thing.

To speak of the Devil, the Small twins plopped down in front of us. Both were sort of dweebish, wearing flannel shirts and beat-up jeans. Oscar, however, had the extra value-add of Coke-bottle glasses. Whereas Oscar was prematurely balding, Frank had enough hair to make Paul Bunyan jealous. Frank gave me half a wave, but Oscar had a serious expression and carried a black leather Bible tucked up under his arm. I had a history with both brothers. To be exact, I helped free Oscar when he'd been erroneously thrown into jail as a murder suspect last year.

Both signed my cast when a look at the clock showed fifteen minutes before tipoff. The team jogged back into the locker room for one last powwow and would reemerge when it was closer to game time.

"Don't look now," Justice groaned, grabbing my hand with a steel-vice grip. "Mister Himmel just entered the building."

Red had been speaking to Rookie and ended the call right as I muttered, "Oh, shiz."

"What?" she asked.

"My teacher. Mister Himmel. He's here."

After I pointed out the troll to Red, she squinted and focused in. "Baby, I know him."

"You know him?" I said.

"Yes. He goes by the nickname of Art. I deposed him a few years back on a hit and run which occurred in front of a restaurant he happened to be eating at downtown. His brother is actually a judge in Mack County. His name is Gilbert Himmel. Rookie doesn't particularly like him."

Cue the clueless. And if Rookie didn't like Himmel's brother, then the psychotic, anti-social tendencies just might run deep.

Valley High School's gymnasium was the size of a college arena. Mr. Himmel could be headed anywhere, but I swear he made eye contact with me and grinned from ear to ear as he descended the far stairs. Grinned, for Pete's sake. My PTSD came back with a roar, and the hot dog I'd just chowed traveled north up my throat.

Down, I told it. *Down, down, down.*

The closer Mr. Himmel got, the more he didn't look like himself. His blond hair had been greased back in an attempt at a sophisticated GQ style, and he wore a black sports coat overtop a tailored white dress shirt and black slacks. While Justice, Bean, and I fidgeted, Mr. Himmel climbed up the eight steps to our row and squatted down directly in front of Red. She met his gaze with a smile. Forced on her part, but Red's smile normally blinded like the sun anyway. I wasn't sure anyone would notice.

"Hi, Doctor Himmel," I said. Zero response. In fact, his eyes and ears acted as though he hadn't even registered the noise. "Hi, Doctor Himmel," I said louder.

"Hey, baby," he said to Red. "I'm so happy you could join me." Oh. Lordy. The man had not ignored me because he despised me. His face said Red was the Hope Diamond, and he wanted to fondle the rare.

Justice burst out with deep laughter. Me? I sat there like a knot on a log.

Mr. Himmel frowned flirtatiously as Red opened her mouth and closed it. "Don't you remember our romantic evening?" he said, touching her knee.

Red didn't attempt to remove his hand. "I apologize," she replied, again with a semi-genuine smile. "If I would've spent an evening with you, I most certainly would've remembered the romantic part." Red had a strange look on her face.

"It doesn't surprise me you're a little foggy," he said chuckling. "But then again, we were busy doing other things. It's Art, baby. Art Himmel."

Here was where Red was supposed to call up her redheaded roots and tell Art-baby to kiss her a-s-s. Instead, she leaned in closer and subtly breathed in his nauseating aftershave. "Your cologne," she said softly. "I do remember you. How could I forget?"

Cologne?? Cologne, I thought. *Wow.* Murphy said Red's stalker stole her mail and doused it with his cheap aftershave. Ho. Ly. Bejeezus. Mr. Himmel had gone cuckoo for Cocoa Puffs, certifiably stalker-in-love with my aunt.

"Anyone got a straitjacket?" Justice whispered. I had to agree. Whatever crazy pill he took, he swallowed a shiz load of it.

"Tape this conversation, Justice," I whispered to her.

"On it," she answered, sliding two fingers in the pocket of her jeans and removing her iPhone.

Dylan's father, Colton, and Principal Unger stood on the second floor catwalk. Willing my eyes to go laser like Superman, I tried desperately to snag their attention because Colton had a concealed carry. Problem was, it was probably outside in his Bentley. Neither noticed me, but by their body language I knew they rehashed the specifics of Himmel's class earlier in the day. Colton was more business-like than normal—his I'm-off-the-job, gregarious self in sleep mode. I knew Colton. He wasn't PO'd, but he definitely wasn't whistling Dixie...and he most certainly hadn't recognized Mr. Himmel trying to mack on Red.

"Why haven't you returned my calls?" he asked Red, stroking her knee.

"I didn't get your messages," she said with a smile.

"Switch places with me," Justice whispered adamantly. "I'll take him."

Justice had a black belt in karate, so she would definitely be our best bet, but right when I barely shifted a hip, things took a macabre turn. I noticed a slight bulge in the waistband of Mr. Himmel's slacks. Shiny. Metal. Something that went bang. Mr. Himmel came packing heat.

Chapter Twelve

LIFE, INTERRUPTED

*B*ean and the Small brothers were so enthralled with the spectacle they zoned out like mother-trucking zombies. Elbowing Justice's ribs, I slowly pitched my head toward the gun in the side of Himmel's open jacket. Red had focused in on it too because as she kept up the flirtatious routine, she occasionally checked and rechecked its whereabouts.

When I didn't carry a purse, I'd store my iPhone in one of my UGGs. I slid my right hand down into my boot, surreptitiously removing my phone. Bending at the waist, I quickly tapped in Colton's number, but unfortunately he ignored the buzz. I phoned again, and that time he actually glanced at the number. He gave me half a stare, knowing where I usually sat, but continued on with the conversation. Buzzing one last time, when he gave me a frown, I thumbed in a text:

S.O.S. Himmel is here with gun! Stalking Red.

"How about we get out of here, baby," Mr. Himmel tried to coax Red. "Pick up where we left off. I would never hurt you, Tabitha, but I *am* anxious to be alone with you." I had a B.S. in shiz detection. Once he got her alone, if he didn't kill her, she'd wish she were dead by the time he did whatever creepy little things he considered entertainment.

By that time, Oscar came to himself, whispering, "We need to do something."

No shiz, Sherlock. But if I created a big spectacle, he might open fire in the stands. VHS had gone through a mass shooting before. I wasn't sure if luck would be on our side again. It almost seemed too much to ask.

"Let's stay for the game first," Red said, handing me her popcorn and grabbing his hand. "I'm here to watch my niece's boyfriend. You know how kids are. If I leave before he gets to be a star, then he'll get his feelings hurt. You do understand...right, baby?" she played along.

Speaking of my boyfriend, where on God's green, psycho-filled Earth was he? A glance at the empty locker room door produced nothing but more indigestion.

The contours of Mr. Himmel's face immediately changed from hopefully harmless stalker, to violent predator who came with a plan. "You can come with me now, Tabitha, or I'll have to use this."

Mr. Himmel drummed his fingers over his 9mm with such ease it was apparent he'd used it before. Yup. He was all in. I glanced at Justice, inhaled, and on the count of three...here's where the whole thing went south. I wasn't sure what my plan would've materialized into because the Small brothers and Bean went ape poopoo in their own version of vigilante justice. Oscar went at him first, Bean jumped over Justice to assist, but then Frank got involved and per usual "franked up" the whole freaking thing. Justice broad jumped over all of them in an effort to grab the gun, employing her black belt karate skills, but someone clipped her knee and DQ'd her efforts.

All four tumbled down five rows.

Me? I sat there frozen...the popcorn raining down like fat snowflakes around me.

Mr. Himmel laughed darkly and his eyes flashed angrily when he saw our dashed efforts. "Come now, Tabitha, or I'll start by murdering your loud-mouthed niece and her friends."

Himmel's words were like toxic chemicals that pollute the soil. I wanted to stuff a rag down his throat and make it virtually impossible for him to ever open his mouth again. I held my chin high and defiant and said something so insanely stupid even I knew it was bad. "Sticks and stones may break my bones, but words will never hurt me."

Omigosh, that wouldn't even offend a third grader...ergh.

Red immediately popped to her feet and stepped in front of me, fearing I'd get a six-inch hole in my chest complements of a hollow point. But seriously, I preferred it to be me instead of her.

"Take me," I said to him, fisting my hands together at my side. "It'll be a Pink Floyd moment for me. Just another brick in the wall. You hate me. It should be an easy kill."

Red cursed next to me.

Mr. Himmel snorted as if the prospect of taking me had been so insanely ridiculous I had to have lost my mind. "No way in Hell," he muttered. "I will not hurt Tabitha. I promise."

He might as well have taken Baby Jesus and dragged him through the streets at high noon. "Can I borrow your rose-colored glasses?" I spat angrily. "My mother was murdered, moron. I know bad people when I see them, and you're bad. In fact, my aunt deserves an extra ring around her halo for surviving her sister's death and for putting up with your stinky cologne."

Mr. Himmel ignored my retort, instead focusing on the diamond bling on Red's left ring finger. "Do you like the rock, baby?" he said in his attempt at a sexy voice. "It took awhile to save for it, but you were worth it."

Dude had totally gone off his meds.

Red's breathing elevated as she glanced down at the diamond the size of an ice skating rink Rookie had given her "just because." No doubt, she wondered what he'd do in the situation, and it was über creepy Mr. Himmel implied he knew it to be a recent gift. Gently grabbing Mr. Himmel's forearms, she leaned in to whisper something in his ear with a lingering kiss on the cheek. His chest puffed out, and his mood morphed from agitated lover to instant happiness. Whatever perverted lies Red told him he bought hook, line, and sinker.

"Okay, Artie," she said, pulling back with a smile. "Leave your gun alone, and I'll go home with you." She moved toward me, and the look in her eyes was fierce with determination. Red wasn't scared. She planned to rip his gonads from their home once she exited the room. "I love you, Darcy."

"Copy that," I whispered.

Red gave me a look that demanded I stay put. I nodded an affirmative I would comply. In fact, I should have espoused it in some sort of ritualistic dance, but I didn't know what the situation called for. Life, interrupted. That's what this was. A girl came to watch a game, gape at well-muscled bodies, catch-up with the besties, and just like that some psycho pants can snuff her life away.

It was a beyond weird situation. The band piped up with the school's fight song, and everything was going on as scheduled. The cheerleaders just completed an opening cheer and tumbled back to the sideline while both teams jogged onto the floor.

Justice jumped to her feet in a growl as Mr. Himmel proudly escorted Red in front of him, a firm hand at the back of her spine.

My eyes darted across the floor to the catwalk for Colton and Principal Unger, but neither was to be found. I resent the same text, and that time copied Principal Unger, Lincoln Taylor (if he was here), and the school's full-time police officer who'd been added after last year's shooting episode. Each student had his number, and he attended every game.

As Red made it to the hardwood floor, I stared in mute horror while my heart twisted in my chest. I blinked back a tear, telling myself only sissies cried and corralled the Smalls, Justice, and Bean. Chances were good Mr. Himmel parked his car in the teachers' parking lot. The four of us would go there, kick his a-s-s in Technicolor, and hopefully set Red free. We were talking crapshoot. Major long shot. But I wasn't a fool. He would not take her to his home. My guess was he had a separate place altogether for whatever perverted atrocities he intended. But what set him off right then? The argument with me? Principal Unger?

While the buzzer signaled time for tipoff, I stole a worried glance at Dylan who frowned in confusion but within seconds was caught up in the middle of a play, dribbling the ball up court. Dude, was it inappropriate to take a moment to appreciate how hot he looked? I took a good, hard look trying to remember his features because if it was my day to bite a bullet, it was his mug I wanted to have on the backs of my eyeballs. But dang, I needed to prioritize the OCD...Himmel, gun. Gun, Himmel. Guns took first priority.

And the misfits had declared me their leader. Why, one might think, would the five of us so willingly march to possibly meet our

Maker? I guess we all lived by the creed the good guys needed to win.

Unfortunately, some of us were smarter than others.

Red and Mr. Himmel never made it out of the building when Oscar launched at them, swinging his Bible at Himmel's head. So here was the problem with that. He embraced his Bible thumper right in front of the student section. Let me enlighten you, heroes were rarely born in a group of teenagers. In fact, someone yelled, "Fight!" and the stands emptied themselves and crowded around us for the show.

Within seconds, we'd been circled in, which created a domino effect of confusion. Justice reacted next, then Bean, followed by an overly zealous Frank. The four of them took Mr. Himmel and Red down in a hard tackle, like a pack of lions downing a zebra. Himmel fought and flailed with a snarl. I dove into the tangle of arms and legs, ready to lambast him with the others. In the blur of bodies, Frank broke wind that by a smell of the methane content just might level a five-mile radius. When someone kicked my broken finger, the pain was almost too much to bear.

Shoving the nausea down, I went for Red—Red, however, fought like a hellcat, pawing, scratching, and shouting profanity that belonged in a girly bar. I took a wham to the gut, lost my lucky hat, whapped arms with Bean, and clonked heads with Justice. Unfortunately, that threw her off her game as she tried to get Mr. Himmel in some sort of chokehold. With the Devil clearly on his side, the man somehow eluded every fist pound that should've incapacitated him.

Here's a reality check for you. I'm a great fighter in my brain. In truth, I sucked.

I thought, surely to God the bad fighting would level out, but the Smalls wound up taking me down again, along with the front row of students. When I stumbled back to my feet, through blurred eyes I spotted a black head, viciously clawing its way through the crowd, yelling, "Darcy! What the..." *Insert some profanity.* Sigh. Dylan. Unfortunately, he seemed like a planet away because every foot of ground he made, some idiot pushed him further back. While Bean helped Justice to her feet, Mr. Himmel finally fired off a shot.

A collective scream was heard throughout the gym. I froze for a second and waited for blood to pool, a scream to materialize, anything, when I realized the shot must not have claimed a victim. Justice quickly knocked Red out of the way and wrestled Mr. Himmel for the gun. Another shot rang out. She elbowed his windpipe, leaving him coughing and sputtering. Next thing you knew, Oscar delivered the coup de grâce of a blow to Himmel's head with his Bible. I wasn't sure that was what God had intended for the Good Book, but that might be one of those sins covered under the Savior's blood. Mr. Himmel went down face first and moved like a bad song—all over the place, making no sense whatsoever. In a flash of speed, Lincoln Taylor threw himself over the side of the second story catwalk in a coordinated jump, lithe and graceful but as powerful as a jungle-born savage. He landed in a crouch and in no time flat had Mr. Himmel's hands behind his waist, his knee dug into his back.

"Back up, you dumbasses!" he yelled to the students.

The dumbasses wisely backed up.

While the school's police officer and Colton had their guns trained on Mr. Himmel's head, Lincoln restrained him with the cuffs the officer pitched over. Once he was on his feet, his pockets were checked and he got introduced to Miranda, but Mr. Himmel had diarrhea of the mouth. "Help me, God!" he shouted in prayer. "Help me!"

Red readjusted her disheveled clothing and strode over to him in stone-cold, beeyotch attorney mode. She stood several inches taller than Artie and glared down in his wide-eyed confusion. "You're going to pay, you idiot," she seethed, "and I have it on very good authority Heaven does not want you to live."

I wiped my mouth on the back of my hand, tasting blood. By that time, Dylan was huffing and puffing next to me, checking me up and down for wounds. "You're not hit, are you? Please, tell me you're not hit."

"I'm good, but I'm not adverse to a full-bodied frisk if the mood hits you."

Dylan stared at me like I'd grown a new head. He next patted down Red, Justice, and gave a visual to the Smalls and Bean. "Mother of God," he prayed, and then his eyes landed on Mr. Himmel's gun that Lincoln handed the school police officer.

"The threat has been neutralized," Colton warned, tracking Dylan's gaze.

Someone in the crowd actually said, "Thank you," because Colton had issued those words as a broad PSA. I, however, knew they'd been meant specifically for his hero-complex son.

Dylan raised his eyes, not his head, and with one deep grunt pulled me into his side.

I met Mr. Himmel's gaze as he was led away. His eyes were the kind of black people experienced when they stumbled to the bathroom in the night. It wasn't only dark. It was hazy and uncertain. Bless his heart. He was certifiably deranged and insane. I should probably care...but I didn't.

———

A cold sleet dotted the Bentley's windshield at nine-thirty, Monday night. No way in the world would I take a pass when Valley's finest stormed Mr. Himmel's condo, so I hitched a ride with the Taylors while we did our own version of stalking. The game had been postponed (shocking), and after my misfit crew and certain members of the crowd had been questioned, Lincoln and Colton felt the need to close the loop with Mr. Himmel who'd been carted off to jail.

And may I just cry, *Huzzah for Lincoln Taylor!* Lincoln had apparently come to the game with Colton but had left him and Principal Unger to talk in private. When Colton finally read my text, he showed his father, and they banked on the fact Himmel didn't want Red dead. So he, Lincoln, and the school's police officer planned to apprehend him once they'd left the building. Rookie had been phoned as soon as the plan was underway, but of course my misfit crew foiled it.

Overall, I felt pretty darn good, no signs of lasting mental trauma other than Frank Small's intestinal issues. But I was hungry and in dire need of a Coke. Before we parked ourselves discreetly on Mr. Himmel's street, Colton ran through the drive-thru and ordered five bags of White Castle sliders. His Bentley smelled like trans animal fat and crude oil caffeine.

Regarding police searches in general, authorities cannot go into a person's home without probable cause. Police had probable cause enough to enter Himmel's pad since he abducted someone and discharged a concealed weapon in public, but Rookie and Valley's Police Chief wanted the case ironclad. Once Red and the detective answering the call gave the details to a judge, a broad search warrant had been issued to enter Himmel's home to look specifically in drawers, closets, crawl spaces, photo albums—anything the man owned that could cement him to Red as her stalker. Rookie likewise had the muscle at Rafaeli Investigations tearing Red's apartment apart, checking for bugs since Mr. Himmel seemed to be privy to private details of her life. A necessary overkill, but no doubt Rookie was antsy the crime didn't occur in his personal territory—where he could control things.

Huddling next to Dylan in the backseat, we chowed on burgers and watched as one detective exited the home carrying several sawed-off shot guns and hand guns, while one followed after mouthing, "Oh shiz," to his partner with the makings of a pipe bomb. Stacks of girly magazines and cameras with long lenses were recovered along with two desktop computers and a laptop. All of that was play-by-played by Lincoln's high-powered LA-issued binoculars that had some sort of night vision thingy. Himmel was a Grade A scumbag...about as shocking as water was wet.

"While we've got time to blow, I suppose we should debrief on what went down tonight," Colton murmured, his diplomatic way of disciplining me. Murphy already had me in his crosshairs. I suppose Colton could take a shot at what was left.

I bit into my burger, getting a tiny onion caught in my teeth. I picked it out with my pinky nail, attempting a diversion. "Yeah, nice jump from the second floor, Linc. You really upped Dylan's street cred in the badass department."

A small chuckle from Dylan. "I need two ibuprofens," Lincoln groaned. "In my mind, I'm still sixteen. My body, however, feels like it's a hundred."

I wiped my mouth on a napkin. "All things considered, it was pretty anticlimactic. I thought it ended well."

"You didn't have a plan," Colton added.

"It would've come to me. I didn't think a solo mission would work, so I took backup."

"And the backup you chose was not skilled," Colton said in a tone that was not a criticism, just an observation.

"Justice was skilled," Dylan murmured in my defense.

"I'll give you that," Colton agreed.

"Then let me clarify something," I said. "Oscar jumped Mister Himmel. That's not what I had in mind. I, uh—"

"Aided and abetted," Colton said chuckling.

"And provided the mastermind," Lincoln grunted.

Dylan raised his voice. "Put that way it sounds criminal, and Darcy did not break the law." He was angry, but I didn't want to take the time to unearth if it was at his family or me.

Snuggling closer into his side, I dumbly tried to make light of the situation. "Is this an intervention?"

"Would it make a difference if it was?" Colton asked.

My situation called for a great lie—unfortunately, I wasn't feeling creative. "I would like to think I'm results-driven, Colton. I'm sure you can appreciate a go-getter."

"Of course," Lincoln said sarcastically. "How can we not appreciate an overachiever?"

Dylan didn't find the humor. "Point blank, you were tied up and couldn't answer her text, Dad. Darcy thought she was Red's only hope. I do not like that she was in jeopardy, but Darcy is Darcy. She'll try to help someone rather than watching him or her become a victim. I hate it. It makes me sick. I worry all the time I'm going to lose her. But at the same time I admire her like none other. It's the very reason she's my girlfriend because she just...cares."

The car went quiet for a few breaths as everyone digested the vulnerability and truth to Dylan's words. He made me sound noble. I wasn't sure I was noble. I was nosy, I hated bad guys, and my excursions seemed to be a win-win for my personality type. But let's be real. Dylan hanging with me was being up shiz creek with no paddle. I wasn't sure how long a sane guy could convince his brain that was normal. But consider Rookie...he was still doing it...and somehow on this side of the dirt.

Lincoln broke the building tension. "Son, she needs training if she's going to continue to be Darcy."

"I would agree," Dylan said softly.

Lincoln went Yoda, focusing his words solely on me. "Come to

LA, dear, and move in with Lex and me when you graduate. You can go to the police academy. Paddy and I will take care of you. What if Colton wouldn't have read your text? You had four people banking on your brain when I know your plan was simply to show up and improvise."

"There's nothing wrong with improvising," I said. "In fact, that's my motto: utilize all twenty-four hours of each day, three hundred and sixty-five." Just not in schoolwork.

Lincoln groaned something about wanting to shove me in a cage and throw away the key. "Just think on it, Darcy. You and Dylan can work things out. At least, let me teach you how to make plans."

My opinion? That was death to a verb. "D?" I asked, wanting his take.

Dylan wadded up the paper on his fourth slider, stuffing it in the takeout bag. His body was rigid, a telltale sign he didn't care for the subject matter. He took a deep breath and angled my chin toward him, but it sounded as though his mouth was full of gravel. "I support whatever makes you happy and keeps you alive."

A silver Benz SUV parallel parked right in front of the condominium. Two silhouettes sat inside. I was intimately familiar with that car. I'd fallen out of it last year. My high heel got caught in a metal grate, and I fractured my left ankle in three places. The car was Rookie's. Could be good. Could be unbelievably bad. He had met Red at the police station while I hopped into the Bentley with the Taylors. I'd spoken with Red twice, but I assumed they were on their way home. Obviously, they couldn't shut down the worry any more than we could.

Rookie opened the driver's side door and slid out into the frigid air. He stood there for a moment and gazed blindly ahead of him, like he didn't know whether to jump back in his car and ride to parts unknown or tackle something he knew would be a tough job. The warmth coming from his nostrils clouded in front of him as he fobbed his ride to a lock and briskly strode to a detective who'd just opened the back of a black van. Dressed in the stately clothing of a gentleman, his dark slacks and long, black coat showcased a six foot four frame that was an argument for genetic cloning. His high cheekbones and coffee-colored hair topped off a lean, hard-muscled frame that didn't require one day's work in the gym. Good thing. He happened to be a junk food junkie like me.

"Holy hell. Who is that, Jackal?" Lincoln muttered, addressing his son by his nickname.

Colton chuckled deeply, placing his takeout coffee back inside its holder in the center console. "That's Rookie, Dad. You've golfed with him. Please tell me you remember."

Lincoln snorted and took a bite of burger, talking with a full mouth. "I'm not that senile, son. He just looks different at night... but then everyone does. Watch a man walk by himself in the dark, and you discover the confidence level. Rookie carries a lot of power in his gait. He's Red's husband, right?"

Colton stuffed a slider in his mouth. "Ex-husband. Darcy, are they still married?" he asked, turning to find my eyes. "I swear, I know they're supposed to be divorced, but I can't bring myself to push when things go gray between them."

Swallowing down a sip of Coke, I answered as honestly as I could. "No, they aren't married," I groaned, but Rookie oddly still wore his wedding band. Staying together for them had been as difficult as trying to pick up a jellyfish. But Rookie's love was without borders.

Funny thing was, every time there'd been a divorce, Red's hair changed from its natural red to whatever color she felt at the moment. Over the course of the past few years, her hair had been jet-black, medium brown, light brown, and at the moment blonde. Why? It was a final dig at Rookie who loved her original hue.

Sigh. Love...or the end of it. It made people do crazy, crazy things.

"He still loves her," Lincoln murmured. I wholeheartedly agreed, but Red had a problem with being happy. At least, that was Murphy's theory. When things got too good, she would self-destruct and nuke everything around her. Come to think of it, maybe she changed her hair because she thought it would make her unattractive to Rookie. Who knew?

"Please, don't go in there, son," Lincoln muttered subliminally to Rookie. "Jackal, you might have to stop him. If he tries to exert some authority, he's going to screw up this case."

No kidding. Rookie going badass-mofo-prosecutor would screw Red's case to heck and back.

Colton had one hand on the door when Rookie stopped in front of the van, said a few words to a detective, nodded, and then strolled back to the privacy of the Benz. He fobbed it open and peered inside, saying something to the silhouette of whom I could only assume was Red. After a few headshakes, he closed the door, beeped it locked again, and turned toward the Bentley when Colton flashed his headlights in greeting.

"Smart man," Lincoln said and chuckled. "He gave them a message he's watching but didn't attempt to muscle his way inside."

In five determined strides, Rookie made his way to the driver's side of the Bentley but had an OCD moment and checked Red again, refobbing an already locked SUV.

Colton struck the button thingy on the side of his door, rolling down the window. "Rookie, if you and Red want to go home, we'll keep our eye on things," Colton told him.

Rookie squeezed his shoulder in thanks, giving an answer I wouldn't have expected in a million years. "I might take you up on that, Colt," he murmured, palming the back of his neck. "We're beat. Thank you."

After Rookie thanked the both of them for their part in apprehending Mr. Himmel, he made nice with Dylan for a bit and then focused his whiskey-colored eyes on me. "Hey, baby," he said, ducking his head into the backseat. "I love you, and thank you for looking out for my wife. Are you okay? Do you want to come sit in the car with Tabitha and me? If you want to spend the night, I'll get up and take you to school."

Holy heart failure, Batman. Rookie's BP had skyrocketed, and his hands shook when they reached for mine. I squeezed Dylan's fingers and then opened the passenger side backseat door. Rookie needed a hug—like he teetered on the edge of a cliff and was moments away from another "Red coma" there was no escaping.

I jogged to his side, the cold boring into my bones like an oil drill going for liquid gold. "Is Red okay?" I asked. Rookie pulled me into his arms in a possessive hug, kissing the top of my head.

"No," he murmured.

"Mister Himmel definitely has a few screws loose."

"She's not worried about herself. She worries that you seem to have no regard for your life. She's cried for the past hour, talking about you, Gemma, Marjorie...damn."

Tears welled up in my eyes, but I somehow stopped them before they slid down my cheeks. "Don't worry. There's a bright side. Now we know why he hated me so much."

Rookie squeezed me like his life depended on it. Red's, Marjorie's, and my happiness was the barometer by which he measured his days. If something were amiss with one of us, he would remove whatever he considered an obstacle until his world stabilized.

"By the time I'm through with him, he's not going to be able to hate anyone," he said. "That's a promise."

Chapter Thirteen

CURIOUS GEORGE

$\mathcal{M}$y cell phone buzzed, signaling a text was on deck. Fumbling around for the noise, I found my iPhone underneath the covers, tangled up in the sheets. I pulled it to my eyes, squinting at the screen.

Hi, the text said. *Fisher said you could help me.*

Fisher...Fish-er...Fisher Stanton...it took a second to remember Fisher had promised me another client, but I decided in an instant fifty bucks underpriced my particular services.

I can help you, I thumbed back, *but my fee is $100. Double if I deliver early.*

Here was the returned text:

Money is no object for Trudi Hatchett. That's T-R-U-D-I. And if you verify what I think is true, then I'll triple.

Trudi Hatchet. Yay! (NOT).

Trudi was a real snooty patooty who insisted on spelling her name upon introduction. But let's just say if she were North Vietnam and I was the United States, I would napalm her butt in a heartbeat. Trudi conjured up zero sympathy in my brain, and she hung with other entitled clones I referred to as the Skank Squad. But here was the thing...the Skank Squad had money.

I quickly thumbed in a response before she could change her mind:

Meet me at locker twelve with the details.

I stumbled out of bed and into a cold shower the flavor of Icelandic frostbite. My dealings with Trudi were not even on an as-needed basis. I avoided her like a porta-potty in the August heat. But I needed to do some pre-meeting recon before we spoke, and only one person in her inner circle wouldn't mind to dish—Jagger Cane. I didn't consider it a breach of confidentiality because we at Darcy Walker Investigations didn't break the confidences of our clients or put them in a compromising situation. Besides, Jagger would give me the details simply because he thought it would super-glue us together. Did that make me a user? Yeah. I didn't give a rat's bald butt about it either.

After I dried off and did a quick blowout, I finger-combed my hair, dotted some blush on my cheeks, and swiped my lashes with mascara. While I stood in my closet hoping my clothes would talk to me, I dialed Jagger and placed the call on speaker. I chose a pair of skin-tight Citizens of Humanity jeans with a white long-sleeved T that cut off my oxygen supply. Overtop, I pulled on a black Ramones T-shirt, a size too small.

When I laced up my Chucks, Jagger answered. "Give me five minutes to get ready, babe, and I can be at your house in fifteen."

"I need information," was my greeting.

"So this wasn't a call for a ride to school?"

"Listen, bud, my dance card is full."

"With Taylor?"

"He *is* my significant other."

"I won't tell if you won't," he whispered conspiratorially.

Ugh. "I may be a lot of things, Jagger, but a cheat isn't one of them."

"Thanks for ruining my day," he mumbled. "I'd been hoping your union was a mere moment of temporary insanity."

"Nope. Still going strong."

Jagger lost some of the charm. "Then name it, Darcy. I have to grab a shower before I start another nauseatingly boring day at Valley."

Trudi was a good friend of Ivy's. If anyone knew the intricate details of Trudi's life, by default it would be Jagger. I led the conversation with, "Exactly what is going on between you and Ivy, Jagger? She was dating Grumpy as of seventh period yesterday, then you swoop in, deal out your Jagger Juice, and he gets dumped."

"Why do you care, babe?"

"Call me Curious George."

"To sate your curiosity, George, I missed Ivy. Trudi and I had a thing, but it was subzero from the start and as boring as watching paint dry. Ivy and I spoke after seventh period, and we decided to give it another go. End of story."

Um, wow. So that was why Trudi had contacted me. She'd betrayed girl code by dating her girlfriend's ex, and when she got the heave-ho, she obviously had payback on her mind. But IMHO, she should've known better. Jagger was a hit-and-run boyfriend. There were some girls that never seemed to bother, but they all were the same type—ditzy, superficial bimbos.

"And that's gospel?" I asked, grabbing my black leather jacket.

"Honest injun, babe. I'm going to make you a promise. I'll always tell you the truth...and I expect the same from you."

My God—for some insane, idiotic reason I believed him. But if he was going to be all *you show me yours, I'll show you mine*, then I had a laundry list of things I wanted to ask starting with Rudi and Dylan. Problem was, I heard Dylan yelling downstairs that he'd brought coffee and a danish for breakfast.

I mulled over Jagger's words for half a second then muttered, "Deal," into the receiver and cut the call.

"Let me get this straight," I said to Trudi. "You want me to break into Ivy's home, disable the alarm, and sneak into her room to see if I can find the knockoff Chanel sunglasses you bought for ten bucks?"

"On Canal Street. In New York," she said proudly.

Trudi had dark hair and eyes, money out the yin-yang, but disproportionate features that belonged on an alien-human hybrid. For some reason, she landed dates with cute and semi-cute guys. Like Ivy, she had a sense of self-entitlement and would do anything to lock a guy down. My mind didn't choose to theorize on what those selling points would be because I was positive I'd need a barf bag. But hips the size of a tractor aside, the girl could dress. Wearing a cropped blue sweater with a black cat on front, her threads rivaled Ivy's and Brynn Hathaway's.

"Did you allow her to borrow them?" I asked as a follow-up.

Trudi twisted a strand of black hair around her finger. "No, but she was in my Jeep the last time I wore them. She left, and the sunglasses left too."

"Describe the glasses."

"Oversized and white. And you know how she likes white."

True. Ivy wore white clothing daily, and her naturally blonde hair had recently been bleached as cold as frostbite. Stealing a pair of white Chanel sunglasses was highly possible. The girl even drove a white MINI Cooper.

"Does she have a reason to be angry with you?"

Trudi held her bony chin high and leaned forward, looking intense and stealing my personal space. I'd never officially had a conversation with her that hadn't been forced. And after our gig was over, I didn't anticipate that changing. "She's angry Jagger and I had a thing," she said haughtily. "Well, we used to. We broke up yesterday."

I didn't want to rub salt in her wound, but she happened to be the "other woman" asking me to find out if the former "legitimate woman" was a thief...when her relationship with said opposite sex had always been on the DL...*twisted*.

"I'm sorry," I said genuinely.

Trudi acted unaffected, her lips freezing into a pouty expression. "It's on principle, Darcy. Surely you can understand that."

Sure, I could understand it. Thing was, I observed her chatting with Ivy on the sidelines while they cheered. "You and Ivy seemed awfully chummy last night," I said, glancing over my shoulder for Dylan. If he discovered my plans for a B&E, I was hosed.

"I had to keep up appearances," she said.

"When did the sunglasses disappear?"

"About a week ago."

"So you think Ivy's been sitting on the knowledge that you and Jagger had a thing?" She stiffened with a nod. "What are you going to do with this information once I provide it?"

An evil wench smile. "I'm going to take her down publicly. Everyone will know what a two-faced, lying thief she really is."

File that in the *OMG File*. Maybe situations like these were why I sometimes preferred guys. They didn't take pot shots at people or try to cut them down behind their back. They just hit a person instead. Regarding Ivy, I was thinking everyone already knew she was a two-faced, lying thief. She'd been stealing Hello Kitty merchandise for years. Not my problem. I just delivered the goods.

"This has to be top secret," she added. "Promise to keep it between us."

"Cross my heart, hope to die, stick a needle in my eye."

Brynn Hathaway picked that moment to slither—I'm sorry, "let her booty work"—up next to us, acting as if she were privy to what we'd been talking about. She didn't seem shocked. She didn't seem nosy. In fact, she just stared, almost as if she deliberated whether I was as good as the reputation that preceded me. All I knew was the top secret plans to break into Ivy's home were not so secret if Brynn knew. And if Brynn knew, she would tell Dylan. She was the goody-goody type, which usually meant she was a tattletale.

"Hey, girlfriend," Trudi gushed. Trudi, I think, was Brynn's lapdog. Made me want to bark just to rub it in her face.

After some revolting sorority girl hug, both of them held hands while Trudi launched back into skank-mode, losing most of her mock niceness. "So it's a deal?" she snipped snottily.

"Dial it back a notch or two, Trudi, or the deal's off," I surprisingly said. Trudi opened her mouth but then quickly snapped it shut with a frown. She wasn't used to being called out on the mean girl attitude, and frankly I wasn't used to being the person to do it. "I'm going to need half up front of my fee," I added, reminding her Fisher gave me the Ben Franklin recommendation.

After Trudi provided the location of Ivy's room inside the Morrison home, she whipped out a Louis Vuitton checkbook, while Brynn supplied the burgundy Montblanc ink pen. I held up my hand. "No paper trail," I said, reciting the acceptable forms of payment. Trudi dug around in her purse, removed a wad of bills, and placed them in my palm. Glancing down, I took note she dispensed the full-amount, plus a double bonus. Trudi must've read the confusion in my face. "I trust you can deliver," she said.

I folded up the three C-notes and placed them in my purse.

"Did you hear?" Brynn asked Trudi.

Trudi had one eye on Jagger's locker across the hall, the other on Brynn. "Hear what?" she said.

Brynn glanced over her shoulder to check for privacy. "Jagger gave Ivy a ruby promise ring last night that looks like a meteorite."

Trudi gave one slow, drawn-out blink. "Seriously? The most he gave me was a burger from McDonald's."

Brynn shrugged in apology. I wasn't sure why that morsel of gossip should surprise Trudi. One day Jagger and Ivy were all over one another like swans that mated for life. The next, I heard how she dumped his fastard butt for...well, for whatever relationship crime he allegedly committed. But here was the interesting part. After what Jagger propositioned me with earlier, it sounded like the promise had already been broken.

Brynn glanced longingly at Dylan's locker, like an addict looking for a fix. Cue the awws. I took advantage of the opportunity to really get a read on her. Dressed in black riding boots and jeans that hugged her butt, she was a genetic explosion of perfection in a pale pink sweater that showcased perfect boobs. Clutched tightly in her small hands was an AP math book and a worn-out copy of *Anna Karenina*. We'd read that book freshman year, which meant it was a reread. I didn't want to think she was a deep thinker, but that book suggested otherwise. My stomach clenched at the thought there might be a person worth knowing beneath all the pink and the self-made burden to look like a runway model.

"How are you, Brynn?" I groaned aloud.

Brynn unloaded her trademark, flirty smile. "Fine," she answered. "And you?"

"Living the good life," I said, wondering if she'd ask about the night before's chain of events.

Instead of diving into the juicy stuff—like, *Hey did you get shot, Did your aunt get shot, Did anyone get shot?*—she glanced at my jeans with an envious smile. "Nice jeans."

"Hand-me-downs," I explained and shrugged.

"Oh," she said surprised. "Well, whoever bought them has great taste." She dropped her eyes to her own ensemble. "It's stressful looking this good all the time, you know?"

Oh, the cross she has to bear.

Hanging my purse on the hook, I grabbed my math book, pencil, notebook, and the morning paper. Shutting the door, all of a sudden I felt self-conscious. My clothing, hair, posture, teeth—everything seemed wrong. *Don't do this, Darcy*, I told myself. *You're a good person. You're loyal. You're kind, and at least a six on a scale of one-to-ten. Okay, maybe a five point nine...but you're def above a five.*

When I said nothing, Brynn piped up in an overly saccharine voice. "I had a question about homework. Do you know where Dylan is?"

I sighed so hard it actually hurt my throat. Dylan was in a basketball meeting. I had no plans to lie, but I wouldn't give up his whereabouts either. "He's with the guys. Is there a message I can pass along?"

Brynn held her chin high, her tongue basically dripping drool as her eyes fell on Dylan's class ring, dangling from my neck. "I'll wait," she said curtly.

I thought of a naughty word, but out of my mouth came, "Have at it."

Glancing over the heads of students cruising the hall, there was no sight of him. Dylan was so huge he was already a head and shoulders above most who were probably full-grown. When my eyes swung back to Brynn, I was rewarded with a grin. Ugh...she could not easily be offended.

"Hey, we should go out some time," she purred. I swear to God on the Great White Throne, my mouth dropped wide. "I'm serious," she said, eyeing my reaction. "We should check out that new place. Club Need."

I had no desire to play besties with Brynn, but the girl just played her high card. "Club Need?" I verified.

"Yes. Have you heard of it?"

Act dense, Darcy. Pull on the dumb. "Yeah."

"A body fell out of the wall there on Friday." She pitched her head to the morning paper tucked up under my arm. "The details are in the lead story. Creepy, but I feel sorry for the victim."

"Oh, wow," I whispered. I hadn't read the morning paper but planned to during downtime. Dylan had retrieved it from the driveway earlier. After a scan of the opening paragraph, as Brynn claimed, the lead story penned by Tito Westbrook identified Lyric Armstrong as the victim. In fact, Tito even mentioned the coroner's theory that Lyric had tried to sneak in through the ductwork, which turned out to be a quote-unquote "unstoppable death march" when she lost her way and toppled into a room with no way out. Schematics of the original structure showed a location behind an air conditioning unit where she more than likely gained entrance. Tito dropped a mortar round by mentioning Lyric had been concerned over her best friend Ryder Beck, who'd disappeared last seen entering Club Need.

Brynn amped up the chatter. "We should totally go. It would be fun. We could go in a group or just us girls."

Brynn needed to issue an APB for her brain if she thought I'd accept, but the best of manipulators usually thought too highly of their skills. She simply wanted to slum with the peasants because she believed Dylan would accompany me. I made a mental note to get nervous when I had the time, but right then, I pondered Tito's next move.

"Think about it," she pushed.

Brynn then broke a cardinal rule by touching me. She might have legendary looks, but she didn't outrank me on the smarts, and I wasn't easily manipulated...even by force. I pulled on my mean-girl face. "Listen, Brynn, you're selling, but I'm not buying."

"Buying *what*?" Dylan murmured, coming up from behind. Dylan placed his left arm around my neck, tugging me to his chest and kissing my hair.

Brynn swallowed, suddenly uncomfortable. "See you in class, Dylan," she muttered. Turning on her designer shoes, she gave her hair a dramatic flip and waltzed off.

"What were you two talking about?" he asked. I couldn't help but take a gratuitous moment to peek over my shoulder at his six foot two batch of brawn. He'd dressed in a white button-down shirt that lay untucked outside faded, loose-fitting jeans. His shoes of choice were flip-flops on a cold February morning in Cincinnati. No surprise there. Like me, Dylan didn't always color between the lines. Let's be real. He'd been dating me.

"Nothing, really. She said we should hang some time." Dylan

made a what-sound in his throat. "I know," I said, frowning in confusion. "Today is not short on weird."

When Dylan tunneled his fingers through my hair and nibbled down my neck, a very loud, embarrassing gasp broke free from my lips. Dylan totally pushed the limit of the school's PDA policy, which basically was keep your hands to yourself, walking at a respectable distance à la the Amish. "Seriously, D, are you trying to *kill* me?" I moaned. "You're going to kiss the very last, unfulfilled, tragically-dead-at-sixteen life right out of me."

Lifting his muscled arm from my neck, I pivoted and placed both my hands around his neck. They didn't even span the circumference. Dylan laughed and gave a quick yank of my ombré-blue hair.

"No, Darc, that's not the way I would get rid of you." He grinned devilishly, flashing perfect rows of pearly whites. Honestly, if I had to think about it, his mouth might be the best part of his body. *Nah*, I quickly retorted. The way he filled out his jeans was.

I went back to scanning the paragraphs of Tito's article. "Chinese water torture...bamboo shoots under the fingernails kinds of torture?" I asked offhandedly.

"No, I'd do something more slow and barbaric. Something along the lines of Genghis Khan."

"Head on a stick?"

"No," he murmured. "I actually like your lips a little too much for that. And on that note, show me some love."

"No."

"Yes," he said, a big smile in his voice.

I closed the paper with an exaggerated snap, placing two fingers over his lips. When he opened his mouth with the same one-worded command, the vibration of his voice on my fingers did strange things to my equilibrium. Cupping my face in his hand, he pulled my chin up within millimeters of his mouth—pouring on the seduction. "D, you totally push the boundaries of the kissy-face rules," I said, still keeping my fingers as a defensive gesture between us.

"Mmm," he murmured.

"You have major dog breath." My attempt to bulldoze the moment did nothing.

Patting myself down, I eagle-eyed the floor for the pencil I must have dropped. For some reason, I'd been losing them all semester. Right then, Dylan pulled it from behind my ear and held it above my head, hustling away when I made a grab for it. "You are such a bully," I said, laughing softly. "Give me my pencil, or I am exiling our mad, passionate love to the frigid land of Siberia...while I serial date the soccer team."

Dylan immediately stopped, eyes hard as nails. "You're playing hardball."

"I'm playing hardball. Besides, the soccer team has some really cute guys."

He grumbled and finally placed the pencil in my hand as a peace offering, turning and grabbing his math book from locker thirteen. As the tardy bell rang, he landed on my mouth like a paratrooper on a big, black X. And let me make something clear. His idea of slow and torturous was definitely *slow* and *torturous*.

Heart palpitations, broken breaths, sentence fragments, and animal sounds came out of my chest all at once as I fisted his shirt in my hands. I shook my head, attempting to clear it, realizing I was in the general population of a very public place. "Later, lover," he murmured into my lips. As I stood there hormonally flustered, Dylan turned me toward my class, giving me a scoot forward by pushing my lower back...and spanked my behind.

Chapter Fourteen

BREAKING AND ENTERING

*H*ere's the thing with Dylan and me. Our lips weren't logically made for one another, but thank God the logical part of his brain had gone fully AWOL.

Hotfooting it to class in a jog that left me winded, I skidded into Mr. Gordon's room right as the tardy bell busted me for being officially late. Even with his back turned, Mr. Gordon drawled out, "Glad you could join us, Walker."

I sputtered out, "You're welcome," and fell into my seat in front of Rudi.

Mr. Gordon glanced over his shoulder, his short-sleeved plaid shirt and gray pants heavy on the nerd, especially with black horn-rimmed glasses. Scarecrow-thin, his face was shaped like a pelican's with a nose two sizes too big for his other features. Chalk stains smeared the pockets of his pants, and after he tried to rub out what I assumed to be a headache, they then shaded the shine of his bald head. "Did I just get chalk on my face?" he asked.

"Either that or it's cocaine," I muttered.

Insert some mumbling. "You worry me, Walker. I read somewhere that you meet seven psychopaths a day. Himmel might've eaten up six, but the seventh is reserved for you."

I unzipped my backpack with my teeth, unable to use my useless broken finger. "You were there?" I mumbled behind the zipper.

"Everyone was there. It was a big game."

"It was definitely a stellar moment in the *Darcy Walker Playbook*. But don't try it at home. I'm a professional," I dumbly said and laughed.

"Monday night could use a do-over," he muttered, "but I'm going to go out on a limb here and say you're one of the good guys. Himmel was heavy on the cray-cray." I cocked my head to the side at his attempt at teenage vernacular while the rest of the class snickered. "Did I fail with the delivery?" he groaned.

"It's the thought that counts," I said and smiled.

"Darn, I'm trying to be relatable but rarely hit the mark. Get to work, Walker, and if anyone sees my giraffe stapler, please let me know."

Mr. Gordon's stapler had been a no-show for two weeks. He'd been obsessing over the loss.

Math assignments as usual had been chalked onto the board. Flipping open my textbook, I thumbed to the appropriate page and felt the heated gaze of Ben Ryan. Chairs were on a first-come, first-serve basis, reminiscent of festival seating in a rock concert.

Unfortunately, Ben thought his festival belonged up in mine.

My opening sentence? "I need to find Gabrielle Allen."

"And you need this why?" he asked, confusion tingeing his voice. Ben had helped me gather information over Christmas on Coach Wallace's wife when I suspected her of trashing his ride. Ben had proved then he had a vast array of resources at his disposal. His father was a ranking general in the Air Force. And yes, Ben's use of those resources had probably been illegal and treasonous but not my problem.

I gave him a quick cutoff. "Do you need a reason?"

Ben and I had a moment where he attempted to understand my brain, and I basically wished his sorry butt good luck. "The last time I helped you it nearly ended with you getting bullet holes in your gut for Christmas," he said. "And after I read this morning's news, and seeing how the gym is still crawling with detectives, it sounds like you've thrown another log on the *crazy* fire."

Ben's British accent was heavy—a trait that surfaced when he grew perturbed.

The crime scene at the gymnasium had been processed the night before, but a new set of detectives was on the scene when we rolled in first period. Yellow tape cordoned off both entrances and exits and was the number one picture trending on Valley's Twitter page and Instagram feeds. Unfortunately, a copy of my butt also made the cut and a shot of Red's black bra, captioned with a "Yowza," had more favorites than VHS had seen in months. Everyone else involved was a blur of motion.

"Don't dwell on the negative, Ben."

After a few breaths of stalemate, he sighed and buckled. "Is that still her name?"

"Don't know."

"Did she attend Valley?"

"No clue."

"I love it when you're prepared," he groaned. "I'll dig around in the newspaper archives to see if she surfaces, and if not?" he paused. "God only knows."

When Ben scrawled the name in his notebook, I realized his love of the pen and not the sword might actually come in handy. Ben had only attended VHS for a few short months but was named editor of the newspaper when the senior in charge decided he wanted to be in charge of the girls selling advertisements. Apparently, his hands were found in compromising situations, and the publisher had to make some changes that didn't require unsteaming windows and praying STDs were merely a myth.

"Remind me to send you a thank you note," I said, rolling my eyes.

Ben lifted up one corner of his mouth in a smile, his normal uniform of khakis, a light blue oxford, and penny loafers looking too prep school for Valley. Ben refused to morph into anything other than what he was—perhaps that was why I found myself drawn to him—he refused to conform. "Anything for you, angel, but I'll think of a way you can repay me anyway."

Cue the red cheeks. In the immortal words of my potty mouth, I blurted out, "You are such a frigging blowhard."

"And a cute one at that. Give me a few days."

Ben definitely had a healthy self-esteem, but when his quips became flavored with self-indulgences toward me, I cut off the drive-by antics. He somehow held on to the torch he could break Dylan and me up, but I had a feeling if he was ever successful, he'd move on to someone else who was unavailable, merely as a challenge. Why? At the end of the day, I believed his words to be total BS. Ben was a serial dater like Finn Lively. And if the rumor mill served correctly, he'd gotten to know Ivy, Clementine, and—big gasp —Brynn. All three girls still spoke to him freely, so if there were breakups, they'd been amicable. But Brynn seemed unnaturally proprietary when I was around. Go figure.

Ben flirting with me caused the ripple effect…

Grumpy grunted, "She's taken, dude," when he sat down across from him.

Finn added, "Yup," when he settled in behind Grumpy.

Insert a villain. "And I can't figure out why," she sneered. Those words were Ivy's.

In the grand scheme of things, Ivy's words meant nothing, but after Brynn trying to legitimately muscle me into doing as she wished, Ivy could kiss my big, white, redneck a-s-s. I kept my face neutral as though the words didn't sting at all. "How are you, Poison? I mean, Ivy?"

"I'm hearing The Baha Men," she said, and then launched into her rendition of "Who Let the Dogs Out."

Ugh, that was a good one. "Shut the eff up, Ivy," Finn glared, irritated of her goad. "You're voice is giving me a headache."

No kidding, she had a major case of munchkins in the *The Wizard of* freaking *Oz*.

"So you're under her spell too, Finn?" she guffawed. "Really, what's this world coming to when Darcy Walker is all of a sudden everyone's dream girl?"

Want blood to spew out of my eyes? Put me in a room with Ivy Morrison. I could feel the mechanics of her mind turning, trying to find a weakness to exploit. She glanced at my Ramones T-shirt, jeans, and black beanie and compared it to her white lace skirt and *Flash Dance*-esque cut-off she'd designed herself. The ensemble looked like it would disintegrate if water hit it, highlighting a set of store-bought boobs that punctuated how flat her butt was.

"I like the Ramones," I shot back.

Ivy unloaded a smile that was nothing but shark as she leaned into Finn's personal space. "You smell yummy, Finn. What cologne are you wearing?"

"Hate," he muttered, opening his math book.

"New on the market?" She smiled.

"About five minutes ago," he deadpanned. Ben bent down to laugh.

Ivy batted her eyes so much I almost puked in the process. "So creative," she said, settling back into her seat and picking up a pencil. "And here I thought I was the most creative person in this school...it just goes to show someone else can have a creative moment when they want and it looks like Darcy had one last night or maybe she didn't and that's why she almost got killed."

"For crying out loud, use a freaking period," Grumpy groaned.

Grumpy referred to the monotonous, sanctimonious speechi-fying only Ivy was capable of. Her conversations were one big run-on sentence peppered with self-edification and public putdowns. Things were definitely frigid between them, and I hoped it would be where Grumpy permanently clued-in she hadn't been worth the brainpower.

Ivy rolled her ice-blue eyes, too arrogant to be offended. As usual, she began first period with her standard gossipy line, telling me why Dylan and I would never work. Funny she used Brynn as the ammo when Brynn was in the know about my little B&E project.

"You're sure Dylan is committed?" she asked.

"I'm the old ball and chain," I explained, scratching the back of my neck with my cast.

"I only ask because I care." She crinkled up her nose, opened her mouth to speak, but then changed her mind at the last minute with a smirk—like she considered shielding me from something painful but couldn't quite mask her amusement. "I was under the impression he and Brynn were exclusive," she blurted out.

What the what?!

I scratched even harder, her words feeling like an outbreak of pus-filled blisters. Finn groaned, leaning across the aisle and handing me a *Pokémon* card he knew I'd been after for months. Ivy snorted at my juvenile obsession I had no desire of getting under control. "Blue hair and *Pokémon*," she said. "I'm not sure what should be more embarrassing."

By God, she added a hair flip.

"Maybe having a boob job at seventeen should be more embarrassing," Rudi actually said aloud. Rudi leaned forward and touched me on the shoulder like a protective lioness, prepared to take down the predator who threatened her baby cub.

"What did you say?!" Ivy snapped.

Rudi opened her mouth for a repeat, but Jagger plopped down right at that time and spoke overtop her. "Shut up, Ivy," he barked, grabbing my eyes with a heated gaze. "Nothing is going on between Dylan and Brynn...promise."

He then leaned across the aisle and lifted my chin on the tips of his fingers, giving me a face that said, *Feel better now?* I think my mood could only be bettered by some seriously illegal narcotics... but not my thing.

"You're asking for trouble," Grumpy said, referring to Dylan.

Jagger didn't care, and his gaze hadn't faltered as he hammered home the point Dylan was a faithful boyfriend. It wasn't that I didn't trust Dylan. It was just that with Ivy it was a daily struggle to not hit the panic button. If you hear the same propaganda over and over, it eventually became a type of psychological warfare. You believed it despite what you knew to be true.

Jagger looked totally diesel beneath his red polo and had just trimmed his hair in a buzz cut that accentuated the sharp lines and angles of a face that held secrets. Backing out of his grasp, Ivy's loud groan reminded me of her frequent jealous rages, and although I appreciated Jagger's sentiment, I didn't want to be the bullet in her loaded gun. She attempted to pack on the lovin' after his rude retort, but he didn't seem interested. She gazed at me and mouthed, "I hate you."

I gazed at her and mouthed, "Ergonomics."

The new and improved Darcy had begun to return the barbs. Obviously, going "ergonomics" on her butt had only been badass in my brain.

Letting out a, "Hmpf," when Jagger refused to acknowledge her touchy-feelyness, she commenced to tell us she'd be out of town for two days while her father took a quick trip to Las Vegas. That would fall under the category of *Tell Me More*.

"Sin City?" I asked.

"Yeah, for two days," Ivy's vermin-infested soul replied. "We're flying out as soon as I get home, and then we'll be back on Thursday."

Here was my opportunity to earn some cash from Trudi, and when opportunity knocked, I sure as shiz would answer the door. All I had to do was get past Murphy and then get Vinnie onboard. Bean had never done a B&E...heck, I'd only performed one...but Bean might crack, and it would be as easy as breathing for Vinnie Vecchione.

After I got particulars like what airline she'd be traveling and the actual departure time, Ivy gave me a, "Ta ta, dahling."

Here's what I want to say, *Buh-bye, hope to not see you later, and please let the door slam on your flat a-s-s.*

Here's what I said. "Have a great trip."

Because I was going to break into her house while she was gone.

———

When you're a verb, you don't always plan your excursions. They just sort of happened. It was the first trip, I admit, that I had to plan. The time ticked at eight o'clock. Murphy and Marjorie had just pulled into the driveway from a trip to the library. To safeguard against getting busted, I clocked in with Murphy five minutes earlier and told him I was with Dylan. I clocked in with Dylan and told him I was with Murphy. Wearing commando-black, my lucky hat, and Chucks, I quietly lifted my second story window and shimmied my way down the bare maple tree. Jogging to the entrance of BTCC, the air cut through me like a sharp knife on butter.

In the spirit of duplicity, the sky was two-faced like the moon. The east was cloudy, the west a midnight blue with a blanket of stars. I jumped up and down as the chill settled into my muscles, and at fifteen minutes past eight, Vinnie's pink VW Bug sputtered to a stop in front of the big buffalo sign I hid behind.

That was what I liked about the misfits—when someone told them to masquerade as someone else or break into private property on the sly, there were no questions, only a, "What time?"

Vinnie was game when I'd called...thank the Good Lord.

"Home for the weekend?" I asked as I leaned forward to warm

myself from his heater. The Bug had one foot in the grave, blowing air so cold it rivaled the chill factor outdoors.

"Yeah," Vinnie answered. "Yolo."

I was no college student, but logic said he was at the beginning of his week like everyone else. Could he legitimately have flunked out of school when he'd probably only gone to a few week's worth of classes since the semester began? I slid an inquisitive gaze over, but Vinnie was Vinnie—his only complex thought being where his next moon pie or Red Bull would come from.

He looked like a tattooed meth head. His arms were covered in colored hieroglyphics and his fingernails glowed an electric-blue. His brown hair had been styled in a permed Mohawk with a Fu Manchu mustache. Obviously, it was the look for his new movie, and since it was called *Fat Men from Venus*, he decided to pile on the pounds to be more believable in the role. Pre-movie career, he weighed close to three bucks. Right then, his butt was so big it needed to be on National Geographic.

At the risk of sounding offensive, I asked about the official rating of the movie...his answer? It didn't have one and may not get one at all. Not good in the movie business. It either meant the flick would go straight to DVD or wouldn't be released to reviewers because producers didn't want it panned, *or* it was so hard porn it would only be advertised in the underground.

"Just tell me it's not porn," I mumbled.

Vinnie slid his brown eyes over in a chuckle. "It's not porn."

Vinnie's brain was a fruit cocktail of things that were true, wished, and lied-so-good only another trained deviant could out him. I decided to take him at his word.

It took thirty minutes to arrive at the Morrison's on what should've been a fifteen-minute trip. Vinnie's Bug ran, but it was more like a fast walk. We ditched it a half a mile from the entrance and crawled up the fence of the gated community. Easy for me—extremely hard for Vinnie. He never received the memo about how a fit body helped a person excel athletically—a fact that made me ponder how long he'd hang on to his scholarship.

Once we made it to hole fourteen, Vinnie disarmed the security system, an alarmingly easy process, and trailed after me snacking on a moon pie as I made my way throughout the darkened first floor.

Ivy's penchant for entitlement came from her mother. Upon introduction, her opening sentence was, *Hello, I'm Bunny Morrison. I live
on hole fourteen at Valley Links Golf Club.* Ivy's father had obviously
been Bunny's ride on the gravy train. Albert Morrison hadn't been
snatched up due to his roguish good looks. In fact, he was a short
Gollum-like creature with a thatch of black hair on a face frozen in
a bug-eyed scowl.

"V," I whispered, "are you sure we aren't going to get busted?"

"Dolce, I've got a lot of tricks up my sleeve. We're good."

Listen, the only thing up Vinnie's sleeves were moobies that
belonged on an episode of *Double Divas.*

"We're not going to hit any motion detectors?" I asked.

"I know that type of unit. I disabled everything."

I never inquired how he knew that type of unit, but no one had
busted us yet, and a complementary call from their security
personnel hadn't rang on the Morrison's telephone or alerted local
authorities.

Trudi said Ivy's room was on the second floor, a right up the
staircase and then a left-left-right into her room. The Morrison's
home was modern with a pale color palette, simple design, and
geometric shapes as art. Overall, it felt cold—fitting for the
Morrison household, as I knew them.

Crossing the threshold into Ivy's room, it came as no surprise
the furniture was white and ostentatious. A comfy couch had some
sort of laminate coffee table caddy-corner in front of it. On top sat
a smorgasbord of snack food: pretzels, cheese popcorn, and half an
eaten pizza. There was a smell of grease, and a can of Mountain
Dew. The couch groaned with Vinnie's weight as he collapsed on it
and picked up a slice of pepperoni pizza.

The bed was unmade, the sheets rumpled together in a mound
at the foot of the bed. A pillow lay on the floor. A half-empty bottle
of white Sally Hansen nail polish perched on a nightstand along
with four cotton balls and polish remover. I had the same polish in
my locker. I usually swiped on a coat while walking the halls. Overall, Ivy's room resembled any other teenager's room—the abode of
someone who hoped her parents didn't realize the roach trap she
actually lived in.

Holding my flashlight in my teeth, I opened and closed drawers as Vinnie told me about his personal—and way too intimate love life —with Donatella. I rolled my eyes in my brain, praying he ran out of gas.

"That's great, V," I lied through clenched teeth.

"She's the one, Dolce," he said. "And by the way, I'm still digging around for the guy driving the yellow Dodge Charger."

Vinnie was the only person I'd told about my quest to find that man. He'd been helping me track him, but so far our luck had been worse than the Irish.

Finding nothing out of the ordinary, I moved on to the chest of drawers and plunged my gloved hands in the top section, stifling a grimace as I sifted through G-string underwear. Evidently, Ivy only wore one type—red.

Closing the fifth and final drawer, I slid open the mirrored door that led to an immense walk-in closet and switched on the light. A eureka slightly mixed with LOLs bubbled out of my mouth. Ivy's closet looked like King Solomon's mines. Hello Kitty merchandise was neatly strung on hangers—necklaces, shirts, and bracelets— some of it still with price tags attached. Underneath sat a white filing cabinet, top drawer slightly ajar. Sliding a finger in the gap, I pulled out the top bin stacked to capacity and uncovered gel pens, colored pencils, paperclips, and Mr. Gordon's giraffe stapler. *Ivy, Ivy, Ivy*, I thought, *you little thieving beeyotch*.

Instantly I mobilized, clicking off pictures on my iPhone for evidence. The second drawer contained a variety of candies and unwrapped pieces of gum and suckers. Things, my guess, she could slide in her pocket easily and undetected. In the bottom drawer were various unwrapped CDs of Beyoncé, Mumford & Sons, The Beastie Boys, Death Cab for Cutie, Justin Timberlake, Paramour, and Ed Sheeran still in cellophane (Dude, so wrong to leave Ed Sheeran in cellophane). Stacked underneath lay a bunch of T-shirts and photographs. As I quickly thumbed through the pile, I snapped pics and nearly swallowed my own tongue when I uncovered white Chanel sunglasses in a matching case. Wow. That was incontrovertible evidence, and let me just say, *cha-ching!* An even bigger surprise was my own dang Cincinnati Roller Girls T-shirt!

Ugh! The wench!

Anyone with an IQ above plant life would deduce Ivy was a true kleptomaniac. It wasn't a mere obsession with Hello Kitty. It was an obsession with anything that beguiled her at the time. When I walked into the adjacent restroom, I immediately came to the conclusion Ivy's family just may be aware of her penchant for stealing. She had a prescription for a drug I recognized as one that treated impulse behavior on the white granite countertop.

When my mother left the Earth, my OCD burst to the forefront, and I began to count things. I went to a therapy group for children where everyone talked freely about what bothered them—one tactic on the quest for being cured. Well, *they* mostly talked. I mostly listened and wondered which one of us was the most screwed up. Anyway, one of the group members took that drug and said it was because she couldn't stop stealing merchandise at her local Dollar Tree. It didn't matter what it was. If it caught her eye, she'd put it in her pocket. That behavior emerged due to what our therapist claimed was a verbally abusive childhood courtesy of her stepfather. I realized then that all of us may come wired with specific tendencies, and while some surfaced at birth, others appeared after a massive stress triggered that particular trait in our gene map.

Ivy obviously had some issues hidden beneath her Barbie-doll persona because first of all, the girl had no reason to steal anything considering the bank account of her father. Looking at Ivy's inventory, it wasn't general theft either because she plainly couldn't resist the urge to steal anything. The why for Ivy? A good question...one beyond my skillset. Was she the rich girl who felt no power and stealing provided it? Or was she trying to reclaim a part of her childhood Hello Kitty represented? Only the Devil knew, but I had a tendency to believe it to be power alone. My reasoning was due to her past and current behavior. Ivy liked to have the upper hand even in conversations. And it wasn't just dominating them. It was putting me beneath her feet with a stilettoed stomp.

"Vinnie," I whispered, "I've got the money shot..."

I put a cork in my flapping mouth when I heard Vinnie talking to someone.

*T*here was some mumbling I couldn't make out, and then Vinnie murmured, "Do you trust me?"

I screamed soundlessly, *No!!* Tiptoeing to the crack in the door, honest to God the shadow could've been Whistler's Mother, but odds were it was Ivy. She hadn't gone with her parents, and here we were caught with our hands in the legendary cookie jar.

Ivy expelled a hollow laugh. "You might be one of the few people I trust, Valentine. You've never been dishonest, especially in the time when we were together."

Interesting. Very interesting, agreed?

I needed a moment to park my brain around a couple of things. Number one, Vinnie and Ivy evidently had a thing in the past. I had a hard time thinking of them doing anything together, or worse yet, shtupping; and number two, I needed to digest the fact Ivy actually sounded...well, genuine.

"You look beautiful," he murmured.

"I think so too," she said.

I birthed a healthy eye roll here. Ivy had dressed for bed in a long white billowy gown, her hair piled high in a ponytail with no makeup. Gazing up at Vinnie, her big blue eyes were awash with an emotion that looked a whole lot like respect. Grabbing Vinnie's chubby hands, she pulled them to her lips in a soft kiss.

I felt a possessive growl vibrate low in my throat. I considered Vinnie mine. Not in the sense I considered Dylan mine, but Vinnie was mine to love and protect. Whoever he wound up with in the soulmate arena would have to get my stamp of approval. An ice-cold panic seized me when I thought of him and Ivy together. If he began a relationship with her (again), I'd have to come to terms with seeing a lot of Poison Ivy on a personal basis. And although she appeared legit at the time, I wouldn't let that muddy the waters. It was merely a veneer to throw people off the trail of who she truly was.

They were huddled together like two old lovers reminiscing about Auld Lang Syne. At one time, she'd genuinely cared for, or at the very least, been immensely attracted to him. Sure on the surface that appeared odd, but I was one of the few who truly knew Valentine Vecchione. He had a talent for worming his way into someone's heart and staying there.

Before too long, Ivy's face glazed over like the recently dead, and she fell into his arms. "Why are you all alone?" Vinnie asked.

"My parents decided to leave on a business trip before I got home." Ouch. "I would've really dug Vegas, but it's kinda cool to have the place to myself, ya know?"

Vinnie gripped her chin, tilting it upward. "That doesn't hurt you?"

Ivy had a look on her face like it was all normal when the rest of us would be crying child abandonment. "I'm okay. I'm just going to take an Ambien and crawl into bed. Why are you here? You're the last person I would've expected to find camped out in my room." Notice she didn't ask how he got in, nor did she dial 911, or punch him in the nutters. Vinnie was Vinnie. Everyone knew he had ways of doing things, and they weren't questioned. "I thought you and Darcy had something on the side," she finished.

"Darcy is with Taylor," he told her.

Ivy frowned and rolled her eyes. "And that's a little piece of news that still blows my mind."

If Ivy pureed my name one more time, I'd send her some anthrax in the mail.

Vinnie jumped to my defense. "She's a good girl, Ivy. A little flighty but so good I don't think Taylor will ever let her go."

Ivy took some time to mull over Vinnie's words. Finally, she sighed and said, "Maybe."

"I'm going to be bluntly honest," he said. "I have a great girl-friend, but you're the one who might've gotten away. Is there anything left between us?"

Bloody Ivy looked down at the ruby meteorite Jagger had given her and stonewalled. "I'll have to think about it. Call you?"

"Just text me if it's a no. I don't want to hear your voice because it'll break my heart."

Ivy talked like she'd gargled with helium. Vinnie didn't want to hear her voice because he valued his eardrums. Right then, he spotted me through the crack in the door, giving me a chin jerk to hightail it to the Bug. Let's just say Vinnie began sucking all over her like the best Hoover on the market. Maybe he cared for her, or maybe he was just trashed on moon pies. When Ivy's hands migrated close to his coin-slot butt crack, I grabbed the Roller Girls T, stapler, and Chanel glasses, slinking out the door before I barfed. Sorry what that tidbit of information might do to your appetite. God knew it killed mine.

———

Close call. Too close for comfort.

Once the Bug was back on the streets of Valley, I laid into Vinnie on his choice of girlfriends. "Seriously, V. A real Hallmark moment back there."

"I like the broken ones, Dolce."

Scrolling through the pictures I'd taken, I realized Ivy was far from broken. She'd had a choice in every one of these photos and historically chose wrong. Granted, maybe her medication didn't always work, but here's what I knew to be fact...she was mean to boot, and with that she lost mercy points. "I don't happen to think Ivy is so broken," I said quietly.

Vinnie changed gears on a car that protested movement of any kind. "I don't either."

Both of us let that thought germinate. So why did things end? Vinnie was worlds away from being Jagger Cane. He didn't have money. He didn't have the polish, and God knew he didn't have the body. But Vinnie had something—something a girl couldn't help but fall in love with.

"Why didn't you go public?" I asked.

"She wanted to. I didn't."

Still. Having. Trouble. Digesting. "Then why didn't you tell me?"

"Dolce, it's common knowledge you two aren't BFFs. For me, it was a fling, but if I would've known exactly how horrible she was to you, I would've ended it a lot quicker than I did."

"For realz?" I grinned.

"Nah, I'd probably would've just lied to you," he said and chuckled.

I burst out laughing, leaning across the console to punch his shoulder. My phone picked that moment to break into "Talk Dirty to Me." Ohhhhh fuuuuuuuddggggee. Just like that, all the humor was sucked out of my smile. My guess was Murphy had issued a BOLO, and my boyfriend played retriever.

"Where the," *bleep profanity*, "are you?" he growled when I answered.

I dove right in, headfirst. "Does Murphy know?" I mumbled.

"No, but I had to do some fast thinking. I don't like lying to your father, Darcy. That totally sucks. It was a first, and it will definitely be a last."

I glanced over to Vinnie whose blubber gut bounced like a beach ball. Mentally shrugging, I decided to tell him the unadulterated, uncensored truth. "It feels wrong to lie to you, so I'm going to give you the naked truth. I inked a deal with Trudi to find out if Ivy stole her bogus Chanel sunglasses. I know, bogus shades, but it was a job. Anyway, Vinnie picked me up after I lied to you and Murphy. He drove me to Ivy's home at Valley Links, so we could break into her house. He disabled the alarm, but things got a little hairy because it turns out Ivy was there. So to save my butt, he made out with her while I snuck out with the evidence. And guess what, she had my stinking Cincinnati Roller Girls T-shirt and Mister Gordon's giraffe stapler. I don't feel bad...about anything."

Wow, confession felt good. Dylan, however, acted as though he'd just had an enema.

"I'm proud of you," he said sarcastically. "You've proved you're one heck of an entrepreneur. Plus, you're so damn deviant I'm almost impressed."

"Yeah," I said, stupidly giggling. "If what I did was wrong, I don't wanna be right."

"Valentine is with you," he said lowly.

"He's here physically, but I'm thinking he'd rather be here in spirit."

"Put me on speaker," Dylan snarled.

I put him on blast while Vinnie's grin grew wider. "Valentine," Dylan seethed. "If you assist my girlfriend in something like this again, I'm going to permanently smash out your teeth. You feel me?"

Vinnie actually laughed. "I feel you, man. Would you prefer me to get the A-Okay from you in the future? We both know there'll be a next time."

Pauses. "I'd prefer you talk her out of going."

Vinnie slid a wary gaze my way. I sheepishly shrugged. He knew that went against my DNA. "Sure," he said. "I'll give it a shot."

Dylan switched gears—still trying to navigate our new relationship by being a protective boyfriend while being a supportive best friend. I didn't envy his position. I could accept Dylan for whomever he decided to be. He, on the other hand, wrestled with too much Boy Scout and a hero complex. "So you walked away with proof?" he asked.

"About fifty photos' worth. I'm not sure how I'm going to proceed at this point."

"Go home, Darc," he murmured, totally exhausted. "Sleep on it, and for God's sake, tell me next time."

A long moment of silence. All at once, I was slammed with enough guilt to keep a priest in business for decades. "You sound angry," I mumbled.

"I'm not angry, but it's like I'm addicted to the fricking adrenaline. Here's my theoretical kiss good night, sweetheart. Enjoy it while I try to force a dream that my girlfriend has been home painting her nails and doing her homework." That theoretical kiss lit up my insides like molten lava even through the phone.

"Would you have gone?" I asked. Dylan's lack of an answer didn't tell me anything I didn't already know. He and I both knew he could and would never participate in a B&E. The following words went through my mind: OMIGOSHIHATEYOU! YOU'RE RUINING MY LIFE WITH GUILT!!! *door slams*

Instead, I muttered, "I'm sorry," and hung up.

Gazing over to Vinnie's told-you-so mug, I let out a jagged, confused sigh. I'd found success, but in the process I'd disappointed the cutest boyfriend on the planet Earth. As I stared out the window, I wished I could be in any galaxy other than the Milky Way, but all I saw was a mushroom cloud. A mushroom cloud signifying a lot of fallout coming my way.

————

Indigo Chase? Check. Ivy Morrison? Check. Lyric Armstrong? Uncheck.

Considering I was several hundred dollars richer, one would think I'd be in jubilation. Instead, I was confused about my next steps. First up on the agenda was to confront Ivy, which was the exact reason I wore the Cincinnati Roller Girls T-shirt. Call it my game-ON look. I'd lost that sucker last semester. It literally disappeared out of my locker, so what had she done? Snatched it when my back had been turned?

I'd had time to think about Ivy and her particular problems and wasn't without mercy. She probably operated as the thieving beey-otch we knew because of her parents, but the things she'd stolen needed to be returned. Problem was, if they were returned, the intelligent victim would want to know where they'd come from. Did I actually want to see Ivy publicly taken down? I wasn't sure. Privately? Yeah, you do the crime(s), you do the time. Second up on the agenda...figure out if my boyfriend was still in love with me.

Bleh, I might not like the answer.

Snow fell like powdered laundry detergent on Wednesday morning, and the windows on the Beemer were almost at a whiteout. Just in the ten minutes we'd been on the road, the fall had intensified and so had the feelings between Dylan and me. There was love, lust, confusion, and an elephant in the room called silence. Realizing my fascination with his lips might make me crazily land on top of them, I zipped up the black North Face I'd snagged at the consignment store where Justice worked. After a few seconds to find my nerve, my eyes circled back around to his gorgeous mug.

"I'm sorry I hurt you," I blurted out.

Coming clean was the key to a successful relationship, according to Murphy. If dating me aged Dylan, one hundred percent transparency would drive him to an early grave.

Dylan leaned over and tucked my hair behind my ear, briefly putting his thumb in the dimple of my chin. "We're solid, Darc, yeah?"

"It depends on how you define solid. You're not exactly walking on sunshine."

He frowned. "When I love someone, my first instinct is to keep them close, so I can protect them. With you—"

"Your love is on a balance beam."

A deeper frown. "Don't put words in my mouth."

"But it's true. I'm like a beagle off its chain."

A small grin. "If you weren't, I'd probably be bored out of my mind. I don't want you to change."

"Are you sure about that?"

"No," he finally said, "but I love who you are and what you stand for."

Dylan looked like he'd just encountered some post-traumatic flashback. Here's the problem with his logic. Dylan rarely forgot a slight. He was forgiving—he could move on—but he always filed that stuff under the premise, *If you're disloyal once, you'll be disloyal again.* Lying to the boyfriend was disloyal, and with me, he was constantly reinventing who he was.

"That's a schizophrenic statement," I reminded him.

"Perhaps, but I just need to figure out *how* to react...and *when* to react."

Listen, he'd be a fool if he didn't react to what I did. It was illegal. The majority of the world would frown upon it. "That doesn't seem fair." Eh, because it wasn't.

"Our relationship is a marathon, not a sprint. I'm not interested in keeping score, Darc."

By that time, we idled in his designated parking space in front of VHS. After he switched off the ignition, he leaned forward and placed both of his hands on my knees. Ah, shoot. I was going to pass out. Breathe through my nose? Out through the mouth? Sweet, Lord...he smelled like hormones...was I actually *panting*?

"A little tongue-tied, sweetheart?" he murmured.

My eyes ran over Dylan's black hair, his eyes within inches of mine, and down to his knees that were practically in my seat. Seriously, his car suddenly felt the size of a phone booth. "My tongue is just fine. Besides, your kisses taste like varnish remover," I laughingly lied. "I'm not interested."

Dylan giggled into my lips. "Are you sure about that? You've never complained."

As with everything since Dylan and I'd begun dating, he was the one doing most of the compromising. Me? I continued to be Darcy...but things felt off. My relationship with him was off. Having legitimate sympathy for Ivy was off. In fact, it was so far off, it might've circled around into "on."

I kissed him thoroughly, deciding to unravel the confusion later.

———

That kiss with Dylan came with a heat warning.

Funny how my body went iceberg-cold when I came face-to-face with Ivy. We stood outside first period math, and I was prepared to call her out on her deviant ways. I'd already returned Trudi's shades, and surprisingly, she vowed to keep it secret like a Swiss bank account. Although I was sure she'd eventually retaliate in some form or fashion, right then, my main concern was that Ivy became aware the world was onto her.

Looking at Ivy, it was a kill-or-be-killed moment.

She gaped at my Cincinnati Roller Girls T and immediately connected the dots. "Aren't you subtle," she seethed. Oh, boy. Shots fired!

"Yeah, I'm a master of the obvious."

"You were in my home. That's illegal."

"And thou shalt not steal is not just a suggestion," I countered.

"I'm not very religious," she said indignantly.

"Shocking," I scoffed. "Even if you don't respect the Almighty, Valley PD says it's law."

"So you're going to put me on blast?"

I snorted in my head, making note no apology lay anywhere. "You're so tone deaf, Ivy."

"Me? Don't you know what people say about you?" Ivy threw figurative nunchucks at my head, but I refused to go down like a sissy. When she saw the lack of a rise, she stepped closer and seethed, "How much?"

"How much what?"

"How much is it going to cost for you to keep this a secret?"

"A bribe?" I laughed.

"I understand you're quite the businesswoman."

I lifted an indifferent shoulder. "I'm not interested in your money. You either return all of the merchandise by tomorrow or I squeal."

"This conversation is an admission you broke into my home."

Uh-huh. "With Vinnie," I added. Ivy blanched. "Do you want to do that to Vinnie?" I pushed. No answer. The beeyotch. I wanted to go ghetto on her but knew it would be top of the gossip food chain by the end of first period. Besides, I knew her survival instinct would kick in, so I pulled out the big guns. "Do it, or I tell Jagger everything."

Ivy went cadaver-white. I forced myself to watch her panic with a numb detachment. Normally, I crumbled at the sign of someone's pain, but Ivy panicked merely because she feared being caught. It was her MO. Her feet hit the floor in the morning, and she was vicious. It was a given. Just like human stupidity.

"You would do that?" she asked, again with no remorse to be found.

Honestly, I wasn't sure, but Ivy should've considered ramifications before she issued the five-finger discount on whatever wasn't nailed down. But it was an interesting feeling to have her fate in my hands when she'd destroyed so many other girls' self-esteem over the years. Two texts barraged me within seconds of one another. Ivy stared at my iPhone like it was the key to Fort Knox when I pulled it out of my jeans. "Don't even think about it," I snapped. "The picture evidence is already on the Cloud."

Ivy sneered some unprintable swear words. Another text hit me. That time, I glanced down at the number—Dylan.

Do you need backup? was number one.

Call me or I'm leaving class, demanded number two.

Number three...*At least tell me you're alive.*

I thumbed back, *I'm closing the deal.*

Ivy went with a full-court press. "I'm going to tell Vinnie. He'll vouch for me and swear it's all a lie...because it is," she added.

I stared in wide-eyed stupefaction while I slid my phone back into my jeans. "Denial ain't just a river in Egypt, but go ahead. You might be surprised Vinnie's not so into you anymore."

"Exactly what is your problem with me anyway?" she hissed.

"Alphabetically or in order of importance?"

Ivy's face went Maleficent. The last time we stared at one another so intently we wound up rolling around on the floor in a catfight. I wasn't much of a fighter, but hand to God if she swung at me, I'd make a fist and connect.

I broke the standoff first. "One choice, Ivy. Return them to their rightful owners, or watch the contagion effect happen."

She looked confused. "What contagion effect?"

"Jagger is going to be as disgusted with you as everyone else already is."

Now the real Ivy surfaced. Her eyes trained on me like a hawk's on a field mouse. I felt myself shudder but hoped I was cool enough she never picked up on the nerves.

"I can't," she said woodenly. "You don't understand..."

Ugh, now I felt bad. I called up my inner-rehab counselor and said, "Enlighten me." When Ivy said nothing, I expelled an exhausted sigh, throwing the girl a bone she didn't deserve. "Give them to me along with a list of who they belong to, and I'll return them."

"So you can be a hero," she said snorting.

Oh, no you dit-ten. Like I said, giving her sympathy had been a waste of brain cells, but I wasn't going to issue a get-out-of-jail-free card unless she went by my terms. "I prefer to work in the background, Ivy. But if I were you, I wouldn't bite the hand that just gave me a way out."

"You're serious."

"There are 86,400 seconds in a day. That's all you've got before I tell the victims who stole from them. And word to the wise..." I paused for effect. "If you hurt Grumpy again, I'm not saying bad things will happen, but the threat does hang heavy in the air."

With that, I turned on my heels and strutted away, misfit head for once held high.

————————

It was five minutes after the witching hour Thursday morning and insomnia had me in its grip. I'd gotten off the phone with Rookie an hour before, fell asleep, and had just jerked awake in a cold sweat. Rookie delivered bad news. Mr. Himmel had been arraigned and made bail. Arraignment was when the person accused of a crime stood before a judge and heard official charges against him or her. Mr. Himmel was charged with kidnapping, attempted murder in the second degree, and found in violation of the concealed carry law. There were a couple of other charges, but I honestly couldn't make it past the first two. They were capital offenses with major jail time, but somehow the weasel scored house arrest where he'd wear an ankle bracelet, promising to never leave his condominium even if it was on fire...not really, but here's to wishing.

Apparently, it was beyond rare for someone who kidnapped a victim and fired a gun to be given the extra privilege of house arrest while he waited out his court date. But Rookie's feelings were his judge brother pulled some strings and made it happen. A black and white had been posted outside Himmel's house to ensure he stayed within his perimeter, but even with around-the-clock surveillance, it didn't leave a person with the warm and fuzzies. As a result, Rookie didn't have *one* foot in insanity. He had *two*.

Mr. Himmel pleaded "not guilty," and rumor claimed he had a bigwig Chicago attorney prepared to prove he and Red had a relationship before he took his stalking past friendly crush to the predator level. The obvious defense would be a crime of passion. Um, right. Red had been attracted to a *Jurassic Park* reject the size of a troll...so believable.

I discovered my next tidbit of information via Zander, Dylan's little brother. Zander was the biggest eavesdropper known to humankind. Fortunately for me, I was the person he always unloaded his gossip on. Out of respect for Lincoln's badge, the detective running the show Monday night stopped by the Taylors' and told Lincoln Mr. Himmel was one of those survivalist, end-of-time types with canned goods, detergent, and other sundries stockpiled in his basement. Along with his grocery store stuff, a black nylon duffle bag had been found that included a blindfold, duct tape, rope, and nylon cable ties the detective referred to as a kidnap and "maybe" murder kit. To top off the creepy, multiple photographs of Red, Rookie, and me were tacked to the walls in his own brand of psycho surveillance. Eeeuw. I was not supposed to know those things, but it would come out in Discovery anyway, which was the next phase of the court process for Mr. Himmel.

Speaking of criminal activity, I'd not forgotten about Lyric, and more than anything I wanted to prove to Tito I could hang. When I nonchalantly asked Rookie about any updates with Club Need, this was what he said: *My wish is to shut them down permanently. It doesn't feel right, and God Himself only knows what ghosts are within those walls other than Lyric Armstrong.*

He continued by saying he had a stack of missing and murdered persons who had a connection to the club. And as Jaws had banked on, the death of Lyric Armstrong would get some manpower from the Cincinnati PD because she came from a wealthy family. One of his assistant prosecutors would be taking the lead since he was so ate up with what had been going down with Red. Problem was, until Ben provided Gabrielle Allen's whereabouts (who would hopefully provide information about Lyric), I couldn't narrow down the field of suspects (that I didn't have) until each had been interviewed. So I was back to square one...hoping the universe would give me a hint.

Chapter Sixteen

TRIPLE THREAT

arek Ransom called at late o'clock.

It took all of five minutes to realize he still planned to do the underground fight club for a monetary reward. Like me, he wanted his own ride. Here's to hoping he didn't get killed in the process. The fact it was underground meant there were rules that were unsanctioned and probably only partly observed. That bothered me. It should've bothered Marek, but I got the feeling he lived in the moment. Who was I to judge? I lived life as a lit firecracker.

All I knew was Darcy + Marek x Sleep Deprivation = Bad Idea. I'd all but confessed I was in the L-word with Dylan—he was the only person who'd ever gotten my screwed up head—but I couldn't tell him he had a monopoly on my heart.

Marek's advice? Girl, grow some.

Simple enough, but nothing with me had ever been cut and dried. So I buried those unsettling emotions into the deep recesses of my mind—the part I dug through on rainy days when I felt sorry for myself. Sort of like me digging through the pile of crap Ivy had FedEx'd to my house earlier. Murphy hadn't gone to work when the box arrived because we had a two-hour delay due to snow and ice. When he went outside to shovel the drive, he immediately came back inside, lugging in three gigantic boxes dropped off on the front porch addressed to "Witch."

Only Ivy spelled it with a B, of course.

"I'm assuming this is for you," Murphy grumbled, his chocolate-brown eyes defensive and unforgiving that someone had addressed me that way.

My father's eyes took people places that would make a momma shriek and a daddy dig a grave. His body was thick, with hands that could palm an entire face and crush the last breath out of a person. Plus, his nose sat slightly off-center, deviated to the right from a bar fight when he was nineteen years old. Evidence he'd used his strength before. If Ivy were a guy, Murphy wouldn't care about the age difference. He'd kick her you-know-what and bury her in cement. He'd always had trouble navigating the murky waters of mean girls and trying to remain a gentleman. Seriously, join the club.

Grabbing a Coke from the refrigerator, I texted Bean to come over and help sift through the booty and then crashed in the middle of the floor, pseudo-explaining the "why" to my father.

Murphy immediately scratched the back of his neck like he had fleas.

"Rewind, kid," he grunted, so I told him the story again. "Hit the stop button," he said when I'd finished. "So Ivy stole these things, and you're returning them to their rightful owners. Would it be beneficial for me to know how you came upon this evidence in the first place?"

I looked up with one eye as I tore through the packing tape with my teeth. There comes a time in a woman's life where she needs to stand up and tell the truth. One look at Murphy, and I decided it wasn't that time. "If you mean did I break into her home and search for specific stolen items, then the answer might blow your image of me as the model child. If I were you, I'd save myself the indigestion."

Murphy pulled a cigar off the countertop and lit it up. Murphy smoked enough cigars to keep the Kentucky cash crop at least partially legal. "Listen to my DNA, kid," he muttered through a puff. "Since we aren't technically having this conversation, then I won't technically tell you that if someone knocks on my door tonight and arrests you for breaking and entering, I'll technically tell them to throw away the key."

"Technically, I'm saying I understand," I said.

While he mumbled to himself there was an embarrassing mug shot in my future, I ripped off the packing tape with a snap and opened the first box. Inside was a spreadsheet of items that had been tagged like a detective would mark them, along with the name of whom it belonged to. The whole thing had been a dumb idea once I thought about it. It would eat up my day when I needed to phone Tito about Lyric.

Ten minutes later, Bean sat in the middle of the floor with me yoga-style, putting things in piles representing people we knew and people we didn't. On those, at least Ivy provided an address...how thoughtful.

"This is mean," Bean muttered. "Do you think people will forgive her?"

It seemed Trudi had (maybe), but personally I didn't think people truly forgave anyone. I think they just had short memories.

Bean plunged his hand down into the third box, removing the last item, which was a black baseball cap of Mr. Pongo's and white nail polish belonging to yours truly. Ugh, I should've known the nail polish by her bedside belonged to me. Bean didn't take the news quite as well as I had though. He shuddered like he had a case of quivers from a horror movie, holding Mr. Pongo's cap like it unlocked the mysteries of the universe. And that was why Ivy and I would never, ever, *ever* be best friends. First off, Bean was a nobody to her, and it was pretty lame she stole from his dead gerbil. Secondly, she stole from innocents; and thirdly, as a result I had to figure out how to get Bean out of my lap he was then sitting on.

––––––––––

We had everything catalogued after thirty minutes. For the Valley victims, we merely stuck the merchandise inside their mailboxes while Murphy played chauffeur. Thankfully, the sun appeared to be on our side because it was still dark and Murphy's silver Toyota Camry blended in with the snow. Murphy, "technically speaking," had no idea why we stopped at random mailboxes, so he hummed and listened to talk radio.

What could I say? It worked for me.

For the Hello Kitty merchandise, I walked into Claire's

Boutique, claiming the jewelry and shirts were Christmas gifts my little sister couldn't wear...which Marjorie, God love her (as she stood next to me), swore was correct. When I didn't have a receipt, the young woman working the register was puzzled as to how she would return them. I simply told her to restock them or gift to charity.

By that time, another snow front moved in, and school was called off completely. Consequently, Bean hung out with us for the day, and after we dropped him at his home at dinnertime, I took matters into my own hands regarding Tito. Call me a genius or call me an idiot, I got extremely aggressive, *67'd *The Cincinnati Enquirer,* and simply asked for him. I sat in bed, pulling a sweatshirt over my head because I'd just applied voodoo cream to my flat chest. My nanny, Claudia, had made it her mission that I grow some boobs. She created some Puerto Rican cream I slathered on during the crescent moon. Call me a hopeless romantic, but I wanted boobs Dylan would kill for by morning.

"Jester," was my greeting.

"Sweet Lord above," he said, laughing when my name jelled into place. "Where have you been hidin' since I spoke to you last?"

"You didn't exactly act as if you needed my help."

"I didn't exactly think you'd take my advice either. Your sources worry me, Jester, and therefore I worry about you." Heck, I didn't even have a source yet.

"I got the feeling you have a personal connection to the story at Club Need, Tito. Unless you're going for a Pulitzer, the victim discovered—or someone attached to them—means something to you other than the lead story."

"Have you read my stories recently?"

"I have. And regarding the first one, you went to print the Saturday morning *after* Lyric Armstrong fell from her grave. You either penned that story immediately or it had already gone to press. Funny thing is, Saturday is not a big news day. So unless you blew her out of the wall yourself to get some traction to your story, it seems to me you tried to draw someone out. Someone you might've been looking at for quite some time."

"I only wish I was that powerful," he muttered and chuckled.

"I know this isn't the first time you've chased this story, Tito. I found an old article of yours on the Internet." No response. "Let me shoulder some of the burden. I'm here to help you, okay? But first off, I need to know the name of the person or persons you're trying to draw out."

"Absolutely not," he barked.

"So that's an admission of what you've been trying to do?" If it was, then he and Jaws were pretty much doing the same thing. Trying to draw someone out that had chosen to remain hidden.

"I didn't admit to anything," he said.

"Kids at my school go there, Tito, and I'm smart enough to know you might need someone like me to feed you information. And since your article claims teenagers have been a target, then I'm actually doing you a favor."

"A favor."

"Yeah. I'll do the dirty, heroic work. Consider me Joan of Arc."

"I don't know," he said. "Things didn't turn out too well for Joan."

True. "Think about it. If I brag, then that could draw attention to me. I don't want to wind up as your next lead story of the girl-gone-goodbye or have to live in some sort of witness protection program."

Tito gave me the silent treatment. After a few beats, he finally went live. "Two rules. You *do not* go there by yourself, and nothing is emailed. Keep your ears open this week, do your thing, and call me from a payphone on Saturday. Tell the operator to reverse the charges to me at this number." He spouted out some digits I quickly penned on my palm. "If you don't get me personally, *do not* speak to anyone else other than Sophie."

"Sophie," I repeated.

"That's right. Give me your name, darlin'."

I giggled loudly. "Nice try, but Jester is all you're getting. And I still need the names of who you're targeting."

A heavy sigh. "Jester, I cannot tell you how important it is that you do your best work here. This is deadly."

"I specialize in disturbing. So about those names?"

An even heavier sigh. "Do you have a pencil? This list is long."

———

My earlier buzz fizzled like last year's fireworks. I'd turned over every godforsaken rock in the bloody town looking for Pierre LaFayette, Mahesh Singh, Jared Ming, and Igor Guskov and came up with a big, fat goose egg. I phoned last names, performed Google searches, and even joined a criminal investigation site for $19.99 to run a prison record check. My eyes were bloodshot, my body weary, and my brain like baked bananas. If the universe didn't throw me a bone, I was done.

I'd failed. And even worse, if I didn't supply the name of the man who killed Lyric Armstrong to Jaws, he'd never give me information on my mother. And although the guy had a soft spot for me (and was sort of sexy), he enjoyed stringing me along more. That was what happened when I did business with a psychopathic schizoid. I had to watch my back in case he wanted to stab it.

So Friday morning was like any other morning really. I looked for something Hostess or Little Debbie in the pantry, and when I found nada, the next move was to drown my sorrows in coffee. I slid a stainless steel travel mug underneath the Keurig as Dark Magic, Extra Bold took the southern trip into it.

Five solid knocks on the front door. I yelled, "Enter, stud," knowing it had to be Dylan. When he knocked even more violently, once again I shouted, "Enter, stud!"

Twisting the lid on the mug, the door slammed wide and boomeranged off the wall. "Darcy!" he said frantically.

At his frenzied reaction, I knocked over the mug, the lid popped off, and I gaped horrified as the last stream of coffee in the casa drained across the countertop to the floor. Prediction? The day was really going to blow.

"In here," I mumbled. "You just made me spill my coffee, moron. I officially hate you."

Dylan's huffing and puffing could wake the dead. "Are you okay?" he shouted.

Grabbing a dishtowel, I mopped up the mess and threw everything into the sink. *Not really*, I thought, because coffee was like my wonder drug.

My super sexy, make-me-wanna-swing-from-a-grapevine boyfriend thundered toward the kitchen, his leather shoes pounding on the hardwood. "Do you know what I feel like when I can't get to you?" he said. "I hate the feeling. It reminds me of last spring..."

He trailed off when he made it to the edge of the kitchen, his amber eyes burning like butter in a hot skillet. I wasn't exactly killing it in the looks department, but I think he appreciated what I'd chosen to wear. He started at my feet and slowly made his way up to my head in a lascivious grin.

Thud...yup, my heart just bottomed out.

"Dylan likes?" I said, laughing and pirouetting in one of my more expensive ensembles. I had on a pair of low-slung boyfriend jeans that had been slashed at the thighs and knees. I'd worn them before and never got sent home for a dress code violation. There was a good chance the powers-that-be didn't find me overly sexual (shocking). Upstairs was a silver tank top that emphasized the girls and a knee length gray crocheted cardigan overtop. Ankle boots.

Dylan sauntered toward me like a cat on the prowl. "Dylan *really* likes."

I actually licked my lips. "Are you going to kiss me?"

"I like it when you beg," he murmured, grinning wickedly.

Dragging in a breath, I parked my lips in the curve underneath his ear. "Two can play that game, bud. I can hold out on the kissing détente as long as you can."

At first, Dylan expressed indifference—not even twitching—but when I nipped his neck in my teeth, he growled like a wild animal. "Someone needs to buckle," he said, voice suddenly tight. "If I don't take the edge off, I'm going to be in a cranky mood the rest of the day."

Solid point.

"Go ahead," I said, smiling and taunting him. "I'm not stopping you."

"And that probably will be a mistake." Tiny beads of water glistened in his raven-black hair that somehow was even more onyx than his choice of clothing. Dressed in the bottom half of what looked like an expensive black suit, once again Dylan had dressed for game day, pairing it with a perfectly pressed white shirt and striped patterned tie. The shirt tugged at the sculpted planes of his chest. Yeah, my boyfriend did the suit and tie thing like a pro.

Again, my tongue shot straight to my lips. "Are you going to keep licking those lips, or are you going to use them?" he murmured.

I felt my cheeks burn. "You're such a pig," I said giggling. "On three. One, two..." Dylan never made it to three. He slammed me against the wall so hard my teeth rattled in my head.

I'd always considered myself a good little feminist on the rise, but when Dylan went alpha male, I had to admit it melted me down to my bones. He raked a hot breath across my neck, making me tremble, still delaying the touching of our lips. Figuratively breathing into a paper bag, I buckled first and landed on his lips with the force of a meteor striking the earth.

Somehow Dylan and I wound up on the hardwood, neither of us caring we would probably be late for school. His lips were in the driver's seat, breathing hot one hundred percent male messages straight to my heart. He bruised my mouth with hard kisses while he tangled his hands in my hair and pulled. For a split second of pure insanity, I allowed myself to be transported to a place that was just the two of us.

My blood pressure sailed through the roof, my ears ringing and banging with each pump of my heart. The human brain contained approximately one hundred billion neurons and all of mine screamed Dylan Taylor's name. He had me...*gone*. Like three-sheets-to-the-wind gone. My hands yanked his shirt from his slacks, and then they dove underneath—running up and down the exquisitely shaped pectoral muscles inside. Dylan was sweet but always hungry—teasing me with little, when he knew I wanted more. He lifted my leg at the knee and had almost all of my hair in his right hand. When my eyes stuttered open, I noticed his were heavy-lidded but somehow wide—wanting to kiss me while watching for a response.

Did he even have to ask?

I was pretty sure I had firecrackers behind my eyelids!

I felt his heart pump into my chest with a strong boom-boom, but when the kissing neared the NC-17 rating, Dylan reluctantly sat up and pulled me between his legs—both of us panting like two greyhounds that needed to be put down.

"Crap," he muttered, his voice thick with emotion. "How did that just happen? I'm sorry." I needed to mop myself down it was so blistering hot, let alone find the words to answer. "You're okay, yeah?" he asked. He slid his gaze down my body while he pushed locks of hair behind my ears, trying to help the strands find a style.

My heart jackhammered behind my ribs. After Dylan's version of a kiss, I nearly face-planted in hypoxia. Pulling us to a stand, he popped open the refrigerator and grabbed a bottled water. He drank down half. I finished it out. Three gummy bears later, I grabbed my long wool coat from the closet and slipped one arm inside while Dylan helped me maneuver my broken finger through the other sleeve.

"No coat for you?" I asked.

Dylan twisted the knob, and the wind slapped us in the face with another cold day. My face instantly burned, and the hairs in my nose stood on end. Sad thing was, it smelled like snow was imminent. If you lived in a cold climate long enough, you learned to recognize the smell.

"I'm too warm-blooded for a coat," he said and winked.

"That explains a lot. Must be why you have so much hot air."

He pulled me into the warmth of his side as we jogged to his car. "No, sweetheart. Hot hair, hot lips, hot body. Take your pick. I'm a triple threat."

"Do you ever stop beating on your chest?" No answer...just a laugh.

After he beeped the Beemer open, we both grabbed our seats, and he immediately attempted to fluff my hair.

"It's bad, right?" I asked with a grimace.

Another devilish grin mixed with a male pride that knew no bounds. "You might want to find a brush."

———

Five minutes at our lockers, my phone blew up with texts like the Fourth of July. The first came from Bean who wondered if Ivy had plans to beat us both up. The second originated from Vinnie, regarding the man in the yellow Dodge Charger. He claimed he had a solid lead—can you say, *Hollah!!*

OMG, I was so geeked up I bounced around during my return keystrokes like a ping-pong ball on pavement. I heard Dylan expel a jagged sigh and then a click of his cell phone hit the atmosphere as he snapped a picture.

I gave him my patented, air-headed huh-face while I told Vinnie I loved his fat gut and for Bean to duck and run. Coffee in my left hand (yes, Dylan bought me an extra large at UDF), I bounced on my feet like a boxer. "Why the pic?" I asked.

"You're up to something," he growled.

"No, I'm not."

"Yeah, you are. You look wired. You always look like you've taken a hit of speed when you're up to something."

"It's just PMS," I said, stopping to laugh.

Dylan's pulse skyrocketed as he rolled his eyes. "Keep shoveling, sweetheart, because you're about to be in fricking China by the depth of the hole you're digging."

"I suppose you'd prefer me to be honest."

He arched a brow. "I thought that was a given, but if I'm forced to answer, then yes."

I told him the truth, ninety-nine point nine percent of the time. That other point one percent would put him on a slab in the morgue.

"You're cute when you do your possessive caveman thingy," I said, giggling and trying to redirect the questioning, but my attempt was useless—Dylan dug his heels in deeper.

"Look at my face," he murmured.

"Why?" I asked.

"I think I just got my first wrinkle." I burst into laughter.

Dylan ran both hands through his hair and actually pulled. "I don't know why I love you, but I do." With that statement, he pivoted on his heels and broke the crowd with a little more force than was probably necessary.

"Dude, rainbows exploded behind my eyelids when you kissed me!" I screamed, laughing in a throaty laugh. "It was awesome, D. Like baby-making stuff...or at least a naked game of Twister."

Dylan abruptly stopped on a dime, and I swear I watched his body quake in laughter. "I'm your freaking *love slave*," he shouted over his shoulder, emphasizing the last two words. He casually resumed his walk down the hall and waved over his head.

I was cheating our relationship. I normally dropped my walls with him, but he'd never understand what I was doing. Even *I* didn't understand why I got involved in the situations I did. Was it boredom? Sure. Was it because I had talent enough to figure things out? Make that another sure. Could it be because I couldn't stand for wrongs to go unrighted? Yeah...no one did that for me. And I was reminded like a punch to the face since the countdown to the anniversary of my mother's death ticked-tocked like a bomb. Sucked. But time soldiered on, not taking the time to remember anyone.

Chapter Seventeen

TIME WARP

A fire broke out in my metals class when someone tried to solder a statue of C3PO's hand to the naked bust of a female Pilgrim—may I ask why? That had my third period class scrambling for the gym while that side of the hallway was hosed down and fumigated. I'd thread one earbud into my ear while I sneak-texted Dylan with a *Hello, Lover*. He quickly sneak-texted back, *I have more love than you can handle, babe*. Let me tell you folks, the winner—by unanimous decision—me. I needed to dive into an ice pond with the vision that conjured up.

Thing was, I wasn't alone. Jagger was here. He'd taken the bleachers two at a time to sit beside me—no, practically on top of me.

I scooted a foot over. "You look nice today, babe," he said with a grin. Jagger loved the word "babe." If you were halfway decent looking, somewhere during the day a girl got a babe. Then if she were masochistic, she'd fall for it, and then wonder how she'd temporarily lost her mind. Oh, he was good-looking enough, but underneath Jagger's beauty was a dark edge, an edge that could cut a girl if she wasn't careful.

And are you sitting down?

He and Ivy broke up...*AGAIN.*

I'd always thought them to be a perfect love match. Why? Because some people in life never had their cages rattled. And if they did, they'd been lucky enough to land on another perch. Some of us had simply gone to the bottom and stayed there. Jagger and Ivy, however, both always got what they wanted. Even the problems they created, they talked their ways out of and stayed popular in a school as large as Valley. And here I'd just added to that Teflon factor because I didn't turn Ivy in for being a thief. Ugh. I should've derailed her crazy train, but I just let it roll.

The gym had foldaway bleachers, but the side where Jagger and I sat was stationary. It was your typical gym, having white walls with red bleachers and black and white paint accents. A buffalo had been painted in the middle of the floor, with VHS on both walls. While I listened to Superchick's "One Girl Revolution," I munched on a bag of Grippo's barbecue chips, listening to Jagger whine he was in the market for a new GF.

He grabbed my dangling earbud and placed it in his ear, humming along. A little too intimate for my taste, but with Jagger you had to pick and choose your battles. "You live in a musical time warp, Darcy."

Point made. Whatever classic rock tunes the Apple Store didn't have, Finn Lively in all his glorious geekiness created for me. Flipping open to chapter eleven in my science book, I answered questions that would probably be assigned next period. A substitute had taken Mr. Himmel's place, and I was determined to make the man love (or at least tolerate) me.

Once finished, I thumbed through my economics book, reading two chapters on the bull and bear markets. There'd been hints of a pop quiz all week, and since I already had an A—shocking, but thank you, Jesus—a little bit of an effort might help me keep it.

The gym class was finishing the hour with suicides. When Coach Wallace noticed a few of his basketball players passed time on the bleachers, he ordered them to jump in and participate. So they ditched their suits and Finn, Grumpy, and the others obliged, but Jagger was Jagger...ignoring the command.

When the last gut was busted, Grumpy pulled a navy hoodie over his head, schlepping across the floor and up seven bleachers to collapse in front of me. I handed him my bag of chips, and he cocked his head back, dumping the crumbs into his mouth.

"What's that smell?" he asked, grimacing and scrunching his nose up.

Once I sniffed in a big whiff of air, it registered what he'd smelled...*voodoo cream*. I'd OD'd on it before I hit the sack, and all the sweat in the gym must've sparked some sort of chemical reaction.

"Cough medicine," I said, coughing out a lie.

Grumpy shrugged it away, narrowing his eyes. "What's wrong with you, Walker? You seem a little too studious. Are you worried about something?"

I closed up my books, shoving everything into my backpack. Leaning back until my head rested on the bleacher behind me, I threw an elbow over my eyes, instantly overwhelmed. Maybe I *was* worried. God knew I had a lifetime of thinking about what the future would bring. Having no mother to cheer me on put a damper on what I felt my success rate would be. *But I have this one*, I told myself. I could freaking taste it.

Jagger reached out and touched me on the knee. "Don't worry, babe."

"Get lost, Cane," Grumpy grumbled.

Jagger ignored him, all of a sudden sounding self-conscious and cautious. "I really didn't want to have this conversation in front of Bradshaw, but I'm not going to be able to rest tonight if we don't. It's about the Valentine's dance next weekend. I'll pick you up at six p.m., take you to dinner, and then we can enjoy the dance or catch a movie. I've been *dying*," he emphasized, "to take you out. Actually, it's been nerve-racking. In fact, maybe I should take you home after school. I'd like to meet your father and do this thing the right way. I'd appreciate that if the roles were reversed."

Pardon me for laughing, but I actually looked up to see if Jesus was in the sky.

"You're serious," I said, halfway giggling and sitting up.

"As a heart attack. That's not like some bombshell, babe. The Devil himself knows I've had a thing for you."

Time and again, he never failed to shock. When Jagger saw my face, he pitched his head back and laughed. The sound was like crushed velvet. It traveled the length of my body, touching and warming parts too intimate to be shared unmarried and in public.

"I'm not sure I'm..." I said, then paused and looked at my feet—like the right word would come up and smack me in the mouth—"...your type," I decided on. "Besides I eat, sleep, and breathe all things Taylor."

All he did was grin. Now that didn't make me feel comfortable, folks. It really didn't.

Grumpy picked up my backpack, pulling me from my seat by the wrist. "She says *no*, Cane. Let's go, Walker." Grumpy was right... an exit would be good. What was one way to tick off your alleged soulmate? The answer was by mackin' on one of his enemies and ruining your girlfriend factor for-like-ever.

"Darcy might want to switch teams," Jagger murmured and chuckled.

"It would take a whole lot of Prozac to make me forget Dylan," I mumbled.

"Man, do you have dementia?" Grumpy said, unloading a death stare.

"Of course not," Jagger answered.

"Then I suggest you grow eyes in the back of your head," Grumpy advised. "She's with Taylor, man. Oh, I'm sorry. You don't understand the term 'with someone,' do you?"

The air crackled with metaphorical fists longing to find a target. The tension between them was so thick I needed a hacksaw to cut through it. Jagger had humiliated Grumpy by stealing Ivy right out from underneath him, and as much as Jagger had quasi-found a way into my heart, he'd never be Grumpy. I looked at his beautifully dark, good-looking face and realized a part of Jagger was uglier than a goat's butt.

"Jagger," I said, preparing to unveil my true feelings, but Grumpy mumbled something under his breath and pulled us down the steps as though he tried to stop another holocaust.

"There's no expiration date on that offer, babe," Jagger shouted from behind.

Prevailing wisdom said if you repeatedly turned someone down, the person would never ask again. Jagger was never swayed by the umpteen refusals I'd disbursed weekly. But as I stumbled down the steps, I glanced back and observed something I wasn't prepared for. His eyes were panicked—as if the bottom fell out of his plan, and he didn't have a contingency. My pulse leapt to my throat because the look of desperation mirrored the one I'd seen in Mr. Himmel. It was a look that said he was capable of something really, really dark and stupid. I'd think about that later... much later.

———————

"Tell me you love me, angel," Ben flirted.

Grumpy dumped me to sulk in private, but like chum in the ocean, I'd somehow attracted Ben's shark. I raised a brow at his comments and shoved my Spanish IV book on the top shelf of my locker, carefully lining its spine up with the others. As long as my sorry butt lived, I'd never get used to guy's hitting on me. Like I'd said, my ante as a female had been upped since Dylan put a ring on my finger...otherwise, I'd been as invisible as Ivy's conscience.

"No," I muttered.

"Come on angel. Tell me you love me because I just found Gabrielle Allen."

My chest thumped like a scared rabbit. Holy. Jeezle. That was good, but Ben had gone for my hand three times, and touching him was like sticking my hand in a tiger's cage. I glanced over my shoulder to scout for Dylan. Thankfully, he hadn't surfaced, but I could feel him...somewhere close.

"You found her while you were at school?" I asked.

Ben chuckled, his British accent heavy on the flirt. "I can multi-task, Darcy." Not a shock. His normal uniform of khaki pants, penny loafers, and an oxford screamed the managerial type.

Patting myself down for a pencil, I gave up and grabbed a new one from the top shelf. "Where is she?"

"Right here in town. She goes by Gabrielle Spencer now. Two failed marriages, but she's in the process of having her maiden name restored."

"Should I ask how you received this information?"

Ben's smile quirked up at one corner. "I plead the fifth on the grounds I might incriminate myself."

Made sense. "I need to see her, Ben. Would you take me?"

Ben raised one eyebrow and gazed heatedly down his nose at a forty-five degree angle. "Why, Darcy Walker. Are you asking me out on a date?"

Ben just endured a mini stroke if he thought I'd asked him out, but I'd be remiss if I didn't acknowledge Friday and Saturday nights equaled date nights for all the lovers. "Would it have to be a *date*?" I grimaced.

"It could be whatever you wanted it to be," he answered. Ben took one step forward, and my upper lip beaded with sweat. I grabbed my worn copy of *The Scarlet Letter* for English lit class. We were to have it read and see the new Hollywood adaptation releasing during the weekend and compare/contrast them in a type-written paper—double-spaced and all that—by the following Monday. I'd read it four times even before it had been required.

What can I say? I'm a hopeless romantic for a doomed love story.

"File thirteen the date, stuff, Ben. I'm with Dylan. Any other guy would be a runner-up."

Ben reached out to touch me again, but I backed away. "Why is she so important to you?" he asked, changing gears.

Removing a makeup bag from the top shelf, I snagged a scrunchie rubber band I used when my hair went to crap. Flipping my head over, I gathered my hair up into a ponytail. Ben knew a single father had raised me, but he didn't know the whys of the situation. I couldn't tell him the details—I couldn't tell *anyone* the details—and I wasn't sure Ben would do this "just because."

"Just trust me, okay? And I swear I'll tell you when I have everything figured out. Do you think we could see her tonight?"

I stood back up, shocked when a glimmer of romantic hope surfaced in his eyes. "I'm available," he said.

"Good, but don't break out the champagne yet. This thing between you and me," I warned, motioning back and forth between us, "it's all business."

The cocky grin grew. "For now, but after one date with me I can promise you're going to be saying Dylan-who."

"What about Dylan?" Dylan asked, coming from behind. The Big Man put his left arm around my waist and pulled me so close I could've counted his vertebrae.

"Later," Ben said, laughing with a promise, and I saw it in his gaze he'd text me with a time to see Gabrielle later that night.

Just for the record, that had bad idea written all over it, but I couldn't deny it was freaking nirvana. I made a mental note to get my self-destructive life back on track, but right then, fate was knocking at my door...or should I say, *Gabrielle Allen's*.

By the grace of God, I'd convinced Ben to stay in the car. Not an easy task since he was a control freak, but he'd brought something to read and said he'd give me twenty minutes, or he'd break the door down. Ben Ryan was the dangerous, Svengali-kind of demanding, and if I were in the market to protect my heart, I had a feeling he would steal it one way or another.

A rainy snow swirled in the wind as I jumped up and down, attempting to stay warm. Who I assumed was Gabrielle opened the door in a three-inch crack, peering outside as I performed some idiotic jumping jacks. "May I help you?" she asked.

My nose was hit with the smell of something savory in the oven...or a crockpot. "Yes," I answered, instantly hungry. "I'm, uh, Jester. I'm not a weirdo with a pickaxe. I'd just like to talk to you."

"Talk to me about what?"

"I work for your landlord. We're going to be doing some renovations," I lied.

Gabrielle narrowed her eyes for a split second, surprisingly unhooked the chain, and invited me inside.

She lived in a modest three-room apartment on the outskirts of Valley. Shorter than me, she had long, wavy black hair, brown eyes, and a genuine smile that seemed emotionally tired. The way she'd dressed, she'd either come from work or a job interview because a crisp résumé in ivory paper stock lay on the glass coffee table.

If she was in the middle of a divorce as Ben claimed, appearances led me to believe she merely rented the place and wouldn't be getting the house. Furniture was sparse, the only seating being a well-worn fabric couch and old wicker chair. Gabrielle motioned for me to take a seat. After five minutes of small talk and a cup of burnt coffee, I confessed I'd come for another reason—that I thought Lyric might be the victim of murder. Gabrielle looked like I'd cracked her in the face with a lead pipe.

I held up my hands in a surrender motion. "Wait, wait," I said nervously. "I'm just trying to find answers. That's all."

Bruh, not even close to the truth...

Sometimes I wasn't a patient person. Okay, I was *never* a patient person—especially when something in my gut started to nudge. I went full steam ahead. "Have you read the papers in the past week? More specifically, the stories by Tito Westbrook?"

"I have," she answered strangely, like I'd broached a subject she didn't want broached.

"Good, then you'll know what I'm talking about. I found an article on the Internet where you spoke of Ryder Beck's disappearance years ago. You said Ryder would never run away...that you felt certain something had happened to him. I think the same thing might've happened to Lyric."

Gabrielle had a strong affection for Ryder because she stopped and glanced up wistfully, recalling fond memories. But as quickly as those memories washed over her face, just as instantaneously they'd been replaced by something distressing and dark. "I believe that too," she said. "I loved Ryder very much. In fact, I've destroyed every relationship since him because I can't fully commit. If we just had a body," she whispered, "maybe I could move on."

My stomach had officially traveled north to my mouth. "Could there be any reason Ryder would want to skip town?"

She vehemently shook her head. "Absolutely not. Ryder and I were close. He and Lyric were close. His home life wasn't the greatest, but I can tell you this...he would've never left me. *Never*," she said with an adamant confidence. Gabrielle found her feet and paced the small apartment. "Ryder and I hadn't broken up," she continued as she walked, "but something was driving a wedge between us. I didn't know what it was until after he was gone."

"And what was that?"

"Ryder had gotten involved in some sort of fight club."

No freaking way. And let me just say again...*no...freaking*...WAY. Whatever had gone down decades earlier was still happening—or trying to be resurrected—in the present. And here Marek was primed to dive into the octagon the next day. "Why would Ryder want to get involved in something like that?"

She shrugged. "I've asked myself that a million times. Maybe the thrill? He wasn't big into monetary things, so that could only leave his ego of never wanting to be beaten. He was a good athlete."

"Was he a cocky guy?"

"Confident," she said defensively. Girl, I understood cocky. Dylan vacillated back and forth between cocky and confident, but that was only on the playing field. Anywhere else, he was the consummate gentleman.

"I have information that a fight club might still be happening."

Gabrielle's face instantly sobered. "You're sure?"

"One hundred percent positive," I vowed.

Gabrielle placed her hand over her heart, gently patting it. "Ryder never spoke to me of it, but he had to Lyric. It was a secret society of some kind. He told Lyric he was getting out, but when he tried to gain his freedom back, he was never heard from again. That was the story Lyric had been chasing."

Ding, ding, ding! Lyric had been chasing a story? For Tito, perhaps? That'd make sense why he specifically told me to keep my nose to myself. He didn't want another dead source on his hands.

"I know someone considering lacing up his gloves. A fight club was advertised at Club Need last weekend on a flier. In fact, the first match is supposed to happen tomorrow. The manager pulled the flier down because he wasn't backing it, but it wasn't soon enough."

Gabrielle dropped an, "Oh, God."

"Did Lyric ever tell you *who* she thought to be responsible for Ryder's disappearance? Did she give you any names?"

"No names. In fact, we were supposed to meet the night she disappeared. I've worn myself out with the police department. I've told them everything...all of my suspicions, but I gave up years ago. Lyric's family hired PIs, but no one came up with anything except more questions. Opening up Lyric's case is probably just going through the motions anyway."

Gabrielle picked up the beaded crucifix lying on the coffee table in front of us, winding it tightly through her fingers. Drawing it to her lips, she kissed it like it was the only salvation she had left in a life that had dwindled down to nothing.

It wasn't that I didn't believe in God, it was the "will" part that always made me wonder. Wonder how it was okay for murderous lunatics to walk the face of the Earth, unchecked. But I'd chase

Lyric's murderer down if it was the only way to find my mother's killer—even if I had to dance with the Devil to do it.

Gabrielle briefly left the room and returned with a worn, leather-bound journal. "Here are my notes," she said, placing them in my hand. "Every lead and every dead end are detailed inside. I wrote down anything that seemed suspicious over the years."

There was a big gulp on my part—make that a whale-sized gulp followed by a forced feeding of the play-it-cools. In that notebook was a photograph of Ryder. He had duel-colored eyes, one ice-blue and one an Atlantic Ocean-green. More notable than his rare eye color was an expression that said he was eager to take on the world.

I stared in dumbfounded pleasure while Handel's "Hallelujah Chorus" started blaring in my mind. The hunt was on, and I was feeling like a hound dog.

Chapter Eighteen

THE DEATH KNELL

The traffic came to a screeching stop right before Ben and I turned into Buffalo Trails Country Club. An accident was up ahead, and a wrecker was hooking its tow onto the back of a crunched up beige minivan.

I'd debated the depths of little white lies versus black lies for the last ten miles. Dylan had texted, repeat texted, phoned, and attempted a FaceTime in the past three hours while he traveled two hours away for a basketball game. I held him off with a message that said, *Call soon. I'm a busy beaver*. I even added a beaver emoji to top off the lie. Unfortunately, before I could say no, Ben pulled into LaRosa's Pizza and ordered a large pizza with everything and a JoJo's salad. I stood there speechless because I wanted our not-really-a-date over. In Ben's mind, however, it had just moved into fifth gear.

He didn't push for particulars on my conversation with Gabrielle, but I could tell he'd bitten his tongue off in the process. I used that time to grill him on being a five-time MMA champion. If anyone understood an underground fight club, it would be Ben. So for two hours, he reaffirmed what I already knew. Fighting wasn't illegal. It was the unsupervised tax-free gambling that was. It was also illegal because they weren't sanctioned, meaning there were no rules of fair play. Anything goes without professional supervision, and no doctor or trained personnel were usually on site, telling opponents when to quit sparring. Ben said a lot of guys got involved in the underground because they'd been kicked out of the organized circuit. The main reason for that happening was usually fighting outside of the ring or breaking the law. And the underground circuit could be either MMA or traditional boxing, just depended on the venue.

Unfortunately, my interest made him think I was enamored of his accomplishments.

He leaned over the steering wheel, craning his neck to see the accident closer. While his brows remained furrowed, it struck me how good-looking his parents must be. Every once in a while, a couple of average people hit one out of the park and birth an other-worldly face, but more often than not, it was just good genes reproducing themselves to make the rest of us feel like crap.

My mouth opened and blurted out, "Your parents must be gorgeous because you look Photoshopped. It's not normal to look like you, ya know?"

I slammed my hand over my lips, longing to rip my tongue out because I had such little self-restraint. Ben grinned broadly, leaning over to remove it. "Angel, angel, I think you have a crush on me."

"No, my mouth has no filter," I said in an ugh.

The Valley police officer securing the scene motioned us through after three cars went by, and suddenly it was nothing but awkward silence. Ben glanced over with his cocky grin predictably quirked at one corner. "Silence is a good sign, Darcy. That means you're having trouble surrendering to what we both know is meant to be."

Not quite. Silence meant I realized I was an idiot.

When we pulled into my driveway, I literally jumped out of the car while it still moved and scrambled inside. Tapping in the security code on the garage door, I padded past Murphy's car and dumped my things on the floor in the den. The house felt and sounded like a morgue. Murphy was in mourning, and I didn't know if that was because I was out with someone other than Dylan or if he mourned the loss of my innocence.

Dude, that had come and gone by the time I was six.

His favorite recliner sat to the right side of the fireplace. Sitting stoically inside, he narrowed his brows and made eye contact once, ravaging his preferred dessert of banana pudding, whipped cream, and wafers. After I watched him drain the bowl, he snagged the paper from the armrest and pretended to read.

Marjorie, clad in blue polka-dot underpants and tap shoes, asked, "Did he kiss you?"

She made some kissy-kissy sounds, and if I weren't so mentally drained, maybe I'd have done something about it. I dropped onto the couch, throwing an arm over my face to hide. I had a habit of biting my nails when backed into a corner. I'd ripped off every nail on my right hand, and the pinky nail on my left was down to a painful nub. I brought that nail to my mouth and tried to suck out the pain.

"No," I muttered, wondering if I should be offended she'd even asked.

Murphy aggressively snapped the page, grumbling behind it with a copious amount of sarcasm. "Maybe you should count that as blessing."

"Excuse me?" I mumbled.

"That's such a dumb retort I'm not even going to dignify it with a response."

True, I looked like a cheat. Heck, I *was* a cheat...I think...or at least Murphy thought I was with my not-so-secret, hypothetical relationship with Ben. Thing was, Murphy didn't like change. Change was what was under the cushions of your couch. Change was what you did to your flat tire, and change was what happened with the seasons right at the moment you got tired of the one you were currently in. Change wasn't your daughter switching boyfriends when she'd just gotten one around Christmas. I wasn't changing. Dylan just wasn't so, uh, *beneficial* to me in times like these. He had too much of a conscience. Eh, I was going to Hell.

"Mark my words, you're going to regret this," he grunted.

I sat up, wincing. "Did Dylan call? Did you tell him?"

The pizza I'd just eaten was in the back of my throat. "Nope and nope, but God has a way of laying our sins bare." I agreed. God and I could really use some face-time, but I feared what He'd say if I got detailed.

———

"Meet me outside," he murmured.

"Huh?" I yawned.

"You. Me. Outside. Now."

I was a notorious insomniac, but when I would sleep the four horsemen of the apocalypse could thunder by, and I'd miss the hoof beats and world-ending stuff. Pulling my iPhone up to my eyes, I squinted to see the time. Ho. Ly. Canoli. "D, it's one a.m., Saturday morning!" I croaked. "Do your mom and dad know where you are?"

My voice was scratchy with sleep, but even though I was bone-tired, Dylan could always breathe a breath of air into me. He ignored the question and disconnected with a deep chuckle. Shaking my head to clear it, I slid my glasses on my nose and stumbled out of bed in black leggings and a ratty white T-shirt. I found a hoodie in a pile at my feet and coaxed it over my head and cast. Next, I clumsily punched my feet inside my UGGs and tiptoed down the stairs to Murphy snoring like a jet plane.

Turning off the security system, I creaked the front door open and stepped outside to the mother-trucking tundra. The cold wind slashed across my face like Jack the Ripper as I sprinted to the Beemer. Dylan quickly beeped the door ajar, and I dove in. His hands immediately went to the strings on my hoodie, pulling me forward into an aggressive yet instantly tender hug. That had become normal for our type of relationship. Hot. Heavy. Highly physical that had my heart screeching Code Blue.

"Are we good?" he whispered into my lips. "I swear, Darcy. I feel like I'm about to throw up, and I couldn't close my eyes without getting my hands on you."

"We're always good," I said, sleepily yawning.

I wrapped my arms around his waist and lazily kissed his chest. Dylan packed some major mojo power. When he hugged me, my body got hotter than the Sahara. "You're the best friend I've ever had," I said, squeezing him around the middle.

Our relationship and its seemingly shaky future had been eating away at me too. I'd attempted to phone several times before I hit the sack, but the calls went straight to voicemail. Dylan would never screen my calls. More likely than not, cell phone service was "iffy" because he was two hours away in the heart of Indiana. All I knew was according to the nightly news, he'd scored an all-time high in points, breaking the school record, and nearly toppling the state record that had stood for over fifty years. And it wasn't that he'd been a ball hog. Dylan led the entire game in assists. He was just that good. Dylan Taylor was destined to be someone who defied the odds of what normal meant to the rest of the functional working world.

"As you are mine, sweetheart. I love you."

I dispensed a stupid grin because per usual I still could not return those three magic words. Twining my fingers in his, I whispered, "I'm proud of you. I hear you had a great game."

Dylan kissed the top of my head in thanks and immediately focused all his attention on me, tenderly rubbing my back. "Were you working on your paper? The one Mrs. Conner wants you to make up?"

"Yeah," my voice answered before I could stop it. Oh, God, lie number one.

Another kiss to the head. "Did you get everything squared away?"

"Close," I answered. Someone shoot me...lie number two. Lie. Lie. Lie!

"Good," he murmured, "but I sense something is wrong." My body betrayed me because I stiffened and tried to pull away. "I'm right, aren't I?" he said.

How could I explain I worked for Jaws who dangled a carrot over my head with information of my mother's murderer? He'd tell Murphy, and I'd be placed in permanent lockdown.

"I don't really know how to talk about it," I said truthfully.

Dylan tucked a tendril of hair behind my ear. "Did someone hurt you?" he murmured.

"No."

"Hurt your feelings?"

"No."

"Is it school?"

"Not really," I said, lifting a shoulder in a shrug.

Dylan's subsequent frown said his worries were mounting. "Family? Friends? Work?"

"No, D," I answered.

Inhale...Exhale...Inhale...Exhale. "That only leaves you and me."

"No, no," I said quickly. "You'll always be my best friend."

He furrowed his brows event tighter. "Boyfriend?" he asked gruffly.

My smile grew wide. "The boyfriend is a bonus I don't intend on giving up. I promise. My feelings for you haven't changed. Pinky swear."

An impish glimmer returned to his gaze, but he still looked pensive—like he halfway listened to me and one hundred percent listened to something else in his mind.

Dylan winked. "Then whatever it is we'll deal with it together. I'm here when you're ready to talk, Darc. I'll always be here."

My boyfriend might as well have written those words in blood because I knew he meant them. He drew my fingers to his lips. "Remember I'm flying out this morning to spend the weekend with the football staff at the University of Florida. I'm not sure when we'll be back. Probably late Sunday afternoon." As much as the initial information floored me, evidently I'd shoved it way down on the *Must Think About List* because I blinked a few times for it to register. I'd been concerned with how I'd get Dylan to agree to watch Marek fight later that night. Right then, the point was moot. "You remember, yeah?" he murmured.

"They must really want you to have something planned on a weekend."

Dylan shrugged as if it was no big deal. "Is there any way you can get out of work and join me? I can have Dad call Murphy and give him the details."

Here was my dilemma: Go with Dylan, and I'd blow my chance of recon at Marek's fighting debut. Stay at home, and I'd probably get in trouble and more than likely hurt my boyfriend's feelings. Unfortunately, I went with the latter.

"A girl's gotta work, D. The Double-B is expecting me."

A grimace touched my eyes with the lame excuse because it wasn't like my first day on the job where I had to show up bright and early, ready to set the literary world on fire. And Marek aside, I didn't relish thinking of Dylan and me separating—maybe for good —next year. Call me an avoider.

We both sat in silence, and about a dozen heartbeats passed while I wondered if I'd just heard the death knell on our relationship. While the Beemer purred, Dylan caught me staring at the stars.

He pitched his head in the direction of my gaze. "What's captured your attention?" he asked, stroking my face with the back of his hand.

I pointed out the window to the beautiful cluster of stars arranged in the shape of a lopsided square. I'd been a stargazer for years...one way I tried to find my mother, I think. "Lyra," I answered. "The harp of Orpheus."

Dylan leaned in for a kiss. "Come here, and let me taste your mouth, sweetheart. You look sad. I can promise you I'll never give you a reason to look sad."

Dylan's words could completely shred me in two.

So here was the part where we steamed the windows to the Beemer.

Before I could say, *I think I need deodorant*, Dylan's hands found my hair, pulling me into his lap. My back cut into the steering wheel, sending a sharp pain down my hip, but a team of wild horses couldn't tear me away. Dylan tightened his grip and kissed my neck, rubbing it raw with his hunger. Trying to get even closer, I threw my arms around his shoulders and cracked him in the head with my cast. "Sorry," I said laughing.

"Quit talking," he murmured.

When I repositioned myself, I got twisted in his seatbelt and inadvertently smacked him in the jaw. "Ow," I said, giggling again. "It comes off soon."

Dylan's answering growl said he couldn't care less. He kissed every one of my fingertips like he savored something delicious and migrated up to my mouth. My lips parted underneath his touch, and he found his way inside my soul.

Now imagine that yourself...it was pretty awesome.

———

Cue the fist pump.

I couldn't have scripted a better ending to the previous day and start of the next. As I lay in bed, I'd come to terms with the fact the only way to sometimes get the info I needed was to...gulp, lie. Yes, I said, *lie*. I liked to think of my actions as creative investigation, but what I'd found out was if you told one lie, you had to tell another to cover up the previous offense. By the time Dylan said goodbye, I gave up counting how many untruths I'd birthed.

And that nervous giggle I normally had when I fudged on the truth? Uh, nowhere to be found. Conformation I'd taken my first step into sociopath.

Crawling out of bed, I coaxed my arms into my fluffy white robe and peeked in Marjorie's room. She was MIA, so I moved on to Murphy's. His room was as quiet as an empty grave, but instead of turning to leave, I paused at the door.

Stepping inside Murphy's room always brought an incredibly sad feeling. It wasn't the room he'd shared with my mother. Their master bedroom was downstairs, door closed, and had remained that way for seven years. Thing was, sometimes I could feel my mom—even smell her—when other times it got harder and harder to remember. But I can sure as heck tell you one thing: if she were around, she'd be royally ticked off I'd been partying in my own transgressions.

Ugh...que será and all that.

When the laughter of voices tingled the air, I took a quick dip in the shower before joining them downstairs. Trudging back to my bathroom, I cranked on the spray and dropped my clothes. Stepping inside the glass enclosure, I lathered up with Bath & Body Works shower gel and let my mind linger over my mother.

There were things in life that defined you. Unfortunately, my mother's murder still defined me seven years later. I'd been diagnosed with ADHD early on into grade school, but after her death, those characteristics magnified tenfold. I continually had the urge to move. Move even if there was no place to go.

I could always be found at the pencil sharpener, talking to people in the halls, making nice with custodians, and merely staring and willing the day to end. Spending so much time trying to get my body to obey left me a couple of pages behind everyone else. And it wasn't because I couldn't grasp material. I'd been a great student before my mother died despite the ADHD. It was simply that after she passed, my brain went on system-overload. My mind swam with answers, but I couldn't get them from my head to the Number 2 pencil, let alone have them meet the paper in a logical fashion.

Out of the blue, I developed OCD tendencies—counting, categorizing, and performing meaningless rituals because my brain couldn't find the off switch. I also birthed nervous tics and the occasional seizure—seizures my Grandmother Marjorie (Murphy's mother) apparently suffered from. Call it stress or another tragically meant-to-be occurrence, all I knew was when I came out on the other side, I learned the value and power of the sense of humor. It didn't always cure a person, but it could Band-Aid you while you scrambled for safe cover.

More often than not, Dylan was my safe cover.

I found myself telling him things I would only confide in my mom. Things like *I had a bad dream*, or *Can I hold your hand?* Or *What do you do when xyz happens?* He never laughed or pulled away physically or emotionally. In fact, he learned to predict what was on my mind before the thoughts even made it past my lips. There were days I didn't know my own name...*but I always knew his.*

Unfortunately, everyone didn't handle my particular tragedy like Dylan. Most shied away from things they didn't understand, and when they didn't shy away, they overtly stayed away. Bargaining with death along with ostracizing peers never made schoolwork easy. When I wasn't dealing with people who hurt my feelings, I preached peace, love, and happiness to my brain. And my brain was, eh, stupid. Some teachers offered support. Others like Mr. Himmel seemed to delight in pointing out my deficiencies.

Shutting off the shower, I toweled off and dressed in my Belinski's gear, walking downstairs with a shudder when I realized the son of Satan himself was the breakfast subject of choice.

"What do you mean he tried to break out last night?" Murphy barked.

"I mean the dumbass sawed off his bracelet and was stopped by the black and white positioned at the corner of his house, Murphy."

"Last night?" he asked.

"No, last Easter, moron. He was right out there with the damn

Easter Bunny." Red mumbled something to herself but deep-six'd the talking to gaze at me. "Sit. We need to talk. And yeah, good morning, baby," she said, half grinning.

Red rose from the kitchen table for a kiss, wearing tight jeans that hugged the butt of a teenager. She'd paired them with an even tighter black sweater, which showcased boobs that were certifiably real. Her blonde hair had been pulled back in one of those sleek ponytails, highlighting perfect bone structure. No wonder Rookie temporarily lost his mind. Her ovaries operated like a tractor beam to the gonads.

Murphy had gotten his Kentucky on and cooked ham, green beans, cornbread, and okra with tomatoes. My mouth salivated like a rabid dog as soon as my butt hit the chair next to Red. Spooning food onto a plate, I leaned over to hug Marjorie, my brain instantly barraged with a memory of when I was ten years old. I woke one morning and decided I needed to know how to change a tire. For God's sake, that defined bizarre because I wasn't even close to getting my driving permit. But I'd dreamt I'd broken down somewhere with a flat and wanted to be prepared. Rookie spent one entire morning teaching me how to jack up a two-ton car until the obsession was laid to rest.

My obsession needed to freaking die, or it would put me in the ground. But I was only one person—proverbially outgunned and outmanned. My band of misfit PI wannabes weren't even in on the caper...not even Vinnie, really. In retrospect, leaving him out had been wrong, not to mention careless.

Maybe I should call the whole thing off. My dishonesty threatened my relationship with Dylan, and I didn't want to wind up like Rookie and Red...one of us suffering in silence at the hands of the other. I tried a new tactic. I hadn't touched the subject of my mother for years...*years*, I say. I shoveled a piece of okra in my mouth and broke the dam.

"Is anyone at this table ever going to tell me what happened to my mother? Gemma Walker. You do remember her, right?"

One would've thought I'd just called God a four-lettered word. "Please tell me you did not just say that," Murphy gasped.

"I said it," I answered, and in fact I repeated the sentence again. Here were my thoughts on the subject. When the doctor told you that you had a malignancy, you eradicated it...you didn't take part of it...you took all of it, or it would come back and bite you again later. They had no idea I planned to be their cancer until I had answers.

Murphy's cell phone sat next to his plate. He snatched it up and fake dialed, mimicking a high-pitched and sarcastic beep-beep-beep while his index finger struck the keys. "What are you doing?" I asked.

"I'm mobilizing a search party for your sense of timing," he growled.

I stabbed the ham with my fork. "Maybe they should look for yours while we're at it. I've been waiting for it for seven years."

He slammed the phone back on the table. "Watch the mouth, kid," he bellowed. "This is not the time."

"Then tell me the time, Murphy. My calendar is wide open."

Murphy buried his head in his plate, trying to wish me away. "You know enough."

"I don't know anything."

"Yeah, you do. You had a front row seat."

"And a nine-year-old perspective. I'm not going to go away."

"Yeah you are," he seethed. "My conversation on this subject is a single serving."

"Clever."

"I swear, Darcy, you're a *48 Hours* episode in the making. Why do you insist on replaying the worst day of my life?"

I slammed both fists on the table, rattling my glass of OJ. Marjorie reached her little hand out and snagged the glass before it tipped over. "You aren't taking me seriously!" I screamed. "I know Robert 'Butch' Lawrence was her stalker, and I know you'd just left to walk the perimeter of the building with some other huge muscle you'd hired. It was just mom and me. Red kissed us both and left to pick up Marjorie from the baby sitter's when this nice looking man walked in. From out of nowhere a gun appeared, they fought, and he shot her in the chest at close range. All while some black diamond cross dangled from his neck. She stayed alive best I can remember for about four or five minutes. But all of that seems too simple. Mom knew him. I don't believe he fell in obsession with her from afar. And the way you've avoided this subject for years makes me think there's something else to the story. I believe people outside this room know the true story too. I swear, Murphy—"

He angrily jerked his head up, pointing his shaking fork in my face. "Don't forget your little sister is in this room, Darcy Winston Walker. You should be ashamed of yourself."

"Me?" I said, snorting self-righteously. "It's *you* who should be ashamed. You told me nothing. Was it the worst day for you? Try living it the way I did and then having the people who are supposed to care about you the most guard it like the nuclear football!"

The key to Murphy's silence lay in what his duty had been that night. When Red introduced Murphy to my mother freshman year in college, Murphy had just begun the narrow road to redemption as he backed out of the bookie life. My father, in short, was good at thug work. When The Minstrel Cramps took off, he headed up her security detail. Talk about survivor's guilt. Without saying it, I knew he felt he'd been out of practice too long.

"What's wrong, baby?" Red asked, tenderly stroking my hand. I jerked away, refusing to play nice. "Is something wrong between you and Dylan?"

I leered at her like an angry cat when someone doused it with water. "Not yet," I said, "and I've never seen you without an opinion. You know I have a beef with you too."

Marjorie glanced up from her Cap'n Crunch. "Please, don't fight," she whispered in a small voice.

"I'm not fighting," I answered because if they'd just give me the necessary information, I could tell Jaws to kiss my fricking can. Maybe I'd eventually help him, but right then I resembled a sports car with no brakes—capable of the extreme, especially if no one was reining me in.

Red looked like she was negotiating with a suicide bomber. Honestly...pretty darn close. "Baby, just calm down," she soothed.

"Tell me about the man who murdered Gemma Walker, and then I'll calm down. You're privy to information I don't have."

Red opened her mouth with a sigh but then looked to Murphy for a bailout. When he did nothing but continue the icy stare, she glanced back to me with a look of apology. I didn't know if that meant she sympathized, or if she merely apologized because she had no plans of giving me anything substantial either.

I stared in shock, then with anger. The anger quickly morphed to hot tears as I gazed at the two people who were always supposed to tell me the truth. I pushed away from the table so fast I knocked over my own chair. I'd already catalogued Red's hoop earrings to be as large as silver dollars. Her fingernails had been polished in an American manicure. One light bulb had burned out in the chandelier overhead, and the dark brown leather boots she wore stood at three inches tall. All were things I didn't want to observe, but my OCD brain couldn't stop observing if I tried. The more upset or agitated I became, the more information my mind absorbed, even if it was mundane...and then the mundane became maddening.

"I've lost my appetite," I said, sniffling and knowing I needed a change of venue. "Good to see you, Red, and don't either of you bother driving me to work. I'm taking the bus."

"It's twenty fricking degrees outside," she said softly. She slid over her keys. "Take my car."

I raised my chin defiantly. "I only want one thing from you, and you aren't willing to give it. I'm not nine anymore, and with the glories of cyberspace, my little sister knows enough to probably have questions too. And guess what, she's smarter than me. You. Owe. Us."

We had a stare-down where I prayed she'd cave...no such luck.

"That's what I thought," I said sadly and grabbed my coat and rushed out the door.

Chapter Nineteen

THE PRESSURE COOKER

I've been told I leave a path of destruction behind me. That wouldn't be a problem if everyone would just get out of my way.

Despite the buzz working an undercover op provided, on some level I'd hoped to confess everything to Murphy and Red. The lump in my throat told me that probably wouldn't happen. Luckily, I'd been able to escape the house arrest a disagreement such as ours probably warranted. Red's closing argument? *Take my car. Take my bloody car*—that's all she wrote. She and Murphy both phoned The Double-B, but the conversation had been less than desirable. Their words were fraught with *I love yous* and *We understands* but still offered nothing to ease my mind. So basically, we were at a stalemate. The race against the clock had alienated me from my family. I feared Dylan would be next.

Feeling like a pressure cooker about to blow, to preserve what remained of my sanity, I vowed to find answers that night—answers Marek Ransom just might inadvertently provide. I phoned Vinnie to see if he was game, but unfortunately he claimed he was in dire need of some "Donatella time" but would meet up Sunday to chase the man in the yellow Dodge Charger. Backed against a wall, I did something Dylan would never understand. Instead of contacting Justice—or even Finn or Grumpy—I phoned Ben Ryan. So here we were...in his Audi...at nine p.m. on a Saturday night. Club Need the final destination.

I'd just dialed Murphy from Ben's cell phone because I'd fled ground zero so fast I left without my iPhone that morning. "I know you've had a bad day," Murphy said, "and I don't totally understand why you're doing what you're doing, but just remember if you play with matches, you're going to get burned." A reference to him thinking I was deep in the process of cheating on Dylan. I admit it appeared that way, but alas, it wasn't that simple.

"You can also drive a horse to water, but you can't make him drink," I countered.

Murphy mumbled to himself how I'd obviously hit my self-destruct button. "Glad to know we're on the same page," he grunted. "You call me when you get there, you call me when you're leaving, and you call me when you're on the way home from the car."

"Am I supposed to *call*?" I giggled.

"Shut up, Darcy."

"Tell me again. I forgot."

"Just do it, kid, but I'm going to go on record as saying you're going to regret this." Murphy ended the call with one of his standard lines, "I could be wrong...but I'm usually not."

I'd just darkened my soul. That counted as one of those lies of omission. It wasn't like saying I'd brushed my teeth before bedtime when I hadn't, or I'd taken my vitamin when I'd spit it out in the trash. Problem was, my OCD had jumped out of an airplane and was trying to avoid the ground. To be honest, I wasn't exactly sure I looked Club Need ready either. I'd ditched my uniform in the break room and pulled on a stash of clothes I kept in my locker when Dylan would take me out after work—dark jeans, a gray turtleneck with lace sleeves, and oversized red beanie.

Ben was so...*Ben*. Dressed the same with his rocker snarl turned up at one corner. The closer we got to our destination, I realized how unnatural being together felt. I didn't feel comfortable changing radio stations. I didn't feel comfortable inserting a CD. I didn't feel comfortable being quiet if I wanted to be quiet. I felt like I had to make conversation when I didn't want to do anything except veg and formulate a plan on how to find Marek and watch him fight.

Ben maneuvered his ride down the icy slope of a parking garage, reaching for my hand when he shut down the engine. "No h-hhand," I stammered, suddenly panicked.

"Let's clear the air then. Is this a date? Or two friends who *missed* one another," he said grinning, "catching up?"

Ben's mind had one frequency, and I needed to scramble it. Leaning toward me, he unleashed a gaze that'd melt the flesh from your bones. Sheesh. Ben just might be as determined as Dylan...not a good thing. "Listen, if you're looking for emotional or physical compensation, it ain't happening," I told him. "And before you judge me, let me wrap my head around a few things, and then I'll field questions."

Ben dialed back the Casanova thing. "Does this have to do with Gabrielle Allen?"

I zipped my coat to my chin and placed my hand on the door, recycling Jaws's sentiment. "She's a means to an end."

I stared at Ben, Ben stared at me, and my snoop bonded with his snoop. We were a match made in Heaven. Okay, probably not Heaven, but at least Purgatory.

———

Club Need's music roared like a fighter jet. Once again, we'd gained entrance without a cover charge—although I'd come prepared, counterfeit ID in hand. Last summer, Dylan and I'd gone to Cowboys, a club in Orlando, which was the venue where I helped O-Town police nab a child abductor. The fuzz had provided counterfeit IDs...I wasn't a fool. I'd held on to that sucker like it was a block of gold.

Club Need's older demographic dominated once inside, but there was no regards to age or stereotypical boundaries on hookups...um, yuck. A few teens had been granted entry like us, and even parents of kids I knew with dates who weren't their spouses. But among the over-forty crowd, one thing was constant...Botox.

Lars van der Hart stood onstage next to the DJ, still in all-black attire. His stature was aristocratic and his smile beguiling, possessing just enough star-quality one couldn't help but stare. I pitched my head toward him as Ben got acquainted with the surroundings and a bass sound of "Turn Down for What" that needed to be lowered before my eardrums burst. "He's the owner!" I screamed as we danced.

Ben answered with four words. "His bodyguard looks familiar."

The seven-foot goon was stationed next to Lars van der Hart. He had an Italian mob look about him, wearing a dark designer suit with matching turtleneck and Aviator sunglasses. Call it stupid or good detective work, but I stared at him like fresh roadkill, wondering if his brain was as dead as his expression. I gave him a cheesy grin but couldn't make out anything past his mirrored shades.

"You hungry?" Ben asked over his shoulder, leading us off the floor when the music transitioned.

"I'm always hungry."

"Any requests?"

"Deep-fried and dead is always preferable," I answered.

Ben and I slid into a booth, but before we opened a menu, a stunning woman who introduced herself as Delia came to take our order. Delia looked early thirties and had long, chestnut curly hair with a medium height and build. With full red lips and green cat eyes, she oozed a sex appeal that would make the monogamous toy with the temptation. Her uniform was a short black miniskirt, fishnet hose, spiked heels, and a simple white fitted shirt.

"First timer?" she asked with a grin.

"Second," I said...and, girl, that was the least of it.

While Ben ordered two soft drinks and an appetizer sampler, I gazed at the gyrating dancers, individuals mingling at the bar, and those going to a party upstairs. I could understand the love of the nightclub. The ambience vibrated to perfection with rotating disco balls and strobe lights bouncing off the shiny black floor. But the feeling was not as it had been last weekend with Dylan. Then was all about hard lovin'. Being with Ben was all about business. I had no desire to dally in the meat market.

Ben's affections hadn't been deterred even though I'd doused the goodnight kiss. He'd gone for my hand—and hair—multiple times but stopped dead in the water when Jon Bradshaw and Finn Lively slid into our booth.

Busted. Crap.

I offered them both a sheepish smile and spit out the Coke I attempted to swallow down. "Is this a lynching?" I coughed guiltily, wiping the dribble from my chin.

Grumpy's eyes volleyed like a tennis match, bouncing back and forth between Ben and me. "Taylor's gone, right?" he grumbled.

I saved my breath. It was obvious, or Ben wouldn't be behaving that way...nor would I be here semi-cheating on my hunk of a boyfriend.

Finn laughed hollowly as he appraised Ben and me in a Scottish dialect. "Oh, lassie, so if you admit to nothing, then you're not guilty, aye?"

Heaven must really hate me because right then Ivy walked by. They say imitation is the sincerest form of flattery, right? Freaking Ivy made her hair a Kool-Aid red...ombré style.

"Original much?" I muttered.

She slid into the booth with an even snarkier expression than normal, melting into Grumpy's lap. They'd come together. I stared a hole through his dumb-butt skull and said, "Fool me once, shame on you..."

Grumpy lowered his brown eyes and completed the proverb. "Fool me twice, shame on me. I'm sure that's a phrase going through Taylor's mind right now."

Touché.

Giving Grumpy a quick kiss to the neck, Ivy then focused on me while she twirled her hair. "Ooh, problems with Dylan?" she said and grinned. "How juicy."

Ivy made Regina George from *Mean Girls* look like Snow White. My anger instantly boiled. "No," I seethed. "The only story here is that PETA missed dousing you with cat piss because you've got a dead animal on your back."

Yeah, I said the P-word, and it felt goooooood.

Ivy wore one of those longhaired vests overtop a white turtleneck—she looked like an anorexic yak. "Sticks and stones," she sneered. "Sticks and stones. You do know Brynn is with Dylan, right? It's all over her Twitter feed. I guess they visited Florida today."

Wait. What did she just say? Dylan. Brynn. Together? *But...How?*

"Well, aren't you sweet for letting her know," Ben muttered sarcastically, jumping to my defense.

"Hey, I'm not knocking it," she said, flirting with Ben when she'd obviously come with Grumpy. "Backups are a smart way to do business."

My word. She'd basically called Grumpy an insurance plan...and he'd let her. Was I subconsciously doing the same thing? Murphy was an underwriter, and he always preached one should plan for a rainy day. My life in about five seconds flat had become a freaking thunderstorm.

My brain scrambled for a second, recycling the bliss-inducing make out session from the night before, trying to convince myself it meant something other than hormones needing an outlet. Per usual, Ivy tried to wind her vine of self-doubt around me, but she'd always been of the opinion Dylan and me dating was at the height of ridiculousness anyway.

Surely, that was a pack of lies...er, right?

Refusing to look at Grumpy, I sought out Finn's gaze for corroboration. "I call BS," I said quietly.

"'Tis true, lass," he said even quieter. "I don't know the details, but I *do* know he texted Bradshaw and me both wondering where you were. It seems to me the two of you need to have a talk."

Finn offered a smile, but it never reached his eyes. Something twisted in my chest, and darn Ivy Morrison, she knew it. When her evil grin grew, I slammed the brakes on my emotions and wished her a case of intestinal parasites. I had the perfect opportunity to put her in her place—tell the world just who her lying, conniving, stealing sack of shiz true self was. But I feared if I opened my mouth, a cry of desperation might crawl out. But here's what I knew for sure. When the time was right, I'd bring Grumpy up to speed with Ivy's pastime. I think she registered it in my face because she quickly backpedalled on the Joker smile.

"We're outta here," Grumpy said, sliding himself and Ivy from the seat. "This place reeks of Grey Goose and infidelity."

I didn't smell anything other than my own guilt...and broken heart. "Since when did you become the long arm of the law?" I muttered, shifting in my seat.

Grumpy gave me his bros over 'hos look. "When you forgot all the rules."

———

Seriously. Does. Not. Compute.

When a server delivered our food, I excused myself to answer nature's call and walk off my embarrassment. Finn would never lie to me, so beyond a shadow of a doubt, my boyfriend had spent time with someone who'd wanted him in the Biblical way for years. Was I doing the same thing? Not exactly, and although that little angel on my shoulder swore there was an explanation, I didn't even possess a phone to call Dylan and rake him over the coals. Was I upset? Yes, but I'd watched my mother get slaughtered at age nine. That'd put me in a grave long before Dylan Taylor and any brand of infidelity would.

I went Twisted Sister as I made my way to the restroom. "I'm not gonna take it..." I sang.

I stopped when a guy covered his ears and cringed.

The hallways of Club Need had been painted red and were as crowded as the New York subway. Once I juked around the biggest bevy of people, I bumped headlong into what felt like a brick wall. "Ugh," I wheezed out. "This day sucks."

Shaking my head to clear it, I glanced up and stared straight into the shades of Lars van der Hart's seven-foot goon. Far away, he resembled your typical security detail. Up close and personal, he was your worst nightmare—big, bald, and sweaty. "Hey." I blinked. "Sorry."

Goon said nothing but made no move to get out of the way either. In fact, he backed me down a side corridor until I stumbled and caught myself against the wall. Right then was where I knew for sure I had no sense of self-preservation. I should be scared. Instead, annoyance was the major emotion. "Is there something wrong?" I asked. "I don't have time for anything except my own personal panic attack."

As God as my witness, Goon started reciting the lyrics to "Rock You Like a Hurricane."

"Come again?" I asked confused.

Goon not only recited them...but opened his goon-mouth and sang them. I must say, that was the first time ever someone went Scorpions on me.

The human mind was a crazy thing. Most usually had a little voice in their head that would file the episode under the category of *Kick Him In The Happies And Run*. Call me a fool, but my little voice just stood there with its mouth open. I threw my head back and burst into giggles. In fact, it was so *high*larious I doubled over in pain, caught between laughing my head off and crying my eyes out over Dylan.

"I don't think what I said was funny," he said robotically. I somehow righted myself, turning to leave. Goon, however, grabbed me by the elbow, determined to get cozy.

My eyes slid north to his mirrored shades. "Seriously, I'm flattered, but you've been wearing shades too long. I've got the sex appeal of an onion."

"I like what I see," he said.

"I'm thinking you need a stronger antiperspirant man. Just sayin'."

Unfortunately, Goon gazed at me like he'd hit paydirt. Glancing to his hand that almost doubled around my arm, I spied a tattoo. It had the face of a dragon and body of a snake wrapping around his wrist. I had one of those ah-ha moments because Gabrielle Allen's notes spoke of similar ink Ryder'd received mere days before he'd disappeared. I didn't give much credence at the time, but her description was eerily similar.

At that moment, I heard a deep groaning—and soon after the groaning, came a bleak whispering, "Help me."

My spidey senses started tingling. "Hey," I said. "Did you hear that?"

Goon gave me a strange, even darker look. Although he sported sunglasses, I felt his eyes break through the plastic and attack my sanity. Okay, I'd finally begun to experience the appropriate worry. *I'm not going to lie to you...a little bit of pee came out*...especially when I heard the voice say again, "*Please.*"

What the freakity freak?!

Van der Hart exited the office at the end of the hall, whistling. It took a few beats for his eyes to focus and subsequently rake over Goon and me together. In three long strides, he hovered at my side. "Excuse me," he murmured politely. "Is there any good reason why you and my bodyguard are outside my office?"

"I'm just here doing God's work, bro," I joked. "If you don't mind, I'd like to use the restroom, so I can look for my friend."

"The restroom is in the other hallway," he said, narrowing his green eyes.

"Yeah, about that. Goon here thought I needed a little detour."

He raised a brow at Goon. "Did he now?"

Unfortunately, my mouth had its own agenda...to make me look stupid. "He's not big on manners," I said. "Besides, I have a shizzle of a man piece at home, so I'm not interested in his hurricane. Now if you'll both excuse me, I need to visit the little girl's room and round up my friend."

"A friend?"

"*Was* a friend," I grumbled, stating Marek's pending status. "I'm going to kill him if I lied to my father and lied by omission to my boyfriend to see him in a fight he bailed on."

Van der Hart continued with a customer-service smile. "Sounds like you have a lot of problems."

I repositioned the beanie on my head. "You don't know the half of it."

"Tell me about this fight. Perhaps I can help," Van der Hart said.

I glanced at my watch for the time. "Marek said he planned to throwdown tonight in an underground fight club. Anyway, he was supposed to meet someone here, so I was hoping to run into him. Unfortunately, I've not seen hide nor hair of him."

"Did you phone him?"

"That's the thing. I'm without communication tonight, and it kinda screwed up everything. Which begs the greater philosophical debate, how in God's name did civilization ever survive without cell phones?"

The wheels in Van der Hart's head turned. I could almost smell the burn of the gears. "Haven't we met before?" he asked. "Last weekend? In fact, we actually spoke about this fight club, correct?"

Cleverness said I could play it coy or play it cool. I think I wound up somewhere in between. "I'm Darcy Walker."

There was a brief pause, and then recognition slowly bled into his eyes. "Ah, yes. Darcy Walker. Are you enjoying yourself?"

"Goon here thinks my shama lama wants his ding-dong. I don't."

Van der Hart laughed so loudly it made Goon angry. "It's not a joke if both people don't laugh," Goon seethed.

I rolled my eyes. "Check your math, bud. Two out of three laughed. That's a sixty-six point six, six, six percent success rate. I'd say I hit one out of the park." The guy was on my very last unstable nerve.

While Van der Hart continued to chuckle, his looks changed. Last time we spoke, I noticed four one-inch scars on his right cheek —one running so deeply a layer of flesh seemed to be missing. The scars had grown red in his laughter, reminding me of the agony he must've endured when injured.

I tiptoed up and touched them. He winced in pain or had merely been taken off guard. "Sorry," I said, suddenly embarrassed. "I didn't have a right to touch you."

"You're tender," he said smiling.

Nah, just stupid...

"How in the world did you acquire such deep gashes?" I asked out of curiosity.

"Sometimes things that are worth it...*hurt*." Ouch and sado-masochistic were the two words to initially come to mind. He glanced at the cast on my hand that went to my forearm. "Are you on the mend?"

I'd become so used to the cast, I sometimes forgot I had it. "Yeah, I'm cool."

Van der Hart had changed out of his black shirt into a crisp white button down. Red lipstick smeared on the left side of his collar. Guess he'd had company. "So what's going on out here, Eight Ball?" he asked his bodyguard with a serious face.

"That's your name?" I asked Goon.

Van der Hart smiled and answered for him. "Let's just say that sometimes you don't want to be caught behind him."

A chill snaked down my spine, wondering what he was capable

of. "We were having a private conversation, Boss. I'd like to finish it," he muttered.

Van der Hart placed a palm on Eight Ball's chest. "Down boy," he murmured, chuckling with humor. "Why don't you check on things up front?"

Eight Ball stiffened, raked a lustful gaze over my torso, and reluctantly thundered back to the dance floor.

That's not suggestive, is it? (Hint: It is. It really, really is.)

Glancing at my watch, the time reminded me I needed to scram, but I would've sworn on a stack of Bibles I heard someone behind the wall. "Hey, did you hear anything earlier?"

"Like what?" Van der Hart asked.

"Someone crying for help."

Van der Hart cocked his head to the side, totally speechless. "Seriously?"

"Yeah. It sounded like it came from behind this wall."

I knocked on the wall to my right but was rewarded with silence. Van der Hart frowned and ran his index finger around his lower lip, deep in thought. "Who's your server, Darcy?"

It took a minute to remember. "Delia."

"Tell her Lars said it was on the house. You're not leaving, are you?"

"Yeah. My date is probably going bonkers. Are you sure you didn't hear someone?"

"No, but I promise I'll look into it. Have a nice evening."

The lights went off quicker than a prom dress.

Here's a word of advice for you. If you're ever stuck in a night-club when the lights go out, pray to God you're by the exit sign. Thankfully, Ben and I had one foot outside when the entire block's electricity went poof. He grabbed my hand before we were trampled in the rush and led us into a night air cold enough to freeze you into a snowman. It was past midnight. I'd missed my curfew, but Murphy was in no position to lecture me because I had no cell phone. Texting him from Ben's phone, I informed him we were homeward bound. As expected, he texted back with a, *Grrr. You're dead.*

I didn't want a date with God...not yet. But then again, God might be friendlier than Murphy.

I blew warm air into my hands, bringing it up to cover my nose. "Did you see anything suspicious?" I mumbled behind my fingers.

"A few tattoos on hands," Ben said. "But they were only on the good-looking servers who seemed brainwashed."

Hmmm. Eight Ball had a tattoo...he'd jive with the brainwashed part but certainly not on the good-looking part. I scanned the crowd for Marek. All I saw were bodies scrambling for cars and cops trying to corral the chaos of intersections without traffic lights. The bottom had fallen out of my plan, and the fact Ben grabbed my hand wasn't so great for my reputation, especially when students from VHS noticed with dropped jaws. A spike of adrenaline hit me, chased by hot tears screaming I was a cheat. Yanking my hand away, I stepped off the curb, but a car came from nowhere, revving its engine. Ben cursed and pulled me out of its path, and I quickly shifted my gaze up to glimpse a yellow Dodge Charger. The driver peeled rubber on a long *vrooooommm*, paused, and turned the corner, almost like he'd acknowledged I'd seen him.

Don't cry because it's over. Smile because it happened.

—Dr. Seuss

Chapter Twenty

JUDAS KISS

*L*unch was a burnt grilled cheese sandwich.

Stuffing the last bite in my mouth, I chased it with a can of Coke and stared at the clothes in my closet. I hadn't seen Dylan since our early morning make-out session, and I wanted to make sure my body said *Kiss me, stud* instead of *Trade me in*.

When I crawled into command central the night before, I discovered he'd texted eight times, FaceTimed twice, and even left a video—a video wherein the cap on his head was positioned and repositioned numerous times, evidential proof he was under duress. As I'd waited for sleep to claim me, I eyeballed the video half a dozen times, wondering how we'd come to such a place in our relationship. I'd tell you why...sometimes I had good ideas. Sometimes I had bad ideas. Long and short of it? I. Sucked.

Here was what the video said:

"Darc, it's me. I can only assume you're still out with Ben Ryan. I'm not sure what that's about, but obviously we need to have a talk. Please meet me at the four o'clock movie tomorrow afternoon. I'd pick you up, but I won't be back in time, so I'll just meet you there. Just know that I love you, yeah? Know I would never do anything to jeopardize us. My God, Darc, my feelings haven't changed in twenty-four hours. I'm still crazy about you. Nothing and no one will ever change that."

But it felt like something had died. I just wasn't sure who'd pulled the trigger.

As I punched my legs in some super skinny jeans, I threw a gray sweater over my head and *67'd my phone, dialing Tito. Unfortunately, I took a trip to voicemail. Hearing Murphy yell my name twice, I sputtered out a message. "Jester, here. I visited Club Need last night and would swear on the Holy Book I heard someone begging for help behind a wall. I'll phone back later because it's mission critical we speak."

I then phoned Marek. Unfortunately, Marek was more gone than Ivy Morrison's virginity. Sliding my phone in my back pocket, I padded to the bathroom and stared at my reflection. I utilized the mirror only on-demand. I was thin enough, but no matter how many squats or lunges I performed, I couldn't make myself look like the girls who only ate rice cakes. After I fluffed my hair, I swiped on some mascara right as Murphy made it to the door. He'd just wakened from a nap, his hair kinked out like he'd stuck his finger in a light socket and enjoyed the buzz. "Kid, I'm worried about you. You've hit DEFCON 1. Maybe, uh..." he paused wincing, "maybe we need to take another trip back to counseling."

He might as well have thrown boiling water in my face. After I gave him a nuclear-reactor gaze, I placed the wand back in the dispenser and strung Dylan's class ring on a chain and clasped it behind my neck. I refused to think it would be the last time I'd wear it, but I guess I should prepare myself for the worst. "And your reasoning for that?" I asked.

Murphy leaned a shoulder up against the doorjamb, glancing down at his sweatpants and old shirt. If memory served me correctly, he'd worn the same outfit the day before. "You're self-destructing," he said. "You've probably destroyed your relationship with Dylan, and you talked about your mother in front of Marjorie."

Ah, the irony. I snorted to myself. I wouldn't have spoken about my mother if he would've been a little bit more forthcoming in the information department. "If you think I'm going to uncover some repressed memory," I said with a glare, staring at his reflection in the mirror, "you're wrong."

The only thing I repressed was my fist, which wanted to find its way inside his mouth.

"You need to cash out, kid. You need to regroup and think about the things that are important here. Chasing old demons won't do anything except get you hurt and everyone else."

"So you admit there's something to chase?"

Murphy's face darkened. "I didn't say that."

I brushed past him and grabbed my coat on the bed, sliding my feet into nearby black UGGs. "May I have your keys?" I asked. "I'm meeting friends at the movies. It's a class assignment."

Murphy dug them out of his pocket and laid them in my palm. When I made a move for the door, he snagged me by the elbow and pulled me into a hug. A hug I did not return. "Kid, I love you. Trust me on this. Let it go."

_____

I loved my father, but sometimes he was grossly misinformed to what I was capable of. Maneuvering Murphy's Camry into the closest parking space available, I jumped over two muddy puddles and hotfooted it to the entrance of AMC Theatre. A cold knot twisted in my stomach. I had a feeling someone watched me, and if a person could step on my future grave, then they did a dance on it with zero respect.

To pile on the worry, Red phoned at that second and dropped a grenade. She claimed Mr. Himmel had once again gnawed off his ankle bracelet and was running in the wind. "He what?" I asked, stopping at the door to finish the call.

"Art Himmel sawed off his ankle bracelet and is unaccounted for. Valley PD is currently pounding the pavement with bloodhounds looking for his ass. Once he's found, he's going into lockup, but until then, grow some eyes in the back of your head."

Sonovabiscuit eater. Just what I needed. Another crisis sitch. I pulled my coat tighter, feeling the walls closing in. "Ten-four, kimosabi," I said.

"Murphy told me you're at the movies," she added. "A black and white is on its way to shadow you and escort you home. Keep an eye out for them."

Again, I unloaded a, "Ten-four, kimosabi," but shut down the call when she asked how I'd been doing emotionally. How the H did she think I'd been doing emotionally? My life sucked. My relationship with Dylan sucked. That was double-suckage, which was pretty darn bad.

I pushed open the door. The ticket line wound around the hallway like a snake, harboring students from school and folks who'd obviously missed opening night. I didn't see any close friends, but then again, my eyes were instantly preoccupied. Leaning up against the wall, slowly waving an extra ticket back and forth in his hand was Dylan.

Frustratingly, looking as good as ever.

My breath froze in my throat. Dylan Taylor kicked my hormones into high gear, and all those feelings regarding male and female anatomy made me wish he were a Jesuit priest in Central America. If a shot existed to make him look repulsive, then push me to the front of the line.

My legs felt like lead as I weaved my way in and out of the heavy crowd. Dylan seemed bone-tired but managed a smile, wearing a dark pair of jeans and a V-neck, camel-colored sweater—the perfect complement to his uniquely colored eyes.

"Hey," he said softly.

"Hey," I echoed back.

There was a moment here where the Earth stood still. Neither of us knew what to say or made a move to get physical. Personally? I was wrong. I was so dead wrong in going with Ben I didn't even know how to approach the subject. I broke the standoff first with a mealy mouthed, c'est la vie attitude that was horrid.

"Why didn't you tell me Brynn was going with you?" I asked.

Dylan rubbed a palm over an eye, wincing at my lack of affection. "I had no idea. Dad had no idea. Sometimes he gets pulled into situations because of his job."

"Please explain. I'm alllllllll earrrs."

Dylan took a weary breath. "When Brynn's father heard about our trip, he phoned early Saturday morning and asked if they could hitch a ride. Apparently, he has a deal down there going south."

Okay, I'd buy that. "Makes sense," I said, "but what doesn't make sense is why Brynn hitched a ride too."

Another palm to the eyes. "I suppose she's considering Florida as a college also."

Stake to the heart. "How convenient," I answered.

Dylan's temper showed a tiny bit of itself. "And how convenient for you that the moment I leave town you go clubbing with Ben Ryan. I texted you multiple times. Too many fricking times to count and said, *We need to talk. I love you. Please call.*"

True, he *had* made an effort, but I'd been without communication. And when my iPhone was in-hand, all I'd done was read his texts and reply back with an impersonal, "Okay." I should apologize...I didn't.

Dylan's voice turned raspy with pain. "Darc, something is wrong," he said, reaching for me. "Murphy said something is very wrong right now, and it's got him all torn up."

He didn't seem so torn up to me, I mumbled to myself. "You talked to Murphy?"

"Did you think I'd give up trying to find you?" he said shocked.

To be honest, I wasn't sure what I thought. All I knew was I felt so unconnected to him...and part of that...if not all...was my fault. I heard a jigsaw in my head, and by the panicked look in his face, he obviously felt and heard the new jumble. Our destinies were separating. Dylan dropped the hand that'd reached for mine, and I noticed it trembled.

"I assumed Brynn was keeping you occupied," I muttered, immediately knowing that wasn't fair.

Dylan opened his mouth, closed it, and then spoke so slowly it was like he tried to converse with someone who only read lips. "I'm not going to sling mud with you, Darcy. I know you went to Club Need *before* you even found out about Brynn and her father. That tells me something is so wrong you didn't care how it would make me feel."

"That's not exactly true," I said quietly, tears stinging my eyes.

"Then explain it to me," he said even quieter. When I didn't respond, he said softly, "Darc, you told me Friday night in so many words that something was bothering you, yet you refused to be specific. You had to know I wouldn't let this thing go."

Murphy was right. I'd truly hit my self-destruct button. I looked at Dylan's gorgeous mug and offer him nothing but respirations. But here was what I knew to be true: he had no intention of conceding the discussion. He'd poke and prod and wear me down until I saw things his way and even thanked him for breaking me.

A tingly feeling slithered over my arms and legs, convincing me again someone had been watching me. Darting my eyes back and forth, Dylan interpreted my scatterbrained look like my head wasn't in the game—I wasn't invested in the conversation. He massaged his heart like he tried to find a sinus rhythm. "Darc, what's wrong?" he asked, closing the distance between us. "Talk to me. I've felt something wrong between us all weekend."

I swallowed the tears, my body language saying, "Trust me," my dumb-butt mouth saying not a single word. I felt a million eyes and even bigger amount of questions on the two of us. In that second, Brynn came out of the woodwork, carrying an extra-large popcorn and drink, toting a purse the size of a small dog. Ho. Ly. Moth. Er. Did she come too?

"Did you bring a date?" I snapped.

Dylan frowned. "What?" he said. I didn't even grace him with a repeat. Instead, I shot daggers through Brynn and her expensive pink sweater and jeans. She leaned up against the pinball machine with Trudi Hatchett and Jagger Cane. The cool crowd. And by God, she painted on a sheepish smile, like she was all bashful and inno- cent. "Darc," Dylan said softly, "I didn't hear you. Do you want to blow out of here? We can go somewhere by ourselves and talk. We *need* to talk...please." Once again, I couldn't shake the feeling someone had been scoping me out. Whatever feeling of unease I'd had earlier tripled, with a side order of dodge-a-bullet-fast. "You know I love you, yeah?" he murmured with more force.

I nodded, uncertainly. Dylan didn't lie. Still, my self-doubt convinced me it was best to keep my secrets to myself. I would not tell him about my mother...even if that meant...*we parted ways*.

"Want some popcorn?" I heard. "It's a nice golden brown."

Awwwesome...juuusssssst awesome.

Bean had dirt under his bitten-to-the-quick nails, aggressively offering Dylan a handful of popcorn that resembled burnt ash. When Dylan politely declined, Bean offered it to me after Mr. Pongo, of course, took a hypothetical nibble. I held up a palm. Bean meant well, bless his heart, but he had a crappy sense of timing. "Seriously, Bean," I said. "I heard you loud and clear, bud. Nix the popcorn."

Sometimes it felt like the universe conspired against me. Or in my case, maybe it saved Dylan from a best friend who didn't deserve him. To prove my theory, when Bean scampered off to do Bean things, Ben appeared next to Brynn and watched Dylan and me who'd become the proverbial dinner theater. Dylan glanced behind him to see what—or should I say whom—I'd been staring at. "Are you kidding me?" he said lowly. "How the hell did we stop being a couple?"

You couldn't escape the stubborn defiance in his jaw. Crap, shoot, the F-bomb and everything unholy flew through my mind because I deserved whatever would come my way. We had one of our infamous, silent conversations.

What has happened to us? he asked confused.

I don't know, I said.

But why, Darcy?

Hello, Rock. Meet Hard Place. I wanted to uncover the secrets of my mother's death more than I wanted him. Deep in my soul, I knew I was about to do something that couldn't be undone, but I looked at Dylan...looked at Ben...and sniffled out, "I'm so confused."

So yes...

In that moment, it looked as if my problem boiled down to picking between Hot Boy A and Hot Boy B, but I didn't know how to shake Dylan otherwise. A feeling touched his face that I couldn't immediately discern. Almost like he'd never met me before, and it was our first introduction. My feelings were raw, stripped naked. Was it possible for someone to make you want to hurl just by looking at the person? It was. I had some crud in my throat to confirm it. I broke down and bawled in public—right there for the Skank Squad and anyone else who was curious to see.

Dylan didn't care that I'd practically exiled him back to single life. He wrapped me in his arms, giving me his patented I'd-eat-a-bullet-for-you face. "I love you. I'm also *in love* with you. Can you say those words to me?"

In all my years of dysfunction, my gut had never let me down. Fear trampled me like a herd of hippos outrunning a poacher. Someone was definitely watching us, other than the peanut gallery witnessing me nuke our relationship. Taking my lower lip between my teeth, I furiously glanced around, wondering if I should tackle

Dylan to the ground lest a bullet miss me and find its mark in his chest. Nothing seemed out of the ordinary. No Himmel anywhere, but someone was. When I finally met Dylan's gaze, I saw the life drain out of him when I didn't return the sentiment. "I'm sorry," he apologized hoarsely. "I understand I might've forced something on you that you didn't feel quite as deeply as me. I just—"

I panicked, his pain like acid on my skin. "D—" I interrupted in a shaky voice. "Just...give me a sec. Something's wrong here—"

He adamantly shook his head, the expression in his voice like he waited to absorb a blow. "Please, let me finish. If I don't finish now, I'm never going to be able to get the words out. Darcy, can you only be with me?" My God, he referred to Ben. There really was no other way for Dylan to interpret my lack of response other than a turn-down. "It's okay," he exhaled, voice cracking. "You don't love me the way I love you. Just give me time. Give me time to wrap my head around loving you...and *losing you*. I promise I'll get there, but I just need...time."

Hearing him murmur my name always brought me to my knees. But Dylan sad? That could drive me to my grave quicker than anything else. His amber eyes looked like they belonged on a dying animal—beat up, streaked with pain, with a little flicker of life left. These actions were everything that Dylan wasn't. He never backed down, he never surrendered, and he never shared whatever it was he wanted. For the first time ever, I witnessed a crack form in the most confident person I'd ever met.

After a few seconds of disbelief, Dylan gave me the movie ticket and bit back the tears. Cradling my face in his hands, he brushed his lips against mine, squared his shoulders, and split the crowd. Did it make me a loser I noticed he looked amazing as he walked away? Confident, arms strong, head held high—everything that I needed at the moment? Brynn slowly followed after, pitching her head over her shoulder in a you're-never-getting-him-back face.

For once, I feared she might be right.

———

Listen, I came to the movies with a bad attitude and got real generous in dishing it out. I shouldn't be shocked I wound up alone.

I'd stolen into a theater by myself and watched the entire movie—coughing, snorting, gasping, and crying like a lovesick fool. On some level, I thought Dylan would sniff me out and force the issue. My heart completely broke in two when he didn't.

My chest heaved with regret as I dialed his parent's home. Was I embarrassed? Yes. But you know what? Life's a beeyotch, and then you die. I pulled on my big girl panties and forced my inner-idiot back into its cave.

"How was the movie, dear?" Dylan's mother asked when she picked up the call.

"Crummy," I said, swallowing down a sniffle.

"Oh, really?" she soothed. "I'm sorry."

"I need to talk to Dylan," I said sheepishly. "Is he back home yet?"

The sound through the receiver was so quiet you could've heard a pin drop. And it was even quieter here. I wasn't sure what had gone down with Murphy, but I'd heard him shouting thirty minutes earlier—Red and Rookie on the receiving end. M had gone to bed early, my guess due to stress. I wish I was the type that could sleep my problems away. Instead, I lay curled under my covers, your standard breakup kit surrounding me—pint of chocolate ice cream, Oreos, recent photographs, really awful poetry I'd written, and a copy of *Seventeen* magazine telling me how to deal with rejection.

"I assumed he was with you, Darcy. Did you try his cell?"

"About ten times. I'm verging on stalker territory." As soon as my butt hit the seat of Murphy's Camry, I'd started stalker dialing. Dylan ignored my every attempt to reach him, some going to voicemail, some stuck in a repeated ring.

She laughed, and even her laugh was filled with class, femininity, and grace. I sighed deeply. My God, she was Brynn Hathaway. "I was under the impression you couldn't stalk your boyfriend, honey. Maybe he's in a dead zone."

My voice was a whisper. "Or maybe he just doesn't want to talk to me."

"What's wrong?" she murmured, voice getting alarmed.

"He was at the movies, Mrs. Taylor. I met him there, and then... well, things didn't end on a great note."

Gosh, I sounded pathetic, but only a few answers made sense.

Number one, he didn't want to talk to me. Number two, he was with someone who'd more than likely been comforting him. Number three, he'd moved on.

"I'm confused, dear. You're going to have to explain."

"Has he spoken with you?"

"Yes, about ten minutes ago. He was with a group of friends. I assumed you were with him."

"Was Brynn with him? Please," I begged. "Just tell me."

Nothing, and then she said, "Yes." I gasped at the admission. "Honey, would you believe me if I said there must be some logical explanation?"

"Friday, I would've. Today, not so much."

"Aw, Darcy, what's going on? I know the two of you are committed to one another, but Dylan hasn't been himself since Friday evening. I've tried to talk to him, but he's being uncharacteristically tight-lipped with his feelings. Am I correct in saying his change of mood has to do with your relationship?"

"If you mean, am I at fault, then yes." I blew my nose and sounded like a complete loser.

A light sigh. "That's not what I said."

"No, but it's what you meant, but you were nice enough to not say it so offensively."

"Nothing could be further from the truth. He adores you, and you're his first thought every morning."

"You said yourself he was different. Trust me, he doesn't want me around."

I heard the rustling of fabric, like she slid her arms through a coat. "Let me come and get you. I don't like the way you sound. May I speak with your father?"

A gasp fell out of my mouth. "I don't feel welcome there anymore." I broke down and blubbered like a walrus.

"What the hell," I heard his father say. "What in God's name did my son do?"

"Colt, settle down," she said.

I jumped to Dylan's defense. "Nothing. He didn't do anything." My word, had she placed me on speaker?

"A disagreement like this takes two people, Darcy," Colton

murmured. "I've been around long enough to know that, and believe me I know my son lives to have the last word."

"I humiliated him...but I didn't mean to."

Susan Taylor started talking again, but Colton spoke overtop her. "You need to give me more to work with, Darcy," he murmured.

"I was just being me...doing the things I do...and Dylan didn't fit into this particular plan...he was sort of collateral damage."

"Collateral damage," he said.

"Yeah," I gasped. "He thinks I was cheating on him."

Colton didn't miss a beat. "Were you?" he asked in a clinical tone.

"No. God, no. But since we've been dating, Dylan tells me he's *in love* with me. And he told me how much he really cared right when I was in the middle of...this something. Dylan does everything publicly and at warp speed. I didn't know how to...what to...do. I would never hurt him. I just wanted to get questions answered before we got all let's-bare-our-souls with one another. It was totally insensitive and selfish for me to think he'd wait around until I was in the mood for that discussion, but I planned to have it. I swear. Plus," my voice cracked, "Brynn was there. It made me angry. She's always cared for him, and it hurt me that she shadowed him all weekend long while I was in Valley, continuing to be the loser I am." Silence for a bit. "You know I'm playing with a handicap, right? I'm not normal. I do things other people don't do. He should be with someone normal, like Brynn—"

"Aw, dear," he interrupted sympathetically. "Let me break this down. Dylan knew something was amiss and pushed you to open up?"

"Yes, sir."

"So you allowed him to believe it was better off for you two to be apart than drag him into whatever this is?"

"Yes," I said. My word, I sniffled and snorted like a baby pig.

"Do we need to talk about what you're working on?"

I'd already lived through every child's darkest fear...abandonment. Something like that aged you on the spot and killed the instinct that told you when you needed an adult's help. "Probably," I said, sniffling like an idiot, "but I can do things on my own."

"Dammit," he cursed, "I've witnessed the way you do things on your own. I'm calling him."

"Colt," his wife eased, "settle down."

"Why?" he said. "This needs to stop because I can't put up with his mood swings any longer."

Some talking on their end. "Darcy, let me come and get you," his mother requested once more. "I promise I won't interfere, but I'll be happy to sit quietly as you iron out your differences. May I speak with Murphy?"

I rubbed my forehead furiously, an attempt to reprogram my warped sense of values. "Just tell Dylan I care, okay? Our relationship hasn't been some sort of Judas kiss. As much as I don't understand or know how it happened, he's the only person I care about in the way you're supposed to care about the opposite sex. This has been hard for me. Putting him off has been hard for me, and I don't even think he realizes or understands why I've been hot and cold. I'm afraid of how he makes me feel. When he hugs me, he hugs a place deep inside that no one else has ever touched. Something shifts in my soul. Emotionally, I fear him. I fear what he could do to me if he one day goes away."

"He won't go away," Colton said softly.

Another nose blow that sounded like a foghorn. My word, I had boogers everywhere. "Yes, he will," I disputed. "College is around the corner. All three of us know I don't qualify to attend the places he'll want to go...the places that'll offer him the best opportunity. And there's my little sister," I said with a sniffle. "Even if I could, I can't make her sad like I was made sad." And that's all she wrote. I didn't even try to hold back anymore because everything boiled down to my mother. "I can't survive another loss like my mom. I barely made it out the first time. You both know I have OCD because of it. I have eye twitches that might as well be terminal because my nervous system is so freaked up. I never did any of those things until she was gone. I feel a little crack form in my heart each time he walks out the door, wondering if he'll ever return. Dylan brought me back the first time, but who'll bring me back if it's him who decides to go? I can't go there with him. I want to...I just don't know how."

I was pretty sure I heard them both swallow because I'd done everything except officially utter the three magic words. Colton muttered something else, followed by, "Susan, I knew they were close...but not like...I feel sick."

"Please, dear," his mother said more sternly. "You're breaking my heart. Let Colt and me help. These are words my son needs to hear. I can promise he's been waiting to hear those words for some time. Go grab your coat because I'm coming to get you."

I hung up without a goodbye and struck the red button on my iPhone. Then I yanked the house phone from the wall and shut down Murphy's cell, as not to chance him picking up.

If I were to be honest...wait for it, people...I kinda-sorta was in love with my best friend (cough, cough) and how in the heck did that happen? I needed to deep freeze my feelings. Unfortunately, the message never made it to my tear ducts because I couldn't stop the tears. And it wasn't a little cry. It was a snot-rolling-into-my-mouth cry. Dab my eyes. Blow. Blow. Look like an idiot. Dab some more.

Chapter Twenty-One
STRANGER DANGER

*W*ell, that went well.

To make matters worse, I had no idea I was such a cluster mess in the communications department either. Here was confirmation I was unstable. Not only had I broken up with my boyfriend, I'd cried about my mistake to his parents and then shut down all modes of communication, only to call again later because the guilt-slash-regret wouldn't shut up in my brain. But that was me, wasn't it? Darcy Walker was always balls-to-the-wall, never thinking about anything except being a verb.

"D?" I said when he finally answered with a formal hello. "Where are you?"

His voice was nothing but business. "Still in my car. I haven't gone in the house yet."

"Have you talked to your parents?"

"Like I said, I haven't gone in the house."

Not that his parents would've given me a vote of confidence, but the wimp in me hoped they'd broken the ice. "Oh," I said.

"What does 'oh' mean?" he barked.

"It was just a response. No hidden meaning."

"Of course, there's no hidden meaning," he said, snorting in anger. "You've made your feelings abundantly clear. I just never thought you'd be a cheat. I thought we were exclusive, Darcy. What the hell..."

Dylan's mood had gone seismic. Not at all as desperate as he'd been earlier. "Dylan, it's not what—"

"On this one, I choose to trust my eyes," he interrupted. "Number one, you lied; and number two, you went on a date with someone the moment I left town. A guy who has been crushing on you since fricking Christmas. A guy I know still calls you, but I've looked the other way. I can't look the other way anymore."

"I understand what it looks like. Please, you're my best friend—"

He cut me off again, bringing out the heavy artillery. "You took the words right out of my mouth!" he roared. "No matter what, we were never supposed to do something like this to the other. My whole existence has been to protect you, and now I want to..." Dylan stopped, his voice instantly racked with grief. "You're right. You're right," he muttered almost to himself. "The two of us together was a mistake. But I don't know how to go back. You make me feel things I never expected..." He slammed a gridlock on his words again, like confiding in me wasn't as safe as it used to be.

When Dylan got even more emotional, I handled things the way I usually did...by putting my foot in my mouth. "I didn't kiss him even though he tried, D. I swear it."

Gah. I sucked.

"Wow. I feel so much better. The fact he was even close enough to try is the real issue, Darcy."

I patted my thumping heart. "You're right," I said, quickly copping to it. "But just let me explain. It's more complicated than you think."

"I understand fully well. You want to be with Ben Ryan, too, and I don't like to share. I've made my feelings one hundred percent clear—embarrassingly so—and I've become so damn territorial I've surprised even myself. But I've always believed the things worth having are above embarrassment or the judgment of those around me. It doesn't matter what anyone outside the relationship feels or thinks. It's just between the two people involved. It's become painfully clear that the two entities I thought to be in this relationship are not the two who should be—it's just me and my stubborn pride that thought we could be together. I get it now...I get it," he said, his voice suddenly soft. "I know you love me. I don't doubt that at all, but it's not the type of love I'd hoped and prayed for."

Those words came out in a strangled whisper. Dylan always moved me, but my attempt to wear him down with sincerity had been a verbal car crash. Our conversation would haunt me 'til the day I went to the Great Beyond. A crying jag hit me at the worst possible time because I couldn't talk even though that was what I wanted to do more than anything.

"Maybe it's for the best," he whispered. "I can't do this anymore, Darc. I can't do the handholding...or the sitting on my lap...and God knows I can't handle the emotions you stir up in me when you nuzzle your nose into my neck and sigh. I realize things are going to change going forward, but we can write those terms as we go."

My heart crashed into my ribs. "Our rrr-relationship will have t-tterms?" I stammered, because when did best friends ever have terms?

Dylan acted as if he choked on his own oxygen. He began to cry, mumbling over and over, "How in the world did it come to this?"

"D, wait...I need to tell you something." I'd tell him. He'd understand. He'd help me discover the information for Jaws, and we'd figure this thing out together. "D-DDylan," I cried louder. "Listen to me. I need to tell you what I've done."

"Not tonight, Darc," he finished in a whisper. "I can't talk anymore."

Before my mouth could get with the program, the proverbial dial tone buzz-buzzz'd in my ear.

Our relationship just flatlined.

Panic itself kicked me out of bed.

That reunion with Dylan? I tanked that opportunity. Exhibit A, he'd hung up on me. Exhibit B, he hadn't phoned as my wake-up call. Technically, I was as single as a dollar bill. Was it good for my undercover career? Sure. But why couldn't I convince my heart?

After I dressed in clothes to die for, I grabbed the wooden stool from M's and my adjoining restroom and gingerly removed the antique jewelry box on the top shelf of my closet. I hadn't touched it in a year, and hadn't opened it for five. For some reason, I wanted to sift through its contents. Stepping down to the floor, I dropped into a squat and unlatched the lid on the wooden two-by-three foot chest Grandpa Winston had made my mother when Murphy proposed.

Inside were newspaper clippings about The Minstrel Cramps, an unsigned record deal contract from superstar agent Randy Kuligowski and Moon Glow Records, a gold locket from Murphy's mom, concert stubs, a photograph of my maternal grandparents, and fan letters to my mom. Folded up in a nice, tight square was a fuchsia satin cape she'd made for me. I wanted to be a big time wrestler when I was eight...my name to be DEFCON DARCY. Longing to be notorious in the ring, I planned to be the girl who wore legitimate boxing gloves—don't knock it. It made sense to an eight-year-old. Slowly removing the cape from the box, I brought it to my cheek and closed my eyes, hoping to catch a glimpse of my mother. After several seconds of numb wishing, I placed everything back inside and returned it to the shelf, using the same amount of care I'd removed it with and made my way downstairs.

My body ached all over, and if there was such a thing as internal black and blue marks, then I'd gone the equivalent of twelve rounds in a title fight. When Dylan and I fought...*we fought*. Determined to make the day count, I pulled on my Scarlett O'Hara, guzzled down a Coke, and parked my butt at the breakfast bar. Murphy had made biscuits and gravy in enough lard to sink a battleship. I took four obligatory bites and then binged on M&Ms, purging all of my demons...well, almost.

My actions, I feared, were irrevocable. I needed to get back into Dylan's good graces. I'd make one last ditch attempt to resuscitate our relationship, even if I had to yank him out of first period and strip. If that proved to be a no-go, I'd move on until I crossed the finish line for Jaws, and then I'd go at Dylan again like a dog on a bone. Since I didn't want Murphy to know our status was pending, I texted Bean and asked for a ride. Stuffing my English lit paper in my backpack, I zipped my coat to my chin and laced up my Chuck Taylors for luck, heading for the door.

Murphy grabbed me by the hair and spun me around. His face was broad with a smile, a rarity for a man whose normal emotions ranged from PO'd to sort of PO'd. "Remember we get your stitches out after school."

"Yup."

"And try not to worry about anything, kid. This year is going to be a lollapalooza. I've got a good feeling." Oh. Shiz. With Murphy's luck, he could've killed Hitler and got arrested for murder. My guess was he'd just sealed our fates not even knowing it.

"Prophetic," I muttered and then slung my Beats around my neck, kissing him and Marjorie goodbye.

One step outside, and I became a fan of global warming. A huge gust of wind blew ice speckles in my face, and the trees bent at such sharp angles they appeared in danger of snapping in two. Paralyzed with cold, I hobbled-slash-jogged to the entrance of BTCC and waited for Bean and his father. While I checked my texts for a "Roger that" from Bean—didn't find one—I scrolled through a couple unanswered messages from the night before.

Grumpy. Finn. Both Dylan's parents. Red. Rookie. Right as I had my finger on Dylan's mother's text, my iPhone vibrated with another message. Ermergherd, Indigo Chase:

DARCY! she typed in all caps, shouting. *I NEED YOUR HELP. IT'S MAREK. HE'S GONE!*

Indigo wasn't the sharpest tool in the shed, but since I hadn't hooked up with Marek on Saturday, nor had he returned my dozen or so texts, I dialed to see if her definition of gone was the same as mine. Straight to voicemail.

Ugh. My brain flip-flopped. I quickly thumbed back a message for her to meet me at locker twelve and accepted a call from Vinnie when Kongos's "Come With Me Now" broke the silence.

"Hey, V," I muttered, dancing back and forth to keep warm.

"What's wrong, Dolce?"

"Dylan and I broke up." A silence the length of the Gobi Desert ensued. "Yeah. You heard right, and I could use a drink."

"You don't drink."

"Today might be a good day to start."

"Did you wear makeup?"

"Affirmative."

"Then don't cry. Looking good is the best revenge. Do you want me to kick his ass?" There were milk cows that moved faster than Vinnie Vecchione, but if anyone could kick Dylan's tush, it would be him.

"I'm hoping for a reconciliation."

"Your fault or his?"

"Whose do you think?"

More silence. "I can't imagine him ever not forgiving you. Hold on, Dolce."

I didn't get to tell him I'd seen the Dodge Charger myself, but it was first on the docket when he came back live.

BTCC was one creepy-butt neighborhood in the dark. Sunrise was close to seven-thirty this time of year, and I had about twenty more minutes of the moon to suffer through. A black stretch limousine pulled into the front of the neighborhood and stopped. The driver rolled down his window and lifted his phone to his eyes, like he checked a GPS address. Around sixty or so years old with a butler look about him, his arms were thin and sinewy as he gripped the wheel, his hair a salt-and-pepper gray as it peeked out from a black chauffeur cap. Someone must be going on a business trip. No one would come into BTCC with a limo for a reason other than that.

"Sir, are you waiting for someone?" I asked. He took one last gander at the phone and then smiled at me. No answer. "Sir?" I asked again. "Maybe I can point you in the right direction." I went back to Vinnie, rewarded with a dropped call.

"Dang it," I muttered.

When the driver didn't do anything except tilt his head toward me, I pulled a complete-180 on the conversation and decided to dial Bean. It rang twice and went to voicemail. Scratching my forehead with my cast, I pulled out my necklace and gave Dylan's ring a kiss then nerded out and played *Clash of Clans* while I waited. I had only a second's warning before the back seat of the stretch opened and out popped a man close to seven feet tall dressed in black, wearing a toboggan. It took a few beats for my brain to catch up to my eyes, but when it did, I realized right then was a capital OMG moment. I gazed into the dead-eyed stare of someone who'd lost his soul many years before.

Eight Ball...

Mother-trucking Eight Ball had come looking for me. And he had on leather gloves. Just a stab in the dark, but my guess was that wasn't a good sign.

I took off at top speed toward Bison Boulevard, but Eight Ball was at my heels like a wolf charging a sheep. Dropping my backpack and purse to the ground didn't free me up fast enough because he lunged for my hair, dragging me back toward the limo like a caveman. My Beats fell off. My necklace with Dylan's ring snapped and tumbled to the ground. I screamed. I screamed like a gosh-danged monkey. Pawing behind me, my arms flailed like a dying fish on the wharf. I tried to fight like a badass chick, but my butt-kicking skills were silenced when he dropped an elbow to my head. The bang hurt so much I sucked in air through my teeth.

I thought, *This is the time you learn to pray, Darcy.* I wanted my conversations with God to be meaningful, but all I could mutter was a, "Holy heck, this guy is bonkers."

Ergh. A freshman attempt.

It should probably be scary, but sad thing was I was angry I actually looked good. I'd flossed, flat-ironed my hair, doused myself with body spray, and had on a black crochet hoodie sweater that made you theorize on what was underneath. But then douchebag Eight Ball had to go and ruin everything. I continued to kick and fight against his savagely powerful grip, breaking out the passenger side window with my foot. In a one-handed throw, he tossed me in the backseat with the force of a thunderbolt, holding me facedown. Realizing I still gripped my phone in my hand, I spoke my address into the GPS, hoping someone would ping my phone and realize I'd been abducted in my own neighborhood.

After Eight Ball instructed the driver to, "Take us home," he then bent down into my ear and said, "Who's the joke on now?"

I'd hoped *him* because I'd hit the record button, attempting to record the conversation. Craning my head backward, I looked into his black eyes and saw...nothing. Nothing but a machine. I shoved my phone under my torso and left it there when I felt a sharp pinch in my hip, and then it was lights out to his psychotic hum.

———

I read somewhere a child goes missing every forty seconds in the United States. And during that abduction, the first three hours were the most crucial because seventy-five percent were killed within that timeframe. I wasn't sure how long I'd been out, but my contacts were plastered to my eyeballs, and I sat in a room so dark I couldn't see my own hand.

I mentally patted my body down, inspecting for injuries. Being a female, one could imagine where my mind went first. I was all about fornication in the right setting with the appropriate bling on your finger, but the number one requirement would be for me to be conscious and agreeable. My lady parts felt intact, so I was pretty sure I was still a virgin, but whatever Eight Ball injected me with left me fairly incoherent. Just picking up on the context clues, I'd say it was some sort of knockout drug. All I knew was Eight Ball had been the one to throw me in the backseat of the limousine. And unfortunately for me, his tastes went far beyond the normal vanilla. I remember him humming, "Rock You Like a Hurricane."

As far as I was concerned, he could keep his hurricane to himself.

The accommodations weren't exactly five-star. The homespun whackadoodle had me sitting in a wooden chair, my hands and legs bound behind my back with duct tape. Okaaaay. I'd been kidnapped —not a bullet I wanted to add to my résumé, still here we were. But it wasn't a wrong place/wrong time sort of thing. How utterly ironic Eight Ball had come after me like Butch Lawrence had shadowed my mother. As they say, *Life is stranger than fiction*.

A scream tore from my chest, but after several more minutes of expelling cries for help, I realized all I'd done was wear myself out. My only hope would be to get in his head and help him find a conscience—or twist him up so badly he started to make mistakes. With what strength I had left, I hopped backward until I hit the wall and scooted and bounced all around the perimeter of the room, feeling the space with my legs. Best I could tell, I sat on a concrete surface, probably a basement—maybe fifteen feet by fifteen feet, the cold draft traveling up my black leggings.

I'd been in a few situations before where I believed there to be no way out, but those situations served as a mere warm-up. I was trapped here indefinitely, unless someone took mercy on me. Sleep claimed me until I woke to someone's voice. After a couple blinks, I registered Eight Ball was next to me, pushing my hair from my face.

I stiffened at the contact, deleting the spam in my brain and focusing. "Your phone has been ringing off the hook," he said. "You have messages. I would like to hear them."

So would I, but I didn't want to concede to even the slightest of demands. Still, I needed to hear what my friends and family thought. I wasn't sure how long I'd been here, and listening to my messages would provide one way to fill in the blanks.

I revealed my passcode, and once he thumbed it in, he struck the speaker and held it close to my ear.

"Sweetheart, where are you? Pick up, Darc. It's Dylan. I miss you. Oh, God, do I miss you. And I'm sorry. I'm so sorry I cut you off when you called last night. I was hurt, but I spoke with Mom and Dad, and I get it. I get it, and please forgive me for not taking the time to dig deeper. I came on too strong...I should've picked another time for us to have that conversation, but I wanted you. I wanted you and was overwhelmed. You feel like things are being forced on you? I feel like I'm being forced into decisions when all I want to do is hang with my favorite girl. I just want you back, Darc... however you're able to give yourself to me. I called and called last night, but you just shut your life down. I should've tried this morning, but I was afraid it would end in another argument, so I decided to surprise you. Darc, I'm worried. I'm at your house with Murphy and haven't even made it to school. Something feels off to me."

He knew. My God, he knew what I'd confessed to his parents and somehow managed to still care. I'd dwell on that later, but right then, Eight Ball literally breathed down my neck like a freaking dragon. I'd rather chew a cyanide pill than talk to him about my private life, but if I didn't talk, then I'd never figure out what made him tick. Did he want a ransom? My family wasn't exactly the epitome of massive wealth.

"Boyfriend?" he said. I gave him nada. "Answer me," he barked.

When I said nothing, I got another phone call from Dylan.

"Darcy, please," Dylan begged. *"The police are here. I found your things at the front of the neighborhood. If you're upset with me and needed to get away, then please come home. I'm sorry. I miss you. My mind is going crazy wondering how I can get you back."*

With the flip of a switch, Eight Ball and I stared into one another's eyes. I squinted at the instant brightness, but in a split second, I did a 360-degree revolution of the room. It was dimly lit with red walls and a black shiny floor housing the occasional divot—a dungeon. Chains were shackled on the three walls opposite the door, and a wooden table sat as a focal piece in the middle, containing fetters for servitude. There were instruments for torture everywhere. Knives on a dark wooden, old-world style table to the right, and a whip neatly rolled up next to it.

Listen...I preferred the dark.

Naked from the waist up, Eight Ball appeared as if he'd just come from working out because he had on white athletic shorts and gray sneakers, sweat dripping from his hard pecs in tiny drops. His eyes were dark and stormy...everything that signaled psychotic... mentally incompetent...straight from the crazy farm.

I'm going to let you in on a little secret. The Walkers have some crazy people in the bloodline.

Thing was, we weren't embarrassed of them. Where most liked to hide those kinds of things in the closet, we placed our crazies front and center so everyone could get a load of the genetic pool. Eight Ball made my crazy clan look like Albert. Freaking. Einstein.

Especially since one of his feet stood on top of a pile of bones.

With a touch of his thumb, I heard the mounting desperation in Dylan's voice with a third call.

"It's me. Someone with your description was seen talking to a man in a limousine after seven a.m. If he's with you, then this message is for him. Listen to me, you cock sucking, mother—" bleep profanity. *"If you hurt her, I'll make it my life's mission to make sure you feel pain."*

My chin trembled like a glass of water in an earthquake. Eight Ball noticed my shift in mood and immediately went to the next message.

"Your battery has to be dying, but I want you to fight. Fight and when you can't, then think. It's what you do best. I know you're smarter than whoever this is. My every thought is of you, and when you're too tired to do either, then picture me doing it for you. I'll never get tired. I'm praying that you're strong, and just remember I'll never stop looking. I love—"

My battery died.

I'd been out and/or drugged for quite some time if my battery went DOA. I had a feeling the next time Dylan saw me though, there'd be a toe-tag hanging from my foot.

"Only a boyfriend speaks this way," Eight Ball said, running his sweaty hand down the side of my face. I hardened my gaze, wondering whether I should go bat-poop crazy like Sidney Prescott in *Scream* or use my brain like Clarice Starling in *The Silence of the Lambs*. I used to think my greatest talent was to talk and bargain. What an overestimation of my abilities. I absolutely sucked.

"Can I go home?" I asked.

Eight Ball cocked his POS face to the side, like he was suddenly enthralled with a small animal. "Are you lonely? If you're lonely I can bring you this friend."

Sheesh, Eight Ball was definitely off his rocker. I refused to answer one way or another. Answering would give him even more power than he already had. Plus, if he brought Dylan here, then Dylan would eventually try to take him. I feared he wouldn't be able to, and he'd join the stack of bones at my feet.

Chapter Twenty-Two

STOCKHOLM SYNDROME

*E*ight Ball brought me three slices of bread and water—how very prison camp—and led me down the hall so I could do my business in a dirty bathroom. After ten minutes, he brought me back to my quarters. A goose egg the size of Nebraska dotted the back of my head, complements of the initial abduction, and my jaw was noticeably sore. I didn't know if I'd busted out a tooth when I crash-landed in the back of the limo, or if Eight Ball had clocked my jaw and I didn't remember.

All I knew was since I'd wakened, I'd been obsessed with the little things...my contacts...not having cleaning solution...bodily functions...a shower...brushing my teeth. It wasn't easy telling my captor I needed the basic conveniences, but requesting them had also been a test. I wanted to see how much mercy he'd impart. Eight Ball said I'd be on a two-hour schedule during the day. He or someone else would lead me to the restroom, and he promised he'd score the appropriate products to keep my life as normal as possible. I almost said thank you, but again I wasn't big on imparting words of praise. I simply gave a nod.

My finger was past due to have its stitches removed, and it itched like a mosquito had slipped inside and feasted on my blood. To his credit, Eight Ball didn't flinch when I requested he remove them, and when he rebandaged, he surprisingly showed a tender side. It unnerved me that he'd been affable. I had no idea what that meant but knew enough to train my eye closely on someone who flipped the psycho switch so easily.

That meant there had to be a trigger. My job was to identify the trigger and either defuse it or exploit it.

It also crossed my mind to ask him to remove the bones from my room. I'd counted and categorized the remains but decided at the last minute to pile them up in the corner. If my plans to bust out of here came to fruition, they would serve as DNA evidence for someone gone missing years earlier.

I fell asleep on a cot up against the door with a musty Rainbow Brite blanket. Where the heck had Eight Ball found Rainbow Brite? Hadn't she been retired decades earlier on the toy market? Regardless, I shoved the mat up against the entry. The reason was simple: I wanted to know when someone entered, and they'd have to move me out of the way to do so.

When I woke after a restless night, my stomach rumbled like a thunderstorm. Eight Ball arrived with a duplicate meal, and after some coaxing confessed it was Thursday morning...*the exact day my mother had died*. What a way to relive her memory. I'd found myself in quite a few no-win situations before, and although hungry and in mourning, nothing seemed worse than no goodnight FaceTime from Dylan or wake-up text earlier. I felt him though. I felt him in my bones, willing me to stay alive.

Thursday meant I'd been out for two days before our little get-to-know-one-another session. Marjorie had to be permanently traumatized, and Murphy had probably busted down the door of every registered sex offender close to BTCC. I missed them. I missed M's hugs and Murphy's breakfasts, but I couldn't allot any brain cells to my loved ones. I planned to blow this joint and send Eight Ball and his psychotic brain to the big house.

After the carbo-load, Eight Ball said, "Come." From where I stood, I had two choices: put up a fight or go and accept the inevitable. It was black and cold when I stepped outside my new home. Shielding my eyes with my hand, I blinked back the blurriness until my eyes adjusted. What was ahead of me? Rape? More fake friend conversation? My room had no windows, so I couldn't get a read on the environment, but it was so quiet it was like I lived in a vacuum or better yet, one of those ant farms behind glass. I knew it was important to keep track of the days I'd been gone, so I marked a slash behind the door with a pebble I'd found—now I'd have to add two more days according to Eight Ball.

Question was, *will Eight Ball always be as congenial as he's been today?*

Survey says? No.

Again, he'd dressed as if he'd been working out—no shirt, but right then he had on tiny black Speedos that barely covered the full monty. I gulped at the acreage of him. I didn't want to meet him in the dark, and my mind debated whether I should try to befriend him or stay with my fists figuratively clenched, lest Stockholm Syndrome claim me.

We journeyed around three hundred meters before I heard the sounds of civilization. Dare I think he would let me go? Let me answer the question...he opened a black door duplicate to the one I'd been stowed away in and shoved me inside. I found myself in the presence of other people...like me.

Taking a deep breath, I summoned enough courage to shove down the shock while I watched Eight Ball take his place in the center of the room. Eight Ball was the acting C.O., and I knew immediately it had to be the fight club of which Marek Ransom had referred. Could Marek be here?

Whatever split-second judgment I'd made earlier was replaced by a more grim picture. Men, young and old, stood in a row tanta-mount to a prison lineup while three guards had trained weapons on them, prepared to squash a rebellion.

Eight Ball slowly strutted in front of them with his hands laced behind his back.

Realization came fast this was a holding tank...a place where one's skills were assessed as marketable or not. And if not? Maybe I'd become the pile of bones in my room. That went on for about twenty minutes. Some males had been instructed to go to the left—others to the right. Eight Ball seemed to have lost interest in me, so I surreptitiously trolled through the crowd about two hundred deep, trying to find someone who'd dish. A chatty guard in the middle of the crowd claimed a man named Marx had picked up the nasty habit of kidnapping and using humans for monetary gain while in Russia.

I could only assume the man to be Eight Ball. Eight Ball carried some scary, sociopathic markers. But that wasn't the real story here. Jaws commissioned me to find a man named Marx...Marx he claimed killed Lyric Armstrong. Could it be *Julius Marx*?

When we reached the fifteen-minute mark, dumb or not dumb, I tested my limits Darcy-style. I idiotically went William Wallace in *Braveheart* and pumped an arm. "They may take our lives, but they will never take our freedom!"

Silence...

Eh, no one had a sense of humor anymore...tragic.

What happened as a result was the camp's divides were clearly established. Those going to follow the rules simply to stay alive avoided me like the plague. Those who were Marx sympathizers and obviously fallen to Stockholm Syndrome ratted me out like fifth graders trying to gain brownie points. A few went so far as to kick my legs out from underneath me, taking a shot at my ribs, but what happened on the trip down was a small handful came to my defense, whispering phrases like: *We need to talk*, *Let's get out of this hellhole*, or *Keep that attitude and you just might keep your mind*.

The thought gave me pause because I took note of those who'd lost their brains months, maybe years earlier. They were total animals. Wired. Defensive. Protecting their personal space beyond what was necessary. As the ruckus continued, the largest guard cut a path through the crowd and backhanded me across the jaw. When I went down on one knee, tears stung my eyes, and I immediately negotiated with my estrogen to go into hibernation. I couldn't cry... I refused to show a sign of weakness. By that time, Eight Ball figured out the cause of the chaos was me, and he forced his way inside, attacking the guard who'd struck me to the ground with a loud whack.

He called the guard Blaze. I catalogued him at around three hundred pounds like Eight Ball, as mean as a junkyard dog, sporting a clown-red buzz cut that stood about two inches high. Eight Ball, however, stood half a foot taller than my attacker. They engaged in brutal hand-to-hand combat, blood splattering from both of their mouths as they punished one another with fists to the upper body. Some in the crowd gasped at the violence while others acted blasé, like the show was so mundane they were almost bored. Eight Ball finally took the guard to the floor in a hard uppercut but paid no attention to the tap-out he viciously performed with his right hand. With a savage roar, Eight Ball went Mike Tyson and bit off the tip of Blaze's nose, spitting it to the ground. The scream was in the guard's eyes when he realized what Eight Ball had done, but he somehow swallowed down the panic.

Hellooooo, Hunger Games. That was the brand of crazy we were dealing with.

While Blaze left the room to tend to his wound, another replaced him, and it was on with the show. I was the first picked in organized games of any kind, was undefeated at rock-paper-scissors, and people fought over me for their *Monopoly* teams because of my bizarre ability to acquire prime real estate and never land in jail. I found out pretty quickly it wasn't a compliment to be picked first in the holding tank. That meant you looked beatable. Those separated to the right were thought to have potential—those on the left were the "potentials'" opportunity to prove they'd deserved their place on the hierarchy. I'd been shoved together with a group of three other girls out to the side. I wasn't positive what our station was in their little gig but assumed time would tell.

First up was Slime Ball, according to introduction. I'd clocked on him as soon as I entered the room. He looked like he'd come straight off furlough with greased-back hair, chest hair up to his neck, and more scars on his face than Frankenstein. He picked the scrawniest guy in the loser camp. Scrawny Guy looked like he could use a Big Mac or two, and when he sheepishly muttered, "Can I go home? I promise I won't say anything," my memory went from zero to sixty...I recognized the voice. Scrawny Guy had been the person moaning behind the wall at Club Need.

There was no time for sympathy because Eight Ball yelled, "Take him!"

Slime Ball jumped on Scrawny Guy like a bed bug on a piece of luggage. Scrawny Guy didn't stand a chance, going catatonic as soon as the first punch connected. Going down on one knee, he staggered back up with a flailing punch that hit nothing but air. Slime Ball's fist connected with a southpaw to the jaw. Scrawny Guy went flat on his black and spun around like a dreidel.

Eight Ball said a few words in Slime Ball's ear, and Slime Ball strutted over to my group of females and stared each of us down. My stomach came up to my mouth. Female intuition alerted me like a hammer to the skull what our station in their little game was—the prize. Slime Ball spent a long time on a petite brunette, an even longer time on me, but then parked his prison butt in front of a bleached blonde with boobs the size of Pluto. Listen, I loved the male body, but I couldn't help but stare at the boobs either. The girl looked bone-tired, my guess pulling an all-nighter or longer. She went for the damsel-in-distress approach, and when Slime Ball's grin widened, I was struck with the horror he had a split tongue like a snake. Damsel shrieked at the monstrosity, and I stepped in front of her, shoving my palm in his chest. "Back off, Slime Ball," I ordered. "She's not interested in your anaconda."

Sweet Lord...I sounded like I belonged in a federal prison.

Slime Ball raised the back of his hand to strike me, but Eight Ball grabbed it before he made contact, twisting it behind his back. "Never that one," he seethed. "Never."

I wasn't flattered—I feared why I'd been set apart.

Three more fights ensued. Two won by the Potentials. A Loser surprised everyone and went kung-fu fighter and knocked a Potential out cold. After a third fight, the crowd got into it, like the Romans watching Christians be eaten by lions in the Colosseum. It was some serious underground action because by polling the crowd, the majority of teenagers here should be in school. Shouldn't someone have noticed we'd gone AWOL? When the crowd circled those sparring, the back wall came into view, and I instantly formulated a plan.

There was a window...by God, a window! A window meant I could see outside, possibly get a whereabouts, and when opportunity presented itself, rock 'n' roll and alert the authorities. Perhaps I could even bust out the glass and go right then. I dropped down into a crouch and carefully traveled the length of the wall until I huddled right underneath the window. It had old, metal vertical blinds that had been bowed inward by someone slamming into them. Slipping two fingers inside, I spread the slats but didn't see a soul. No people. Cars. Dogs. Cats. No dogs chasing cats. Nothing but a red brick wall about two feet away that ensured we had no way out. My word, the buildings had been built right on top of one another.

A year earlier, I came down with the legitimate flu. I shook so much with fever Murphy worried I'd crack my own teeth. A shaking spell fell over me that had me almost kissing the floor, but a guard came from nowhere and spun me around into his chest. I blinked. Then I pulled a double because I stared right into the mismatched eyes of Ryder Beck.

One breath.

Two...

Make that three.

It took awhile for my brain to do the math. So in a quest to find Lyric Armstrong's killer, I'd run across the missing Ryder Beck... while I simply tried to watch Marek Ransom fight. Talk about your mixed blessings. It was almost too complicated for me. Or maybe that was the point...maybe it was *easy*...because it was still going on.

"Ryder Beck?" I whispered.

The guard showed no sort of autonomic recognition at all. No blink or frown. No gasp of, "Oh joy, someone found me!" Nothing. But I'd swear on my sorry life it was him. His hair was a darker blond, but he had the unusual characteristic of one blue eye and one green—the tattoo on his wrist. Thing was, he didn't seem so eager to take on the world as he had in Gabrielle's photograph. My guess was something tamed the tiger...or killed it.

"In the wood," he roared. "Now!"

I prided myself on being hip as far as urban vernacular went, but I hadn't a single clue what that "in the wood" thing meant. By the frothy foam coming from his mouth, I had a feeling it wasn't a good thing. Ryder pulled my kicking-and-screaming body past another match and into an adjacent room. With a narrowed gaze, he opened his mouth to speak but was quickly shoved out of the way by Eight Ball who apparently wanted the honors of the "wood" thing himself. Without a word in contest, Ryder left the room and Eight Ball slung me over his shoulder, taking me to yet another venue.

I pleaded into his greasy, sweaty back. "Please, Eight Ball. I'm sorry."

Eight Ball never acknowledged me, and I soon understood the depths of his anger when he deposited me next to a wooden coffin.

It appears I didn't conform well..."in the wood" signifying an undisclosed amount of time spent like a corpse. I tried to talk myself out of the vortex of fear in my brain. *Darcy, this isn't a dream*, I said, briefly closing my eyes. *Think fast.*

I grabbed his wrist, "I'm claustrophobic. If you put me in there, my brain is going to scramble up like eggs in a skillet. Please. I'll be your friend. We can date. I'll even make you a mix tape of some of my favorite songs. And I don't even care that you scare the bejeezus out of me. I'll close my eyes or something."

Dude, talk about killing the sale...but I'd never been forced into a situation where: (A) someone put me in a pine box; and (B) that someone forced me to stay there.

After one long blink to register my words, Eight Ball opened the lid and tossed me into the casket like a bag of trash. The casket came lined with crushed navy-blue velvet. In the middle of a screeching, "No," he slammed the lid shut to the sounds of a buzzing drill and splintering wood. Oh. God. He had plans to bury me alive. First instinct was to pound on the lid to let him know I'd objected. So I pounded. Pound. Pound. Pound. When that got me nowhere, I stuck my fingers through what I deduced were air holes, still trying to alert him of my panic. After I realized the futility of my actions, I felt around the velvet, shredded with rips from those doomed to the same punishment before me.

One bolt was in...two...three...four, five, six. I lost count. Again, I fisted the lid angrily to remind him I was alive. The smell of pine stung like strolling through the forest during allergy season. My nose immediately closed up, and I didn't know if shock had thrown me into anaphylaxis, if it was merely the smell, or if it was fluid that traveled down the back of my throat smothering me.

This wasn't the way I wanted to be buried. I wanted to be buried in the DEFCON DARCY cape my mother made. I wanted the Brooklyn Tabernacle Choir to sing "Amazing Grace," and street dancers to perform on the sidewalk with pants to their knees. I wanted my zits popped, my toenails done in black, my fingernails in orange, and my hair to be styled as lush and full as a hooker on Main Street. I wanted a boob job. I wanted to die with a perfect C-cup showcased in a low-cut black velvet dress. After all of those wishes had been fulfilled, I wanted a Frank Sinatra impersonator to sing

"My Way" as I was lowered into the ground. And last but not least, I *did not* want to die a virgin...NOPE.

I tried to cork the tears, but they wouldn't cooperate. I'd met a slew of crazy people in my life, but Eight Ball brought a whole new level of psycho to the playing field. *Calm yourself, Darcy*, I said. *Relax. Breathe deep*. But Eight Ball was so bad, I knew I'd have to endure something heinous before he'd get in touch with what form of conscience he had, if any. I almost said, *Forgive me, God* for him, but instead muttered, *I hope he rots in Hell* and closed my eyes.

———

I spent the night in a coffin.

The only way I knew I'd actually slept was I woke with the granddaddy of all headaches, and the overwhelming need to relieve my bladder. Eight Ball paced outside, moving back and forth like a leopard in a cage. Thinking. Plotting another psychopathic plan of mental anguish, no doubt, all with the goal of making me conform. I squirmed at the pressure between my legs, commanding the urge to heel. Even worse than sleeping in a coffin, I didn't want to sleep in a coffin and pee on myself at the same time.

I decided to make an appeal to his civility. Even the Geneva Convention said POWs were to be treated humanely, and a regular bathroom break would fall within the lines of fair.

I rapped my knuckles on the lid two times. "I know you're out there. May I please use the restroom?" Nothing. That went on for several minutes with me simply knocking. When my eyes filled with tears, I allowed a small fissure to form in my resolve. I whimpered out another, "Please," knowing even if he gave in I could never feel sympathy for my captor. The moment I gave him a piece of kindness was the moment my freedom would truly be lost.

There were certain smells and sounds desirable to wake up to... the smell of breakfast, laughter, birds singing, a kiss to the lips, but nothing was sweeter than the sound of splintering wood and a drill bit. I stretched as best I could, and the moment the last bolt had been removed, I sailed out of there like one of those catapults the Orcs used in *The Lord of the Rings*.

My goal was to never freeze in life. I'd done fairly okay, but a lot of times I'd simply stolen the air from the real heroes. Let me just say, I froze like a gosh-danged icicle because Eight Ball wasn't the one who'd freed me...Lars van der Hart had.

Holy cow...Eight Ball had merely been the deliveryman.

Van der Hart sat casually with his legs crossed on a foldout cot next to me, one you'd find in an Army surplus store. He'd slept beside me. Wearing dark-washed jeans, a long-sleeved expensive black shirt rounded out the top with dark loafers on the bottom—a more casual look for someone who owned a nightclub and obviously complicit in my kidnapping. His brunette hair had been spiked in a more youthful appearance, and where I thought he'd been attractive earlier, his faint smile was so sick it was nauseating.

"Comfortable?" he asked.

"Yeah, you really know how to treat a girl, and if you don't show me a bathroom pronto I'm going to ruin your carpet."

While Van der Hart considered my threat, I took a quick scan of the room. Warm mahogany furniture stood in stark contrast to pure white walls. Books lined the shelves and an altar sat in the area directly behind him, illuminated by brass lamps and solid gold fixtures. Black ravens perched in multiple cages, staring. In fact, there were so many ravens it would've made Alfred Hitchcock shudder. Even the ravens were prisoners...but what did I expect? That was what happened when your life went DEFCON 1. Was it the lower level of Club Need? I'd be the first to admit I hadn't scoped out my surroundings when the coffin came into view, but I hadn't heard nightclub life or the squawking of birds at any time.

After I'd done my business in his bathroom, Van der Hart said, "I'm sorry about the coffin, but I hear you've been somewhat," he paused, "disagreeable."

A raven blinked at me. "You left me in there all night...I accept your apology."

"I wasn't aware I'd offered one."

"Yeah, well God bless you anyway."

At that Van der Hart smiled. My eyes traced the four one-inch scars on his right cheek. If he rubberstamped being buried alive, God only knew the story behind that injury—I sent my sincerest gratitude to the one who'd inflicted the pain. "I had to make you tough," he said. "The world is a very dark place, Darcy. I have to make sure you're prepared to be in it before I leave."

"You're leaving?"

"Just for a day."

Thank God for small miracles. "So where are you off to? Tell me it's Africa because there's a guy named Ebola Virus I think you should look up."

"Not Africa," he said.

"Ah, then I bet it's Moscow. You know, so you can get some tips on how to run a fight club more efficiently."

I thought his head would blow off his shoulders with my words. Instead, a sly grin slowly lined his lips. "I see you've been doing some detective work. Good for you, Darcy. You make me so proud. I've been following you for years. Thank God, the shooter last spring didn't kill you or the mob when they sent a hit out on Lincoln Taylor's family. Not to mention, the psychopaths you outran last summer. How tragic."

He'd done his homework...eh, creepy. "You don't see a parallel here?" I asked with a snort I couldn't hide.

"I see no parallel, but to answer your question I'm traveling out of town. Moscow simply provided me with a pastime I enjoy. There's something deeply visceral in watching men fight for their lives. I do enjoy the matches—"

"But you enjoy the money more?"

He grinned. "It does have its perks," he said. "I didn't always have a lot of money growing up. I enjoy being on the other side. My wish is you want for nothing. Do you understand why I made you sleep in there now? Why I wanted to make you tough?"

I commanded my face to stay expressionless. I did not want to show him fear lest he use it as a means of submission again. "Seriously. I get the concept, but didn't you think I'd get the message after Eight Ball nailed it shut?"

He rubbed a hand down his chin, deep in thought. "Perhaps I went too far."

"In case you're wondering, you did. You just screwed Maslow's hierarchy of needs to heck and back. I didn't have air or food or water, and I sure as heck didn't feel safe or loved. You don't even have a darn recycling bin here either which shows you don't care about Mother Earth. And the fact I had to tell you I needed to pee was downright demoralizing."

"You didn't touch self-actualization," he said, playfully winking.

"I'm not self-actualized yet, but I plan to rub that in your face once I spring this joint and am looking at you on the other side of prison bars."

"What I did was out of love."

"Is that your idea of a rebuttal?"

"I suppose it is."

I cracked another joke, biting my nails into the palms of my hands. "Sometimes you can't love people into better behavior. Murphy's tried for years."

A muscle ticced in his jaw. "Murphy?"

"My dad."

Van der Hart slowly uncrossed his legs and went vertical, running a hand down my jaw. "That's where you're wrong. I've done all of this for you because *I'm* your father."

Chapter Twenty-Three

DADDY DEAREST

The first two chambers of my heart collapsed. "What did you say?"

"I said I'm your father."

The other two chambers followed suit. I inhaled deeply, fighting a shiver. No...couldn't be. Murphy Walker was my father. We lived at the end of Bison Boulevard in Buffalo Trails Country Club. We were middle-class. My father was an underwriter. He was a widower still pining away for his dead wife. I had a little sister and aunt and uncle I adored. My name's Darcy Winston Walker.

My family wouldn't lie to me.

My knees still knocked, and the room spun until I smothered the shock. I tried to see a resemblance. His eyes were green. A dimpled chin. Tall and thin. But those characteristics I'd also inherited from my mother's sister, Red...*allegedly.* "Listen, dude. You're not my father," I said. "You can write that on your dry-erase board in permanent marker."

Van der Hart frowned. "Don't you remember me?"

"Other than the obvious, no."

When I first met Van der Hart, I *did* have the sense I'd met him before. At the time, the answer danced at the edge of my mind— just out of reach. Right then, something happened to clear up the confusion. He turned to gently shush a quarreling raven, and a crucifix on a black diamond chain tumbled out of the shirt he wore.

The same one he wore when he shot my mother...

My respirations became more pronounced, and my hand shielded my heart as I swallowed down the emerging hysteria. He'd killed my mom. The man killed my mom in cold blood while his so-called lovechild witnessed it. My first instinct was to charge him like a bull. Rip. Pull. Desecrate whatever I got my hands on beyond recognition. He'd ruined my life, changed my family beyond repair, and morphed my father into someone who on some days was hard to witness. I wanted him dead. Regardless if I had his blood in my veins or not, I'd make sure he found the grave I'd been digging since I was nine years old. Could my mother have cheated on Murphy? Seriously, if that was true, I would've sniffed that out like rotten trash years earlier...right? Right??

But how?

When?

Van der Hart didn't look totally the same as back then, although the builds were similar, but time could certainly alter in strange ways. Willing the tears to not fall, I stared Daddy Dearest in the face. "Tell me something only a lover would know. And please, keep it with a parental guidance suggested rating."

He pitched his head back, laughing deeply. "You're definitely Gemma's daughter. She was so witty."

Pointing to a leather couch, he murmured, "Sit, baby. You have to be exhausted."

I ground my teeth at the term of endearment but wanted to hear what he had to say more than the discomfort it caused. "Now where were we?" he said when I sat down. "Ah yes, I'm supposed to tell you something only a lover would know. Gemma and Tabitha were adopted. They were left on the steps of an orphanage."

He'd hit the bull's eye with his first throw. "Who adopted them?"

"An older pastor and his wife. It wasn't an easy adoption for them, taking two children. Both were in their late fifties, but the orphanage was adamant the girls not be separated."

Bull's eye number two, but that information could've been uncovered by a good private investigator. "Tell me something about her personally."

"She absolutely hated disbanding The Minstrel Cramps and

resented Murphy for demanding she do so. It was a point of contention she and I hashed and rehashed whenever we were together. That band was her passion."

I would agree the band was her passion, but his reasoning didn't jive with me. My mother disbanded The Minstrel Cramps when she became pregnant with me...by Murphy. She said she didn't want to travel with a baby, although Murphy apparently didn't care one way or the other. "That's not the story I've been told. She got pregnant with me right along the time a stalker appeared. At first, he appeared harmless, but she didn't want to run into him while pregnant."

Van der Hart leaned forward, resting his elbows on his knees. "A decision I obviously supported." Once again, I kept the thought buried I knew he was her stalker.

"If you're my father, why did you agree to allow another man to raise your child?"

An inhale, exhale. "Good question. Our situation was complicated."

"Complicated? Your story makes no sense whatsoever. My father worked security on my mother's shows. They met one another in college. They were deeply in love."

He nodded in a pseudo-compassionate manner. "At one time they loved one another, but then she and I met through Tabitha. Things quickly changed."

My heart caught in my throat. "So you had an affair? When did said affair end?"

"What we had together was not torrid or tawdry, Darcy. Gemma was my greatest love. We were both unhappily married at the time. My wife," he said with a deep frown, "was a remora. Are you familiar with the remora?"

"Remoras are fish known for their clingy behavior."

"And Gemma was a breath of fresh air. Your mother was one of a kind," he said. "Red was the outgoing one. She solved the problems, but when Gemma stepped onstage," he said, sighing wistfully, "even God bowed down."

Instant migraine because Murphy had pretty much said the same, except he'd never say something borderline sacrilegious.

Murphy feared Hell too much. Van der Hart, I'm pretty sure, had never had an introduction to God...as in ever.

Although his story held some weight, what didn't make sense was Murphy. Murphy was the most paranoid individual I'd ever met. He would've uncovered their relationship, confronted my mother, and cut his losses...*or would he?* Did he love her enough to raise someone else's child? But then there was Marjorie. I didn't resemble Murphy, but M was a mixture of he and my mother. If my mother truly had an affair and I'd been the byproduct, did she and Murphy patch things up and produce a child of their own? And could that have made Daddy Dearest angry enough to kill her? The timeline would fit. M was a little over a month old when our mother was murdered...did Daddy Dearest snap at the introduction of a new child...one who wasn't his?

"When did this affair end?"

Van der Hart closed his eyes as though he relived the worst day of his life. I wasn't totally convinced he was my father, but by the pained expression on his face I'd be lying if I said it didn't cause me to doubt things I'd considered absolute. But I reminded myself Murphy had always characterized him as a stalker.

Stalkers created their own realities...

He answered, "It continued off and on throughout both our marriages, up until her death. When word of her death reached me, I nearly had a heart attack. In fact, it took me several years to recover."

"So what is my real last name then?" Please say Lawrence because if you do, I will nail you to the frigging wall.

His phone chose that moment to bust up our little homecoming and walk down memory freaking lane. As soon as he recognized the voice of the caller, his personality shifted. He became soldier-like, robotic, and nothing but business. He responded with a series of numbers, "33.5000° N, 36.3000° E" and disconnected. His gaze hardened like a diamond straight out of a South African mine.

"Lars?" I asked. He'd gone somewhere else. "We were talking about my mom?"

"Get dressed, Eve," he said abruptly.

"As in the Garden of Eden *Eve?*"

Wherever he'd gone, his brain went back online. With a graceful shake of his head, he chuckled. "I'm sorry. Eve is the name I'd picked for you, but Murphy won that battle."

And right then, he acted like their alleged love triangle was one big happy family. Dude was so jacked in the head. "Why am I getting dressed?" I asked, suddenly nervous I'd have to disrobe.

"I want to show you around The Underground."

First a prisoner...now an honored guest.

He led me to the door of his bedroom, and neatly folded on a huge mahogany poster bed lay a new pair of jeans, black leather boots to the knee, underwear, and an expensive black sweater. When he closed the door to allow me privacy, I performed a quick recon of the space. The room was devoid of clutter. He was either a neat freak or one of his minions performed housekeeping duties. Overall, the place was unintimidating except for the picture of my mother next to his bedside table. I swallowed. Talk about serving up some heartbreak. The picture happened to be my favorite shot of her ever. Her blonde hair whipped in the air, and her face was scrunched up in a rocker snarl as she performed a guitar riff that made her a goddess. Murphy had the exact same shot in his room. After I got my breathing in check, I ventured into the restroom and snooped in the cabinets. Inside were various wigs, tubes of makeup, and bottles of hair color—ranging from black to red to blond. Jaws had been right on the money. This man not only changed identities...he even did the camouflage himself. Afraid Daddy Dearest would enter the room, I quickly disrobed and stepped inside the marble shower. Cranking the spray to the hottest setting, I shampooed my hair, lathered and rinsed, and toweled off in seconds. After I rehydrated my eyes with contact solution laying on the vanity, I combed my hair out straight and changed into the new clothing. Curiosity chewed at me, wondering where we were going, but perhaps it would be some place I could escape from—or hook up with the men I'd met the day before with similar thoughts on a prison break.

When I walked outside, Van der Hart gave an appraising grin along with a, "So beautiful. Just like your mother."

He placed his fist to his chest with his elbow out to the side. I didn't have any recourse but to link my arm through his. Plus, I got the feeling I hadn't been given much of a choice. He wound us through several dark corridors, down another set of stairs to an area where men happened to be sparring. So that was the training ground...they were freaking moles...moles on a leash.

"So you're the ringmaster?" I asked.

"Of just The Underground," he said and chuckled. "Although I'll admit I've been compared to Lucifer." Well, that would certainly fit in with him calling me Eve, wouldn't it?

With the ease of a politician, Van der Hart effortlessly worked the room, meandering through pods of teens and men working out in small groups, addressing people by names, specifically providing minute details on what some could improve. He certainly had a charismatic, charming air about him, but I knew the person underneath.

I gazed at him when he halted near Slime Ball, who worked out some poor chap destined to lose. "I'm not going to lie to you. You and I both know this is illegal for you to keep me prisoner, and by the looks of things, everyone else too. What's the secret to your success?"

"In due time, Darcy. Due time."

"How many fighters are here?"

"That can vary."

"And what would make it vary?"

"The outcome of a fight."

His voice sounded detached, the remorse of a certified sociopath punctuating the lack of emotion. I gulped...no way in the world would he allow someone to resume their normal everyday life topside. To me, that meant live or die. "How do you keep them in fighting shape? The lack of sunlight is one thing...and the crappy menu sucks."

"The fighters eat fruit and grains. If they win, they'll get a full meal once a day as part of the victory."

"If they lose?"

"Back to fruits and grains."

"So if you lose, you not only need to win again for a full meal, but you have to win with a deficit?"

"I like to think I'm instilling the instinct to *always* win...no matter what."

That was certainly one way to term psychological and physical abuse. "Speaking of food, Eight Ball forgot to drop off the fruit portion of my meal. He's been heavy on the grains since I arrived."

Daddy Dearest slid over an ice-cold gaze. "No, he did as directed. Everyone knows you're my daughter. My desire is for you to earn the respect of others instead of my association granting it by default. You'll have to prove you're tough."

The last thing Murphy would ever do was see me go hungry. When a hole of sadness formed in my chest, I cut off the thought of Murphy instantly. I could cry myself to sleep at night. I wasn't sure how long I would have Daddy Dearest's full attention.

"Tell me about Moscow."

I braced for a backhand but got nothing but a nonchalant answer. "I travel a lot in my line of work," he said offhandedly. "A couple of decades ago, I found myself in Moscow and in the company of two former spies named Rodchenko. When the Cold War ended, many soldiers entered the business world. The Rodchenko brothers started a new business by inviting wealthy, urbanite businessmen for a week-long crash course on being a real man."

Translation? The Rodchenko brothers showed the nerdy geeks how to get the crap beat out of them, survive, and then think they had bigger cojones than anyone. "So basically grown men paid for Russians to beat them up in order to metaphorically thump on their chests they were real men?" I clarified.

"In so many words."

"And how did you fit into this?" I asked.

"The Rodchenkos and I became fast friends," he answered. "I visited their establishment just to observe and wound up training some of the businessmen for a while."

From what I knew of world history, the thought pre-Cold War was the only good Russian was a dead Russian. When the walls came down, people realized nice people existed on both sides. So I'd buy that story. "I know enough that the audience lines your pockets. How do you keep them from squealing?"

"You're very clever," he said winking. "Yes, we gamble here, and gambling can be a very risky business. But I've run this place for close to two decades, yet to be discovered. I worry more about the chances of a meteor falling on me than being raided by Cincinnati's finest."

A UFC octagon sat in the middle of the space along with metal benches surrounding it in a semicircle, an exact replica of what one would see in a legitimately sanctioned fight. Overtop were several glass enclosures resembling booths at a professional football or baseball stadium. "Who are the booths for?" I asked.

Without answering, Van der Hart led us up a short flight of stairs, past a restroom, into a booth overlooking the activities of the first floor. It was an area for those desiring a little more discretion than normal. One could leave the glass open or pull a red velvet curtain for privacy. No explanation was needed. That space was for public figures who did not want anyone to know of their sick hobby.

Van der Hart strolled us to the rear of the room and took a cigarette out of a leather case lying on the bar area. Tilting his head backward, he closed his eyes and inhaled one long breath and immediately looked frustrated, like the drawl of smoke never reached his chest. He took three more deep puffs and snuffed it out on the countertop.

His cell phone rang, and when he lifted it from his pocket, an object fell to the ground. Yowza! It was a passport. Pick it up? Leave it? Would a security camera see? Performing a quick eyeball of the room, I found no cameras present anywhere. Dropping to a crouch, I placed it in the waistband of my jeans and pulled the sweater overtop.

As Van der Hart nodded down to a fighter shadow-boxing in the air, I made a motion I was headed to the bathroom behind us. He placed his hand over the receiver, narrowing his eyes.

"Make it quick, Eve." God help me, he was back to the Eve thing.

Swinging my hip into the restroom door, I strode inside and quickly picked a stall, closed myself in, and opened the passport. The booklet was black, marked with "Diplomatic Passport" on the front. From what little I knew about passports, diplomatic passports did not automatically grant you diplomatic immunity—in other words, a massive get-out-of-jail free card because you were important to another country. So who in the heck did Van der Hart officially work for? The United States Government? His face in the passport looked similar, but the hair was blond. The name, however, was the real killer: Julius Marx.

This was big. No, HUUUUGE!

Julius Marx was the name Jaws needed...*I got him*.

Did Jaws know Marx, Van der Hart, and Lawrence all to be the same? Was that why he wanted *me* to bring him to justice? If so, no wonder he didn't unload all the damning details. It would've clouded my judgment.

Question was, how had a passport been issued to Daddy Dearest with a different name than his Lars van der Hart Cincinnati alias? Jaws claimed Julius Marx's passport had been active. That meant he'd traveled recently, shown proof of ID, and had gone through security. How had he survived on the grid as different people for as long as he had?

Thumbing through the pages, I took note Marx was quite the globetrotter. While I memorized the countries visited, I thought of Tito. Tito didn't mention Marx as one of the aliases, which could only mean he'd been chasing another name—probably the one Cincinnati PD initially believed to be guilty in Lyric's disappearance. Here's what I knew: Marx was Jaws's endgame, and if Jaws was as good as I thought him to be, I could provide the names Tito'd been after, and the whole thing would come together. Unfortunately, a good chance existed I may never deliver the information to either of them.

The one hope I held onto was Jaws knew me as Darcy Walker. My name had to be plastered all over the media, which meant Jaws knew my investigation had hit a major snag.

Once I rejoined Daddy Dearest, he was still on the phone. I dropped the passport underneath him. The moment he killed his call, I picked it up and slid it into his hand, giving him nothing but dumb and blonde. When he nonchalantly placed it back in his pocket, my growling stomach reminded me he was the only hope I had of a decent meal.

Throwing caution to the wind, I boldly asked, "May I have breakfast before you leave?"

He tucked my hair behind my ear, cupping my chin in his hand. "Sure, baby. One good deed deserves another, right? You've complied, so the least I can do is treat my daughter to breakfast. What will it be? Eggs? Bacon? Toast?"

The day needed sugar like a car needed oil. "A doughnut and Coke will be fine."

"Just like your mother," he said, chuckling deeply. "Maybe one day you'll come to love me as much as she did and even call me Dad."

I'd put that in the *When Hell Freezes Over* category. "I'm conflicted," was my official response. Murphy didn't raise a fool. Since Daddy Dearest was the psycho from Moscow who started the whole fight club, I needed him on my side...even if only to help me dodge Eight Ball.

———

Ryder Beck brought in a rolling silver cart filled with enough food to feed a third world country. I experienced a sudden pang of guilt, pondering how everyone else in captivity spent his or her evenings. More bread? No bread at all?

On top sat a bowl of fruit containing oranges, strawberries, kiwis, bananas, and grapes. A bowlful of chocolate covered doughnuts perched next to it. Ryder lifted the silver lid from a white china plate, revealing scrambled eggs and toast next to three slices of bacon. Orange juice was by the fork. Coke beside it. I was famished but knew enough that eating quickly, and for that matter *all* of it, would leave me with a massive stomachache.

"Is he coming back?" I asked.

Ryder answered with a stare into nothing. "The Master has been called away. He asked me to give you his apologies."

The Master, I thought. How utterly narcissistic of him. "Care to join me?" I asked.

"The Master would not care for it."

"The Master?" I asked. His reply was a single nod. "Do you mean Mister van der Hart?" Another nod. "FYI, Ryder. Supposedly, he's my father."

"The Master speaks often of his great love, Gemma. I'm happy you two have reconnected after such a long time."

"He's not my father," I said adamantly, although a small part of me feared it to be truth.

Picking up a doughnut, I tore off a piece the size of a dime and nibbled like a mouse. The temperature was warm enough that it melted on my tongue upon impact. I closed my eyes, debating how much food my stomach could hold. I would be fool to believe things were looking up from here. First off, Eight Ball shoved me in a coffin. Secondly, Daddy Dearest didn't object. And thirdly, Daddy Dearest turned out to be the SOB who ruined my life by pulling the trigger on my mother—his so-called lover. Blood or not, as long as I kept my brain, I'd find a way to make him pay. Ryder, however, appeared to have lost his mind years before.

"Can I trust you, Ryder?" Once again, I got that lights-are-on-but-no-one's-home gaze. "Listen," I said, trying for a more direct approach. "I was pseudo-investigating this fight club and was aware you disappeared years ago. Your best friend, Lyric Armstrong, came looking for you but got caught in the ductwork sneaking into the club. Her body was recently found. I believe it was murder."

I honest to God saw him swallow. Thank you, Jesus. I'd put a chink in his psychological armor.

"The Master said it was necessary she die."

"Did he do it?" No answer. "Did she fall in, and he just let nature take its course?" A single nod. Make that two murders I could pin on the man because even if he didn't cause it, he was still guilty if he did nothing to help. "Would you testify to that in court?" I added.

"We will never see a court, Darcy."

"Yeah, we will. I also know Gabrielle Allen. She's never stopped looking for you."

Ryder visibly grew disturbed, shifting back and forth, almost in a fighting stance. Did I think he would attack me? No, but it was almost as if her name triggered some sort of instinct to brawl. "Gabby," he whispered to himself.

God help me, my manners went the way of the Cro-Magnon because I didn't know how long I'd have to eat. I shoveled food into my mouth like a pig in fresh slop—one bite here, one bite there, swallowing grapes almost whole. "Yes," I said, talking behind some eggs. "I've spoken with her. Would you like to know what she said?"

His glazed-over look returned. "The Master said we should not speak of our pasts. We are now a family."

I rolled my eyes so high I almost saw my own grey matter. The human race was interesting. We had the mutual need to belong, feel safe, be loved, and have purpose, even when held captive. Van der Hart capitalized on those needs while servicing his sick pastime.

Peeling a banana, I bit off a third and swallowed it whole. "You're suffering from Stockholm Syndrome, Ryder. You know, feeling sorry for your captors. I have no such desire to travel to Stockholm and intend on busting out of this joint whenever the Good Lord sees fit. If you're with me, then I suggest you start by not calling Lars van der Hart 'The Master' in private. It's not good for your mind. At least in your mind know he's the man who robbed you." When he didn't respond, I said, "Do you want to ask about Gabrielle?"

A look of devotion crossed his face but quickly poofed like the genie in *Aladdin*...definitely Stockholm Syndrome. Ryder's subconscious tried to dwell on an emotion, but his learned behavior at the moment was stronger. "Gabby is in my past," he said.

I hammered home the truth. "She mourns you daily, but here's what's important. She's alive. And she still loves you."

"That part of me is dead."

"No, it's not. The fact you're having a conversation with me and not saying 'The Master' every breath tells me some of the outgoing boy she loved is still in there. A love that deep just doesn't die. I should know...those sorts of commitments transcend time."

Oh, God. The need to cry hit me in a torrential downpour. The emotions of Dylan shook me to the core, and all of the food I'd shoveled down my throat came up in chunks. Ryder quickly motioned to the restroom, and I stumbled inside and emptied the contents of my stomach in four violent episodes. I retched, cried, prayed for God to just-kill-me-now, but after a few minutes it subsided, and I lay across the toilet in a sweaty heap.

"I'm getting out of here," I said, wiping my nose on my sleeve. "I will try my best to make sure no blow-back falls on you, but you need to decide which side of the fence you want to land on when this shakes out."

"The Master won't like this," he said. "*Hart,*" he corrected himself, "won't like it."

Omigosh, I'd definitely placed a chink in his carefully constructed persona of a human android. *Keep chipping away, Darcy. Chip until he breaks out of his shell.* "No, he won't," I agreed, "but my specialty is getting into someone's head. Give me time, but do one thing for me." Unfortunately, Ryder acted as if he'd rather sit in a dentist's chair. "I need to know the various pseudonyms he goes by. We both know him as Hart, and I heard a man in the holding tank refer to him as Marx. Think, Ryder. If you know him by other names, I need that list. Getting those names will link him to other crimes, and once we get out of here, we can nail him to the wall."

If Ryder knew the names, he did not choose to divulge them.

I took a major gamble here that Ryder still had some humanity and free will left inside. But if he was totally a Van der Hart devotee, then I wasn't sure I'd be living much longer. No matter the case, I made the executive decision to not give him the name of Butch Lawrence, the stalker who killed my mother. Even if Ryder gave me up, I couldn't chance Daddy Dearest putting two and two together that I knew he'd murdered Gemma Walker. That would put a bullet in my chest quicker than anything else.

Ryder helped me to my feet. "I'll sneak you in the muffins," he whispered. "I will say nothing. If he lets you eat again, do not gorge. If you get sick, he will not send for a doctor...even if you *are* his child."

Chapter Twenty-Four

THE UNDERGROUND

I shuffled sleepily down a dark hallway, frustrated I couldn't get there fast enough. My legs felt heavy and newborn clumsy, falling over my pink DEFCON DARCY cape that hit me at the knees. The door slowly opened, and I stood center stage with The Minstrel Cramps. They were on their last set of songs, and my mom sung the ballad she'd written for Murphy's mother. Her short skirt and heels made her look like a movie star. Her long honey-blonde hair fell gracefully down her back as her fingers strummed the rhythm guitar. Her expression of sorrow made me want to cry. I closed my eyes and swayed back and forth in my sneakers, trying to feel the emotions she obviously felt. But suddenly, he was there. We were backstage. Mommy talked to him as if she knew him, but he only wanted to talk to me. She told him to leave. She told him Murphy would be here soon and would kill him. The man roared like a lion that he didn't fear Murphy, and Mommy told him that would be his biggest mistake. They argued, and he made a move to take me with him. I stiffened like a scarecrow and pounded on his shoulders with a, "Let me go! Let me go!"

Mommy yelled, "No, Butch!" and they struggled over a gun I didn't know he had. At first, I thought he'd listen, but then his face went angry like a monster, and I saw him pull the trigger on purpose. A bang as loud as a launching rocket went off, and Mommy fell to the floor, gasping for breath. He'd pulled the trigger on her while his fancy black diamond cross gleamed in the air. She gurgled, "Murphy. Run for Murphy, Darcy," but I was frozen, crouched with water running down my legs. I didn't want to leave her. I saw

267

the way the strange man gazed at her and feared he'd take her. After she talked to God for a second, she hummed and sang songs, but then she just stopped.

Something was wrong because the strange man went crazy, screaming to the ceiling, "No!" He pushed on her chest when he realized what he'd done. One, two, three...four, five, six. But he gave up when crunching sounds filled the air. He then slid to the other side of her body and told her he was sorry... then he said it was her fault...that she'd made him do it. When he tried to pick her up, I jumped on top of her and wouldn't let go. He said, "Smart girl," and patted me on the head. When he left, I remember all of a sudden being behind some boxes. I must've pulled her there, so he couldn't find us if he came back. Convinced we were hidden, I curled next to her and kissed each eyelid, telling her to have sweet dreams.

Son of a freaking nutcracker...

If my life wasn't bad enough being holed up in a godforsaken prison camp, I hadn't had that dream in years. Let me just say, thank you subconscious...you mother-trucking ponkey.

And that folks, was a play-by-play of exactly what'd happened to my mother—the incident that made me into the Darcy Walker some loved and some wished they didn't *have* to love. Butch Lawrence worked so diligently trying to revive her that he soaked his suit to the bone, slumping over her body when he'd spent his last bit of energy. Problem was, I counted his compressions for days on end, even after I'd been found and there'd been a funeral—until I finally confessed to Murphy I couldn't stop.

I pushed up on my elbows, weak from lack of food, and covered in an ice-cold sweat. Ryder made good on his vow to swing some muffins, but I still found they weren't enough to sate the constant hunger. Eight Ball had been too dumb to confiscate my iPhone, so I gave it to Ryder and begged him to charge it. When he balked and claimed it would be next to impossible, I scaled down the request with the instructions to abandon it somewhere in public. Ryder never claimed he didn't go topside, and to me it was worth the added risk. If someone charged it and attempted to dial, then the Apple store—fingers crossed—would pick up on the fact my phone was in operation. I knew Rookie. He'd have my phone heavily trolled. Problem was, it still wouldn't be verification I was alive.

Wiping my brow on Rainbow Brite, I pulled my legs to my chest and rocked back and forth, singing a lullaby my mom sang before she tucked me into bed. "You are my sunshine," I sang, "my only sunshine."

A bolt of power large enough to slingshot me to Wyoming launched me in the air. I bowling-balled into the back wall right as Eight Ball entered. "I brought you a friend," he muttered and dropped a large male frame like it was nothing more than a sack of trash. The shadowed body sagged like dead weight...out cold. Oh. God. He'd found Dylan.

And then I recognized the coppery-colored hair of Ben Ryan.

———

Ben had been out all night and most of the day, and I could only assume Eight Ball'd injected him with the same drug he'd shoved inside me. I massaged his pulse points and spoke to him nonstop all night long. I felt responsible, and I really didn't want him to die on my watch. Eight Ball not only acted as C.O. of the fighting unit, but apparently he did rounds—like a counselor in summer camp—to ensure everyone was tucked into the unit to which they'd been assigned. He walked in on me snuggled underneath the blanket with Ben, trying to give him my warmth. Eight Ball didn't appreciate the intimacy of the gesture, picked me up underneath my arms, and lifted me to his dead gaze.

"I tracked the two of you when you left Club Need last weekend, and then I spotted both of you at the movies," he'd said. "I will crush him. I thought he was just a friend. I can see it's something more."

Nausea pitched in my stomach at his words. It wasn't Mr. Himmel's presence I'd felt that night at the theater. It had been Eight Ball's.

Eight Ball unceremoniously dropped me in a heap next to Ben and left the room.

As a result of Eight Ball thinking I'd cheated on him, I'd been stripped of my new threads and issued a light blue prison uniform. Even worse, all they'd given me to eat was a bowlful of rice. It seems when Daddy Dearest happened to be away, my station in life was on shaky ground—or maybe *he'd* decreed that, and I'd find out later. Myles had just delivered two bowls of rice for Ben and me, introducing himself as The Master's top crony, a job he'd held for twenty-five years. My churning gut alerted me he'd driven the getaway car Eight Ball had shoved me inside. His eyes had a gaze that said, *I've seen it all.* After the last six days, I'd come to the conclusion he'd probably done it all too.

"May I serve you with anything else?" he asked.

I muttered, "Some cockroaches as protein might be nice because this carb action is eventually going to pile on the pounds."

Ben had wakened ten minutes before and was about as clear as the London fog. He immediately got with the program in a more mannerly way. "We're fine," he replied quickly. "Thank you."

"Very well," Myles said.

Myles bowed and backed away. My eyes fell on his little red bowtie, packaging a white shirt and black slacks I found a throwback considering the prison jumpsuit Ben and I wore. His getup resembled something Bean might put on Mr. Pongo. These were the thoughts of someone insane. And furthermore, I shouldn't be provoking him. Anything different, however, would be out of the ordinary.

When Myles was out of earshot, Ben said, "Darcy, I've been so worried. Are you okay? Did anyone," he stopped to wince, "hurt you?"

My legs had itched all day from dry skin. Running my hands up the legs of my pants, I felt the prickle of a week's worth of growth. I could add a razor to the list of amenities I'd taken for granted. Ben leaned forward to touch my hand and squeezed it between his, thinking I'd divulge I'd been some sort of sex slave. Not quite, but my circumstances weren't much better. I was victim of a homicidal man who thought he was my father...let's hope he truly was delusional. The only thing that kept me rolling out of bed, so to speak, was my resolve to see him go down along with all of his aliases.

"To answer your question, no one has touched me in the way you're insinuating. So physically, yes, I'm okay. Emotionally, not even close because I've had enough sick games done to me to last a lifetime."

I briefly explained to Ben what "in the wood" entailed and

watched some life drain from his silver eyes. "I'm tougher than I thought," I said quietly.

Ben blinked, fearing that to be a black-hearted lie. "Promise?"

At the moment, I was okay...God only knew if post-traumatic stress would surface and chain me to my home once rescued. "Ben, all we've got in here is our honesty. I will never lie to you."

Ben staggered up and walked the perimeter of the room, pausing to stare at the stack of bones I'd moved to the corner. "Yeah, it's bones," I told him. "I haven't quite figured out why they are all dried out yet. It makes me think they were placed in here as some sort of mind game to keep prisoners in check." Ben ferociously felt around the wall, checking for secret doors, no doubt. "There's no way out, Ben. I've tried. Eat your rice before it gets cold. I don't think a four course meal is on the horizon anytime soon."

Ben began to pace, running a hand through his thick hair. "Where are we, angel? I'm totally at a loss, but I'm sorry you've been alone." Hey, no one was sorrier than me. I took a few nibbles of rice and briefly wondered what Dylan had been doing. How had he handled my disappearance? Did he have a prescription for an anxiety drug? I was pretty sure I'd need one indef once I sprung the place. *Wow*, I thought. How that one argument between us changed everything.

"I don't know. A lower level of Club Need, maybe? Or close?" Ben's mental wheels began to turn. "What do people think happened to me?" I asked.

Ben dropped down beside me and took his black bowl in his hands. "They think you're a runaway," he said softly.

"Swell." A few more beats went by before I opened my mouth. "Did you tell them I wasn't?"

He closed his eyes...opened them. "I never knew what happened until Monday evening. Neither Dylan nor you showed at school, and honestly I didn't know if the two of you had skipped together. Monday skewed toward the bizarre as soon as first bell anyway. Principal Unger was extremely agitated and called an emergency staff meeting with the police accompanying him. It went on for a period and a half. Students aimlessly roamed the halls. I knew something big had gone down."

"Principal Unger is one of my dad's best friends. Murphy must've phoned him."

"Then I can only deduce you were top of the agenda. Tuesday morning I took off to see Gabrielle Allen. I wanted all the information I could find before I went to the police, but I was nabbed outside her home. I never even made it inside."

I placed my bowl in my lap, fighting the rising threat of hyperventilation. "Ben, it's Saturday. That means you were held somewhere else before you were deposited in my room last night."

God. Help. Us. That also meant no one had a clue what I'd been doing or that Ben had semi been in on it. Ben responded with, "I'm glad I have no recollection. So what information did Gabrielle give you, Darcy? And let me add, I don't think she was in on my abduction. I think someone followed me that morning and merely waited for me to get out of the car."

Probably Eight Ball.

I explained to Ben about Ryder Beck, how he'd been caught up in an underground fight club (one still operating), and how his friend Lyric Armstrong had died for information she'd stumbled upon—corroborated by Ryder. I also confessed I'd given Ryder my phone, hoping he'd deposit it some place public and that Ryder appeared to be game. I mentioned my relationship with Tito but never touched the connection to Jaws—there didn't seem to be a justifiable reason to out that relationship.

"Is there any reason—other than whatever Gabrielle provided—for you to be kidnapped? Why *you*, Darcy? Why *me*? As far as I know, Gabrielle Allen is still as free as a bird, and she has a connection to the story longer than you do."

Here was my word of advice to all males: if a girl you have a crush on asks you to take her somewhere, wait in the car, and barely answers your questions why, maybe you should take a pass next time. I picked up a bowl and took another bite of rice. "It was one of those guilt by association things, Ben. I'm so sorry you were blindsided. And to corroborate what you're probably already thinking, Lars van der Hart is in this up to his eyeballs. Thing is, that's not his real name. I found a diplomatic passport issued by the U.S. Government claiming he is Julius Marx. I have no clue who his birth certificate declares him to be, but to me and my family he's Robert 'Butch' Lawrence...the man who murdered my mother."

———

Daddy Dearest returned from his trip and briefly came to my room to meet Ben Saturday evening. He evidently had no idea Eight Ball would bring me a friend, and from the vibe I caught from Myles—which was merely a raised brow—Eight Ball reaped some sort of physical ramifications. Let me make myself clear...Eight Ball shouldn't be expecting a Christmas card. I didn't shed a tear.

Right when the cyclone of insanity couldn't get any weirder, Ben made the situation almost incomprehensible. He introduced himself with a handshake and boldly said, "I'm Ben Ryan, and I would like to fight for Darcy's and my freedom." He then explained he was a five-time mixed martial arts world champion, claiming his name and undefeated status could easily be searched upon on the Internet. At that, Ben scored us a personal invitation to sit in the private box with Van der Hart himself at the evening's matches.

Two hours later, we'd been allowed a shower and were told to dress in designer threads dropped off by Delia, the chick who'd been the server at our table last weekend. I hadn't noticed then—but Ben had—she had a tattoo, the face of a dragon and body of a snake, wrapping around her wrist. Eight Ball and Ryder sported the same.

"What did you have to do to get the tattoo?" I asked.

Ben raised a brow but allowed the conversation to roll. "The Master likes his personal staff to have them," she replied.

Delia's pupils were constricted like the tiny black dot of a BIC ink pen. Her breathing rolled out in shallow gasps, and she had that someone-tell-me-what-to-do-because-I'm-freaking-stoned look. Although beautiful, the woman was about ten pounds underweight. Yup, she was a user, the tremor of her hands sealing the deal. I grabbed her around the wrist and shoved her white long-sleeved shirt up her arm. She gasped at my rudeness and tried to twist away, but I held on like the jaws of a pit bull. There were no track marks visible which would insinuate heroin. So my guess was it was Oxycontin, which made more sense anyway. Those addicted to Oxy could still function...heroin, on the other hand, would make her a nervous zombie.

She yanked her arm away, suddenly self-conscious. "Let me guess," I said, "you started out in this place like me—kidnapped. What's your real name, Delia? Where are you from? Don't you wonder if someone is still looking for you?"

When Delia and I rubbed eyeballs, I knew why she'd so easily left her life behind...she was a purebred addict. Probably only good for the two or three hours she served patrons and then spent the rest of the time drugged up.

I wasn't sure Delia would ever find her will again, but I left her with a parting thought. "We're getting out of here, Delia. I will come find you and help get you clean."

Delia cocked her head to the side, her brain if not *all* gone, at least seventy-five percent cooked. When she left, Ben turned his back as I hurriedly dressed in a little black dress I might find attractive if I actually was going somewhere of my own free volition. It had long sleeves and a high neck decorated with Swarovski crystals. I punched my feet in black Christian Louboutin pumps and stood next to Ben who had on a black Hugo Boss suit. Daddy Dearest had some taste. Unfortunately, the both of us felt like nothing more than a lab rat or guinea pig.

A knock came at the door, and where I'd expected Daddy Dearest, I was rewarded with a visit from Blaze—the redheaded guard who was the unlucky chap who'd lost the tip of his nose to Eight Ball. Someone had performed the search and rescue because it had been sewn back on, rather crudely, but nonetheless repositioned with stitches. Needless to say, he didn't seem to favor me. Ben and I did as we'd been told and followed him in our first official visit to The Underground.

With a group of other prisoners, we were led about a quarter of a mile from our holding cells. We elephant-tailed our way together, holding hands with the one behind us, but Ben's hand was the only one I felt. I wasn't sure how long these people had been prisoners of Van der Hart, but humanity was missing in the majority of their eyes.

Once we'd reached our destination—an arena next to the

training facilities—Ben and I were separated from the others and led up the steps to the Plexiglas booth overlooking the octagon.

Finding a seat, it became apparent pretty quickly the room was made up of bimbos and booze. According to pre-match conversation, Van der Hart was a well known on-the-down-low manager of The Underground. Fight clubs, one would think, only occurred in a very urbanized setting. We were in Cincinnati, though, and like anywhere there'd always be some young fool who needed money that thought himself tougher than his DNA dictated.

When a group of fighters were brought in and placed in a dugout of sorts, I ferociously searched the crowd for Marek Ransom. In all these days, I hadn't run across him, but knowing his temper, it was highly possible he went nuts when first abducted and wound up without a heartbeat.

While Ben and I turned down an offer of booze, music suddenly blared overhead when an announcer grabbed the microphone dangling from the ceiling. "WWWellcommee to the Unndergroundd!" he drawled out. Oh, Good Lord. I recognized his voice as a DJ from a local radio station. I lay a hand on Ben's leg, Ben acknowledging the discovery with a small nod of his head.

The place erupted with cheers as Van der Hart rose above the crowd on a section of flooring in the middle of the octagon. It was about six feet above the heads of the fighters, and the crowd went wild when a laser light show commenced, smoke machines dispensing white fog. Like a politician on a tree stump, Daddy Dearest nodded to both competitors and then addressed the crowd. "You heard the man!" he said and laughed. "Now let's get ready for some blood!"

"Holy smoke, Ben," I whispered. "He's acting like a god."

Lars van der Hart loved attention. He certainly had that messiah quality, but evidently some patrons hadn't assessed he wasn't a redeemer. I had a feeling the group wasn't in the market for redemption though. It was blood, booze, and money in their pockets.

My heart beat like a scared rabbit. I'd never been to a MMA fight. I'd watched UFC cage matches on television, but this here was the real deal. Here's how The Underground worked. Each bout was three rounds only...rounds to last no more than five minutes duration...one-minute rest between rounds. There was no standing eight-counts. Fighters fought until they dropped. If a fighter was lucky, he got a five-minute rest between matches. Just with the sparring I'd already seen, these weren't fights-to-the-death, but they did remind me of Kentucky cockfighting. And those could be so vicious you wished a chicken would just die and get it over with.

First up was Slime Ball, challenging a male I didn't recognize. Slime Ball sported navy satin shorts to the knees while his opponent named One Eye donned yellow threads. Both had a coach in their corner. When the bell rang, they went at it like breeding insects, rolling all over the other and twisted together. Slime Ball had a dominant southpaw, connecting to One Eye's jaw, but One Eye went to the mat twice, refusing to tap out.

MMA fights took a toll, but while I studied the underground circuit, I realized it was suicide if you were unprepared and outmatched. The bell dinged at the end of round two, and when One Eye couldn't find a leg to stand on, Slime Ball's hand was raised as the winner.

As winner, Slime Ball was able to handpick his next opponent and would fight until Van der Hart told him his time in the ring had ended. Slime Ball cockily strutted to the dugout, blood draining from his nose, and slowly cocked a finger at a teenage boy half his size. I didn't want to watch. Slime Ball would make mincemeat of him, and since One Eye didn't tap out, I had a feeling the save-me-card would be majorly frowned upon.

Eight Ball spoke a few words to that teenager when Ben grabbed my wrist in an iron vice. "He's the bodyguard, right?"

"Yeah. That's Eight Ball. He failed charm school."

Ben slid over a wary gaze. "I know the name, angel. I thought he looked familiar last weekend when we visited the club, but I couldn't place him. He used to be a champion about eight or ten years ago. He received a lifetime ban from the sport when he killed Hurricane Cole, his competitor, in the ring."

The rice I'd eaten earlier was right then on my tongue. "Hurricane Cole? Eight Ball hums that Scorpions tune all the time."

Ben narrowed his eyes. "Then he didn't just steal Hurricane's life," he muttered.

"No jail time?"

"Charges were dropped. It was always believed someone bought off the prosecutor."

When match number two started, I left Ben to size up the competition and took my Louboutins to the back of the booth. Around twenty people were in attendance. Some standing. Others sitting. Some with their jailbait girlfriends hanging on them like baby chimps. I picked a squatty-looking man with graying-blond hair and a balding crown. The pants on his brown suit hung ankle length, and he wore orthopedic dress shoes similar to ones my grandfather would wear. His face was frozen like one of those ceramic dolls that were a collector's item—so devoid of personality I hoped he'd gotten dragged into this scene not knowing what it really was.

He strode to the bar and took a Cuban the bartender lit up for him. After one puff, he downed a Grey Goose and clanged the glass on the counter, motioning for shot number two. I touched him on the elbow and crowded into his personal space. "I'm being held here against my will, sir. This is not a joke. Could you take my friend and me home with you? I'm Darcy Walker. I'm not missing like everyone thinks I am."

When he merely blinked his dead brown eyes, I downsized that idea. "If you don't feel comfortable getting involved, then please tell Shepard Johnson I'm alive. He will not prosecute you for being here, but I just want to go home."

Dead Brown Eyes opened his mouth. "I'm very well aware of who you are, Darcy. Allow me to introduce myself. I'm Gilbert Himmel, brother of Art Himmel. Your aunt specifically ruined my brother's life."

Huh...*wow*.

Mr. Himmel's brother had obviously drunk the haterade.

He was a judge...a judge who knew full well what the charges of kidnapping meant and the punishment it entailed if caught. I saw the resemblance: a smile that was downright ugly, dirt-brown eyes, and a troll-like body that belonged on the pages of *Three Billy Goats Gruff*. "I see the similarities," I dumbly said. "Evidently, trolls pack some mighty powerful characteristics in your gene pool."

"Thank you."

I felt like throwing up, but I was hardwired to persist. OCD did that to you. "I mean, trolls can be good...you know, if you're into the troll thing. Ugh," I said exasperated, "I'm pro-troll, okay? I just want to go home. Please?"

My mouth needed to stop talking.

"You are the last person I would help, and just so you know, your aunt will go down for what she did to my brother."

"She didn't do anything to your brother."

"She led him on, promised him things she didn't deliver. By the time I'm through with her and her sordid past with her ex-husband, her career will be over."

I wanted to smack him, but at that point I'd grown desperate. "Hey," I said, "I understand the position you're in, but—"

The bottom fell out of my plan because lo and behold Daddy Dearest and his psycho face ran into the room at a breakneck speed.

He's onto me...I know the look...I know the feeling. "Now, Eve," he murmured. Ugh...back to Eve. "Come and sit with Dad."

Calling me Eve and speaking as if he was my father at least snagged Gilbert Himmel's attention. Unfortunately, not enough for him to uphold the law. He smacked Van der Hart on the back, downed his vodka in two swallows, and took a puff of cigar as his brunette jailbait girlfriend straddled his lap as soon as he sat down.

My walk of shame to Daddy Dearest might be the last jaunt my legs performed. Ben jerked his head when he heard the clickety-clack of my shoes and rose up, ready to throwdown. "I'm sorry," I told Daddy Dearest. "I'm kind of going stir crazy being underground like this. I need sunshine. I think I have that seasonal affective disorder. You know, SAD. Maybe you should get me a sunlamp, or better yet give me your credit card, and I'll go topside and buy one."

My attempt to win him over fell on deaf ears. His eyes drilled into me like laser beams. "Don't be dramatic, Darcy. The desperation doesn't suit you."

"You can't blame a girl for trying," I muttered.

"I do commend you for the effort."

"You are one sick ass production of a father, if I say so myself... respectfully, sir because I don't curse."

"I think you need another trip to the wood."

I'd rather go to Home Depot with Murphy than visit the wood

again. Tremors like the beginning of an earthquake started at my knees and continued upward until my shoulders shook uncontrollably. I didn't want to give him my fear. I thought I'd been strong, but faced with the prospect of being in closed quarters again nearly gave me a stroke. Ben held an air of power I'd only seen in Dylan. He placed himself between Van der Hart and me and said, "Let me fight tonight. I win, and Darcy doesn't go back to the wood. I lose, and *I* go."

Daddy Dearest rubbed the back of his hand down my cheek, gently "shushing" me like he did his birds. "I call the shots here, Ryan," he said. "You have not trained."

Ben held his chin high. "I do not need to train. Put me in the ring, and I will prove it to you."

Van der Hart laughed a hollow laugh. "You stand no chance against my best fighters. My daughter did not learn her lesson the first time. One week in the wood," he said. "She will watch you fight this time next weekend. You win, she will be freed."

Ben was a proud individual. I'd never seen him beg, and I'd certainly never seen him cry. Tears tracked down his face, but his words came out as strong and as powerful as thunder. "Please," he said. "Do not do this to her. I will make you more money than you know what to do with."

Daddy Dearest pulled me into a hug. I stiffened, willing myself to not give him one more ounce of my fear. "I have more money than I can spend in ten lifetimes," he said. "My decision has been made."

So close, man. So close.

Chapter Twenty-Five

THE SECOND AMENDMENT

I spent the next seven nights inside that cheap a-s-s pine box, let out during the day to stretch, use the restroom, and eat a bowl of rice at mealtime. I used to love Chinese food—Kung Pao chicken specifically—now I wasn't sure I'd ever willingly place rice in my mouth again.

Once Daddy Dearest thought I'd been sufficiently brainwashed (that came at three days in some sort of Easter miracle), he extended my daytime hours. After I got over the fact I occasionally lost bladder control, I reminded myself he got off by hearing me panic. If I stopped pounding, then he'd get bored and eventually let me out—the bathroom breaks and mealtimes therefore became longer. While buried alive, I took the time to recite the Periodic Table of Elements, The Ten Commandments, and what I could remember of the U.S. Constitution. I focused solely on my second amendment rights—the right to keep and bear arms. As God as my witness, anyone who hated guns would join the NRA if they endured what I'd just endured. I had plans to blow his freaking head off. Without a flinch.

During that time, Daddy Dearest gifted me with things he considered privileges: a Mrs. Beasley doll, videos of *Fraggle Rock*, *Sesame Street*, *The Love Boat*, and *My Little Pony*...even a Cabbage Patch doll with orange hair. Things more relevant to *his* childhood than mine—*an honest mistake, I'm sure.*

Dude had totally lost his marbles.

Ben and I had been separated since last Saturday night. I could only assume he'd been sparring with the other fighters and prayed daily he'd remembered how to kick butt and take names. Before I'd been released back to my personal cell, Daddy Dearest removed the bandage from my finger. As expected it was stiff, so I stretched the heck out of it—allowing him to believe I performed finger calisthenics when I merely exercised my first amendment right to fly the condor. Daddy Dearest seemed to think his show of compassion bonded us together, so I allowed him to believe we were as thick as thieves. My brain reminded me that mercy with him was the exception, not the rule.

I'd dressed in another long-sleeved LBD Delia dropped off—a mini with flared skirt, mid-thigh. Estée Lauder and Go Glam! Cosmetics were brought in to make me look like a million bucks when as soon as the show was over, I'd be back in the jumpsuit, praying someone would let me take a shower. But that was psychological warfare, wasn't it? Make you think you had a chance for freedom, only for your captor to yank it away with the snap of the fingers? While I dressed, Delia had been the real helpful type—making sure I was zipped in properly and free of unwanted lint. I made an appeal to her sense of self but again was rewarded with a stare just this side of vegetable.

When someone's knuckles rapped hard on the door, I fingercombed my fading ombré-blue hair and threw my shoulder's back, ready to be dutiful daughter, attempting to Black Widow Van der Hart into thinking I was harmless. When my hand circled the knob, instead of being greeted by Daddy Dearest, my visitor was a half-naked Eight Ball in black shorts and Nikes, ready for the night's games.

I gave him nothing. No shock at all. "The Master had to take an important phone call," he said, "so I was sent to fetch you."

Just like a bone, I thought. Instead of leading me to The Underground, Eight Ball closed the door, his dark features immediately morphing into horizontal thoughts. Oh crappity, crap-crap-crap. If things went south, I wasn't sure I could convince myself he was Dylan during anything intimate...but I had no choice but to try. "Let's dance," he said.

Daddy Dearest had taken to piping music in our holding cells. I didn't know if that was customary for a fighting day, or if he'd done it all week long, and being holed up "in the wood" made me unaware of new protocol. Right then, Tchaikovsky's "Swan Lake" played. "I'm a little rusty on my ballet," I said.

Eight Ball had the perseverance of a telemarketer on speed. "I don't know ballet either," he said in his cyborg tone, "but one dance won't kill you." Okay, it wouldn't kill me, but I'd rather blast Eight Ball's crotch with ten thousand gigawatts than share a dance.

Even with heels on, I craned my neck to flip-top league just to see his face. "Shouldn't we get a move on?" I asked. "My father will wonder where I am."

Eight Ball grew visibly PO'd. "Marx doesn't always run the show," he said gruffly. "I'm in control now."

Hmmm. Sounded like trouble brewed in paradise. I pondered what he'd done to Eight Ball to get him back in line. I didn't see any visible injuries, but Daddy Dearest seemed to specialize in mental pain.

"You don't call him The Master like everyone else. Why?"

"Because he doesn't own me."

Booyah! I'd found a weakness I'd learn to exploit. When I offered him a smile like good-for-you, his resulting leer nearly melted the skin from my bones. I swallowed, trying to convince myself Eight Ball wouldn't force me into anything intimate, but I knew that to be a lie. The door echoed with one brisk knock and in walked Ben, escorted by Blaze. The guard's nose had completely healed, but the grudge in his eyes said the rift between he and Eight Ball had only widened.

Blaze's voice was smug, cranking an I'm-better-than-you attitude. "The Master says Redcoat gets a few moments with the girl before the match." Ben...Ben must be Redcoat because they'd picked up on his British accent.

Eight Ball's face went ten shades of angry and then some. "I was not told of this."

Ben gave Eight Ball a tsk-tsk smirk, and then Eight Ball wanted to backhand his tsk. *Ben*, I sighed as our eyes met. His cocky grin quirked up at one corner as he reached for my hand and held it to his chest. He was ready to fight and looked well fed and strong. A small cut lay over his right eye, but other than the minor scrape, he was as pompous and infuriating as ever. Just Ben.

And oh, how I'd missed him.

A shrill whistle pierced the air, and Eight Ball immediately snapped to attention without even looking out into the hallway. Everyone swung their heads to the noise to see Ryder Beck slowly strutting up the hall, giving Eight Ball a no-no finger point a teacher gave a student who'd just broken the rules. And that point spoke volumes because Eight Ball dipped a subservient head and backed down like he'd encountered a crook in a dark alley. Had Eight Ball come to my quarters of his own accord? And furthermore, did Ryder hold a place higher up the totem pole than Eight Ball?

Ryder sported a white Adidas tracksuit with the word "Trainer" stitched on the back. By the way Ben grinned at him, I was struck with the knowledge he must be working Ben's corner. In the week Ben and I'd been apart, he'd somehow gotten Ryder and Blaze in his camp. Smart move.

Rubbing eyes with Ryder, his face was devoid of emotion, but I knew in my gut he hadn't uttered a word about our private conversation. If he had, Daddy Dearest would've covered the offense, and I'd still be in a coffin...or taking full retirement underground.

I placed my free hand on Eight Ball's chest. "Later, Eight Ball," I said, acting as if I'd given him a secret message.

I used to pride myself on the fact nothing shocked me—and after being introduced to a coffin, one would think I'd be beyond surprises. But Eight Ball's kiss came out of nowhere. With an explosive lunge, he yanked me to his side, plastering his mouth to mine. My response was automatic—I shoved against his chest while Ben had a death grip on my waist, pulling me in the other direction. Eight Ball wouldn't concede an inch. I put a deadbolt on my gag reflex and made it through about five seconds of Niagara Falls lip action. I deserved a freaking medal. He'd stolen the breath from my lungs, and I'd basically whored myself out to keep us alive.

I loved Dylan, was imprisoned with Ben, and just might become the concubine of Eight Ball to get us out of here. I had a sinking feeling things would only get worse.

———

Blaze became my ad hoc escort when Eight Ball fell through, and at some prompting divulged some of Daddy Dearest's best customers were flying in to see Ben's debut. I shivered with the knowledge, wondering why the FBI hadn't busted their little setup, or perhaps it was one of those situations wherein they looked the other way since I was pretty confident he worked for some branch of the government—or at least his alias Julius Marx did.

For dinner, Myles gifted me with another darn bowl of rice, but when Blaze and Ryder gave us that brief moment to ourselves, Ben emptied the contents of his pockets, pulling out napkins stuffed with pulled pork on rolls. Evidently, he'd been given a decent meal the night before and earlier in the afternoon as fuel because The Master—I snorted to myself—had high hopes for his career. But if Daddy Dearest was banking on Ben, the operative word there was "banking." He'd placed cash on him, and the only thing that made sense was he'd discovered Ben's undefeated status as an MMA champion. As a result, Ben had been given as much royal treatment as a kidnapped victim could expect.

When Ben slid the contraband underneath my cot, my eyes filled with tears at his generosity. He thumbed them away and swore, "I'll bring you more. I swear, Darcy. I'll make sure you don't starve."

Ben had obviously had to compromise his convictions by eating the full meals he'd won. He was vegan, but by the looks of him, he knew the protein was paramount. Falling into his embrace, I allowed someone other than Dylan to comfort me. When he placed his hand at the nape of my neck, I nuzzled as far into him as I could get without being on the other side. All Ben and I had in the frickin' frakkin' place was the other...and we both knew it.

I'd always been a go-with-the-flow kind of girl. That was the life of a verb. We acted...we didn't plan...we didn't worry about past mistakes. But if I could only have some sort of supernatural rewind, something miraculous to catapult me back seven years, then nothing like The Underground would've happened. I would somehow save my mother, and ergo I wouldn't be obsessed with bringing her murderer to justice. And likewise, Ben and I wouldn't have been kidnapped. But here we were...me rooting for a guy who was trying to win our freedom...Ben overly confident he could get it done. I had a feeling Ben might be too idealistic in his planning. Did I think Lars van der Hart would honor his request? Make that a negative. But right then, that was all we had...hope.

Even as Ben strode in front of me, the energy rolled off of him, churning like a power plant about to blow. The red satin coat he wore had the British Union Jack stitched on its back. It swayed back and forth while he bounced on the balls of his feet, revealing red, roomy satin shorts that hit him at the knees. Four-ounce open-fingered gloves hugged his hands, and white hand wraps were under-neath them. Ben said the open fingers were for when opponents grappled, vying for clinch fighting and submissions. Ben claimed he had two things he did better than anyone—kicking and submis-sions. His words to me? *Pray I've not been out of the ring too long, angel.*

I prayed aloud and made the sign of the cross in spite of my sinful ways—we needed all the help we could get.

Even amidst the turmoil of our lives, Ben had easily slipped back into his MMA routine. The fighting here would be untamed, but Ben traveled with the casual attitude and game day face of a winner. Still, it was gut wrenching to hear the humility in someone as proud as Ben. He was doing everything for me because if he lost? Ryder said he feared I'd become the property of the winning team—to do with, play with, however they saw fit. I wasn't sure I felt the neces-sary nausea, other than the waking fear Ben could be irreversibly hurt.

Ben had been slated to fight someone named Mad Dog. He had a reputation as being crazy and unpredictable. Ben didn't seem worried with the information. He merely nodded, offered me a cocky smile, and retreated into his mind.

By then, we'd made it to The Underground. If I thought it roared the other night, then my ears needed a serious eval on what they considered loud. I could barely hear my own thoughts over the jeering of the crowd. Ryder motioned for Ben to join him in their dugout, but Ben turned at the last minute and grabbed my face in his gloved hands, nuzzling my cheeks with his whiskers. Next, I got the cocky grin.

I half smiled, half wished to God we'd both die on the spot. All eyes in the dugout fell on me when Ben strutted away. It was then I understood what Ryder had been referring to. Ben had staked his claim that I was his. Like a dog, he'd basically peed on me.

Blaze ushered me up the stairs into the glass-enclosed suite I'd been in earlier with Gilbert Himmel. Although he wasn't in attendance, the rest of the clientele was the same...booze and bimbos... with guys whose most attractive thing about them was their wallets. As I made my way to a seat, a hairy gut that belonged on a pregnant orangutan brushed up against me. The man's shirt was a size too small, his waist so thick with blubber the shirt wouldn't tuck into black pants which clung to his thighs like wet dog hair.

"Sorry, luv," he said.

"No harm no—" I said, but his bimbo sidepiece wiggled her pink rhinestone dress between us before I could say "foul."

Chanel No. Five immediately bombarded by senses...too much Chanel because I sneezed on Bimbo's left mammary gland that was exposed and smooshed up in my face.

"Were you looking down my man's shirt, whore?" she hissed.

"Only if I were searching for stretch marks," I muttered.

Bimbo had the cat-eyes of Olivia Wilde, but a squeaky voice like Olive Oyl in the classic *Popeye* cartoon. I think her brain operated in a deficit because she didn't even clock on the slam.

I batted my eyes innocently, measuring my response with diplomacy. "I can't compete with you. He's all yours. I'm just here for the fight."

Bimbo craned her neck around the booth. "What fight? There's a fight somewhere? Baby," she gasped, turning to Fat Boy. "There's a fight."

I stole a glance at Fat Boy who was making love to a sweet roll that'd appeared out of nowhere. I didn't know what was worse: their idiocy, the obscene smacking of his lips, or the violence in the octagon. The slaps and groans of the two in the cage ratcheted to a higher decibel. A redhead named Francis had been trapped underneath the grappling legs of Slime Ball. I winced as Francis's face went blue and then white, while he ultimately tapped out when Slime Ball cranked his arm back so far it snapped at the elbow. The crunching sound of dislocating and breaking bone was enough to make an ER doctor hurl, but point for the redhead, he swallowed it down and nodded once to Slime Ball as the victor.

"Laaddies and gennnntlemen! The winner by tap out is Slllllliii-immme Baalllll!" he roared. After Slime Ball walked the perimeter of the octagon in a disgusting face-rubbing victory dance, he turned to the dugout, poised to pick another victim, but the announcer threw a wrench into his moment of glory. "Let me now introduce you to the newest fighter of The Underground!! This kid is the real deal and will double your bank accounts by the end of summer!"

Daddy Dearest was a presumptuous dickwad.

Slime Ball's testicles shriveled up when Ben jumped into the cage. Ben's hood remained over his head as he shadow boxed on the balls of his feet. A shiver of dread washed over me as Slime Ball stormed out of the ring, mouthing words in Ben's direction that obviously weren't "good lucks" or words of affirmation. Whispers and jeers rang out from the crowd below and inside the booth. Slime Ball had obviously been a crowd favorite. While some continued to boo, the announcer then bellowed, "And here is the promised attraction...Redcoat!"

At the mention of Redcoat, Ben dropped his hood and robe while bimbos in the crowd gasped, swallowed, and then after the shock wore off...ultimately drooled. Ben had an unbelievable body—not that I'd looked. Maybe I'd cheer too if I wasn't so afraid we'd both be at the bottom of the Ohio River by the end of the night. He was devastatingly good-looking, and it was never more prominent than when he was shirtless. While Ryder picked up Ben's robe and went to his corner, Ben took a moment to flirt with the women on the front row I called the psycho super fans. Smart move...he tried to build his reputation and get tons of money on him before the bell even gonged.

I had been under the impression bets were placed beforehand, but then I observed Myles and a couple of other men take bets from the floor and enter them into black portable hand units the size of a checkbook. I could only assume the hand unit was a small computer keeping track of the money placed.

Ben went to the edge of the octagon, holding his hands high, allowing a few of the overly aggressive psycho super fans to grope him through the chained fence. Bile came up my throat as Ben prostituted himself to these women, but when he abruptly swung his gaze to the booth with a wink, a hysterical laugh tumbled out of my mouth.

Lipstick stained his calves and thighs when he made his way back to the corner. While Ben continued to dance around and roll his neck, Ryder said a few words in his ear, placed a mouthguard between his lips, and then left the cage to anchor his corner. Ben's opponent, Mad Dog, entered in a white robe and was met with a mixed response. A couple of inches shorter than Ben, his bald head was too large for his body, and by the puffy look of his muscles, I'd bet someone laced his protein drink with steroids. His eyes had the hardened gaze of a psychopath, and they matched perfectly with the tattooed spikes around his neck.

I stood on the front row of the booth, smoke swirling my head from the idiots next to me who didn't care about lung disease. Listening to their talk, Mad Dog had permanently disabled someone with a kick to the head last weekend. Oh. God. Ben had been given one of the tougher opponents right out of the gate.

When the bell rang, Ben immediately lunged at Mad Dog, striking him twice in the ribs with a right-left combination. Clearly staggered, Mad Dog threw an uncoordinated swing, and through luck alone landed a shot to Ben's jaw. But Ben was so cold, he was almost ice. All he did was blink it away and pound again at his ribs. Mad Dog then kicked a left leg at Ben's knee. Ben dodged a follow-up blow and delivered another shot to Mad Dog's kidneys, followed with a spin and kick to the opposite side.

Mad Dog winced and grunted at the body shot, baring his teeth like a Doberman on the job. With nothing more than a football tackle, he took Ben to the mat, but after about ten seconds on the ground, Ben came out of his clutches like Houdini.

I was on fire, but goose bumps covered my body—I couldn't mouth a word but could only rock back and forth and lean into Bimbo who held on to me for dear life. One of Ben's specialties, I reminded myself, was submissions. He had an opportunity to shut up Mad Dog permanently, but he merely got out of the hold and kept fighting.

Finally, a bell rang alerting the crowd round one had ended. Ben sat on the stool in his corner, sweat dripping from his hair and chest like he'd been in a steam room with a please-kill-me temp. When the sixty-second rest ended, Ryder toweled off Ben's face and returned his mouthguard before he went back into the ring. Once the bell dinged, Ben purposely absorbed a blow to the face and roared like a savage when his right foot connected with Mad Dog's jaw.

Mad Dog went down to the ground, and Ben immediately went into a submission hold, wrapping his legs around Mad Dog's waist. Mad Dog struggled to free himself, but Ben's silver eyes went stormy, and I knew he flipped the metaphorical switch in his brain that made him an undefeated champion. After several seconds of flounder, Mad Dog's body slumped in Ben's arms, passed out.

Goodbye, Mad Dog. I'm not going to miss you.

Ben showed zero remorse when two men carted Mad Dog away. Instead, when his arm was raised in victory, he swung his gaze toward me and unloaded that exasperatingly cocky, rocker snarl.

Ben Ryan was the real Clark Kent type—a total study of looking one way to the world—but the real man was beneath the clothes.

Chapter Twenty-Six

SCARLETT O'HARA

A loud rap startled me awake...

Ben, I thought. It had to be Ben.

Once Ben took two more grown men down in submission holds, fighting ended for the night, and Blaze led me down to the octagon. Ben made it publicly known I was his with a quick hug but hadn't been allowed to leave the premises with me. Instead, Ryder'd paraded him over to Daddy Dearest like some slave from an auction block who'd been a wise investment. I'd erroneously assumed Ben's reward would mean time with me—time where the two of us could put our heads together and think our way out of here. Or at least simply talk to someone who wasn't a lead character in *Lord of the Flies.*

Problem was, when the door opened and I mumbled, "Nice fight, Redcoat," I was shoved back inside with a door slam by the snarling smile of Slime Ball.

Ugh...I shouldn't have answered the door.

Slime Ball had me on my back quicker than a 'ho going for twenty bucks. I clawed and scratched—sinking my nails into his skin—but it was like trying to saw through a redwood with a toothpick. Slime Ball's hand circled my neck, commencing to squeeze. When someone has his hand around your neck, you automatically attempt to remove it. But the more I struggled, the more Slime Ball crushed my windpipe. I was in a no win situation. If I struggled, I'd be dead. If I didn't, my V-card would more than likely be a thing of the past.

"Please, let me go," I coughed out.

Slime Ball cocked his head to the side with an uncharacteristic concern. "Am I hurting you?" he asked.

"Y-yes," I stuttered.

Slime Ball slowly closed then opened his eyes and whatever sliver of humanity I'd conversed with a sentence earlier had been snuffed out. "Good," he seethed.

"You're not my type," I said.

"But I will be."

"Trust me, there's no organic chemistry on my part," I wheezed out.

A shiver rattled my bones when my eyes landed on Slime Ball's right hand—the hand caressing my face like we'd get all up close and personal. It had been marked with the same tattoo Eight Ball and Delia sported...Ben thought only the good-looking wore it. Eh, not the case with Slime Ball.

"What did you do to get the tattoo?"

"Nothing was forced on me that I didn't want...that I did not request."

Without saying a word, the knowledge slowly bled into his eyes he'd sworn some kind of allegiance—he'd made a deal, or done something—that gave him the privilege of going topside. What in God's name grabbed the man's soul and replaced it with one ugly inside and out?

"How did you know where to find me?"

"I stalk my prey," he breathed hotly in my ear.

With every bit of effort in my body, I attempted to push both my hands up through his hold but got nowhere. When I sank my fingernails into his forearms, Slime Ball gave me a glimpse of his forked tongue, running it along my jaw...I screamed. I screamed so loudly I prayed Eight Ball would hear and bust down the door. And did I actually consider Eight Ball a better option? When my throat began to throb like a rotten tooth, I realized no one was near. And if they were, they didn't care one bit about Darcy Walker's ability to live another day. *Think, Darcy*, I said to myself. *Think or*...

All of a sudden, Slime Ball was picked up and thrown into the air like a shot put. As I struggled to stand, I saw Ben coming at him in a blur of motion. Slime Ball's reflexes didn't let him down, and he quickly righted himself and attacked Ben like a tornado in springtime. Ben blocked a series of punches and then pivoted and back-kicked Slime Ball square in the face. Blood spurted from Slime Ball's nose, and Slime Ball went down hard. Ben straddled his sagging, partially comatose body, placing a chokehold around his neck.

Slime Ball jerked like he'd touched a live wire and immediately stilled. "Feel that burn?" Ben seethed in his ear when Slime Ball cracked a lid wide. "That's the strain on your spine. You can't move, can you?" he murmured, laughing darkly. "One move the wrong way, and I can end your life by separating your head from your spinal cord. Your call. You either leave Darcy alone or I kill you now."

"Redcoat!" someone roared.

Ryder Beck.

Ben didn't break stride and never even glanced over his shoulder in recognition. In fact, he acted as if he'd bury Slime Ball alive if he had a shovel. "Ben," I said frantically. "Let him go."

Ben, however, bated Slime Ball. "You'd better tap out," he said. "I'm not feeling very forgiving."

Slime Ball lay facedown, his hands palms-up at his side like the flippers on a seal. He moved the fingers on his left hand in a two-tap, and I knew Ben's goal had been to humble him even more by forcing him to concede defeat. I didn't think that was a good idea. Slime Ball had found me. Had he been allowed to roam free? I'd assumed he'd been placed in lockdown after his loss, but after thirteen days, I still wasn't sure what went on outside the confines of my own cell.

Ryder attempted to ctrl-alt-delete Ben again. "Redcoat," he said firmer. "That's an order."

With a reluctant grunt, Ben stood up and pulled me into his side. "How did this happen?" he barked at Ryder.

"Blaze is dead," Ryder said emotionlessly. "He'd taken Slime Ball to his quarters when he acted up. I can only assume he did not like you, and when Blaze tried to corral him, Slime Ball came out the winner."

"And where is Eight Ball?" Ben followed-up.

"Right here," Eight Ball answered. Dude, seriously, too many guys named Balls (or *balls*, if you know what I mean) to make a girl feel comfortable.

It didn't take a rocket scientist to figure out Slime Ball's intention had been to hurt Ben by attacking me. When Eight Ball put two and two together, his android demeanor changed in a flash. He bent over a completely passed out Slime Ball and snapped his neck without breaking a sweat. I flinched and closed my eyes at the crunch, stuffing my head into Ben's neck. As evil as Slime Ball was, I tried to will breath back into his lungs—but that crunch said it all... Slime Ball was DOA. "Go," I heard Eight Ball say. "Eve has been compromised. Find her another room. I will take care of this."

———————

My name is Darcy Walker. Darcy Winston Walker. I am not Eve. Lars van der Hart is not my father, and neither is his alias Butch Lawrence despite the fact he swears he is. I have a life. I have a boyfriend. I have a family that loves and misses me. Tomorrow I will get out of here. Tomorrow I will see everyone freed. Tomorrow the bad will be brought to justice. Tomorrow...

I realized I'd mumbled everything aloud when Ben squeezed my hand and told me I could stop.

These were things before bedtime. Each night I figured I could curl into a ball and cry...or go Scarlett O'Hara and vow, *Tomorrow is another day*. But my inner-Scarlett had grown weary. Listen, it wasn't the plot for the next Nicholas Sparks novel, okay? These guys were sick mofos who existed in their own twisted counterculture. A culture where I still couldn't figure out the rules. And to survive, one's sense of self-preservation either kicked in and you learned to cope, or one took desperate measures. Unfortunately, Slime Ball took desperate measures for some reason. Would I snap next?

Ben and I were alone in my new quarters, sitting on a lumpy cot with Rainbow Brite's smiling face slung around both of our shoulders. No bones were here, no instruments for servitude, but the stark feeling of loneliness painted the walls. The room was quite a bit smaller, but for once the claustrophobic feeling was comforting. It made me feel invisible, unimportant. I had no idea where Daddy Dearest was, and by the rare frazzled looks on Eight Ball's and

Ryder's faces, they didn't either. But I knew enough that a dead fighter was not something Ryder or Eight Ball liked to deal with... especially if it wasn't a kill Daddy Dearest endorsed. Pardon me, *two* dead fighters—Slime Ball and Blaze. And two dead fighters would eventually smell, so unless they had a woodchopper somewhere to dispose of the remains, my guess was both men occasionally went topside. At least, I knew Eight Ball did. He had his bodyguard gig. But did Ryder? When I asked him to leave my phone somewhere public so it could be found, he never said the request would be impossible. But here's the thing, if he had a sliver of humanity left, why hadn't he gone town crier as soon as he hit the daylight?

"33.5000° N, 36.3000° E," I whispered. "33.5000° N, 36.3000° E." Dear, Jesus. My mouth was playing on a loop.

"What?" Ben said. I repeated the numbers again, my OCD working double time. "Darcy, why are you saying the coordinates for some place in the Middle East?"

Coordinates, I thought. Map coordinates. Of course, that made total sense. Reminding Ben about the Julius Marx diplomatic passport I'd discovered, I explained Daddy Dearest's trip hadn't been long.

"Maybe a trip to Washington?" I surmised. Ben said he could piece the coordinates together for sure if he could score a map, but I knew a day trip to the Middle East would be virtually impossible unless The Enterprise beamed him up via Scotty. Either way, both of us believed he had ties to the U.S. Government. "Do you think Ryder can get us a map? Maybe some newspapers on the days Van der Hart traveled? He's in charge, right?"

Ben scrunched up his eyes in a frown. "I don't know if he can get those things, but if the opportunity presents itself, I'll certainly ask. Yeah, I think he's in charge, but he allows Eight Ball to tend to the fighters at night. At any time, he can usurp his power, but he picks and chooses those instances very carefully. Whatever you do, don't trust Eight Ball, Darcy. We've been playing one another all week, and he doesn't appreciate the fact Ryder has taken an interest in me."

"What has Ryder said to you? Has he told you I requested he get the names of Van der Hart's aliases?"

Ben's frown deepened. "No, he never mentioned your request,

and right now I feel the safest route is to play dumb. You've asked a lot of him. It may take awhile for him to act on it. Either way, I see it as a good sign he's keeping your confidence."

The pipes underground screeched and hissed with the temperature, and a cold draft circled the floor. Snuggling into Ben, tears appeared out of nowhere when he told me Daddy Dearest had promised him we'd be free after one win. As one could see, we were both still prisoners. "We're going to die in here, aren't we?" I whispered. "He's never going to let us go."

As soon as those words fell from my mouth, that nagging little voice in my head whispered, *What if he's your father? What if you're the legitimate progeny of someone who doesn't care about ending someone's life? Maybe even an assassin?* Someone had to know what he did, didn't they? I mean, watch any news show, and they claim the government powers-that-be want to keep the information flowing—sometimes jamming their fingers in their ears and singing la-la-la at the atrocities spies perform in their private time.

"We're not going to die," he promised. "Die tomorrow if you want, but seriously, just not tonight."

He couldn't say for sure we'd make it out of here. Maybe Eight Ball would go psycho again and snap both our necks on a whim.

All I knew was I wanted a night full of Mexican food, crappy reality TV, stalking Instagram posts, and taking selfies with Marjorie. I longed for Murphy to yell at me because I hadn't been studying and for him to hug me when I was sad. I needed Red to mother me and for Claudia to insist I put voodoo cream on my boobs. I longed to gossip with Rudi and Justice about how much our lives sucked. I wanted to plan Marjorie's next birthday party, visit Grandpa Winston in Kentucky, and have an all-night board game tournament with Rookie. I wanted to pester Grumpy, send Snapchats to Vinnie, mother Bean, hug Finn, and I needed my boyfriend...I needed my boyfriend to kiss me and make it all better.

Right then, my system ran on pure guts and the iron-will to see my loved ones again. But I'd be lying if I said the prospect of doing the nasty with Slime Ball hadn't rattled me. I wasn't sure how much longer I could keep one step ahead, especially if the sheer adrenaline of fear ran out. The moment I lost my mental edge, I knew in my gut I'd never see daylight again.

"I just wish Dylan were here," I sobbed. "He'd know what to do."

"I'm going to win, angel. It's what I do. Talk," he encouraged. "Talk before Eight Ball returns. I don't want to leave you like this."

"I need to talk about...*her*."

Ben's voice turned tender. "Your mom?" Score one for Ben. He was the sympathetic, discerning type. I didn't know much about Ben. Okay, I didn't know *anything* really, but I'd come to care for him on a level that was instinctive.

"Dylan is the only one I talk about her with."

"Then act like I'm him. What would you say?"

"I'd say I miss her, D."

"Then what?" he said softly.

"He'd say, take your time, Darc. We've got all night."

"What would happen next?" he said even softer.

"I would say I'm lonely, and I sometimes don't understand how I can be lonely in a room full of people."

"Aw, angel, I'm so sorry."

"He'd say, I'll try my best to fill the void."

"He sounds like a wonderful friend."

All I could do was sob harder. "I would tell him how she was going to make pancakes. She was a terrible cook, but for some reason she could make the best pancakes in the world. I haven't eaten them for seven years, Ben." Three quick gasps left my lips. "I can't even remember what they taste like."

"When we get out of here, I'm going to take you for pancakes, okay?" I sniffled and nodded into his neck. After a few breaths, he said, "Darcy, do you think Van der Hart could be your father?"

"No, but the longer I'm here, the more my mind plays with me. He doesn't know I remember him as the shooter, but I remember he had plans to take my mom's body. I couldn't let him have her. I knew she'd been afraid of him. Afraid for *me*. So I laid on her through rigor mortis. And I lay there so long that when she began to get limber again, I thought God had answered my prayers and brought her back. He didn't," I sobbed. "My introduction to evil was at age nine."

I was found a day later. Butch Lawrence made his getaway in my mom's car, so for a short period Murphy and Red feared we'd been carjacked. In the first sweep of the building, we weren't found, but in a second attempt, I was able to yell back to a police officer.

"Get it all out, angel. It's a poison."

"I'm just always trying to stop bad things from happening. I know that puts me in danger, but if I stop doing it, then what about the people who I actually helped? I don't know how to be someone else, Ben. I was just a little girl," I whispered.

Feelings crashed over me, and I struggled with the intensity. I wanted to say something sentimental but was racked with a sorrow so deep it nearly sliced me in two. Ben's eyes promised things would be okay, but more than his promise was fear—a bone-chilling fear all the way down to the molecular level. He thought one or the both of us would die, although his words said otherwise. I wasn't afraid to die. I'd experienced things worse than death because I'd breathed right through them. One thing I couldn't survive was the fact Ben might die because of something I couldn't let go.

I was surprised he didn't panic when I suggested we give one another our "last will and testaments." We'd just witnessed some-one's murder and then be carted off like a bag of trash. In fact, Ben acted relieved and even more relieved when it didn't spook me into a greater show of hysterics.

I told him, "My family will know I love them." Then I paused, my voice cracking, wondering how I *could* and *should* phrase things. "But I need Dylan to know, okay? I've never...I've never...told him. I was scared."

Ben asked softly, "Why him?"

Whatever was between Dylan and me would always be between Dylan and me. Still, I found myself answering, "Dylan's my default setting, and he never cared that I got weird for a while. He just wraps his arms around me when I can't find the words. He's not who you think he is, Ben. I've felt the tension between the two of you."

"If you care for him so deeply, then I'm sure that means he's worth it, Darcy."

My life felt alarmingly bare. If fate conspired my downward spiral, then witnessing a murder and almost getting raped had been a pretty good start. "What's her name, Ben?" I asked.

"Huh?"

"The girl you love. You're too cute and honorable to be unattached."

If I wouldn't have been snuggled into him, I wasn't sure I would've noticed, but Ben stiffened at the question. "Autumn," he finally said with reverence. "My first love was Autumn."

"Do you still love her?"

A short pause. "I believe I do."

"Then I promise you if *I* make it out, and...you *don't*," I said and grimaced, "I will find Autumn and tell her."

Whatever memories Autumn conjured up—or maybe it was just the heaviness of the conversation in general—Ben's mood shifted. He seemed sad when I wasn't used to him being anything other than all systems go and cocky. "Come here and lie next to me," he said. "I can promise no one is going to hurt you tonight."

Ben and I snuggled down onto the mat, knowing Eight Ball or Ryder would bust up the party after they disposed of the bodies. Before long, Ben's wet tears dripped silently on my cheeks, and I wondered what Dylan would think if he saw us crying, clutching one another so tightly in a desperate attempt to find someone who had your back.

Scarlett O'Hara, I thought as I closed my eyes. *Scarlett O'Hara.*

Chapter Twenty-Seven

OLD HABITS DIE HARD

*N*o man is an island.

People need people. You need people even if you really don't like them that much. Problem was, I attracted the wrong type of people, and I couldn't shake the filth they brought along with them. But now that I'd *lived* with them...I craved the sane.

I woke singing AC/DC's "Highway to Hell."

Now there was a sobering thought. I'd dodged being raped several times, sharing a syringe with an overzealous junkie, and getting the crap beaten out of me by a girl who actually enjoyed being the property of one of the fighters—even though he was dog-butt ugly. My goal, if I ever sprung the joint, was to be boring.

My sleep rhythm had been disturbed. I slept during the day, so I wouldn't think about what had befallen me and stayed up at night because I knew that would be my best chance for escape. One night, Eight Ball left my door ajar when he heard a disturbance down the hall, and I tiptoed outside. I counted at least two-dozen doors before I viewed an exit that had been propped open by Myles while he brought in supplies. When he had his back turned, I scrambled up the steps, and that was when it dawned on me we weren't in downtown Cincinnati. Honestly, I hadn't a clue where we were. Wherever it was, it appeared to be an abandoned section of real estate in a crappy section of town. Oh. Joy. What did I take away with that knowledge? There were massive holes in the security of The Underground, which made zero sense for a man who had remained incognito for years. That meant there were security cameras somewhere, and they hadn't tracked me yet, or the guy was so overly confident he felt he and his pastime were infallible.

I could've gone for it then, but the thought of leaving Ben was like a dagger in the gut. Undoubtedly, he'd have to deal with the wrath of Lars van der Hart, and maybe even worse. When you became the subject of scorn and ridicule in The Underground, it didn't last long...and neither did you.

Suddenly, you just disappeared.

I'd begun to acquire things...the PC way of saying I'd stolen them. I lifted a watch from Delia, a steak knife from Myles, and tried my best to endear myself to these two as Daddy Dearest periodically allowed me to roam the halls. I wasn't sure I'd made any headway, but I kept trying to wear down their psychological defenses. While out and about, I discovered there were schedules in The Underground. All of the fighters did not work out at one time. I used my time in gen pop to find out where everyone had come from. From what I'd discovered, it was about a 50/50 divide of those who came looking for a fight club experience, and those who'd been acquired through a hostile takeover because they looked athletically inclined. Most didn't feel comfortable speaking with me, but when I threw Redcoat's name around, I found out rather quickly those who liked Ben and those who'd just as soon slit his throat. I made sure to pass that information on to Ben each evening.

My goal of the week was to create some sort of false intimacy with Daddy Dearest, outside his psycho ramblings about how we'd finally been reunited...blech. I needed more freedom, but I didn't know how to accomplish that yet, especially when he traveled at the beginning of each week, sometimes several days at a time. On the days he traveled, Eight Ball was up in my business like the thong up Indigo's butt. Thank God, Eight Ball was dumber than dirt.

Ben indisputably reigned as the undefeated champion of The Underground, sometimes fighting three times in a row—which was exactly why he had a target on his back. As reward, he requested I be given one full meal a day to be eaten with him. Although miserable with hunger, I consumed only half and insisted Ben eat the leftovers. My muscles had atrophied and more ribs protruded daily, but I was more afraid of waking up to a dead Ben beside me. The only perk to dwindling away? God's monthly gift hadn't come one time in captivity. Thank my lucky stars I didn't have to deal with the additional hormones.

When Ryder came to see me a few days earlier, upon prodding, he confided the various aliases of Daddy Dearest: Pierre LaFayette, Mahesh Singh, Jared Ming, and Igor Guskov. These were the four Tito had mentioned, and I had the fifth of Julius Marx from Jaws. Plus, Cincinnati knew him as Lars van der Hart, and my family called him Robert 'Butch' Lawrence. I had the mother-trucker in my claws. Now all I had to do was escape. And since Ryder claimed his passports were stored in a safe in his private quarters, that meant when I visited my so-called father again, I'd get my safe-cracker on.

Ryder also scored Ben a map, and since whoever Daddy Dearest worked for sometimes phoned while I was in his presence, I memorized the coordinates and gave them to Ben whenever we shared third meal. With Ben's map, we deduced he'd traveled to (or had business with delegates at) Syria, Afghanistan, London, Lebanon, Canada, and Mexico. There was no way of telling what exactly the travel arrangements had been, but once we escaped, I could establish a trail of his whereabouts or at least a trail of his different aliases.

Research says it takes twenty-one days to form a habit...seven to break it. Another four weeks had passed, and although I'd developed a routine, some habits die hard. As much as I tried to live in the present, I wondered what had been going on in my previous life.

I missed pop culture gossip...did *Kourtney & Khloé Take the Hamptons*? Were Justin Bieber and Selena Gomez back on or off? I missed going on dates with Dylan where I changed my clothes four times because I couldn't find the right look. I missed Valley High. Spring sports had begun, new grass had sprouted up, and the land of blah was turning green. Murphy had probably started his annual diet, and M had hopefully grown an inch. I hadn't realized how much I took the daily grind for granted, but I quickly realized anytime I was awake—even if I was by myself—I really wasn't alone because of a thing called memories. And my memories continued to cast a spell on me, willing me back to my best friend almost as inevitable as a bear to love honey.

Closing my eyes didn't erase Dylan, and telling myself he was uglier than ever didn't either. I knew every line of his body and every curve in his face. Hearing his voice might've given me hope tomorrow would be a better day, but as it was...it was just another day in The Underground.

After my weekly shower in Daddy Dearest's room, I attempted to exercise my once-broken finger, but as much as I tried, it was stuck in a permanent condor. Seriously, it was the only bright spot of the whole ordeal—I now had a legitimate excuse to flip off people I hated.

I dressed in another LBD and stilettos complements of Delia. Like before, I made a plea to her long-gone independence, telling her to help me gain my freedom...I'd help get her clean, etcetera. Delia merely blinked and left the room, but it was always worth a shot.

Daddy Dearest himself waited outside the bathroom while I'd dressed, planning to escort me to the booth personally. He claimed Ben was slated to fight three opponents, but if the crowd was into it and the fights ended before the maximum three rounds, that could grow to five. As always, I nodded courteously and tried not to show the hysteria swirling in my gut that one day Ben would snap under the physical and mental pressure.

I'd begun to worry about his ability to sustain reality. Two times during dinner he referred to Van der Hart as The Master, and I made him repeat back to me verbatim what he'd stolen from us. I demanded he even mention the names of his family members and what he thought they'd been doing. It had been easy for me to retain my sanity because I'd been left alone for the biggest part of the day. Ben, however, had been thrown to the lions and had to survive in psychological and physical warfare. I wasn't sure he could find his norm if we ever escaped without massive amounts of deprogramming.

Concerned for Ben, I even asked Ryder how Van der Hart could win over the smart ones. *Here's what happened to me,* he'd said. *I was told after ten wins I could get out, but when that didn't happen and The Master gained a larger foothold in my life, I grew as overbearing, hard, and unhinged as him. When I was alone, the old Ryder would surface but couldn't stay around long if I wanted to survive. The moment Van der Hart senses your independence returning, he will imprison your mind like he does the ravens in his room.*

Point for the home team, the biggest miracle so far was I'd found a tunnel the night before while walking the perimeter of my quarters. My room was brick and stone, and when I traced the outline of a brick that hit me at the thighs, I heard a tiny click and a portion of the wall measuring around four feet by four feet gave way. Right then, I had plans to enter the cavern, see where it went, and pray to God it was the Bat Cave.

In the past month, I'd read the complete works of Edgar Allan Poe on visits to Daddy Dearest's suite—I'd read them so much I could recite *The Raven* and *The Tell-tale Heart* verbatim and often did when I couldn't fall asleep. When he recognized my boredom, I'd also been given a sketchbook to pass the time. My mother was an artist. She sculpted and painted watercolors. Other than bad eyes, blonde hair, and a good sense of humor (currently lacking), drawing was one of the few things I'd inherited. I drew pictures of every prisoner in The Underground—marking who was sane, iffy, and so far gone they needed a bullet to the brain.

"Let me see what you've drawn, baby," he said when I closed up the sketchpad and placed it under my arm.

"It's a surprise," I said.

"Oh, okay. We've got all the time in the world, Darcy," he murmured. Nausea pitched in my stomach when he didn't fight me —that meant he had no plans of ever letting me go. But thank God for the little things. At least, he hadn't called me Eve.

His eyes softened, and he touched my forehead with the back of his cold hand. "Are you feeling well, Eve? You're being very quiet."

Ugh, schizophrenia might be at work here. "Rice can do that to you," was my answer.

"Did your morning darjeeling not help?" he piped up. "I have no plans to travel for a while, and I've missed you. Why don't we add on some nightly hot cocoa?"

And I was pretty sure he would take me to dinner and a movie if I asked nicely...cue the eye roll.

Before he could 86 the idea with second thoughts, I tacked on some bogus exuberance in an attempt for him to think I truly wanted to spend time with him. Thing was, that would fit into my plan nicely. The mornings we'd drunk darjeeling together, I'd scoped out his place like an Apache scout. The safe Ryder referred to was hidden behind a picture of Daddy Dearest and four other men in military fatigues. And are you ready for this? They didn't look like American soldiers. When I inquired about his past, he went back and forth between thinking he was my father to being a psycho former spook, and after that photograph, I wasn't so sure it was the good old U.S. of A. he called boss.

"I would love that," I said. I even added on a pathetically dumb blonde squeal.

A raven in the cage nearest me blinked twice, like it acknowledged the lie but thankfully couldn't form words. "Wonderful," he said chuckling. "I'll send Eight Ball for you after the fights tonight."

"Tell me about the picture," I asked again, going for broke.

At first he didn't know to what I referred, but when I nonchalantly pitched my head to the photograph, he dumped birdseed in a cage for another raven and smiled. "Ah, they were my best friends," he said. *Were*, I thought. *Past tense*.

"What branch?" I asked.

Again, he sidestepped the detail and launched into how he acquired information and assets for the government.

"That must be rewarding," I said. "You know, protecting American people."

Once again, no divulgence that could incriminate him. Instead, he launched into his daily talk of my mother—telling me how he loved her new haircut, how he'd been disappointed she turned down the contract with a record label, and how it had been a point of contention between them because he longed to join her on the road. He had just enough insider information it made me believe at one time he'd been in her inner circle. But from what I knew about stalkers, they only took things to the next level when they suddenly felt secure in their obsession—like the vic had given them a green light of some kind. He even went on to brag on my mom and how she'd dropped her weight so quickly after the birth of Marjorie. I listened carefully here because he'd never mentioned M before, and I feared he harbored plans of having her join us. Thing was, he sometimes spoke of my mother as if she were alive, and he was so convincing I would've believed him if I wouldn't have been there when she took her last breath.

As per usual, he placed his fist to his chest with his elbow out to the side. I had no option but to link my arm in his and pretend we were one big, happy family. My mind called up a memory of Murphy. Would he understand what I'd been trying to do? At the end of the day, maybe I was doing it more for my father than me. Although Murphy rarely spoke of the incident, I knew it would give him closure if I could say we'd nailed the fastard who shot his wife.

"I've got splendid news," Daddy Dearest said. "There's a new fighter on the circuit. I've put out feelers through a mutual friend that he's invited to The Underground on an open invitation. The male is averaging five fights a night. I think he could give Redcoat a real run for the money. He's undefeated and has put two well-established fighters in the hospital indefinitely. Rumor claims one is drinking a liquid lunch, and the other is communicating by sign language. His management is fast-tracking him."

I swallowed at the possibility of Ben meeting the fighter who had impressed Daddy Dearest. Up until that moment, Ben had been the aforementioned messiah. Granted, he averaged three a night, but it was my impression that was all Van der Hart would allow. Right then, it appeared Ben's place on the hierarchy might be on shaky ground.

———

There is a pendulum of evil in the world in a constant swing. It swings somewhere in the land of choice and meant-to-be.

That truism was no better represented than with Gilbert Himmel. He and his newest jailbait girlfriend sat on the row behind me in the booth, and when I turned for a stare down, his dirt-brown eyes acted as if he didn't recognize me. He hadn't attended The Underground since our first introduction, and it made me wonder what was so special about the evening for him to make an encore. "I take it your brother is still on house arrest," I said sarcastically. "My guess is his attorney doesn't have a leg to stand on, and you're either biting your nails or wishing you could kill him yourself.

I hope you and your stupid brother go down like the bloody fall of Rome."

Again, no *Huh?* or *What did you say?* He simply chewed on a toothpick and acted as if I were merely a fixture in the room, taking up space. Jailbait blinked twice and complimented me on the BCBG Max Azria number that hung two sizes too big when it was my normal size. In case anyone wondered, the boobs were the first to go. I feared my butt would be next, and call me cocky, but I had some mighty fine glutes pre-abduction. The only object in my possession to remind me of my former life was my Chucks. I even wore them to bed because if I was placed in a situation where I needed to run, I wanted to be prepared.

"Do you have a stylist?" Brunette Jailbait smiled.

Fight Club...making otherwise boring misfits fashionable since...forty-one days ago.

"I do," I answered, returning a fake smile. "Her name is Delia, and I'm pretty sure she's an addict, but dang, she's got good taste."

"I'd say," she squealed. "Can I have her number? I need something extra sparkly."

Jailbait had dressed in white with rainbow makeup sparkles on her chest when the only people I knew who did the sparkle thing were six year olds and hookers.

"Sure, I'll have my dad give it to you. Maybe he can throw in a stripper pole too."

God must have a major sick sense of humor like me because He was all about the comic relief. Gilbert Himmel had toilet tissue stuck to his orthopedic shoe. The moment he trained his Velociraptor smile on me, I gave him a poop-eating grin at the faux pas and turned as the bell dinged.

Ben appeared totally different than before. After he played to the crowd during his warm-up, he pivoted and pointed his fist toward the booth, directed at me. Marking me. Telling The Underground I was his. My attention was taken hostage as his smile quirked up at one corner. Ben smiled when he was about to get the crap kicked and punched out of him by some Mexican dude named Widow Maker. I wasn't sure what I was looking at, but it wasn't the Ben of last weekend. He'd either grown scared of what Daddy

Dearest had planned and tried to scare future opponents or Ben had gotten drunk off of the cheers.

After two kicks from Ben, Widow Maker went down like a ton of bricks. Ben showed no remorse as he stepped over his convulsing body, dancing on his feet over to the bimbos in the crowd. He bent his lips through the cage, allowing the prettiest brunette to kiss him. I closed my eyes, willing Ben to keep his brain. How had this happened? What was he doing? I tried to get a read on Ryder's face as he worked Ben's corner, but as usual Ryder was cucumber-cool. But after speaking with him, I suspicioned he got out of the ring personally because it changed him. How he'd convinced Daddy Dearest to only allow him to train was a subject we hadn't covered, but Ryder was a closed book unless he turned a page himself.

A few expletives later, bets were placed in the crowd, and Ben went at a Native American teenager named Black Hawk. Black Hawk came at Ben with four hard blows to the head. Ben's head jacked back, but once he came to himself, he unloaded the kicks he was famous for and took Black Hawk for a little ride on the concussion express. Black Hawk stood taller than Ben, but Ben had a spring in his jump, and after a series of brutal blows, Black Hawk passed out before he even hit the floor.

The crowd went wild.

The booth went even wilder.

Me, I sat frozen at the animal Ben had been forced to turn into.

Like before, Ben approached the screaming women, holding his gloved hands over his head so they could cop a feel of his body. All of the times I'd ogled a guy's abs before made me feel like dirty white trash. These women had no qualms at touching a teenage boy's body, but Ben went with the flow until Ryder entered the octagon and pulled him back to his corner. I couldn't tell if Ben listened to Ryder as he toweled him down and squirted water in his mouth, but he nodded twice, and after a few sucks on an oxygen mask popped up for fight number three.

Fight number three, Ace, went down with a kick to the head by Ben after seven seconds in the ring. Daddy Dearest even joined the cheering crowd at the unstoppable perseverance of Ben, and when Ben said something in his direction, I knew what he was going for. He'd never been allowed to fight more than three fights, and Ben wanted to prove he could go the distance. After some words with Ryder, Daddy Dearest entered the ring and introduced Cash, Ben's next opponent.

Ben's fourth fight went from vanilla to extra violent as soon as the bell ding-dinged. Cash had won two matches last weekend. He was Black and Hollywood-beautiful, and from what I'd seen, his forte happened to be KOs. Cash immediately went at Ben's face. The crunch of his fists on Ben's cheeks made the crowd erupt into cheers, the women in gasps. Ben had let his guard down, allowing Cash to deliver another hard blow to his temple.

Standing up, I could sense the moment Ben had grown tired. I recognized it in his jaw. "You're Ben Ryan!" I screamed. "Fight like the cocky champion you are!"

Sweet Lord...not the thing to do when the name of the game was to stay hidden in plain sight. Daddy Dearest's head whipped around from the lower level of fans. Let's just say if a stare could kill someone, I'd be more shriveled up than my boobs.

Ben's hands immediately went to his face while Ryder reminded him from the corner to, "Guard your head!" Ben had taken note because right in the middle of Cash's next punch, Ben made a leg swipe and took him to the mat in a submission hold. Cash wouldn't concede easily. Struggling to free himself, Cash's face went savage as Ben wrapped his legs around his waist and squeezed harder, baring his teeth at the strain.

In ten seconds flat, Cash tapped out, and Ben was crowned the victor of his fourth match. Ben was running on pure adrenaline and wanted to go for number five. Maybe he'd heard the fighter Daddy Dearest had been following averaged five a night, and an average meant he'd obviously exceeded five on occasion. With a dip of the head, Daddy Dearest agreed, but at the last minute, he swung his eyes to Eight Ball who'd worked the corner of every opponent...and Eight Ball entered the ring.

At first I didn't understand, but when Gilbert Himmel chuckled and said, "This is the fight I've been waiting for," I realized Eight Ball would go up against Ben—a tired Ben who'd already fought four times. Plus, I was pretty sure Eight Ball hailed from the hottest part of Hell, so he had evil on his side. Listen, the math wasn't going Ben's way. He was several inches shorter, weak from lack of food, and Eight Ball had been training non-stop. If Eight Ball unloaded all he was capable of, there wouldn't be enough left of Ben to sop up with a sponge.

When Eight Ball bent his seven-foot frame in Ben's face and pointed to me, Ben became unglued, especially when Daddy Dearest nodded in agreement.

God. Help. Me. I'd been named as the prize, and no doubt it was payback for yelling Ben's real name.

"Looks to me like the key to your city is about to transfer," Gilbert Himmel said, chuckling psychotically. I spit in the man's face. Literally puckered up and spit on his freaking troll head. I'd seen Eight Ball's full monty and decided if Ben didn't win, I'd slit my own wrists with the toothpick Gilbert Himmel had in his mouth.

And why hadn't I made an appeal to those in the booth with me? These people knew. I could feel it...they knew and looked the other way. Sob.

Ben's silver eyes smoldered when they locked with mine, and I saw the new student who'd come to Valley High last December who'd become an instant hit with the girls—a guy whose nosy self came in handy with my particular obsessions. He was just a young man, and an association with me landed him in the middle of the octagon fighting with a certifiable psychopath. Ben, God love him, was fighting for my virtue—something I feared he was prepared to die for. Squeezing and clawing my way out of the booth that had grown rabidly ecstatic, I ran down the stairs, straight for Daddy Dearest.

But it was too late...Ben and Eight Ball didn't even wait for the bell to ding.

Fist after fist split the air. Eight Ball was brutal and barbarous in his assault, and he was so precise with each skill I wasn't sure the man had a specialty. Ben's teeth bore back like a wild animal as he ducked some punches and absorbed those he wasn't fast enough to avoid. My heart was aghast watching the violence unfold, wondering how Ben could take someone down almost a foot taller than him. But with lightning speed, he somehow got Eight Ball in a submission hold. Eight Ball lay facedown, his butt up in the air with Ben's legs around his waist. The moment I figured he'd tap out, he weaseled out of the hold and cracked Ben in the face two times. Ben staggered to his feet, shaking his head, but came at him again with a roundhouse kick he delivered to Eight Ball's jaw. Eight Ball's head rolled back, and he spit out blood with a curse. Ben seized the opportunity to deliver the same blow, opposite foot.

Ben's wince was audible when Eight Ball turned and back kicked him with his right foot. Ben dropped to his knees but took Eight Ball with him, again in a submission hold. Arms and legs rolled in a blur too fast to follow, a tangle of sweaty bodies pumping up the godforsaken crowd like it was the best Pay-Per-View they'd ever seen. Then something happened.

Ben's body went lax on the floor...

A scream fell from my lips as Eight Ball slowly stood, and the announcer raised his left hand as the victor. Ryder jumped into the octagon and immediately began checking Ben. I stood about ten feet from the ring, shaking uncontrollably.

Had I just witnessed my one true friend die trying to save me?

Daddy Dearest glanced at me and then to Eight Ball with a face made of stone. "Your prize, Eight Ball," he murmured. I was struck speechless and at a loss for anything except fear. When my so-called father walked forward and pulled me into an embrace, I stiffened with hatred. Before my last breath, I'd kill the man. I'd kill him with my own two hands. "I'm sorry, Eve," he said. "But I have to keep my word, and you must be taught a lesson."

Oh, God, I prayed. My heart was within one missed beat of a cardiac infarction. I'd be dead by morning, and if I wasn't, I'd sure as heck want to be.

Eight Ball jumped out of the ring and made his way toward me. My heart pumped furiously, and every fight-or-flight instinct I had said to run. My feet pushed into the floor like I gunned a car for one hundred mph, but Eight Ball sensed it and went for my wrist. He latched ahold with an iron grip, and dang it I was toast.

Here's the issue...Eight Ball might've gotten the girl, but he didn't get the cheers he'd expected. The dugout of fighters booed and hissed, especially when Ryder in a rare display of emotion frantically showed the referee the area on Ben's ribs Eight Ball had struck. When the referee examined Ben with a frown, Daddy Dearest slowly strutted through the octagon's door and took a look himself. He said and did nothing, although tiny pinholes of dripping blood stained Ben's abs.

I remembered Daddy Dearest's words regarding Eight Ball when we'd first met: *You don't want to be caught behind him*, he'd said. Eight Ball had done something to Ben while they'd fought. Perhaps something was in his gloves? Ben was a proud fighter. The fact Eight Ball cheated to humiliate him burned me to the core.

Ryder and another fighter from the ring had Ben between them, holding his full weight while his legs hung limp. "This is not fair, Master," Ryder said quietly. "Redcoat was holding his own."

I'd never heard Ryder address Daddy Dearest personally, and I couldn't tell if his diction was defeated or confrontational. I still wasn't sure he was on our team despite the fact he'd given me all of Daddy Dearest's aliases, plus a map.

When Daddy Dearest remained wordless, Ben shakily raised his head. "If you do this to her, I'll kill myself. You'll never make another dime."

"Easily arranged," Daddy Dearest said. "But here's a word of advice, Redcoat. I'm having a championship bout in a manner of weeks. You'd better win the title, or she's dead."

Daddy Dearest turned and ordered Eight Ball to snap the neck of Widow Maker who had fallen first during the night's matches.

The fight bled out of Ben's eyes when Widow Maker fell with a thud into a zombie-like stare. "Please," Ben begged. "Eight Ball cheated. He injected me with something. I feel it in my veins. I beg you, let me fight for our freedom."

Daddy Dearest said, "Maybe I want to keep you, Redcoat."

And there he'd said what we'd both known all along. Ben never wavered in his request. "Then give me five minutes," he said. "I've earned that."

Yanking free from Eight Ball's grasp, I made my way to Ben on legs I couldn't feel. "I'm so sorry," I cried. "This is my fault."

I cupped his face in my hands and kissed his cheeks over and over, finally dropping to my knees in front of him in a defeated posture. We'd lost. There was no way out here. Ben could win...*was* winning...but he couldn't when they changed the rules.

"Zone out, angel," he whispered down to me. "Whatever is to come, just zone out. Your mind is stronger than anyone I've ever known. Do this for me, Darcy. I love you. I will get us out, but I can't survive in here without you."

Glancing up to Ben's drugged face, I saw a tear clinging to the lash of his left eye. He feared the worst for me, but despite what would probably come, seeing him broken was worse than what Eight Ball had planned. "Shhh," I whispered. "I promise..."

Eight Ball yanked me up by the hair before I could finish, and I heard my mother's voice in my ear like it was yesterday. *Focus, Darcy,* she said. *Do exactly as I tell you to do.* When I heard what she wanted me to say, the thought made me ill. Sucking in a deep breath, I prayed Murphy would understand as I followed my mother's decree. "Dad!" I yelled, my lips quivering. "Don't allow him to take me!"

There was a silence as scary as what had come before...and then Daddy Dearest's head jerked around like someone had slapped him. My appeal to his psychopathic wish I be his child had worked.

Yeah, I wanted to gloat but decided to do it in private.

"I love you, Eve," he murmured, coming toward me. Daddy Dearest was dressed impeccably: all black, all designer, all sophisticated, but he held a barbaric tendency in each stride. Striding up to Eight Ball, he put his hand on his chest. "Take whatever you want. My daughter and Redcoat are off limits."

Eight Ball roared, and when he threw a right hook at Daddy Dearest, Ryder came from left field and tackled him to the ground. You had to respect Van der Hart and how he ran a household. I snorted to myself. Eight Ball spent the night *in the wood*.

Chapter Twenty-Eight

THE RAVEN

J'd been radio silent for seventy-nine days.

I missed chocolate, social media, talking to people who weren't certifiably crazy, music, decent food, The Double-B... sheesh, I missed my iPhone and using the restroom in private.

Too many images flooded my vision at once that I shut my eyes hard, trying to force them deep into my subconscious. But it didn't help. I couldn't escape the memories. This place was my new home...without the hugs and bedtime stories.

Daddy Dearest claimed he wouldn't be traveling, but come Sunday evening he predictably packed a bag. While he was gone, Ben and I were often thrown into my room together, bound back-to-back by Eight Ball...untied when it was bedtime. I could report that to my so-called father upon his return, but I feared Ben would take all the flak.

While Daddy Dearest traveled, I made sure to stir the troops and go Bay of Pigs on everyone's butt. I told Eight Ball he should run the show...I promised Delia I'd get her clean if she'd help me escape...I informed Myles he worked too hard and was underappreciated. The fighters I came in contact with, I told them to rise up and revolt. I wasn't sure my tactics worked, but I kept pounding away anyway, hoping for an internal rebellion of some sort.

But as much as I tried, all I'd had lately was a series of hurdles and setbacks. Ryder wouldn't answer if he'd left my phone some place where it could be found, but he'd gotten us a map...so why? Gilbert Himmel had been a total waste of time, and Ben was told if he won, we'd be set free...we weren't.

And so were the days of our lives...

Ben was undefeated—sailing through four matches in record time—but he was not allowed to fight more than four bouts a night. That frustrated him because he felt confident he could win more, and he wanted that notch on his belt when he met up with the other fighter in the championship match. My guess was Ben had been held back to bait his competition to The Underground. Guys who were cocky needed to think they could win, but I had a feeling the mysterious opponent—whoever he was—liked to fight simply to fight.

Ben should've fought him Saturday, but the guy requested a Tuesday night fight. That told me Daddy Dearest wanted him in a big time way. He'd never been one to make concessions...especially for a fight during the week.

I approached the secret passageway to make my way to Ben's room. When I first found the tunnel, I went *Hansel and Gretel* and ventured inside, leaving a trail of wadded-up pieces of my sketchpad every six feet, so I could find my way back in the darkness. Luckily, when I came to a dead end, I listened for voices on the other side. When I heard Ben talking to himself, I pushed on the wall, and his surprised smile met me. As long as I could feel the paper while crawling around, I knew I was on the right path. The main tunnel, however, had several side tunnels, and if I wound up in the wrong room, fate only knew if I'd find my way out.

Ben hadn't stopped by my room for a prematch good luck. I could only assume he was doing some serious meditation or Ryder was doing some serious Mr. Miyagi coaching. No one had come to fetch me for a shower either although Delia dropped off clothing. And oddly, she'd dressed me in red. For once, she seemed sober, and when I thought that would've had her more alert, she'd forgotten shoes and her hands shook like Jell-O when she combed my fading ombré-blue hair and zipped up the back of my dress.

Good luck, she'd said. I didn't know what to say, so I'd hugged her instead when she left.

Dropping to my knees, I retied my Chucks and tapped the brick that would fold the wall back, exposing the tunnel. Once the wall unlocked and creaked into place, I was immediately bombarded with the pungent smell of sulfur. I had no idea how far underground we were, but a sulfur smell could mean water was close by. I feared I'd take a wrong turn and wind up in a bottomless drink of H2O, but sometimes that didn't seem so bad. As much as I wanted to live, in brief moments, death seemed comforting. But death meant I would never see Daddy Dearest go down as the man who murdered my mother.

I might have ADHD, but by God I had staying power.

My hands flinched at the slick, cold feel of the rock beneath me despite the fact I'd made the trek to Ben's room each evening after Eight Ball's rounds. As much punishment as Ben's body could withstand, he was claustrophobic. I wasn't a fan of living like a mole either, but it was the least I could do for someone who fought for our lives. Ben said fighters disappeared daily in The Underground, and it had begun to bother him because some had become allies. So each night I rubbed down his muscles and pumped him up psychologically after the mind games he'd endured. I'd had practice at that. I'd been telling Dylan for years he was the best there was, the world was his oyster, and world domination was around the corner. For some reason, guys needed that shtick more than girls. Girls merely needed to find a guy who loved our bodies the way they were and just listened...pretty simple.

That first night together we talked for hours about life, love, and what we wanted to do when we escaped. Me? My plans were short term. I was headed straight for a Coke and a cookie. Ben's thinking, however, went long term. He wanted to be a reporter—like a big time reporter at *The Washington Post* or *The New York Times*. When I fell asleep next to him, Ben claimed it was the first night he'd slept without waking...so I just kept coming back. I hoped Dylan would understand because he would always own my heart, but I could see how a girl could easily fall in love with Ben Ryan. Despite being hotter than Mercury, Ben was good...down to his core. He talked in his sleep about loving his mom and dad, his brothers, Autumn...and he talked about wanting to keep me safe more than anything.

At the first drip-drop of water in the tunnel, I started reciting

Poe's, *The Raven*. It took exactly eight minutes and thirty seconds to make it to Ben's room, according to the lighted dial on the watch I'd snagged from Delia.

"Once upon a midnight dreary..." I started, and my mind immediately became distracted with the theme of the poem. It chronicled the demise of a tormented young man into madness with the loss of his love, Lenore. The reader doesn't know what happened to Lenore, but whatever it was, her loss eventually made the narrator need a padded room. Why I chose that poem, I didn't know. Perhaps the ravens in Daddy Dearest's room provided inspiration, or perhaps it was the fact Dylan never got to hear me say, *I love you*.

Loving was like the maturing process. One got better at it the longer one was in a relationship. But like anything, the longer a person was in the relationship, the harder it was to let go—especially if you were the one who wanted to hang on. And like the narrator in *The Raven*, I couldn't let go. No matter what, I couldn't let go of Dylan and what "might have been."

All day long I'd felt him beside me. I hadn't decided if that had been a blessing or a curse. Had he experienced the same thing, or did he fear me dead? What had his days been like? Had he picked a college to attend? If I ever blew this joint, I'd encourage him to follow his heart. It was funny how things became clear when all I had were my thoughts, a darn tunnel...and frakkin' rice.

The tunnel tasted like a burnt match on my tongue, singeing my nostrils the longer I traveled. God help me, I splayed both hands wide and felt around, unable to find a wad of paper anywhere. To the right...nothing. To the left...still nothing. My brain sent out an S.O.S. because it appeared I was lost—and I was too dumb to know I should be crying. I decided to laugh because the alternative was a blood-curdling scream. And now that I was lost, I immediately had to pee. I squeezed my legs tight, so I wouldn't wet myself.

The harder I tried not to pee, the more my body insisted on a normal reaction. First came the sniffles followed by an overwhelming sense of claustrophobia—like I was in the middle of a boa constrictor that decided to squeeze. Sweat instantly beaded every inch of my body and fear seized my breath.

"I can't breathe," I said. "I can't th-think."

No, it definitely wasn't the tunnel to Ben's room. The tunnel to Ben's room grew more wide...not narrow, like the one I was in. I backed up and got my geek on, trying to repeat the last stanza in reverse. When that became too confusing, I panicked, and the air around me thinned even more.

Don't get me wrong, I loved Mother Earth, but I sure as heck didn't want to die in a darn tunnel. I'd want Daddy Dearest to find my body. I'd want him to mourn in his own sick, psychotic way and be paralyzed with grief for the rest of his miserable life. But had all of my near misses prepared me for this one final moment? I wasn't used to viewing life existentially. Verbs acted. We didn't dissect or analyze. That was what nouns did.

I killed the debate and regrouped, once again trying to remember where I'd stopped talking about that stupid raven. Backing up about thirty feet, I found a wadded-up piece of paper in a four-way intersection I'd always successfully avoided. The breath I'd been holding exited my body on a hiss. I'd done it! I'd made my way back to the original trail! The moment I turned for Ben's room, however, I heard a noise at the end of the passage I'd just exited. A noise wherein someone yelled, "WWWeellcommee to the Unndergroundd!"

Sweet Jesus, it was like someone had slapped me into consciousness.

The intersection was a shortcut to The Underground—The Underground I could enter secretly and perhaps meet someone who wouldn't be so keen on watching people get destroyed. I'd get help and then find Ben and Ryder if they weren't in the octagon already. I took a few seconds to celebrate but dropped anchor when I heard the words, "Annnnnnnnddddd introducinggggggg, Apollllooooooo!"

Ho. Ly. Zeus. Apollo wasn't a name I was familiar with, but whoever he was, the crowd had gone as wild (or even wilder) than it had for Redcoat. Apollo had to be the fighter shipped in to challenge Ben. Swinging a left back to the side tunnel, I purposely ripped the hem on my dress and removed a large scrap of fabric, leaving it at the intersection. Listen, I metaphorically fell into a hole getting lost the first time but absolutely and unmistakably refused to do it twice.

Making it to the end of the tunnel, I was surprised when I came upon a metal grate instead of a wall that would give way once force had been applied. Pushing with all my might, I removed the grate and crawled out onto the floor surrounding the octagon. The smell of smoke, expensive perfume, and aged liquor instantly inflamed my lungs. The area was cram-packed with elbow-to-elbow people, so tight it was like stilettos and Italian shoes in a sardine can. Going vertical, I could not see the booth, but the crowd was triple the norm. Unfortunately, I couldn't see Apollo either, but I spotted Daddy Dearest immediately.

As I hid in the crowd, my eyes fell to the back of the room where Lars van der Hart leaned up against the wall, conversing with four men and a bimbo sidepiece. To my right, a man mid-thirties was sweating bullets like he'd just placed a second mortgage on his home and was two steps from bankruptcy. He fiddled nervously with his wedding band, rhythmically shaking his leg. To my left stood another group of yuppies with their eyes trained on the elevator they'd just come from, like they feared their attendance was a mistake but were already here. Positioned directly in front of me was a group of five men large enough to play professional football. The bald one was alpha and had the toughest demeanor. As he rubbed a hand down his blond goatee, I couldn't figure out if he was man or animal. He glanced at me and let his steel-gray eyes linger over my clothing. Up and down, up and down his eyes went. He'd noticed the Chucks. Noticed I was out of place. With a dip of his head, he then gazed on the other side of the octagon as though he was bored out of his mind.

Stationed in front of the octagon were the psycho super fans. The fans that came religiously and occasionally enjoyed getting splattered with blood. Mofos...that group was nothing but sick mofos.

When a crack formed between the psycho super fans, I strained my eyes between two females to catch a glimpse of Apollo. When both women gasped and began to jump up and down, I'd felt for certain they'd spotted Redcoat. But suddenly I trembled from head to foot, my nerve endings twisting with anticipation. The echo in my heart and the pump of anticipation alerted me to who was in the ring...

Dylan Taylor, patron saint to crazy best friends everywhere.

My stomach tumbled down like it was on a zip line that just ripped. Nerves? Desire? Both? His honey-colored eyes were darker, smoldering like something burned inside he commanded to go even hotter. Where Ben's prefight routine was to dance on the balls of his feet and feed the crowd, Dylan sat in the corner, eyes straight ahead, palms on his outstretched knees—like he was conserving energy or even bored. A power rolled off of him, electrifying the room. Women either whispered behind their hands or stared dumbfounded at the beauty of his body. My eyes traveled the length of his torso, settling on the little indentions right above his hipbones. Wall to wall tats spanned his rippled pecs, running down both arms and thighs hidden underneath white shorts. The words *God of War* wound around his neck, with other letters of the Greek alphabet, stopping right underneath his left ear. If I didn't know in my heart it was Dylan, I'd be hard pressed to tell the difference. He looked like a god, and he'd had a growth spurt in my absence, at least twenty pounds heavier. His jet-black hair had been buzzed to be merely a shadow on his head. He looked as street hardened as Lincoln...on a good day.

Interpretation for those still not catching on? He looked hotter than *hawt*.

I drank in the changes and fought the desire to run to his arms. *But let me promise you this*...if we ever got out of here, I would seriously acquaint myself with the tattoos on his chest.

I weaved in and out of the crowd until I stood about fifteen feet from the ring—close enough to see Dylan had new bruises and old bruises all over his body. Even beaten up, he was so freaking good-looking I could strangle a bison with my bare hands. I'd lay all the money in the world on Dylan to pull his weight in demolishing the competition, but MMA was not his forte. How long had he been training? He occasionally boxed to let off steam, but that was in his basement with a punching bag. Dylan lived by the creed that you couldn't cheat the hustle though. So what kind of crash course had he undergone? And who'd given it to him?

Right then, his trainer turned...and I had my answer.

A man with orangey-red hair came into view, and his ruddy features pulled me under like I drowned in a whirlpool. Paddy...

Patrick O'Leary, Lincoln's partner and Dylan's godfather, was his trainer. Dressed in black with a white towel over his left shoulder, Paddy sported a tattoo on his bicep of a sunburst flag. *Resistance* was printed underneath. Surely, to God, he hadn't been former IRA... had he? Did the Irish Republican Army even exist anymore? Whatever the case, the tattoo meant Lincoln was nearby. At that moment, my hope intensified we just might make it out of here alive.

Somehow they'd found out I was here and had infiltrated another fight club to gain a reputation. But who had squealed? Delia? Ryder? Craning my neck, I tried to get a read on Dylan's opponent. I'd never seen him before, but I stood next to some guys who had. Slash was his name, and by looks alone he was an infernal male, straight out of the mouth of Hell. Red tattoos covered his body and bald head, making him dark-alley scary. Slash might be as big as a mother-trucking semi, but Dylan wasn't one to be tangoed with. The guys next to me said Dylan, AKA Apollo, had been contracted to fight six, and if he made it through, he'd challenge Ben. Question was, how were these men in the know? That told me there was a very intricate network where patrons were willing to cover for one another to sate their appetite for violence.

My breathing picked up at an irregular pace when I realized Dylan would be fighting the guy who'd kept me alive. For God's sake, no. The last thing I wanted was for Dylan and Ben to meet one another in the octagon. When I searched the dugout for Ben, however, he was nowhere to be found. And for that matter, neither was Ryder.

I gulped down the hysteria. Something was wrong...

Some of the psycho super fans waited as long as they could—like they feared to put their hands in Apollo's cage—but the moment Dylan stood, some females gave him the same treatment they'd given Redcoat. At the last minute, Dylan reached over the top of the octagon and grabbed a blonde from the crowd, pulling her to his lips with both hands. He licked her mouth. *Going, going, gone*, I thought. She'd fallen victim to his instant charm because when he lowered her to the floor, she stumbled into her friends.

A flare of desire sparked in my chest, and I burned with jealousy. That woman had gone under the knife so many times I couldn't take a guess at her age, but then I realized Dylan made a statement he wanted a blonde when he won. He knew Daddy Dearest not only gave a winner the money pot but the female he desired.

Dylan took a seat again, and after all bets were placed, the bell dinged...

321

Chapter Twenty-Nine

COMING CLEAN

*D*ylan didn't even stand at the bell.

Instead, he gave Slash one slow blink...*and yawned.*
Oh. Shiz. Dylan wanted to play. Slash came at him, throwing a series
of punches to Dylan's ripped abs. Dylan didn't flinch, and after a jab
to Slash's chin that nearly removed his head from his shoulders,
Dylan unloaded a heavy left. Slash teetered like he scaled a high
wire, and his eyes rolled back in his head before he fell face first
onto the floor.

That wasn't hitting...that was destroying.

The crowd went Super Bowl-loud.

Dylan strutted back to his corner with a macho swagger I still
found irresistible. I read Paddy's lips. "Patience, Apollo. Ya canna
kill anyone. Ya dad thinks ya won't. Ya grandpa and I know you're
merely lookin' for the perfect opportunity. Play, kid. Let this thing
play."

A dark emotion sparked in Dylan's gaze, but then he head-
butted Paddy as a way of saying, *I feel you.* Right then, the room
went dark. The middle of the floor had given way, and Daddy
Dearest rose up on his figurative throne to introduce the evening's
fights.

Slash had simply been an appetizer.

I knew I had about two minutes before Daddy Dearest came
down off his throne. Slumped at the waist, I zigzagged through the

crowd until I stood behind Dylan. Paddy was crouched in front of him speaking low, telling him to find a weakness and push. Dylan didn't acknowledge his words, and I felt in my soul he scanned the crowd for me. Before time ran out, I tiptoed up and thread my fingers through the octagon's cage, leaving fingertips at his bare waist.

Dylan flinched...but quickly recovered.

Pressing my fingers in deeper, Dylan slowly leaned back to where he trapped my fingers between his back and the cage...he'd understood and tried to prolong my touch. Gentling pressing into his waist with a subliminal, "I love you," I tried to will into his mind that it wasn't just me here. There were others I wanted to come with us.

Fearing Dylan might turn, I withdrew my hand and made my way back to the group of men who'd been gossipy before. They said the next opponent, Dead Dog, had just gotten out on parole—murdered his brother twelve years earlier—and prison life had not been kind. When he exited the dugout after Dylan's five-minute break had ended, I realized his torso was littered with knife wounds. Dead Dog was small—so small he looked like the size of a Smart car compared to Dylan's SUV girth. He took one look at Dylan and gulped, but my guess was a murderer liked to play mind games. Not for one minute did I think Dead Dog to be scared.

The bell dinged, and right then, Dylan charged like a raging bull. With one punch, Dylan KO'd a known killer with a whomping crunch. A deadly silence ensued. The crowd knew they'd seen something they'd never witnessed before because they'd been rendered speechless. They were like flies in a spider's web, pulled into his hypnotic trance.

When Dead Dog was carted off, I glanced at Paddy. He was quiet and tense, and after watching Dylan take grown men down in barely a punch, I knew he feared Dylan would kill someone before Ben and I had been rescued. "Patience," Paddy growled again. "You canna end this in one punch. Make sure ta give them th'fight they're after, son."

Dylan was up for his third fight in what hadn't even been a three-minute rest. Paddy went ballistic, shouting they'd agreed upon a longer recovery time. Dylan went one round with Exterminator, absorbing a series of kicks that rivaled Ben's. As soon as one connected, however, Dylan had his way with Exterminator's gut. Exterminator winced and backed away, and once he'd regrouped, he somehow got his foot up to Dylan's jaw in a roundhouse kick. When he made contact, Dylan's head jacked back, and he spit out blood, but although I knew he could end the fight whenever he chose, he played to the crowd and their hedonistic wishes the fights be longer.

Dylan finished out the round plus the second, but at the beginning of round three, he tapped into his bloodlust and was all over Exterminator like the stink on shiz. Dylan pummeled him in the face, punch after punch until the ring was a bloody mess beneath them. In a one-two combo that ended with Dylan's southpaw, Exterminator literally soared high in the air and was unconscious before he hit the ground.

For the first time since the fighting began, Dylan showed the crowd who he was as a competitor. He raised his arms and roared, the resulting sound rattling the glass in the booth, shaking everyone in attendance with terror.

Dylan was like the alpha male gone wild. You know, the DVD boxed set.

At the unexpected burst from Apollo, Daddy Dearest instructed Eight Ball to produce another victim from the dugout. Dylan strutted back to his corner, the sweat pooling at his waist and dropping onto the floor. Paddy knelt in front of him, dabbing his forehead with a towel, viciously rechecking the tape on Dylan's left hand before the bell did its thing. He motioned for Dylan to squirt water in his own mouth because he couldn't do both during the short rest. Paddy realized the brief recovery time wasn't fair, and a chance existed Dylan would pass out from dehydration long before a punch connected with his jaw.

I'd bitten my nails to the quick by the time Scar made it to the octagon. He was Dylan's size, maybe even taller, and I noticed Dylan stared at him a little more intently than he had anyone else up to that point. In fact, the referee's attempt to explain the rules to Scar was like trying to calm a bloodthirsty beast with a piece of candy when all it wanted was a carcass dripping with blood.

Scar took a look at Dylan's youth and smiled a smile that was born for a straitjacket. When the bell dinged, Dylan immediately had his hands up by his face, dancing on his calves, but he waited for Scar to move first. Scar roared and threw a right-handed punch at Dylan's jaw. Dylan took the punch on purpose and a split developed over his left eye. Fat tears ran down my face like boulders when he allowed Scar to throw another. I commanded the tears to dry up. *Fight, D!* I said in my head. *Fight!* Dylan then threw a punch of his own. Scar's mouth instantly filled with blood that splattered on the octagon floor.

When Scar tried to steer away from Dylan's jabs, he dumbly turned, and Dylan jumped on his back and wrapped his hands around his neck. That sent them both backward to the mat. Dylan pivoted midair and Scar ate the floor, facedown in a submission hold. Dylan then tucked an arm underneath his shoulder, but when Scar bit into his arm, Dylan went off his holy rocker and maneuvered his legs down around his waist and squeezed. Oh, Jesus. Paddy told him to squeeze harder.

Scar, however, wanted to die in the ring.

He did not tap out...and the referee called the first fight of the night when Scar stilled on the floor.

Good night, Scar. Over and out.

Dylan walked slower back to his corner than before. Maybe no one else noticed, but I did. And thank God Scar had passed out because it took longer to remove a guy that big from the ring. Paddy viciously rubbed down Dylan's arms and legs, and where one would've thought Daddy Dearest would awarded Dylan with a longer rest, Dylan barely got a squirt of water when the bell dinged, and Buster was wailing away on his head. Dylan immediately curled Buster into a submission hold, but Buster weaseled out of it, and for once, Dylan was the one in a deficit. Paddy lost his ever lovin' mind, screaming, "N'one canna fight under these conditions!"

But somehow Dylan broke free and won match number five.

Number six with Triple H was pretty much a repeat.

Before another guy could surface from the dugout, Paddy marched over to the referee and grabbed him by his bowtie. He was giving Dylan a chance to rest, forcing the reprieve himself. I wasn't sure what that would mean for Paddy—maybe a knife on the way out—but he'd gone all redhead when the referee finally conceded to give Dylan five minutes.

The psycho super fans began to boo, and I couldn't tell if they booed because they acknowledged Dylan had been cheated, or if they booed the no holds barred action taking a timeout. By the time fight number seven rolled around, Dylan motioned for Paddy to cut his gloves away, so he could go raw knuckles. I wasn't sure what it was, but I heard a click in my head, and I knew bad lurked right around the corner. Eight Ball entered the ring and stood as Dylan's next opponent.

If Dylan didn't beat him, we'd all be dead by morning.

That had been the plan: wear Dylan out, so Eight Ball could be the star. And it was never more apparent than when Daddy Dearest entered the octagon to work Eight Ball's corner...of course the douchebag would. It made perfect sense...*in a Wes Craven nightmare!* Tears rolled down my cheeks because it was like watching a ship go down, and I couldn't do anything about it.

Somehow I crept back toward Dylan and hid behind two psycho super fans reapplying their lipstick. Dylan inhaled deeply then exhaled with even more force, and then he did something unexpected. As if cosmically connected once more, our sixth senses took over. My heart felt *his*. His soul felt *mine*. Dylan angled his body in my direction.

"Apollo," I whispered. "You've got to fight, harder than ever. This next guy cheats, and he's the one who kidnapped me."

Dylan remained still, but his eyes softened into liquid butter. He closed them. Opened them slowly. Haunted. Dylan appeared as if he was in extreme physical pain, but the look on his face said he quickly skipped through it and went to the next level of mental pain. And oh, how mental pain was much more damaging than the physical kind.

With a slow nod, Dylan turned back with laser focus and accepted the water Paddy squirted into his mouth, face, and chest. Dylan made the sign of the cross and then rose up to meet Eight Ball. Right in the middle of me thinking of my many regrets, someone whispered, "Jester, " and pulled me to the back of the crowd.

I whipped my head around so hard and fast I gave myself whiplash. "My name is Iggy," the person said. "Hang tight to me, kid. I'm going to get you out of here when all hell breaks loose."

Iggy smelled like a California forest fire. Dude had to have the beginnings of lung cancer. With a few strands of hair, he reminded me of Mr. Potato Head. I had to hand it to him though. The bimbo next to him wore a see-through blouse, wearing no bra, and he hadn't looked once. It took a moment for the name Iggy to register —he worked specifically for Walter Ivanhoe, Lincoln's mob connection. Iggy lived in Cincinnati, and if Iggy was here, there definitely was a grand plan being executed.

Dylan took an impassive look at Eight Ball, allowing his eyes to gaze up and down his seven-foot bald frame while the announcer reached for his microphone. Before he announced the fight, Dylan slowly sauntered back to Paddy and took the white towel from his hand, throwing it at Eight Ball's feet.

The announcer became giddy with excitement and asked Dylan what he would be fighting for. Dylan looked Eight Ball in the eyes and murmured, "I'll have what he's having."

I nervously pulled on Iggy's sleeve. "What just happened?"

Iggy glanced at me, swallowing. "Apollo threw the gauntlet, kid. It's a submission round. A submission round is to the death."

"D," I whispered, my hand shakily covering my mouth, "No."

Out of the hundreds of people in the crowd, Dylan finally found my eyes. Hand to God, it felt like we were the only two people in existence. His face was full of fierce, savage determination. My God, the demons were probably scared. Drawing a shaky finger to my lips, I gave him a "shhh" sound and nodded over to Daddy Dearest who was taking bets with Myles hand over fist. In that moment, I think Dylan realized I had a personal beef with him, other than being kidnapped. Dylan's gaze hardened into granite. He wanted a piece of him, and I knew he'd never leave the ring until he had it.

When the bell rang, Dylan slammed Eight Ball to the mat immediately with a thud. Goodbye! Unfortunately, the tightness in my chest said there was a good chance he wouldn't stay down. As expected, Eight Ball maneuvered out of the hold, but I saw the stubborn defiance in Dylan's jaw. He allowed Eight Ball to come at him next, but Eight Ball bought a first class ticket to Dylan's fist, his head jerking backward like someone had pulled his strings.

For the first time since being kidnapped, I heard cheers for Eight Ball to get up and fight. He had some fans. When neither could get the other in a successful submission hold, both stood and Dylan immediately pummeled Eight Ball with a series of punches to his abs. Listen, Eight Ball was no willing victim, plus his stomach was harder than iron. When he didn't drop, Dylan immediately went for the jaw, delivering two hard shots to Eight Ball's chin.

Paddy yelled, "Guard your face, Apollo!"

And that was the right call because Eight Ball went at Dylan's head like a machine gun stuck on shoot. I leaned forward, dodging this way and that, coaching him telepathically to steer clear of Eight Ball's right jab. That continued with both trading blows back and forth until the round ended. When the bell dinged again, Dylan was like a caged animal, angry someone had let him out only to leash him. When Eight Ball threw a leg at Dylan's ribs, he caught it and brought Eight Ball down like a sack of potatoes. His head split wide open, and a group-gag went through the row of psycho super fans as the referee tried to assess whether Eight Ball was still alive. Dylan just stood there, bouncing on the balls of his feet, jagged breaths leaving his body in spurts. Like a demon from Hell, Eight Ball got his second wind and found vertical.

After a few useless jabs, the second round was over, and when Dylan made his way back to his corner, Eight Ball jumped him from behind and took him down in a submission hold. A whoosh of air left Dylan's mouth, and I prayed breath back into his body. I was so aghast, I jumped up and down and yelled, "Cheater! Cheater!" In doing so, I outed myself to Daddy Dearest who frantically searched for me in the crowd. Daddy Dearest and Paddy wrestled themselves between the two and pulled them back to their corners.

There were no freaking rules anymore...

As the crowd erupted into boos, that time it was against Eight Ball's tactics. Dylan played that up, standing with hands raised over his head, realizing Eight Ball's fans had just jumped teams.

I'd been so enthralled with Dylan, I'd forgotten about Iggy and his bimbo sidepiece. When Bimbo became extra exuberant, Iggy's phone tumbled to the floor. Right then was my moment...my moment to make sure everyone knew the truth if Ben and I died. The first thing any normal person would do would be to call a loved one, but if I phoned Murphy, he'd cry...I'd lose time...ditto on Red and Rookie. If I didn't make the call, then all my time of living in captivity would be for nothing. Daddy Dearest killed my mom and imprisoned others. I wanted everyone to know and give him the death penalty.

Stealing back inside the tunnel, I hurriedly dialed Tito West-brook. *Please pick up*, I thought. *Please let me get a signal.*

For once I got a freebie from the universe because right at the moment the waterworks threatened, Tito answered with a, "Westbrook."

My heart pounded in my chest. "It's Jester."

There was a long pause, almost like Tito had to reacquaint himself with my voice. "Darlin' where have you been hiding? The last message I received was months ago where you claimed you heard someone trapped in a wall at Club Need."

"I don't have much time. Lars van der Hart has held me prisoner for several months. I'm not sure where I am, but it's some place underground. Ping my phone, Tito, so you can trace me."

Tito shouted something to someone in the background. "Talk."

"I have proof he is all of the men you've been after. I know a guy who swears he can get passports to prove it. I also saw a diplomatic passport by the name of Julius Marx. His hair is blond in that photo, but it's him. What name had the cops been chasing after in Lyric's disappearance?"

"Mahesh Singh. The first manager and owner of Club Need when it went out of business."

"Did you know Van der Hart and Singh to have the same face?"

"Similar enough," he said.

Tito explained for Van der Hart to get a passport, he had to produce a birth certificate, certificate of naturalization, military ID, or driver's license proving him to be that person. A chance existed someone cut him a favor, but here's the thing: he said he's someone he wasn't. Plus, he was getting by with it.

"I think he works for the government," I said.

"That would certainly connect a lot of dots, darlin'. My head is swimming at the moment."

"If I can get those passports, would that help?"

A short pause. "If you can produce his face on the names of those passports, then yes, Jester. He's the man responsible for all the missing kids, and with my notes and eyewitness accounts over the years, we can put him away for good. Jester, let me get you out. I'm sending a squad car over as soon as I get a location on this phone. Make your way to an exit. Can you do that?"

"Probably not, but I wouldn't even if I could. They've separated us."

"Who is *us*?"

"I think there are about a hundred. When I first got here, I counted close to two hundred, but my guess is they're now dead."

"Oh, God. Why would he keep *any* of you?"

I explained Daddy Dearest's sick pastime and how he'd kidnapped the talent. "Of the hundred or so that I know of," I said, "there are only enough rooms to house half. That tells me some travel in and out, which means he probably keeps those of us he thinks would squeal prisoners. Separate those with tattoos. I think that's how you can identify them. Have you heard of Ben Ryan?"

"Sixteen-year-old runaway, new to Valley, five-time MMA...oh, God," he groaned when the light bulb switched on.

"Not a runaway...kidnapped. He's been the main attraction, and we even stumbled upon Ryder Beck. He's not dead. He goes in and out of reality, but his heart is good. I've got to find them, Tito. They didn't show tonight."

Tito cursed and yelled again for someone to hurry up and find my location. "No. Make your way to an exit, capeesh?"

"I can't leave them. If I don't make it, please tell my family and boyfriend that I love them. My boyfriend is fighting right now."

"What's his name, darlin'?"

"Dylan Taylor."

Nothing...and then a prayer he said in Italian. "Holy Mother... Jester...sweet Lord, are you Darcy Walker? Tabitha's niece? Child, she's nearly lost her mind. I should've known...my identity theft... my God, it all makes sense. Colton and I are friends too. Your phone showed up in his mailbox at work along with a note that said, *She's still alive*. There were photos of you in a car. Who was the man?"

I gave him Eight Ball's backstory...bodyguard...kidnapper... former MMA champ who killed Hurricane Cole. "If he makes it out of here, call up the National Guard to bring him in."

Right on cue, I heard Dylan roar in pain...and anger. I scrambled out of the tunnel to view him and Eight Ball in a submission hold that looked like no end was in sight.

"Hurry," I whispered. "Send backup. Dylan's grandfather is a cop and is probably here, but I don't understand why he's allowing this thing to draw on. I'm afraid something has happened to him. Dylan is on fight number seven, and he's getting tired. I know his trainer, and he won't let it go on much longer, but I know Dylan won't leave without me. If I don't make it, tell the authorities to look for Ryder and Ben...and tell Red...tell Red that Lars van der Hart is the man who killed my mom. He's also Butch Lawrence."

Tito said a word so dirty I didn't care to repeat it in my mind. "I promise," he said, and I dropped the phone when a gunshot rang in the air.

Chapter Thirty

SURVIVAL OF THE FITTEST

*I*f there was no God, then that meant we were all locked in some Darwinian fight in a survival of the fittest...trying to make sure we maintained power because no higher power would ever come to our aid. Scared speechless, panic told me I should pray anyway.

Problem was, I wasn't so good at it. Sure I lived like most people, mumbling a "Help me God" somewhere throughout the day, but had I truly been praying? I'd always paid attention in Sunday school, but right when things got interesting—when the stories weren't all about God's love and blah, blah, happily-ever-afters—my mother died. Murphy was still a believer, but let's just say his and God's relationship had been strained...at least of the weekly meetings. He made up for it twice a year at Christmas and Easter, but otherwise I flew without instruments regarding how to address the Big Man on the Throne. Odds were seriously stacked against us.

Murphy said when a person came to the end of himself, though, that was when God took over. Well, I needed him to take over because someone squeezed off six more rounds and people were dropping like flies hit with a can of Raid.

When Iggy lunged for me, I scrambled back for the tunnel amidst more gunfire...but not before a large body tackled me to the ground. I hit the floor hard, like I'd been slammed by an eighteen-wheeler and dragged all the way to the end of I-75 in Florida. But whoever the person was, he cradled my head in the fall, careful to not cause more damage than necessary. Convincing my lungs to work, I blinked into the eyes of Dylan Taylor.

I stared with an all-consuming enchantment.

Yup, stared like a bona fide fool.

I hadn't been that close to Dylan in months, but there was no denying that rich, musky smell on a male who never wore cologne. And then like the idiot I am, I said, "Did you win?"

A roguish wink. "He's out cold."

"Yeah, I knew you'd take him," I bragged. My God, I needed a brain transplant.

While chaos continued, Dylan and I had a moment that was just the two of us. We both dove for a hug at the exact same time. "You're alive," he whispered. "My God, you're alive." Dylan left his lips in the curve underneath my ear, but there was no time for an ILYSM or a what-have-you-been-up-to? We needed to get a move on. Thankfully, I found the needed power. "I can't take the time to hug you, D," I whispered. "If I don't let go of you now, it's going to take the jaws-of-life to do it. We need to go."

He sensed there was a *but* coming, pulling back to look in my eyes. "Talk to me," he said.

More gunshots fired. Dylan shielded me with his body and gazed over his shoulder, glancing through the crowd of screaming women with yelling men. "I don't see Lincoln or Paddy," he said. "Something bad must be going down, other than the bullets."

"Do you trust me?" I asked.

My hopefully *still* boyfriend had a left eye quickly swelling shut, but that didn't stop him from showing his tender side. His lips found their way to my forehead. "More than anyone," he answered. I stared at the tunnel that barely accommodated me comfortably, let alone Dylan who was significantly larger than last time I'd seen him. Dylan read my mind. "Being with you is all the motivation I need," he said. "Lead the way."

Three more gunshots fired, and when I heard Iggy yelling, "Jester," I locked eyes with Dylan and dove inside. Dylan followed and pulled the grate shut behind us.

While we hunkered in the tunnel, I told him my fears about Ben and Ryder being drugged or held prisoner somewhere. Dylan claimed everyone suspicioned Ben had been with me, but Ryder placed a wrench in the plan they obviously hadn't prepared for. "Just stay put, D," I said. "No one will think to look here. I'll go get them and pull them back through. Ben was supposed to fight tonight, and my guess was Ryder went rogue because he wasn't here either. That's a good sign. Maybe he still has his mind. It'll be about ten minutes for me to get there, but on the way back, it might be double."

"No, no," he refused adamantly. "You can't pull two adult-sized men through by yourself, Darc. The physics of it won't work. Plus, I haven't had my hands on you in months. The last thing I'm going to do is let you out of my sight."

On all fours, I took my first shaky steps further into the tunnel. "I'm sorry," I whispered over my shoulder, realizing he was right. "I'm so sorry you had to do this."

"Shhhh," he murmured, rubbing his thumb along my ankle, "Lead us out of here, hound dog. I trust you."

Explaining how I'd found the tunnel and the breadcrumb trail of papers inside, I then admitted I'd gotten lost on the way here and would be looking for a scrap of my dress at the intersection. Before long I'd found it, but then I had to remember which part of the stanza of "The Raven" I was on when I hit that juncture. "I'm getting panicky," I breathed in the dark. "I now feel the pressure I have to get you out too."

Dylan grabbed my ankle, halting me before I could make another move. "You're the smartest person I've ever met...will *ever* meet. You've stayed alive and thought your way out of immeasurable obstacles. Take a deep breath, sweetheart. Have faith. The answer is in your head."

Once I found my center, I began again. "But the raven, sitting lowly on the placid bust..."

We continued to crawl, and after about six feet into a left turn, Dylan said softly, "Keep going. I have my first piece of paper." He continued to squeeze my left leg when he found another.

"...Nevermore!" I said of the poem, ending right when I made it to Ben's room. Pushing with all my might, the wall gave way and I slid into Ben's room. Dylan followed after, and we both fell over the bodies of Ryder and Ben. After several minutes in a black tunnel, it took awhile for my eyes to adjust, and when they did I was stunned, reeling...and I shouldn't have been because these were things I'd come to expect in The Underground. It looked like a bull had been let loose in a china shop. The lamp Ben had bargained for after winning a fight had been shattered, his books and map thrown askew, and the Army cot he'd also scored had been upended and lay facedown...like the both of them.

"Noooo...no-no-no!" I immediately cried.

Dylan bent over both the bodies, two fingers to their pulse points, as I cowered on my knees, frozen. "It's okay. It's okay," Dylan said on an exhale. "I have a pulse on both...weak, but they're alive."

Dylan took a moment to appraise the room, afraid to even comment. He'd suspected we'd lived a bad life, but nothing like what was before him, which was definitely a shift in reality to what he was accustomed to.

Ben wasn't moving, but Ryder stirred as I repeatedly said his name. "It's Darcy," I said, moving closer to him.

"Eight Ball drugged us," he whispered. "I'm not sure why. The only thing that makes sense is he wanted a piece of the fighter himself...or maybe Hart wanted us out of the way for some reason."

I looked at Ben and his lifeless body and realized whatever Eight Ball had dosed them with, Ben got double. "It's going to be okay," I said quickly, touching Ben's hair. "This is my boyfriend, Dylan. He's the best friend I've ever had, and he's going to help us get out of here."

"Redcoat?" Ryder mumbled, struggling to stand.

Dylan squatted down beside us, gently touching Ryder on the shoulder. "I've got him," he said. "Can you walk if Darcy helps you?"

Ryder nodded, and once Dylan had Ben hoisted over his shoulder, we took off for the exit several feet past my room. We passed one door. Two. Three. Four more. And finally on the right, I saw the exit. Ryder's brain waves immediately got with the program, and he scrambled up the stairs, Dylan following...but I couldn't...I was at a crossroads...free myself with Dylan or go for the passports and let all bets ride on Lincoln finding us.

"I can't go, D," I said to his back.

Dylan turned toward me, Ben dangling as dead weight from his back. "What is it you're after, Darc?"

"I need to get Lars van der Hart's passports. They're in a safe in his room." Point for Dylan, he never asked the *why*, and right then so wasn't the time for me to explain Van der Hart had several aliases, one of which was Daddy Dearest, AKA Butch Lawrence.

Leaving Ryder and Ben upstairs in an abandoned building next to us, Dylan and I took off for Daddy Dearest's room, making a pit stop at mine so I could grab my sketchpad as evidence of who'd been killed, who deserved a free pass, and who deserved the death chair. Dylan took a moment to look at the psycho mess I'd been living in. "I'm so sorry," he murmured.

Once I'd grabbed my sketchpad and knife, I said, "Yeah. Home sweet home."

Dylan then spied the slash marks behind my door and added number eighty himself. "Eighty days, sweetheart. Eighty days."

True, it was well past midnight, and eighty was officially my favorite number. Wondering if we'd ever find normal again, I grabbed Dylan by the hand, and after a few hundred meters, we made it into the land of ravens.

"The Raven." Dylan whistled low. "I get it now."

The dozen birds perched in their silver cages, blinking like the dumb-butt fools they were. But maybe they weren't so dumb. Maybe they'd merely grown tired of being prisoners too. "Under the picture," I told Dylan. Dylan slid his left hand down the photograph of Daddy Dearest and his buds, releasing a hinge. As Ryder had said, a safe with a dial was exposed. "Mother Mary," Dylan prayed. "What now?"

I'd had a lot of time to think about this moment. Whatever cycle of the crazy express Daddy Dearest was on, my mother happened to be the current obsession. I had an Edison light bulb moment and spun the dial right, two times left, and ended with a right of my mother's death date and the safe popped open. "How did you know?" Dylan gasped.

"Long story—" A nervous feeling stirred in my gut when I removed the last passport, and in two blinks and a yell from the hallway, I realized Dylan would get the answer to his question with a personal touch.

"Eve! Where are you? We need to leave. Now!"

Dylan shoved me behind him right as Daddy Dearest came running in, carrying a gun. Our odds of survival just took a nosedive, but Daddy Dearest stopped dead in his tracks when he clocked on Dylan.

"Hello, Apollo," he said, his jaw ripping with anger. "Or should I say Dylan? I've been tracking you. Your grandfather is one very smart man."

Dylan did not acknowledge the statement about Lincoln, but he did take Daddy Dearest on. "We're leaving here," he told him. "You can either let us do so or take your last breath."

"And yet I'm the one with the gun."

I hitched my chin high. "Let Dylan go first, and then I'll go with you."

Daddy Dearest walked toward me. Dylan went medieval. "If you lay a hand on her, I'll fricking rip your arm off and feed it to you."

"Come now, Eve, and no harm will befall him."

Oh crap...what now? Verdict? Let it all hang out. "I'm not Eve!" I screamed, coming out from behind Dylan. "You're not my father! You're Robert Butch Lawrence, the man who murdered my mother in cold blood." The bloom was definitely off the rose. Maybe it wasn't the time to confront him, but I felt my mother's presence so strongly I needed to speak on her behalf.

"You remember," he said.

"I remember everything."

"Then you also remember it was an accident. I loved her...I love *you.*"

As expected, Daddy Dearest regurgitated the same crap. "It was too your fault!" I refuted. "Whatever your grief is coughing up, you had a split second of choice...I saw you willingly pull the trigger... did you feel bad? Maybe, but you chose to pull the trigger anyway."

"Now, Eve. We don't have time for any more of your stiff-upper-lipped arguments. My enemies are closing in."

When I took another step toward him, Dylan latched on to the back of my dress. "I know about Julius Marx," I said. "I don't know what you did as Marx, but I have a friend who is going to take you down because of it."

He tipped his head as if he hadn't a care in the world. "A lot of people know of Marx and just let Marx be. I'm not worried about a sixteen-year-old girl who happens to know another life of mine."

I didn't back down. "But you've had several lifetimes, right? Julius Marx, Pierre LaFayette, Jared Ming, Igor Guskov, to name a few. You were also Mahesh Singh, and Singh killed Lyric Armstrong."

"Lyric Armstrong became too nosy. She fell into her own trap. I just left her there."

"How'd you do it? How did you convince the Cincinnati PD that Singh was dead?"

"I have several people who look like me. I chose one to die, and we swapped DNA in the lab. I'm *a lot* of people," he continued, "and you're going to be a lot of people too once I change your looks. Unfortunately, you resemble Tabitha, a woman I could barely stomach."

"Do you work for the government?" I asked.

A cunning grin. "I work for several governments."

Dylan didn't say anything, curse, or even drop the mother of all F-bombs. He merely went still—like the lull in the air before a tidal wave decimated society. Before I could say no, Dylan had thrown me out of the way and wrestled Daddy Dearest for control of the gun. A scream fell from my lips as they landed hard on the floor. Furniture upended. Screeched across the floor. A shot squeezed off, and it became clear Daddy Dearest had the strength of a seasoned pro. The gun fell to the floor, but with them moving like a tornado, I couldn't find it. In seconds flat, Daddy Dearest had Dylan in a headlock, working him over like a new recruit in a dojo. Dylan looked brutal and barbarous with his teeth bared back, but he'd also been purposefully dehydrated.

I glanced furiously for the knife I'd brought with me, finding it on a table nearby. Problem was, whenever I took aim at Daddy Dearest's back, he and Dylan would switch places, and I feared I'd stab *him*. When there appeared to be no end in sight, at the squawk of a raven, I turned and opened a cage, shooing it free. Then I freed the others, one by one. When Daddy Dearest heard the noise, it provided just enough shock that Dylan got the upper hand, forcing him into a submission hold. But the ravens didn't immediately go for the door. Instead, the bulk of them went for Daddy Dearest's eyes.

I heard a desperate, tortured moan, like a wounded animal near death. "No!" he said, attempting to swat them away...right as Lincoln and Paddy entered the room.

"I see you started the party without me," Lincoln deadpanned. Lincoln looked scarier than shiz, his tattoos covering more real estate than Dylan's. At the sound of his grandfather's voice, Dylan released his hold and quickly rolled out of the way, diving for me. With one swipe at a raven, Daddy Dearest took one look at me and then went for the gun he and Dylan had been lying on. Lincoln unloaded two bullets to the chest. There was a slight pause and blur of movement, and then Paddy, I think, unloaded a third. The body bounced with the force and stilled on the floor. *Yeah, eat it, Butch.* Robert Lawrence's eyes were fixed and dilated in a dead-eyed stare as blood pooled around him in a fast-flowing circle. Just like that...it was over.

———

As I watched Ben and Ryder be placed in separate ambulances and members of The Underground corralled by uniforms and detectives in suits, I underwent a very intimate pat down by some rookie cop that caused Lincoln Taylor to bark out a profanity. "She's the effing vic, you dumbass!" he yelled. Whatever...I was just glad to see the light of day, and sunrise was just around the corner. I couldn't tell where we were, but I could smell and hear the Ohio River. I knew what that meant. People had been shipped in and out via barge, and maybe disposed of that way too. The river didn't always give up its dead.

While Rookie and Colton came screaming their ways toward me, the eighty days of fear, disappointment, and regret came crashing down like a tree in the forest.

"Is it safe to cry?" I asked Dylan.

Dylan's chin trembled as one tear slid down his cheek. "Yeah, just let go. Let go and feel what you need to feel, Darc. You've been strong enough and can be tough tomorrow. I've got you. I promise I'm going nowhere."

The moment he hugged me, I unraveled.
See you later, Underground...it's been real.

Chapter Thirty-One
THE WALKING DEAD

*A*fter two hours of nonstop crying—so much that my rice made an encore appearance—a nurse knelt at the side of my bed along with Dylan and convinced me to take a sedative. I still feared not being alert, but a girl could only take so much snot rolling in and out of her mouth before she caved.

Slipping out of bed, I rolled my IV pole to the window and pulled back the drapes. I'd taken my freedom for granted—something I'd just told a sobbing Murphy right before I fell asleep. He, Marjorie, and Red were in Kansas City, Kansas. Rookie had given them a weeklong vacation to Great Wolf Lodge, an indoor water-park, to help Marjorie get her mind off of missing me. The broader reason, I was sure, had been to get them out of town when the plan was in motion. Right then, they were on their way home as soon as they could get a flight.

I watched the traffic outside my room...a man on the sidewalk... a little boy holding his hand...I watched the darn pigeons and how they pecked at the concrete looking for food that wasn't there. I'd always thought pigeons to be really dumb birds...maybe they'd learned to just hope for the best. Since I'd wakened a half an hour earlier, I found myself taking random moments where I just breathed. My chest wasn't so tight anymore, and I craved the feeling.

After a beat, I padded to the restroom, scrubbed my face, and gazed in the mirror. I was so thin I saw my heart beating through my skin, and my head looked like the first stages of decomposition. The nurse had felt sorry for me and scored some makeup, so I applied blush, saturated each lash with mascara, and rolled on some clear lip gloss. I wasn't exactly bringing sexy back, but at least I didn't resemble an extra on *The Walking Dead.*

Altogether I'd lost eighteen pounds, made some friends, more enemies, and after a tune-up from the doc-on-call, I'd been informed I had two cavities. Not to mention, I'd shrunk a bra size. My Barely-Bs were Almost-As, and that almost sucked more than getting kidnapped.

Dylan was dead asleep in one of those chairs that fold out into a bed. I did everything every girl on the planet wanted to do...lean over his naked chest. "D," I whispered, touching his cheek. He jumped like he'd been hit with a hot poker. "It's okay," I told him quickly. "We're okay."

My best friend was still on hyper alert. After his breathing regulated, he whispered back, "I'm sorry. I haven't slept in months, but with you by my side, I think I finally relaxed."

Um, wow, I'd forgotten how smooth he could be—even when he wasn't trying. "You're due some ZZZs," I said, smiling and sliding back under the sheets.

Dylan sat up and tenderly pushed the hair off of my forehead, placing the gel pack he'd held on his left eye on the bedside table. He'd fallen asleep with it in his hand. After a teary reunion with Rookie and Colton—wherein Rookie whipped out a NDA for everyone to sign (a nondisclosure agreement was SOP for Rookie)— Dylan stayed with me while they'd gone home to change. Last I remember, he was on his second bag of fluids. His IV was gone. I could only assume he was back to fighting shape.

"Good morning, sweetheart. Or afternoon," he murmured, glancing at a bedside clock. "I can't tell you what it means to hear your voice."

When he looked at me that way, all others always faded away. "Missed you," I said.

Dylan pulled my hand to his lips in a quick kiss. "I've missed you too," he murmured. "I've never prayed so much in my life, especially when fighting last night. My internal GPS told me you were in trouble, Darc. When the first gunshot went off, I spotted the back of your head in that red dress immediately."

Dylan's omnipresent talent to show up when I needed him had not been severed. Maybe the Big Man Upstairs heard my prayers after all...*thankyouverymuch*.

I explained red had been an unexpected color...that I'd always worn black, which insinuated Delia had been trying to point me out. I knew in my gut that had been done with good intentions. I rolled on my side toward him. "Cough it up, D. How'd you guys find me?"

"When you first disappeared, Marek Ransom came to visit. He said you'd promised to watch him fight and wondered if you'd somehow gotten sucked into something bad. He'd come down with the flu and couldn't attend."

Taking a deep breath, I explained that was the weekend Dylan had traveled to Florida. I waited for the bad memory to surface, but Dylan remained zen. "I didn't find a fight anywhere," I said. "In fact, Indigo sent me a text Monday morning that said Marek was gone. For a while, I thought I'd run into him in The Underground."

Dylan snorted. "Indigo's an airhead who is back with Fisher Stanton. God only knows what her definition of *gone* is."

"Wow." I whistled. I needed a crash course on what had gone on in my absence, pronto.

Reaching under my pillow, I pulled out an open bag of cookies and put two in my mouth. I was on a strict diet that slowly reintroduced solids—eh, I wasn't following it, and I'd recruited a certain male nurse to help me break the rule. Problem was, his shift had ended, and the female nurses were rule followers.

Dylan didn't lecture, simply pouring me a cup of water. "The FBI got involved," he said. "They staked out Club Need due to Marek's information, but understandably when the niece of the County Prosecutor goes missing, the information flow dried up rather quickly. Lars van der Hart was all of a sudden a clean living man. That got Dad to thinking because he remembered you said you'd been working on something the night you phoned to talk to me. He knew you must've stumbled upon something criminal and figured it out before the cops did. Lincoln took a leave of absence because he didn't like the way things were progressing, but he doesn't really play well with others," he said and laughed. "So he hooked up with a detective here in town, off the radar. They tracked Van der Hart, and Lincoln even spoke to him on one occasion while he grabbed a drink at his bar. Lincoln has rubbed shoulders with various filth over the years but said Van der Hart was one of the most evil men he'd ever run across. In fact, as the conversation progressed, Van der Hart attempted to contract Lincoln out for a hit on the same detective he was quietly working with."

I swallowed down some H_2O. "Impressive."

A slight chuckle and head shake. "Lincoln is Lincoln, sweetheart. God knows how he does the things he does. He then talked to Iggy and filled him in. Iggy had heard of The Underground but honestly was too afraid to wade into something that had been operating undetected for years."

"Did you come in by boat?"

"Yes, but Iggy told Lincoln The Underground was actually connected in a series of mile long tunnels underneath Club Need. So you were still technically in the city but in the outskirts, right above a building occupied by the homeless." The perfect cover. The homeless weren't always on their A-game to report anything suspicious, and the cops probably let them be anyway. "Once we knew what we were dealing with," Dylan continued, "Lincoln told me that I needed to be prepared for anything. So Iggy got Paddy in touch with a similar fight club on the West Coast."

"Lincoln hadn't heard of it?"

"Believe it or not, no...but the LAPD had agreed to let it operate until we had you out. I trained with Paddy for the last two months—even before we knew definitively you were being held prisoner—taking on anyone with a big mouth and undefeated status. We had a plan to draw Van der Hart out because we heard he likes his trophies. We wanted him to want me, and it worked."

"But none of that told you I was in The Underground."

Dylan's jaw hardened. "No, but Gilbert Himmel did."

My jaw dropped...all the way to freaking China. "No shiz."

Dylan poured more water in the cup, taking a drink himself. "Yes, shiz. He approached Rookie a little over a month ago and said if Red went on record as saying she had an affair with his brother, then he would give them your whereabouts."

I sucked in a breath. "Blackmail?"

Dylan nodded soberly. "Yeah, it would've been the end of her career, but she agreed. Rookie would only allow it after Himmel delivered up picture proof you were alive. He said he'd get it, so Rookie placed a tail on him. One weekend the tail tracked him entering Club Need, but he didn't leave after closing. We knew then we were on the right track, especially when we received a tip to keep plugging away and not to worry about the Himmels anymore."

Insert a head scratch. "Why were you told to not worry about the Himmels?"

Dylan opened his mouth, closed it, but finally answered, "Because they were at the bottom of a retired rock quarry."

My stomach bottomed out. "I take it they weren't swimming," I whispered.

Oh crap, that had to have been Jaws. When I'd quit communicating with him, he'd figured things out like I'd expected. That meant he'd been tracking everything going on in my life...and even in Red's. "Do you want to venture a guess who that tip came from?" he asked. "It was left anonymously on Red's phone."

Listen, I was historically lousy in the honesty department, but for once I told Dylan the truth—that Jaws was a man I occasionally talked to when I needed the down and dirty on someone, and I suspected he was Cincinnati mob. "I have not met him...at least seen his face," I said, "nor do I know his real name. I sought him out sophomore year when I chased the Northside 12 gang. And before you ask, Vinnie and Grumpy set it up, but it wasn't their fault I continued the relationship. Jaws watches out for me. He's like that fairy godmother who knows my every move."

Dylan was all about the one hundred percent transparency thing, but I wasn't sure he could stomach it once I offered a big bite. "Pinky swear?" he said. I twined my finger in his and squeezed. After a deep breath, he nodded. "I can accept that."

"Will you keep his name between us?"

Without hesitation, Dylan replied, "Yes."

He'd not only grown bigger and stronger, but something had evolved in his voice. I'd expected a come-to-Jesus meeting and got a guy I barely recognized. "This is new," I mumbled.

Dylan shrugged, as though the weight of the past was something he still couldn't quite rid himself of. "I've had a lot of time to be without you, Darc. I have no interest in arguing...about anything. But to wrap up the conversation, as they say, the rest is history. When I won, I was to name my prize. Paddy told Van der Hart I liked tall blondes, and he said he already had someone in mind with long, blonde hair and green eyes." *Some dad*. I snorted to myself. "So were you after him all along?" Dylan asked quietly. "Darc, we didn't know he was the man who shot your mom. If Lincoln knew, the knowledge came late in the game."

Or they kept Dylan out of the loop because they feared he'd blow his part in the sting. "I've always been after the man who killed my mom. You have a wonderful nuclear family, D. I used to, and it's eaten me up inside that her crime went unanswered. And it ate at me even more the way Murphy and Red handled it. But did I know Van der Hart was actually Butch Lawrence? No. This was fate conspiring for me...or against me...I haven't decided yet."

That thought hung in the air while I debated how to unload the specifics of my actions. Right or wrong, I omitted that Jaws and I had blackmailed one another. Did I fear what Dylan would think of me? I wasn't sure I wanted to dwell on it, to be honest. But I feared what he'd think of Jaws. Jaws lived by a different moral code, and although I understood it, I wasn't sure Dylan would...but perhaps I'd underestimated him. Look what he'd done earlier, but that had been to save *me*. For Jaws and me? Instances like the one with Lars van der Hart were a way of life. Regardless, Jaws and I needed to have a convo about his grudge match ASAP. The biggest question? Why didn't he do things himself? He obviously had the resources.

So why use Lyric Armstrong's death to open up this case?

I prayed my relationship with Tito would serve as truth enough. I started fidgeting—wringing my hands like a wet towel—expecting things to blow up in my face. "I realize this might be a deal breaker for our relationship going forward, but here's how I got involved in the first place. I'd been doing some undercover work for Tito Westbrook. I've known him since Christmas when I fed him info on his identity theft. I answered Rookie's phone...I posed as Red...and our relationship snowballed from there." I explained how Tito'd been at Club Need the night Lyric's body was discovered and how I'd subsequently worn him down until he confessed he'd been tracking certain aliases he believed to be responsible for her death. "When he gave me those names," I said, "he didn't tell me they were Lars van der Hart's aliases. They were merely names he'd been trying to tie to Lyric's disappearance. It was not in my active plan to get kidnapped, but I only solved this thing because I *did*. And regarding Butch Lawrence also being one of Van der Hart's aliases? Like I said, this was fate conspiring for me, or against me."

Dylan voraciously rubbed the back of his neck. "Whoa," he said in shock.

"Yeah, boredom can really suck," I said, attempting to explain my behavior. I then clarified I didn't think Daddy Dearest even knew I'd been working with Tito—that he claimed he'd come for me because he was my father, he'd been keeping tabs on me, we'd had a face-to-face at Club Need, blah, blah, psycho, etcetera.

Dylan was speechless...and that might be a first.

There were a lot of *firsts* happening with my best friend. He still looked the same: the sculpted jaw, cheekbones of a stud, but there was a darkness in his eyes that was new...new to someone whose optimism used to be the biggest thing about him.

"Thank you for not giving up on me," I said softly. "I was worried the whole time you fought. A submission round is to the death, Dylan. Eight Ball is bad. I saw him kill two people and rip the tip of the nose off of another."

"I wouldn't have lost," he murmured. Make note he did not say that with arrogance. It was a mere statement of fact.

Dylan's mother had sent me a bouquet of daffodils in some fancy crystal vase. He ran a fingertip lightly around its base, almost like he took extra care of something especially fragile. "I didn't know what he'd done to you, what you'd endured, but I was prepared to die so it wouldn't happen again. Are you okay?" he whispered hoarsely, not making eye contact. "It's been eating me up inside. Every day, all day long, especially at night."

The ache in Dylan's voice nearly sawed me in two. "No one raped me, D. There were some close calls, but whatever you're imagining are just mental pictures of your worst nightmare. Don't fill in the blanks."

"Pinky swear you're okay," he said softly.

"Wouldn't you be able to tell if I wasn't?"

"I think so, but I know how good of an actress you can be, Darcy. If you weren't, you wouldn't be here today."

"Pinky swear," I vowed. "Although being locked up in a coffin I'm sure will breed some pretty bad PTSD when I least expect it."

Dylan lunged at me, hugging me so tightly my lungs almost collapsed. When I felt his tears soak through my hospital gown, I knew whatever was to come I'd make it—just like when Dumbledore's phoenix cried onto Harry Potter's wounds, Dylan always healed me. I found myself praying our destinies synced back up.

I touched his face when he sat back in his chair. The smell of fighting still clung to him...and wow, what a turn on. I decided to be bold. "Do you still feel the heat between us?"

"My feelings have not changed," he said quietly.

"But you want to ask me why, right? You want to ask why I was willing to throw it all away?" Dylan lowered his lids, nodding. "Best friends don't leave, D. Lovers do. And no matter how you say you accept me, I'd always felt my actions bothered you more." Dylan opened his mouth, closed it. Repeated the sequence again. I tried another angle. "Why did you pick me to be your girlfriend? You could have anyone. You even had that crowd eating out of your hand last night."

Dylan's chin trembled with an uncontrollable wave of emotion. "Because of what you did for eighty days. You're like a rock in a pond, sweetheart. The effect of you striking the water ripples out to everything around you. I've missed being inside the ripple...your heart is the most beautiful thing I've ever seen."

Sonovagun. Cue the waterworks. As long as I lived, I'd never forget the look of awe in Dylan's face. "I'm in love with you," I blurted out, wiping the cookies from my mouth. "I know I'm a hot mess, and it's not the setting I would've preferred, but I hope you can overlook my lack of creativity."

Dude, that was about as subtle as a flying axe...but I wanted to kiss him so badly my teeth hurt. Dylan burst into tears, gasping like a car trying to start. Tears blinded his one eye and leaked out of the swollen other in a slow drip. "I love you too," he said roughly. "I didn't even dare believe you'd ever say that to me. I just wanted you back...I didn't care how..."

I sucked in a shaky breath. "Why would I quit caring? We're a team."

"You've just been gone for so long. Eighty days," he whispered. "And Ryan...oh, God...I wished it would've been me...I resented him...but when we discovered the fight club, I knew his past...I knew what he must be doing, so I found myself praying for him because of the pressure he must've felt."

And that, in itself, was the main reason I loved Dylan. At the end of the day, he never failed to do what was right, and above anyone, he'd always have my back. I took a moment to comfort him, kissing the top of his head and tenderly wiping his eyes. The moment my mouth closed over his, the dam that had emotionally separated us finally broke. The kiss was soft...slow...and then it deepened as the air around us became frantic. Teeth knocked and tears fell while Dylan dissolved into me with a moan, taking my face in his hands. He was still under my skin after all the time apart, and I'd take whatever he'd give because my body was ravenous for affection as much as food. Wrapping my hands around his wrists, I dragged him into bed with me. A jolt of desire passed through us, my head buzzing like a light bulb on the fritz. I wanted him closer than my own thoughts, my own skin. Did I have self-control issues? I never said I didn't...but Dylan pulled away when he began to shake.

Three words? Wow. Wow. Wow.

I licked my lips...and prayed he didn't walk away with cookies in his mouth because I'd been all over him like bugs on a windshield.

While Dylan pulled himself together, I convinced my inner-Dylan-whore to get a grip and settled into the crook of his neck, not able to resist brushing my lips against him again. Tracing the outline of a tattoo on his chest, I dropped my defenses as usual—embracing the feeling that I didn't have to be on guard 24/7.

I was the first to speak. "I know we're out of practice talking to one another, but I want to be able to tell you my heart, like always. Is Ben okay? Please don't take my interest as romantic, but he wouldn't have been in The Underground if not for me. I used him as a ride to Club Need. That was it...nothing more. Eight Ball saw us together, tracked him, and brought him to me because he knew I was lonely."

Oh, God, that was where Dylan should've been repulsed. Frankly, listening to it myself might've been the most repulsive thing I'd ever heard, especially when I admitted I also took advantage of Ben when he helped me find Gabrielle Allen. Instead, Dylan kissed the top of my head, delivering answers. "He's still unconscious, but he's expected to make a full recovery."

I lifted my gaze to meet his. "Would you walk me to his room? I need to tell him I appreciate what he did. He fought every night for me. He kept me from being..." I stopped and squinted my eyes together.

Dylan knew exactly what I referred to because his body tensed up.

Taking my hand, Dylan led me down the hall to Ben's room. Ben was out cold, his long beautiful copper hair arranged like a darn J. Crew model on the white pillow. The machines he was hooked up to beeped in a rhythmic pattern. He'd gotten more of the hospital treatment than me. That worried me, but when someone still hadn't wakened, overkill was the name of the game.

Dressed in jeans and a sweater, a gorgeous blonde-headed woman had his hand in hers as she spoke gently to him. Her head darted up when she sensed us, and I knew it was his mom. "Darcy?" she asked.

Truthfully, I didn't know what to expect from her. As far as I knew, she might consider me the Delilah to his Samson, the female who practically ruined his life...eh, pretty darn close. She stood up quickly, extending her hand. "I'm Desirae Ryan," she said to me, blinking with the same silver eyes as Ben. "And you must be Dylan."

After the introductions, Dylan and I pulled up a seat next to her. Realizing she was dying for a slice of what Ben's life had been like, I told her what he did every day, every night, how he'd bartered for me to have food, and how he'd kept me living and breathing as the dysfunctional Darcy Walker that I am. Her face nearly burst with pride. "You've raised a good son, Mrs. Ryan. No matter where life leads us, he will always be one of my best friends. And he might be angry with me for saying this, but he talked about Autumn in his sleep. Have you phoned her?"

"I have," she said quietly.

"Tell her what I said. Ben is very proud. I don't know what happened between them, but he still cares."

"You know my son very well," she said, smiling thankfully.

I shrugged. "When neither of you have had deodorant for months, you tend to look on the inside for someone's beauty rather than the outside. I would sneak to his room at night, so we could sleep next to each other. Please, don't take that the wrong way," I said, squeezing Dylan's hand for reassurance, "but The Underground messed with Ben more than me because he had to fight so much. I worried about him constantly, and I guess we would've rather died beside one another than wake up alone and wonder what'd happened to the only friend we had."

That was like dropping the A-bomb and expecting everyone to survive. When she began to cry, I followed suit, and after a few breaths Dylan found his voice first. "I am forever indebted, Mrs. Ryan. If Ben ever needs anything—"

She interrupted with a deep smile. "Your father stopped in earlier and expressed the same sentiment. Thank you for your part in getting them out, Dylan. Words cannot express my husband's and my gratitude. Your mother and father raised a very fine young man themselves."

Pushing to a stand, I rolled my IV to the bed and leaned over Ben's body, dropping a reverent kiss to his forehead. A rush of emotion took me by storm when I realized what all we'd endured, what all we'd overcome. "We're free, Redcoat," I whispered into his ear. "We're free."

Chapter Thirty-Two

FATE, LUCK, OR THE WILL OF GOD

"*I* love you, Darc," Rookie murmured through the phone. "I'm going down to the station to direct traffic to make sure this thing is nice and tight. I'll sneak in some junk food this evening," he said chuckling. "Is that good?"

"Roger that," I groaned. "I just choked down some hospital dog food. An outside meal would be awesome...like Twinkies...and Coke...and hot dogs...and maybe some McDonald's french fries. My body has really missed empty calories and trans fats."

Listen, I'd batted my eyes at every male specimen I'd encountered, and no one had been willing to score an escaped kidnap victim a little bit of the vices she'd missed. Of course, they'd done it with my best interests at heart.

Insert a wee bit of sarcasm.

I'd been watching the news, trying to reacquaint myself with the world I'd missed. Dylan had just gone home to shower when Rookie phoned, bringing me up to speed. Delia and Myles evidently were at the police station to be interviewed, and Rookie wanted to start with them to get a clear feel of who was complicit...and who was a victim. Basically, if they talked, they might get a deal. Delia would probably get one...plus a trip to rehab. Myles, however, was an accomplice in kidnapping, false imprisonment, and cruelty—and that was just with Ben and me. I suppose anything was possible, but he'd be hard pressed to prove his innocence.

The upside to the conversation? Rookie discovered Eight Ball and Daddy Dearest's connection from talking to one of the fighters. Apparently, Daddy Dearest had been at the match where Eight Ball killed Hurricane Cole and recruited him. Thankfully, Eight Ball was behind bars with several murder charges. The downside? Ryder and the other fighters were also being held until interviews and psych evaluations had been made. Some deserved twenty-five-to-life as a minimum, but for the others? Here was my problem: civilized society was now making them prisoners too.

If it weren't for Ryder, there wouldn't be visual proof of the passports for Tito and Jaws. I knew the cops would balk at me taking pictures, so when we heard Cincinnati's finest clearing the rooms, without question Lincoln and Paddy expeditiously clicked off pics until every page had been documented. And the pièce de résistance? We uncovered an old passport under the alias of Robert "Butch" Lawrence.

The fat lady just freaking sang.

I recradled the phone and took a deep breath right as Red walked through the door, escorted by one of the big men I'd hid behind during the championship round. They were part of the private investigative firm she'd worked for during one of her many-divorces-that-didn't-last from Rookie. Apparently they'd pulled some OT.

As I'd suspected, Rookie confirmed Red and Murphy had been kept in the dark. If Red knew, she would've told Murphy. If Murphy knew, he would've insisted on pulling the trigger himself. Red touched my face, and anger inside me grew like a three-headed monster. I'd held a grudge, but my heart betrayed me. I leaned my cheek into her touch and sighed. Red's voice cracked when she took a seat. "By popular vote, we've all decided you should be homeschooled. No dates, no trips to clubs, basically nothing except sitting at home with no contact with the outside world."

"That sounds fair." I smiled...silence for a bit. Red started at my face, eyes traveling to my torso and bony arms, trying to assess just how much muscle mass I'd lost. I'll answer that...everything that made me look like a girl. Her jaw hardened, her emerald-green eyes figuratively slicing through Daddy Dearest's gut. "Rookie told you we got Butch?" I asked. "And before you consider lying to me, I know he worked for the government."

Red opened her mouth and stopped, fiddled with the gigantic diamond Rookie gave her, and then dissolved into tears...her makeup dripping onto her expensive white sweater. "Murphy and I owe you an apology," she gasped. "We're sorry, baby. We should've told you more about Butch. He was a friend of ours. At first, we never suspected him to be Gemma's stalker, but Gemma began to feel some funky vibes. I got someone to watch him, and that's when we found out he'd been the one sending Gemma all the creepy stuff that forced her off the road in the first place. I think he knew we were onto him because he disappeared for ten years, until the night he shot her. Once again, he went AWOL, and with his job, I prayed someone had killed him. I had no idea he was even involved in your kidnapping—or in the city—until Rookie told me about the passports this morning. You got the man who murdered your mom. Murphy was just afraid—"

"Of where your mind would go," he murmured. Murphy held Marjorie in one arm and stood in the doorway...afraid to come in... afraid to go out. He was still huge like a tree trunk, but his curly brown hair had grayed around the temples. "I almost murdered our pilot," he grumbled. "He flew that jet slower than molasses."

Marjorie jumped out of his arms and bounced into bed with me. "I mithed you, Darc," she whispered, kissing me on the mouth. "I've been so bored. Daddy won't play naked Barbies. He said it was inappropriate. Only Vinnie and Finn will play, but then they put names on the girls and said something about safe words, and it got kinda weird."

Holy crap. I've never laughed so hard in my life.

And that provided the icebreaker we needed to get in touch with the dueling emotions of anger and happiness. Soon the four of us cried like I had while watching *Futurama*—when Fry's dog waited twelve years outside Panucci's Pizza for him to return until he died. Murphy fell on me like he'd witnessed someone rising from the dead, telling me over and over how he loved me. "Kid," he exhaled, sitting on the side of the bed and taking the crappy hospital tissue Red offered. "I was so afraid I'd never see you again. I've missed you being inappropriate at the worst of times and making me laugh until I cried. The house just hasn't been the same."

There was a deep well of love locked up in Murphy's heart if one ever cared to poke around. Shutting out the rest of the home team, my father and I had a poignant moment. He'd kept our family together, cuddled me at night, wiped my tears while I cried, and somehow managed to not hold a grudge when I'd gotten into various messes over the years. The truth lay in his eyes—he thanked me for nailing the man who'd murdered the love of his life, but he was even more sorry for the tension between us. He tried to speak but couldn't. Instead, he went for my once broken finger.

"I worried about your finger, kid. In fact, I got so obsessed I began to have sympathy pains. But I woke up this morning, and the ache was gone. Did it heal?" I attempted to make a fist. Although I'd exercised it daily, the digit had frozen in a half-mast condor. "You've got to be kidding," he said and chuckled.

"Nope, but I've kinda grown fond of it," I said shrugging. "As long as I can still throw and catch a ball, I say it stays."

"Have at it, kid," Murphy said, smiling and holding my hand in his. "Now you have a cover if someone's mean to you."

Red tugged Marjorie onto her lap, so Murphy and I could get closer. M, however, wasn't ready to let go, grabbing ahold of my hair and making a braid. "Dylan loves you. Did you know that?" she said and smiled. "He called me every day."

While I assured her Dylan and I were still together, Murphy took a deep breath, attempting to explain his actions. "I worshiped Gemma, and when she died, I bled, kid. I rarely talked about her because I couldn't keep opening a vein...but I should've anteed up. My greatest fear had always been that Butch would come back and try to take you again...somehow tarnish her memory...but maybe if I'd given you tools to cope..."

Listen, Butch came into town on the crazy train and never looked back. Even if I would've known, I wouldn't have stopped until he'd been brought to justice.

"Was he my father?" I blurted out. "He claimed he was. I almost asked Rookie this morning but figured I'd ask you personally. No matter what, that won't make you any less my dad."

Murphy dropped a JC. Eh, maybe I should've delivered that

question a little more eloquently because Marjorie looked like someone told her Barbies were porn stars. "No, kid, he's not your father," he answered quietly.

"Swear it to me."

"I swear it," he said adamantly.

"Is this true, Red?" I asked because God knew I got the crazy gene from somebody.

"I swear it on everything I believe," she answered. "And I would tell you if he was...even if it hurt Murphy, and he's my best friend. I told Murphy when you first went missing that we had to come clean because we'd obviously misjudged how this affected you...was *still* affecting you. For the longest time, we thought you'd run away. Dylan swore you would never do that to Marjorie."

"But what if you're wrong?"

She set her jaw as I glanced to Murphy. Yup, the cat still had his tongue. "My sister and I had no secrets. She loved your father deeply. I had to endure many conversations of their crazy love life," she said, laughing hollowly. "If Gemma cheated, she couldn't have kept it to herself. She would've told me that too."

I hesitated, but finally said the obvious. "I don't look like Murphy. I look like you."

"True, but your brain is all Walker, baby."

I bit my nails to the quick in a matter of seconds, smiling inside when I noticed Murphy doing the same thing. "Butch is dead, Dad," I said, trying to ease his pain.

Murphy blew his nose, pausing to wipe a tear. "You are my heart and soul, kid. When you have a doubt, realize you've always seen the world the way I have. We think alike, and that's genetic. And I just want you to know that your mom would've been so proud." In true Murphy style, he changed the subject when his feelings began to inflate. "Okay," he said, adding a chuckle. "Now that we've got that out of the way, I think you're grounded."

I threw my head back laughing, stopping when Murphy produced my iPhone out of his jacket. "See this phone here? It's mine until I say you can have it."

"Good Lord," Red said and laughed. "Let the chaos reign."

I held out my palm. My God, that was cruel and unusual punishment. "Give me my phone back, Murphy. I could get eaten by a bear and not be able to call for help." Murphy closed his eyes with a grin. "What are you doing?" I asked.

"Praying bears move into the neighborhood."

———

"Just curious, but do you know your IQ, honey?" Detective O'Brien asked.

I was supposed to be sprung from the joint earlier, but my blood work came back shoddy and the medical team ordered I be treated onsite for anemia. Bored out of my mind, I rearranged my room because the feng shui was off, thought it looked stupid, and when the nurse's eyes bugged out of her head, I changed things back. As a result of my lockdown, a Cincinnati detective decided to give me the official treatment in my hospital room. Detective Christian O'Brien had interviewed Dylan and me months before at Club Need and was the man Lincoln had been working with on the sly— the man Lars van der Hart preferred to be pushing up daisies. I glanced at the new sparkly Reef flip-flops on my feet. Dylan's mother brought them when she picked him up along with new jean capris and a vintage Cat Woman T-shirt. Just like that, I was nerd girl official again.

"My father was told it was 160," I muttered, "but I think they made a mistake."

Detective O'Brien was model handsome but had not seen a shave or sleep in weeks. His brown hair was askew, and his matching eyes had enough bags underneath them to down an airplane. "I would agree," he said. "Mine is 165, and I couldn't have thought my way out of your situation on a good day. Since you're not going home this evening, are you up to answering some questions?"

Red hadn't left my side. Murphy and M had gone to the business department to take care of insurance stuff. I was sure that would be an interesting conversation...Murphy'd probably insist the city pay half.

"The question is, will you be able to stomach the answers?" I said. "The first story starts with Eight Ball nailing me inside a coffin." Red shifted next to me and expelled a profane prayer. Detective O'Brien didn't move a muscle.

"I didn't think we'd have great bedtime stories," he said, "but I can promise if you lived to tell the tale, the best I can do as a human being is to sit through the retelling."

"I remember every day...verbatim."

"As long as you have words, I will listen. And while it's on my mind, if you ever need anything...a job...help with a problem...call me personally, and it's as good as done."

Hey, it beat working the drive-thru.

Right as I nodded and said, "Okay," a brisk double knock struck the door and in strolled Tito Westbrook. He shut the door behind him...and stared. The air sucked out of the room. "Darcy, I need to hug you," he finally said. "Please, let me love on the girl who has had my back, and I didn't even know it."

For a moment, I actually considered lying that I was Jester, but when Tito's chin quivered, Red pushed me to a standing position. I must say, I did appreciate that he didn't out my alter ego's name though...that meant we were still in business. Tito had on jeans and a white polo, wearing a two-day old beard, or his five o'clock shadow was twice the normal man. His olive-complexion had seen its fair share of the sun, and tiny laugh lines surrounded the corners of his eyes.

The affection went epidemic because my chin trembled when his arms wrapped around me. After the I-love-you stuff, Tito settled into an empty seat, still clutching my hand. "Tell me about Lyric," I said.

Tito closed his eyes, breathing deep. "She turned out to be a sacrificial lamb, darlin'. I did not want the same for you."

Tito's face filled with pain as he explained she'd been feeding him information about the fight club and Ryder's disappearance, which he'd subsequently passed on to Detective O'Brien years earlier. Although the club closed under Mahesh Singh's owner/management, Tito'd discovered the building changed ownership every so many years. Those new owners would in turn keep up the Club Need trademark. Thing was, all of the buyers used the same inspection company to walk through the building before closing on the sale. Therefore, there was no opportunity for an outside set of eyes to discover underground tunnels, let alone Lyric's body. And all the names on those real estate purchases had been the aliases Tito had been chasing—the names on the passports.

"Before we get started, I want Ryder Beck to get a deal," I told Detective O'Brien. "He has information on Lyric's death, and I'm sure Tito and you combined have enough notes to prove he's been a victim. The Underground definitely took its toll, but he did the right thing when it counted," I said, explaining how I believed him to be the one to place my phone in Colton's mailbox. "I want him out. Fix it."

Detective O'Brien said softly, "That deal can only be given by the prosecutor, honey. I'm thinking you may have some pull there."

Maybe, maybe not. "Rookie is the fairest person you're ever going to meet. I've already told him my feelings on each person I met, but he'll want to lock up everyone and throw away the key if it will keep Red from crying. If you agree with me after you hear what everyday life was like, promise you'll speak on his behalf." Red and Tito laughed as Detective O'Brien and I had a visual duel. He buckled first. "Deal," he said and grinned.

Red handed me my sketchpad. I started at page one as two detectives entered the room with laptops. I had to say, I had the time of my life.

———

Waking up at four a.m. was only worth it if Dylan Taylor was next to you...*he wasn't*...Murphy was...with a string tied from my ankle to his.

Some guard dog. I laughed to myself because Vinnie had just snuck in and cut the cord. He'd been here earlier with the rest of my friends, crying his eyes out, and had just returned dressed incognito in scrubs...leading me to some top-secret meeting with the man in the yellow Dodge Charger. The venue? The chapel. I found it odd the chapel had been the chosen place, but it brought to mind the existential debate: had my success been by fate, luck, or the will of God? All I knew was I hoped the room didn't implode with Vinnie's and my sins combined.

"Do you know Dodge Charger Man, V?"

"No. Jaws set up this meeting, and even Jaws won't let me see his face. Hug me, Dolce. Jaws had me combing the streets for you. I think I might've lost my pass to Heaven."

Vinnie's look had changed from months earlier. Last I saw him, he resembled a tattooed meth head, arms covered in colored hieroglyphics and his fingernails glowing an electric-blue. His brown hair had also been styled in a permed Mohawk then with a Fu Manchu mustache. Vinnie had recently shaved his head but kept the Fu Manchu. When I pushed for a why, he said his movie career was "on hold." Hugging him as we made our way down the hall, I realized how creepy hospitals were in general. The food sucked. The ambiance sucked. And they were colder than a morgue.

"Tell me you had nothing to do with the disappearance of the Himmels," I mumbled.

"I had nothing to do with the disappearance of the Himmels," he said and chuckled. I took that as truth and not a rhetorical response to the question.

The chapel lay on the far side of my floor, past Ben's room, and housed four pews facing a statue of Jesus and the Mother Mary. Vinnie and I lit a candle because that seemed like the chapel thing to do and waited in the front row. After a few beats, I felt the presence of someone behind me and nearly jumped out of my skin when the person touched me gently on the shoulder.

"Hello, Darcy," he murmured.

I jumped into Vinnie. Vinnie dropped a cuss-word and immediately issued an apology to Jesus. *Darcy, Darcy, Darcy.* I sighed. *A few seconds ago, you were ready. Now you aren't so gung-ho.* My reasons were threefold. One, I was chicken. Two, God was watching. And three, I wasn't sure what I'd do with Dodge Charger Man now that he was a captive audience.

"I understand you got rather close to Julius Marx," he murmured. "I'm so sorry, Darcy, but I need the goods on him. Can you give those to me?"

My manners understandably were fashionably late. I continued to gaze straight ahead, my eyes glued to a flickering candle until Vinnie elbowed me in the ribs to answer. I had the goods. Once Murphy gave me back my phone, I texted Lincoln and told him I needed the passport evidence...he sent it to me, no questions asked.

"Am I allowed to turn around?" I said.

"By all means."

Squeezing Vinnie's hand for moral support, my first thought when I turned? Oh. My. Flipping. Gosh. I'd forgotten how huge he was, nearly taking up the entire pew. Like last time, he sported black fatigues and a faded ballcap. His hair was the same color as Dylan's, and his dark eyes were amused, attached to a Romanesque face that was the epitome of every-woman-wants-me. In fact, his pheromones functioned like an atom bomb, destroying everything in its path. It hadn't just been me he had that effect on. Even Vinnie had his head cocked to the side, wondering if he were man or beast.

Sure, he defined all things gorgeous, but nothing was more gorgeous than what he held in his hands: a UDF coffee, a Coke, and a cookie...the man obviously had his ear to the ground because it was a peace offering of my favorite things. I muttered, "Thank you, God," and giggled, placing them in the seat beside me.

"I take it the cuisine here isn't exactly what you consider three-square," he murmured.

I swallowed down a big gulp of coffee in agreement. Handing him my phone, he scrolled through the picture evidence of Daddy Dearest's identities, preserved for eternity on the Cloud unless someone hacked into my personal files. After he sent the last pic to himself, he deleted them from my device and remained speechless for a few heartbeats. "Thanks, babe. This one has been a long time coming."

Coffee dribbled down my chin onto the Victoria's Secret PJs Red had brought before bedtime. I attempted to wipe it off, but all it did was smear. I shrugged. I should be embarrassed. I had the manners of a sloth. "I'm going to need a name," I said, "and I'd think you know by now that I can keep secrets." Vinnie chuckled next to me, taking a bite of my cookie as he talked to the statue of Jesus.

Dodge Charger Man extended his hand for a shake. "Thorne Sutherland."

My hand was completely swallowed in his, but here's what I learned from the handshake—power lay inside. But it had a tender edge reserved for certain people. "Nice to meet you, Thorne. A very aristocratic name."

"That might be the only aristocratic thing about me," he said, laughing and placing his hand back in his lap. "But I accept the compliment."

"Now let's get down to business," I said. "What's your interest in Julius Marx?"

Vinnie chuckled louder.

Thorne leaned forward and let his arms dangle over the back of the pew. "Marx and I, or maybe I should say *Butch*, met Tabitha and Gemma while they were in college. We all became fast friends. We were already a few years into the organization, and at the time, I felt him to be a trusted confidante. Things on my missions, though, began to systematically unravel right along the time Gemma's stalker surfaced the first time. Details I'd planned to precision, which could only mean a friend on the inside was giving me up. I spent a lot of time proving I was loyal until I realized he was the one undermining me."

"How did you do that?"

"I shadowed him the first time Gemma's stalker surfaced because he'd given her some strange vibes. When he was out of town on assignment, I broke into his home and found detailed things not only about her but about my missions."

"You spoke of 'the organization.' I'm assuming that was your bosses. They wouldn't let you take him out for the betrayal?"

"No. I had to tolerate his existence, but the organization kept us apart. And since the Butch Lawrence alias had been retired, I had trouble tracking him. He surfaced again at Gemma's ten-year reunion concert. I knew it in my gut he'd pulled the trigger. I went after him, and that's when my life went to Hell." Thorne grew silent for a beat, continuing after a deep breath. "That fight club in Moscow? The one he learned about as Julius Marx? A guy on the inside told me Marx was his newest alias, and I tracked him there after he killed Gemma. I had him in lockdown, but the man had a talent for chewing through a leash. With the help of someone else I thought was my friend, he imprisoned me for twenty-two months. I had to fight my way out."

At that, Vinnie flinched. "I'm sorry," I whispered.

Thorne exhaled deeply, like he tried to rid himself of a burden that refused to budge. "No one is sorrier than me. My life had been turned completely upside down by the time I got back into town."

I didn't want to go there...but I knew what that meant. Red's relationship with Rookie had been wrecked not only by my mother's absence, but by an unnamed man I called Boyfriend Zero. One look at the gorgeous mug of Thorne Sutherland, and I knew he held the title. Doing the math, Red had married Rookie a year and a half after my mother's death, which would jive with the twenty-two months Thorne had been in captivity. He'd come back when she was still a newlywed and found out he'd lost her. How tragic, but I loved my uncle more than life itself. "You're Red's Boyfriend Zero, aren't you?" I said softly. "All of us knew he existed, but she's protected you like a tree hugger on a sequoia. I promise I'll never ask her about you, but is that why you've watched after me?"

Thorne's eyes briefly softened, but just as quickly he buried the feeling. Thorne Sutherland liked to guard his feelings. "Yes, and as far as my relationship with Tabitha, that's her story to tell. Just know that whatever means something to her will always mean something to me."

"My uncle is good to her," I said quietly.

"I am aware," he said resolutely.

On instinct, I reached for his hand. Thorne Sutherland had been screwed...and Lord, did I understand the feeling. "You said your bosses wouldn't let you take him out," I said, changing the subject. "Why?"

"Diplomatic immunity," was his answer. "He was a double agent. I couldn't kill him without a good reason, although the guys we work for have a very gray view of what is right and wrong."

"You needed permission?"

"For the most part, and I enjoy oxygen a little too much, babe. My bosses have a way of finding out your dirty, little secrets."

"Do you play for the home team?" I asked, meaning the U.S. Government.

"Yes. Marx played many sides, but his allegiance has always been to himself."

"How did he get the scars?"

A crafty grin. "Before he left Moscow, I made sure to do something that would be hard for plastic surgery to correct. He altered his appearance often, but no one had been able to totally correct what I did."

When I asked Thorne about Daddy Dearest and his penchant for reciting coordinates, he explained that was probably the way his handler communicated—which meant he had a target at those locations or was supposed to deliver a package to a specific person or vicinity those coordinates represented.

"So what is Jaws's connection? I haven't spoken to him since rescued, but the only thing that makes sense is he knew Lars van der Hart was Marx."

A faint smile appeared. "Getting hooked up with Jaws in the first place was a twist of fate because you sought him out for help with the Northside 12 gang. And for that matter, our first introduction was looking at the dead body of Alfonso Juarez. God, you're a trouble magnet, babe."

"What was your interest with Juarez?" I asked suspiciously, remembering the mobster whose dead body I'd accidentally stumbled upon.

His face became grave, regretful. "I needed information, and in exchange for a new identity, Juarez was going to get it for me." Thorne had a voice that stripped people of their will, reminding me of a cobra's trance that could leave someone dead. He paused, carefully considering his words. "You look exactly like Tabitha. I knew it the first time I saw you. It's bizarre." He shifted in his seat, realizing he'd digressed, or maybe he'd just called up a painful memory. "To answer the question," he finally said. "Jaws is my brother, and he's been seeking revenge on my behalf. We look too much alike for him to have gotten close to Marx on his own, but yes, he suspected Marx and Van der Hart to be one and the same. Jaws was in the club when Lyric's body was discovered, and that's when his wheels began to turn. He planned to tie him to Lyric's death, draw him out, and grab his government papers, so I could prove he'd been in Moscow when I'd been imprisoned. Someone in the organization had already told me Marx and Mahesh Singh were one and the same, and Lyric was an innocent. Although we do some pretty dastardly things, the organization doesn't like it when we perform hits that aren't ordered. And the fact that Marx threw the agency's best sniper in a Russian fight club was the straw that broke the camel's back. I was told if I could prove it, then he was fair game."

The agency's best sniper...whoa, a question for another day.

"Listen, babe," he continued softly. "I know Jaws has an unorthodox way of doing things, but I'm all he has. When I was gone, he nearly tore apart the United States looking for me, but I wasn't even on home soil. I'm so sorry. I had no clue he'd asked for your help. He knows I would've forbidden it."

I'd always take a win, and I didn't care how I got it, but that also meant Jaws knew Daddy Dearest—AKA Lars van der Hart, AKA Julius Marx—was the man who shot my mom. I'd suspected it, but it was totally different once someone corroborated my suspicions. "I'm going to kill him," I muttered.

Thorne threw his head back and laughed. "Ah, babe, please try. I think you actually scare him, and he's carrying around so much guilt I almost feel sorry for the guy. Please believe me when I say he was just after your skillset."

Once again, fate had it out for me. "You don't seem as sociopathic as him."

"I'm just a better actor," he said and winked.

"Did you help get us out?"

"I came in late to the game, but rest assured I did my part."

Men like Thorne Sutherland like to right the wrongs done to them. If he did his part, that only meant one thing. "You were the third shot, weren't you? There was a brief pause after Lincoln fired, but then I saw the body jump with a third bullet. I'd just assumed that was Paddy, but it wasn't. You shot him with Paddy's gun, didn't you? He and Lincoln allowed you to get your pound of flesh."

That faint grin of earlier? It grew to showcase a porcelain smile. He did not confirm, nor deny, and I suppose that served as answer enough. That also insinuated he worked with Lincoln...at least toward the end...and unfortunately, it wasn't something I could ask about.

"And you're sure we got him?" I asked.

"The agency picked up his body at my request. Once his identity is confirmed, I'll get word to you."

Our conversation put the last of the puzzle together, but if he thought I'd go away easily—without some sort of concession—he didn't know I was Darcy Walker.

"You owe me," I said, smiling big. He threw his head back again, bellowing out dark laughter. "I could've blown you out of the water by telling the authorities to put an APB out on a yellow Dodge Charger when you shoved me in its trunk. Give me something, so I can consider us even."

"The Charger?" he paused. "I'm not the owner, babe, and I don't always drive it."

So it was Jaws's car then. Huh...still not enough. "I need more."

"Kellan," he said, grinning devilishly.

Thorne shifted all his weight to one hip, pulling his phone out of a pocket and hitting a speed dial. It took a moment to untangle the turn in conversation, but then it hit me like a jujitsu move to the head. "Jaws?" I said, adding a big smile.

"Call him," he said, placing the phone in my hand. "He's nearly gone insane, and I think he might've killed a few people thinking they took you."

Oh, crap. We were right here in front of baby Jesus. I wasn't so sure he should've said that out loud. After two rings, I was greeted profanely...Jaws wondering "why the eff" Thorne hadn't called because he hadn't slept in "forty-eight effing hours."

Only he said the whole F-word.

"Kellan Sutherland," I said, giggling loudly. "You don't call. You don't write. You don't send flowers. I'm beginning to think you're not as invested in this relationship as I am. That hurts my feelings, bud, and I've got a bullet with your name on it."

There was a lengthy pause and then Jaws chuckled deeply with, "Missed you, babe," and killed the call.

EPILOGUE: WILDCARD AND PIXIE

*S*ummer Break: When students forget copious amounts of information they've learned, prowl the night like vampires, and sleep all day until someone wakes them up.

Except for Dylan and me...our summer break sucked.

Dylan's mother had homeschooled him up to a point, but for the assignments we'd missed, Principal Unger worked with us on our junior class requirements. Both of us had online courses to finish before senior year began. I'd finished most of them—even the paper I'd written about my mom for English lit—but my mind couldn't help but recycle the eighty days where I'd been imprisoned.

As suspected, there'd been an intricate network of people who knew of Lars van der Hart's particular pastime. All had been arrested, along with the local DJ announcer, and thrown into jail. As far as key players, Delia went to rehab and got long-term probation because she only pieced things together when I entered the game... despite her tattoo. Myles was pulling some jail time, but would be eligible for early parole because of the information he'd provided on Lars van der Hart's aliases and business dealings. And those fighters living on the edge and victim of Stockholm Syndrome? Along with Ryder, they'd been slowly reintroduced into society in some sort of halfway-house deal. In fact, Ryder was doing so well, he claimed he wanted to complete his high school equivalency. He'd also begun to date Gabrielle. Still others were so far gone counseling would probably be a waste of taxpayers' dollars, but they were being rehabbed anyway in a psych ward because they feared people in general. As I'd suspected—and as Thorne had corroborated—those with tattoos were deep into the life of Daddy Dearest. They went straight to jail, did not pass go, and did not collect two hundred dollars. Fine by me, but I dreamt of that mark and knew if I ever ran across it again, I'd better run for the ends of the Earth.

Scrawny Guy, together with Cash and Black Hawk, had become fast friends. All three had been kidnapped like me and had gone back to their respective families, but I chatted with them regularly and inducted them into my personal mob. And there had also been five teenage girls found who had a homecoming with their families. Unfortunately, there were about fifteen people in my sketchpad unaccounted for, and we could only assume they'd been killed.

Biggest plus? Jaws phoned that Daddy Dearest—or Julius Marx, rather—had been definitively identified as the dead body Thorne had his bosses pick up in the morgue. So life, as I knew it, was back to normal. Unfortunately, my normal needed a serious overhaul.

I'd like to say I'd been living pre-The Underground, but not really. Maybe suspended was more like it, stopped exactly where I'd left off when my mother died. I felt some closure, but the pain of her death had resurrected itself as raw as the day she'd died. Maybe that was the road to healing, but it was nice to be able to talk openly about things with Murphy. Needing a break from Valley, Dylan and I spent a long weekend in Orlando with his family but then flew to LA to visit Lincoln and his wife, Alexandra.

Dylan's mother, Sydney, and Zander were dropping Benjis on Rodeo Drive, and Dylan, Colton, and I were headed to the family bakery to meet up with Lincoln. The family bakery served as command central for Lincoln and his undercover counterparts, and from what I could tell, things had reached a fever pitch in the world of Pixie, Lincoln's informant in the Turkey Cardoza case. *All the good it did me*, I grumbled to myself. My level of involvement had always been late night recaps when Lincoln was feeling extra chatty. I *did* visit the police academy a couple of days earlier and filled out an application and gave them my fingerprints to start a background check in case I decided to make that my career. I'd talked to

Murphy and Marjorie about the prospect of moving to LA after high school and both wanted me to give it a go.

All in all, it had been rather easy...maybe that was my problem... I was used to hard.

Dylan had just worked out and was showering while I scrolled through pop culture articles of the last few months on my phone. Don't get kidnapped, people. There were too many Hollywood divorces to track, Taylor Swift tunes, and professional athletes beating the crap out of their wives.

"Darc?!" he yelled.

Some things in life were inevitable: death, taxes, and Dylan Taylor's gravitational pull.

Clicking off my phone, I pushed off the bed and straightened my clothes: a T-shirt and my favorite jean shorts, Dylan's class ring back around my neck. I'd gotten back to my fighting weight rather quickly, complements of Murphy and Dylan's mother's cooking. Lacing up my Chuck Taylors, I strolled into Dylan's room. *Purrrrr!* He was shirtless...you know, awesome with a side of kickass. His temporary tattoos had worn off, and I missed them. Still, I loved watching him get dressed. It was intimacy at another level altogether. Handing him the black T-shirt on the bed, he pulled it over his head and stepped into a new pair of gray sneakers. "I yelled your name three times, sweetheart. What's wrong?"

I shrugged. "Nothing really."

Dylan sat down on the edge of the bed and tied his shoes, pulling me between his legs when finished. "I sense a *but*," he murmured.

"No *but*. I just really missed you," I whispered, referring to our time apart.

"Same," he murmured, running his hands up and down the backs of my thighs. "It's been a wild ride, yeah?"

"Yeah, but I get afraid the you-and-me-together part is doomed."

Dylan's voice was soothing, like a warm blanket on a cold night. "I'm all in, Darc. We're merely moving on to another chapter."

Dylan still hadn't committed to a college. Something written about almost weekly in the sports pages, but it was also a reason why we'd traveled west. He'd come to tour several colleges. Not only states away, but two freaking time zones away. Oy.

"Did I tell you I loved you today?" I asked.

Dylan winked. "About a hundred times, but I'm not complaining."

I'd uttered the L-word phrase nonstop since returning from The Underground. I didn't think it was from insecurity, but who the heck knew? Females would always be insecure when our significant other was better looking. Holding his gaze, I cradled my arms around the back of his neck and leaned my forehead into his. Passion crackled between us. I'd also become the aggressor in all things physical—I think Dylan feared I'd break—but I so wasn't in the mood for things all neat and proper. When I kissed his neck, Dylan's breath caught in his throat.

I lifted my gaze to his. "I'm not going to break, you know. I've got some new things in my repertoire I'd like to show you."

A feral growl. "Is that right?"

"Yeah, I'm here to demolish the stereotype of the girl that doesn't know what she wants."

Dylan grinned, highlighting two dimples framing some breathtaking lips. Things started as gentle as a spring shower but quickly evolved into a skin-on-skin massacre. Dylan and I were never a slow burn. He wrapped me in his arms and made sure I felt the Dylan Taylor treatment. My lips parted at his intensity, and my fingers wound through his hair. In fact, every hormone in my body screamed out to be quenched. Unfortunately, Colton kayoed our little getting-to-know-one-another session with his big, fat mouth.

"Are you two ready?" he shouted.

Blergh. Argh. Dylan chuckled and leaned his forehead into mine. Normally I'd giggle, *Wow, throw another log on that fire, tiger*, but the fear of Colton coming upstairs was like trying to dodge a flamethrower.

In thirty minutes, we'd braved LA's traffic-from-Hell and were in Alexandra's family bakery in West Hollywood. She'd help run the place since before she was a teenager. Outside had a pink awning. Inside sat wall-to-wall glass cases she could barely keep stocked throughout the day. She was closing up shop and a little neighborhood Mexican girl had come in who evidently visited most afternoons to sweep the floor. On the top of one glass case was a big box of rainbow candy sticks that had powder in them. Lincoln gave her one, and she grabbed a chair, quiet as a mouse.

Colton snagged a handful of powdered cookies that had been dipped in chocolate and stuffed with jam, offering me three while I snagged a chair by the little girl. I took a big bite while Dylan ripped into the baklava.

Lincoln patted himself down, looking for something, right as Paddy entered with four other men discreetly trickling in behind him. Once everyone was inside, Paddy flipped over the "Open" sign to "Closed" when Lincoln directed him to. "Where's my wallet?" Lincoln asked anyone that would listen. "Darcy?" he said accusingly.

I giggled. "If you're suggesting I took it, first off...*flattered*...but secondly, I have an alibi...your grandson."

Paddy and the other four men bit into cookies Colton threw at them. "Like he honest to God wouldn't cover for you," Paddy said snorting. "I'm not sure who is more crazy, you or the boy." Paddy pulled up a seat from underneath a small white metal table, sitting beside me. "I just spoke with Iggy," he said.

"And?" I asked.

"Iggy said you collapsed the stent in his heart," Paddy said laughing.

"Maybe God's telling him to quit smoking," I muttered.

"Where the heck is my wallet?" Lincoln asked, searching the floor.

"Anything on Pixie?" Paddy asked him.

"No," Lincoln said, still grumbling. "And she's too quiet. Something's up."

The case keeping Lincoln up at night starred a mobster named Turkey Cardoza. That was the case I'd meddled in while we vacationed last summer in Orlando. As a recap, Cardoza represented an unnamed businessman who bullied the notorious Carlotto and Bonnano LA crime families into giving up some of their business. In order to fulfill his quest of owning LA, the man ordered hits on members of the Carlotto and Bonnano families himself—hits carried out by Turkey Cardoza. Lincoln became concerned it would be the turf war of all turf wars if it wasn't squashed, and he wound up ticking off Cardoza's boss so much he decided to hit Lincoln a little too close to home.

Translation? Hurt his family.

Lincoln was positive this man—once again, vis-à-vis Turkey—had arranged a car accident involving the Suburban Dylan, me, and two of our friends drove on the first day of school. We were T-boned by a car driven by Weasel Bonnano. So what that told me was this third crime family had somehow gotten a rival Bonnano to do its dirty work. After Weasel's car struck us, I catapulted through the windshield and our buddy, Jon Bradshaw, sailed through the passenger side window. We'd both been pretty banged up, but before I went out cold, I was able to identify Weasel as the man who'd hit us.

Here's the thing. Weasel Bonnano was discovered dead on a park bench barely a day after our attempted murders. One shot to the chest. Inconvenient for him. And even more inconvenient for Lincoln. He didn't get to gaslight him with a single question.

With Lincoln strong-arming anyone who had air in his body, the Bonnanos and even Carlottos, swore Weasel had acted alone. And both claimed they hadn't seen Turkey Cardoza in months. That meant: (A) the Bonnanos either killed one of their own because he made them vulnerable with the LAPD; or (B) Cardoza did it.

Which one did I lean toward? The letter B. Weasel had a reputation for screwing things up, so I was inclined to believe Cardoza knocked him off by order of his unseen boss. Why? The answer was simple...*we didn't die.*

The odd thing was, I was pretty sure Cardoza wanted Lincoln to know he'd sent Weasel. I'd seen the "sent by" message in Weasel's eyes, and unbeknownst to me, he'd tossed an empty bottle of Wild Turkey bourbon whiskey in the backseat of the Suburban. Call that clue number one. Clue number two came by way of Lincoln's informant, Pixie. Pixie somehow knew all of Cardoza's moves—moves orchestrated by his mysterious boss. Directly after the accident, Pixie got word to Lincoln that Turkey was indeed the man who ordered Weasel to kill us. She'd then went dormant for almost six months but came out of hiding right before I'd been abducted. Once again, she'd gone dark.

I'd been thinking about Pixie since we'd touched down. Lincoln

—without saying—feared she'd been swimming with the fishes. Honestly, the likelihood was high, especially since we'd found out last summer that two Turkey Cardozas actually existed. Since Turkey was accused of crimes in one venue but found on the other side of town with legit alibis, I suggested there might be two men with the same face. A facial recognition program proved the theory correct.

While Lincoln yelled for Alexandra to help him find his wallet, I stole a look at the little Mexican girl, shoveling the candy powder in her mouth while she picked up a broom. She'd dressed in a navy plaid private school skirt but with light up princess sneakers that should've been retired years earlier.

"You might want to slow down because you're going to have one heck of a headache," I said and laughed.

She grinned sheepishly. "Sorry," she said. "Alexandra lets me have as much as I want, and then I sweep her store for her. She gives me ten dollars a week. I'm trying to buy shoes."

Well, I could always appreciate a little girl with entrepreneurial spirit. "What's your name?" I asked, taking a bite of Dylan's baklava.

"Penelope."

"Where do you live, Penelope?" I asked.

"Real close. I live with my dad and grandma, but she's sick. She probably won't last the summer. When she dies, I guess the city of LA will take care of me."

"Your dad won't?"

"I don't want him to," she said quietly.

My appetite took a little TO after that because the little girl reminded me of Marjorie. She couldn't be older than twelve, at the most, with black hair and eyes and frankly looked underweight. "I'm sorry," I said, but then Lincoln's phone chimed with a text, distracting me. He bit into a cookie and nonchalantly glanced at the image someone had sent him, narrowed his eyes, and dropped the mother of all curse words.

"Boss?" Paddy asked.

Lincoln tossed his cell phone over that contained an image of two dead Turkey Cardozas—both with shots to the head—and a dark-headed woman bound and gagged next to them, along with a message. I glanced at the screen:

MacArthur Park. Come alone if you want to see Pixie alive...Crash Falcon.

———————

MacArthur Park, close to downtown Los Angeles, looked beautiful when I googled it on my phone. There was water, seagulls, ducks, palm trees, and beautiful buildings, but in person I immediately got the vibe that'd merely been good photography. Lincoln said the mornings here could be peaceful, but as the day wore on, the park became a world of drugs, gangs, and a campground for the homeless. As such, I think it was one of those areas people stayed out of unless they were doing business like we were.

Lincoln was in one H of a mood, wondering how Pixie had been fingered especially if both Cardozas were dead. A follow-up text came that gave the whereabouts of both dead bodies, and when Lincoln and his crew left to investigate, they'd both been positively identified as Turkey and his doppelgänger once they hit the morgue. That could only mean that the man who ran the third family—presumably Crash Falcon by the text—wanted a little meet-and-greet with Lincoln and used Pixie as bait. Lincoln was game because he was tired of the man pulling his strings, plus he owed Pixie. He'd long suspected she'd been inside the organization, but something must've happened to make the third family decide to take everyone involved out of commission permanently. Lincoln was to meet Falcon and Pixie at the park after midnight where he'd get Pixie in exchange for the promise to back off. Lincoln would never back off, but that was a part of the plan I wasn't privy to.

ETA was in five minutes according to Lincoln, so here we were: me in a building with Pete overlooking the park, Richie in a van controlling communication, another undercover walking his dog, still another chatting on his phone, and Paddy disguised as a wino on a bench (a location he'd held for two hours).

Here's how Lincoln's words went down to me at the bakery: *You've been cleared*, he'd said.

What? I'd asked.

You passed the background check, dear. If you want to see what I do, then I will find you a perch, and you can feed my men information.

Am I allowed? I asked.

You're allowed if I say you're allowed, and I trust you to do as I say.

Not a moment's hesitation on my part. I was, however, shocked Lincoln had granted me the privilege. It hadn't exactly been martial law where Dylan and I were concerned, but his family and mine hovered a little more than usual in the past few months. Upon talking to Colton, he'd fed his father information when he was younger and so had other select cadets in the academy Lincoln had handpicked because of their skills. I'd expected Lincoln's men to balk at the invitation, but if anything good came out of being kidnapped, it made others realize I wouldn't buckle under pressure. My job was to watch...report...and repeat that on a loop. Dylan, once upon a time, would've pink-slipped my trip. This evening, although stone-faced, he'd hugged me fiercely and wished me luck.

So far, I'd done as I'd been told...a new leaf, and all that.

It was well past midnight. Pete and I were on the third floor of an apartment building, lights completely off overlooking the park. Lincoln had just strolled out in the middle of a grass clearing to face off with Falcon and presumably Pixie with a gun to her head. To the right, I saw nothing but some collapsed homeless people and Paddy. To the left, however, I viewed a pair of sneakers lighting up the sidewalk in rhythmic pink blinks. I refocused my binoculars and recognized the little plaid skirt I'd seen at the bakery earlier. Son of a beast. Penelope. But why? When she began to run, it only took a few seconds for the answers to materialize.

My God, I'd figured this thing out.

"It's a trap!" I gasped to Pete. "That's not Pixie with Falcon! Tell Lincoln to bail!"

I quickly explained my suspicions to Pete who immediately focused in on Penelope and then back to something else in the field. "Dammit, Darcy, I've got five people walking toward Linc as we speak. I can't tell if they're resident homeless, flunkies, or envoys of Falcon."

Frantically, I corroborated Pete's words with my own set of binoculars. Five men made their way toward Lincoln from all directions, and they didn't look particularly friendly. Penelope would compromise the operation, and things had been choreographed to precision. The way things went, Richie and Pete were never to leave their posts because Pete was the eyes, and Richie the proverbial ears in the van ensuring everyone stayed in communication. That left two other men in the field, plus Paddy. Lincoln needed them to have his back.

Unfortunately, that left me.

"I'm on it!" I yelled, bolting for the stairs.

"No!" he barked behind me. "Stay Put!" Believe me, I wanted to, but I didn't see any other recourse because Penelope, God love her, was systematically making her way to Lincoln, hiding behind trees. Whatever the girl was up to, she was bound and determined to get to Lincoln before Falcon and the woman with him.

I heard Pete yell into his mouthpiece, "Wildcard is on the move. I repeat. Wildcard is on the move."

My experience had mostly been with psychopaths. The men ambushing Lincoln were professionals. They wouldn't walk away until they'd performed the deed their next paycheck required. And I'd bet my sorry life the female masquerading as Pixie was some bimbo they'd hired or blackmailed into doing so. Hitting the pavement, I ran toward Penelope, debating whether it was a stroke of genius or stroke of stupid. The debate suffered a premature death because I soon heard the rapid sound of feet behind me. I didn't think I'd picked up a tail, but in one breath, I found myself tackled to the grass.

"What the bloody hell do ya think ya doin'?" Paddy seethed in my ear.

Ugh, the ground was hard. "Dude," I gasped. "You just killed my kidneys."

"Speak," he growled.

Paddy pulled me into a crouch beside him. "The little girl from the bakery," I said in a pant, "she's tailing Lincoln."

Paddy and I heard Lincoln's voice elevate as he told the woman to trust him, and it was just enough time for Paddy to latch ahold of Penelope, place his hand over her mouth, and drag her back to the van with Richie, me tailing behind.

The van was gray with a ladder on top, complete with state-of-the-art James Bond equipment inside. It was tall enough for people to stand inside too. Richie had that look like we'd just screwed the whole operation to Hell and back as he turned dials, making sure communication with everyone in the field was still intact. Lincoln's microphone was still transmitting. In fact, he said, "Nice to meet you, Crash. Like me, I guess you've grown tired of the charade. Let me have Pixie, and we end this tonight."

Penelope's eyes were glued to the soundboard. "Where's your grandma?" I asked her.

Penelope turned to my voice, although her mind was somewhere else. She'd been crying. Her brown eyes were bloodshot, but I wouldn't let that deter me.

"Darcy," Paddy said softly. "The kid loves Lincoln. She heard us talking this afternoon. Just cut her a break. Penelope," he said to her. "I have to go back outside to keep Lincoln safe."

I ignored Paddy. "Your dad is dead, isn't he?"

Another pause from Penelope, but she finally said, "Yes."

"Darcy," Paddy growled, but I grabbed him by the wrist, alerting him to let the conversation play.

"Your dad died today, yeah?" I asked. A headshake, added with a slight trembling chin. "He pretended to be someone else. Someone named Turkey Cardoza?" An embarrassed nod, and I had a flashback of how mortified I'd felt when I thought my mother's murderer had also been my father. Not a great feeling. And this kid was living the real deal. "You do realize that even though *he* did bad things that doesn't make *you* bad?" I said. "And it's okay to not like what he did?"

"I know," she said, "but he did very bad things to nice people." Then as God as my witness, she jumped into Paddy's arms and held on tight. "She's not Pixie," she blurted out. "Not Pixie."

I reminded Paddy the facial recognition program had proved there'd been two Turkeys, a fact the text of earlier corroborated with visual proof of two dead bodies. Penelope, I'd bet, had lived with the impostor. The little girl would show up every day and sweep the floor for Alexandra...eavesdropping just enough to know that Lincoln was a target of her father's. Lincoln gave her candy... more specifically Pixy Stix.

Penelope was Pixie.

Paddy gasped, "Oh God," and then ordered Richie to instruct the men in the field to cause a disturbance, that the operation was off. And here's where the shiz got real ugly, real fast. We heard arguing between the two men and then gunshots. More gunfire... still more, accompanied with Lincoln and Crash Falcon accusing the other of an ambush.

It was a frighteningly fast experience, especially when I hadn't taken a breath in God only knew how long. Did I like it? No. Many no. All the no in the bloody world, but the little girl would be dead if I hadn't intervened, and Lincoln would be saving someone who more than likely would gut him on the way to the van. When the unending gunfire stopped, we were left with silence. So much silence that I closed my eyes. Lincoln was dead...I knew it.

Before I had a chance to grab a Kleenex, Lincoln nearly blew the door off the van with his anger, entering with a scowl he didn't attempt to hide. "Wildcard is on the move. The five words you swore to me I'd never hear. What was your assignment, Darcy?"

"Watch. Report. Repeat on a loop," I said calmly.

"Exactly," he barked. "I swear, Darcy, I love you, but right now..." he trailed off.

"First off, it was offensive that Wildcard was my code name. It's like you set me up for failure."

Pixie was still hiding behind Paddy. "Linc, you might wanna take a breath, brother," Paddy told him.

Lincoln was having none of it, still focusing on me. "What were you thinking, dear? One of my bullets hit him right in the chest. Falcon's dead, and although that's a good thing, I would've liked to have squeezed him until he talked! My men only make a diversion when the process has all gone to Hell. I'm assuming you were driving the bus."

I'd rather run headlong into a freight train than deal with Lincoln, but such is life. "It was a setup, and I accept the apology you owe me once it comes out of your mouth," I said. The joke expired by lack of attention, and unfortunately, that made me want to turn the screw. "Maybe you should take that breath," I told him.

Lincoln tried to be patient but came up short. Paddy had no recourse but to step aside and leave the real Pixie front and center. Lincoln's hands were behind his neck. He slowly dropped them when he clocked on the little girl. Blinked. Blinked again. It took a second for his mind to do the math here, and then his face looked like someone just hit him with a karate move. He dropped an F-bomb as he removed his black toboggan, shoving a trembling hand through his hair.

While Richie made contact with the two men in the field, and Pete gave everyone the coast-is-clear signal to make it back to the van, Paddy explained that I'd seen Penelope, pieced things together, and acted because no one else was available since Lincoln had been surrounded.

"Oh, ye, of little faith," I said.

Lincoln opened his mouth, immediately asking Penelope for information on things only "Pixie" would know. It was the strangest thing to witness. She hitched her chin high, her voice morphing into that of a young woman as she recited information about secret drug drops, money laundering, where Lincoln would find dead bodies, etcetera. Honestly, I was impressed...maybe a little scared. When she answered to precision, Lincoln slowly slid his eyes to me in a sly smile.

There were no celebratory high-fives or horn honks, but his grin said I'd just helped him close a case that had been eating him alive. I'd been self-assured, focused, and decisive. I mouthed back a playful, "I'm better than you," my inner-verb doing a nana nana, boo-boo victory dance.

Knock-knock, LA. You got served.

NOTE FROM THE AUTHOR

Thank you so much for reading DEFCON Darcy! If you read this book and enjoyed it, I'd be honored if you'd recommend it to other friends or readers' groups and leave a star rating at the retailer in which you purchased the book. Your words mean so much to authors and help other readers discover new worlds.

ABOUT THE AUTHOR

A.J. lives in Cincinnati with her husband, two daughters, an ADD dog, and a spoiled hamster burial site in her backyard. When she's not writing, she's reading, binge-watching the heck out of some show or eavesdropping-slash-creeping on those around her. And maybe searching the skies for aliens whenever the mood hits.

For more books and updates, connect with her on social media and at:
https://www.ajlape.com

ACKNOWLEDGMENTS

To God, thank you for being faithful and pulling me out of the oh-crap zone more than once. Without you, not one thing I've attempted would be possible; to my family, thank you for letting me talk about Darcy like she's real even though you think I'm weird. I love you beyond words; to my editing team of Jeff LaFerney and CR Everett, you guys make me better; to my beta readers, Debbie Brooks, Justine Littleton, Heather Mcguire, and Melanie Osmond. I hit the lottery with you girls. Thank you for sticking with me until we got it right; my Street Team for helping me keep Darcy's name alive on social media. You are the happy spot of my day; Dawn Barnhart Erckenbrack, Randy Grubbs, Jon Johnson, Greg Ramey, and A. Marie Silver. Thank you for patiently answering all my dead body, forensics, law, and government DEFCON questions. You make me look smarter than I am; and to the YA Ninjas, Indie Scribe, Secret Sisters, bloggers, and fans for their friendship and social media shares. Darcy and I have nothing but mad love for each of you!